CW00417475

RONIN FLIGHT

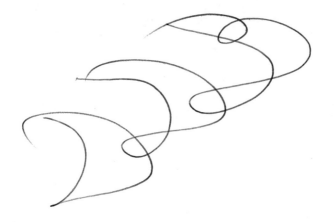

RONIN FLIGHT

D. D. BRAITHWAITE

NEW REPUBLIC ARMED FORCES ROSTER

Traditionally this page is used for dedications but I decided to break with tradition. This story is and its people are based on the people of the gaming clan New Republic Armed Forces (Stylised in the game as [NR] for short) who mainly competed in the space flight simulation game Tachyon: The Fringe. This page is as complete a roster as I can find of the gamertags of each pilot. Thank you all for making the gaming experience as great as it was and for the friendships we forged along the way.

Firehawk	White Knight	Semjasa
Pollock	Gonzo	Brutus
Hellbringer	Ellen	Susan
Nate Dawg	UmmaGumma	AceTachyonPilot
Sexy Kitten	Olam	5th Element
Punk Rocker	Teutonicman	Duo Maxwell
Ved	Himself	Ludicrous
Ice Assassin	Diceman	Moric
Striker	Silver	Bitchslap
Killerklown	Rogue	Kinfolk
Novatiger	God T-Rex	Valor
Detonator	Stray Bullet	Goose
Richthofen	Aran Thule	Cowboy
Master Blaster	Heatt	Thundercracker
Wraith	Red Rum	Hellfire
Redship Rory	Mcloud	Maverick
Teral	Chacal	Hooney
Vador	Bullfrog	Crimson Shadow
Warhammer V	Quantum 5	Burnmaster
Elsgared	Dark Vampire	Red Knight
Razzle	Reactor	Big Dawg

Authors note: some of the characters names, callsigns, personalities and appearances may be different in this story than the real life counterparts.

ACKNOWLEDGMENTS

There are so many to thank for getting me to this stage over the years either directly or indirectly. Without your support, advice, friendship and everything else over the years I wouldn't have been confident enough to even do this, thank you all. Sorry if I have forgotten anyone.

FAMILY

My wife Gillian and son Corran, my niece Nicole, my father Norman, my mother Catherine, my brother Douglas, my father in law Stewart, my mother in Law Alison, my brother in law Gordon, all my aunts, uncles, cousins and second cousins who have been there for me at various times, most notably Benita, Rachel, Ifor, Wendy, Thomas Nicola and cousin in law Tracey. Also my sons Godparents to whom I consider family as well, John "He-Ro" Scott, Jay Gallacher, Jade Austin and Elizabeth Scott.

SPECIAL THANKS

Anthony Greene, Aileen Gormley, Stacey McDonald, Jason "Rifleman Harris" Salkey, Angela Thomson, Angela Hamilton, Kirstin Turner, Sharon Scally, Marco Piva, John Nelson, Kharin Klepp, Rachel Taylor, Jack Berry, Stephen Cameron, Kwaku Adjei, Suzanne Rust, Matt Weston, Phil Marriott, Gareth Holland, Debbie Craig, Lauren Fox, Tracey McCulloch, Siobhan Robertson, Stuart W. Little, Iain MacIntyre, Linda McCabe, Frank McKenna, Marco Calleri, Daria Cotugno, Kimberly Benson, Richard Divers, Alix Brown, Colin Waldie, Keith Campbell, Scott Crombie, Chris Brown, John Sneddon, John Corry, Alex Nicol, Sister Martina, Father Gerard Maguiness, Kitty Gahagan, John Bell, Mo McCourt, Rhys Kay, Luke Murray, Claire McCafferty, Bianca-Louise Little, Sinclair McCall, Brian McLaughlin, Gerry O'Donnell, Ian Gowrie, Haider Dar, Alister Speedie, Chris Cowie, Kimberley Ferguson, Amy Speirs, Gary King George Thompson Smith, Peter Dunne, Chic Anderson, Scott Walker and everyone I worked with in security and with the regular staff especially at the Esquire House Glasgow and at Tesco Extra Wishaw.

RONIN FLIGHT

CHAPTER 1

Matt Easton was nervous as he sat in the waiting room of GalCorp Area Director Gladstone, a veteran of the colonial civil war between United Earth and the Hexstar Alliance (A Secessionist government made up of six powerful and wealthy colonies) he wasn't prone to nerves easy, in fact when he was in a fighter cockpit he was as confident and calm as can be, outside the cockpit..that was a whole different story but he wanted to make a good impression. Galactic Corporation (or GalCorp as it was more widely known as) was a huge company that had its hand in many efforts in the colonies and as such required a security fleet to protect its assets and were eager to recruit anyone with military experience. It was a hard decision to make but the flight from Earth to Galcorp Prime, the large space station with the sleek lines, it looked like ring with a spherical centre and it orbited the GalCorp funded colony Carnarvon that also served as the headquarters for the companies colonial efforts. Matt realised how much he missed flying as ever since the war ended four years ago the military had been scaling back its operations , he thought he could just go back to a mundane civilian life but the itch to be up in space got too much he guessed, Easton smoothed his GalCorp issue two tone light grey with blue trim flightsuit carefully and ran his fingers over his close cut black hair. Me wanted to make as much of a good impression as possible to the director, making awkward small talk with the receptionist had ended in disaster. After what seemed like an hour Director Gladstone emerged from his office, all smiles.

"Greetings Mister Easton, glad to finally meet you." Gladstone said as Matt got up and initially attempted a salute realised he wasn't in the military any more and shook his hand instead

"its an honour to be here and i hope to serve the company well." he said while trying to fight his own nerves. Gladstone nodded and his grin got wider, he was a short man with neatly trimmed ginger hair with a touch of grey at the temples , he ushered Matt into his office.

"Come in, have a seat, and don't worry we are all one big family at GalCorp." Gladstone said, Matt relaxed a little as they walked into the office.

It was a very sparse room, a large desk with some chairs dominated one side of the room in front of a large monitor. One side had a large window looking out to onto the rest of the station and the planet below.

"Well," Director Gladstone said, bringing up Easton's file "your war record is exceptional both in and out of the cockpit, numerous medals and citations, but you left them to join us, why? Do you want back in action? Because you will get that and more especially if I grant you the assignment on the SS Ramesses like you have requested," he got up and walked around the desk to get closer to Easton, propping himself on the desk "So why did you come to us?" .Weston looked up at him thoughtfully before taking a deep breath and saying.

"I joined the military out of duty to protect those who couldn't protect themselves, after the war operations were scaled back, I wasn't able to protect as well I could, hearing about the troubles the outer colonies have and seeing our military do no more than a token effort, I had to do something," he sighed "At least here I'd be doing something, may only be GalCorp colonies and bases but its something and I just want to do my bit." he noticed the directors smile seemed a little more forced, but he stood and looked out his window, his back to Easton.

"That is.. admirable, its rare we get such a pilot who is as committed to protection as yourself and on hearing your eloquently stated reason I have decided your efforts will be best served, for now with the SS Amenhotep, they are conducting security checks of our mining colonies in this sector," he turned to see Easton's shoulders sag a little and added in a hopeful tone "Now don't be discouraged, The SS Ramesses has its full fighter compliment, and your name is up there. The SS Amenhotep is not due to leave until tomorrow, so please take this opportunity to relax, its going to be a long tough flight." and he held out his hand, Easton stood and took the hand in a firm shake.

"Thank you sir." he said in a subdued tone and left.

That night in the stations bar, Matt sat alone nursing a beer, the main lights were dimmed making the blue strips of light that seemed to be everywhere on this station stand out more, drawing attention to the curve of the bar, the outline of the doorways, it was as striking as it was relaxing. Easton had been wondering if he truly did make the right move, he also was puzzled by what he felt was a change in attitude in the director, why did he assume Easton was some bloodthirsty fly boy and was his reply to the question of why he signed up the true reason he was given a lesser assignment? It just didn't make sense, nor did the simulations they ran him through during the GalCorp assessment tests.

His thoughts were broken by the cheers going up at one of the larger tables, the crew of the SS Ramesses had just recently returned from their latest run to the outer territories and seemed in good spirits, one of them, a pilot by his attire, his dark skin contrasting with the lightness of the flight suit, hair kept neat and short and eyes that suggested he had saw more than his fair share of combat, went up to the bar to order another round of drinks when he saw Easton, he smiled and held out his hand,

"Corbin Hayes, callsign Omega, commander of the SS Ramesses fighter squadrons, I see your a new recruit." Easton had heard of him, in the war he was one of the top aces, Matt took his hand.

"Matt Easton, callsign White Knight, say are you the same Omega that took out ten Hexstar fighters on your own with no backup?" Corbin laughed and nodded as he tried to attract the bar staffs attention.

"Well it wasn't ten, more like eight.. seven if you discount the one my wingman shot down before he was hit but yeah..I'm the same guy, so, you joining the ranks of the SS Ramesses?" Matt shook his head.

"No, been assigned to the SS Amenhotep."Matt said mournfully as Corbin patted Matt's shoulder.

"tough break," he said as he indicated to the girl serving him the same again for his table "its six months of sheer boredom, running escort for shuttles perimeter patrols its no fun for veterans like us," he indicated to the gold military wings they both wore "I'm sure you'll be eventually be fighting off ..undesirables with the rest of us in time, care to join us?" Matt drained his glass and stood shaking his head.

"Sorry but I'd be poor company." He said. Corbin shrugged and was heading back to his table when an announcement came over the comms,

"Corbin Hayes to the directors office, Corbin Hayes to the directors office." he shook his head and went to see what it was all about.

Corbin entered the directors office and saw Capitan Joseph Miller standing with Gladstone at the office window admiring Miller's ship, the SS Ramesses as it sat docked at the station, the sleekness of the lines giving the ship a predatory look, almost like a shark, they both turned and acknowledged him,

"so" Gladstone said with a wide grin "I hear I owe you thanks, Miller just told me about your work securing that new asteroid mining operation" he gave Hayes a playful slap on the back, he smirked and replied,

"I can't help it if those dumbass colonists won't accept our claim to the mining rights can I? Before you ask, though I'm sure the captain has already said, we left no witnesses. I'll let my pilots know you appreciate our handiwork," Hayes smile dropped a little "Director, can you tell me why we have a military trained pilot getting assigned to babysitting the SS Amenhotep, it has been a while since I've had any new pilots I haven't had to retrain myself?" Miller also looked at Gladstone looking for confirmation. The Director told both men how Easton replied to his questions to which Miller shook his head.

"So we got a boy scout have we? Damn." he said, Hayes also looked surprised and added,

"Can only hope he gets bored after six months of nothing, though maybe tell the SS Amenhotep captain to keep an eye out on his progress, a guy like that tends to ask questions he shouldn't." Gladstone nodded, he knew

Easton's type, if he found out about the Directors activities in the outer territories could have repercussions. Gladstone's personal comms screen lit up.

"Incoming message from Mister Vulpine." his secretary announced.

"Finally," he turned to Hayes, "you can go now, thanks again for your work." Corbin smiled, tossed a lazy salute and exited the office.

To say the station landing bay was large would be an understatement, Matt had rarely saw any bigger outside of the ones back on Starbase home orbiting earth, he had come down to see if his ships comms had been fixed as he had problems with it on the journey, he couldn't see a technician near so climbed into his Apophis class interceptor the sleek curved wings when viewed from the top made the ship look like a cobra ready to strike, he opened the cockpit canopy and climbed in and after a quick power check, tested his comms equipment, all he received was static

"damn." he shouted hitting the console before retrieving a toolkit from below the seat as he set about repairing it himself, he always found it calming working on a ship, he remembered how he used to tinker with his old Military FA 280 while others in his squad would be sleeping, he turned it on again and after a few seconds of static heard a voice.

"..I really do appreciate your help Remus.." that was Gladstone's voice. "and don't worry your regular payment will be on its way as agreed" another voice came over the comms,

"Always a pleasure Gladstone, though might need help from your boys with a few of the more stubborn colonies.." That voice sounded familiar, heard in news feeds everywhere, It sounded like Remus Fox the leader of the Silver blades A pirate organisation in the outer colonies, but that would mean... He checked his instruments, yes he had been recording the conversation, he slumped in his seat and let out an audible curse.

"Damn." suddenly there was silence on the comm feed, then Matt heard.

"What was that? You said this was a secure connection Gladstone..." Matt panicked, switched off the comms and reached behind to grab the spare helmet stored behind his seat, he knew they'd find out who was listening in, he had to get out of there, he ran through a quick flight check, out of the canopy there were technicians running towards him arms waving, but he just initiated takeoff and at the earliest chance throttled out of the bay with full afterburners.

Gladstone marched out of the office with Miller behind.

"Unauthorised launch detected." was being repeated over the comms. Gladstone shouted to Miller.

"It's that Easton, I'm sure of it, damn we can't risk him telling people about our operations" they got there in time to see Matt leave, three technicians ran up to them.

"Sorry Director..." the lead one said, all Gladstone could

do was glare at were Easton's ship had been...

Matt was in survival mode, he could wee the perimeter defence fighters heading to intercept, activating the light drive, he had no time to set coordinates, a blind jump away was the best option, he could see the station scrambling its own fighters too, his ship was rocked with a few blasts, the patrol ships were in range, he stayed his course, the lightdrive lights went green, pressing the activation button, and he was gone, the last few shots hitting nothing but empty space.

Gladstone was about to order more ships to launch when he saw Matt's fighter fly off in the distance and streak into lightspeed.

"Dammit." he cursed as Miller came up to him about to say something but Gladstone stopped him "I know, we need to do something about him.. and quick.

Easton had only jumped to the next system, but had to think quick, he didn't know how high up this collaboration with the pirates went and if he could trust any of the authorities, he realised his best option may be to take the evidence to outer colony leaders themselves and show it, maybe something could be done that way, his navigation computer calculated it would take five jumps to reach Wayland station, gateway outpost to the outer territories due to the range the lightengines had on a fighter this size and the fact he would probably damage the engines doing so, or run out of power whichever came first, but he may be able to get passage from there to those colonies, Easton prepared for the first of many jumps as he again activated the lightengines...

Director Gladstone turned to the Engineers, his mind forming a plan. One engineer was explaining what happened.

"...we did everything we could Director..we really did...",Gladstone held up a hand,

"I don't blame you, it was unfortunate." he typed a command to Millers personal comms device "you weren't to blame, Easton will be caught to face his horrible crimes." Miller took a position behind the technicians, one of them looked puzzled and asked.

"what horrible crime?" Gladstone just smiled sadly.

"I'm glad you asked, you see in his escape ..he shot..and killed three Galcorp employees," and nodded to Miller, before any of them could react, Miller had drawn his sidearm and shot all three in the back of the head, Gladstone continued, without a hint of irony "Tragic loss, of life," he turned to Miller all business "I'll put out wanted alerts, inform all relevant authorities there is a dangerous criminal and that we are giving out a reward for his capture and delivery to us." they headed to the shuttlelift to set their plan in motion.

CHAPTER 2

Waypoint station was an old angular shaped station and was the last civilised outpost on the edge of the outer territories. It reminded all who saw it like am octagonal wheel. It was as ever a hive of activity, many ships entering and leaving the region and this day was no different. The Waypoint station security patrols were especially vigilant as today as the station was expecting a large shipment of ore from the outer territories to dock, which meant a high chance of a pirate attack, Red patrol were on duty lead by Luciana Valdez, more commonly known in and out the cockpit as Angel, she as joined in Red Patrol by Andrew Douglas, a Scotsman who was an unconventional pilot who used the callsign Firehawk. He was followed closely by Phil Marconi, who flew under the name Semjasa and was the latest in a long line of Marconi's involved in law enforcement and then there was Rob Hellman, a pilot with an easy going demeanour and answered to the callsign of Pollock. They were only one of four such flight patrol groups but they were generally and unofficially considered the top group.

"Keep an eye out for unusual activity Red patrol." came a call over the comms, the station administrator, a rather jaded middle aged ex-pilot by the name of Gustav Nevland pointed out what, to Red Patrol at least, was stating the obvious.

Andrew sighed and shook his head and fought back a sarcastic comment, the cockpit of his old Dynamic Astrospace Vanguard starfighter was cold, like everything else in Waypoint was obsolete and badly needing upgrades or at least decent repairs. The ships themselves resembled swans in flight with the long fuselage and wide weapon loaded wings, he ignored the stiff feeling in his knees as eased the throttle to hold station on Angels wing, he had a problem with his knees and had a doctor dull the nerve endings to reduce the pain but it still bothered him from time to time.

"Here it is.. right on schedule," Said Angel through the comms as a large cargo ship jumped in from lightspeed, the logos of Starcore Mining, one of the biggest mining companies in the business, faded yet prominent on the sides as it lumbered towards the station "If something going to happen it will be now" just then another ship jumped in, a freighter and it looked badly damaged.

"Waypoint station this is the Captain Harkness of the SS Goldrush... request assistance... heavy damage to ship by pirates, cargo volatile.." static came over the comms, Gustav's voice came over the comms, suddenly alert.

"Red Patrol, can you assess and report damage to SS Goldrush and report back with a recommendation?" The thinly veiled order was obvious, if it looks like it will explode don't let it near the station.

Angel was wary of the situation but decided not to argue, however she decided to be cautious "Semjasa, Pollock, stay with the StarCore vessel, Firehawk and I will investigate." both ships gunned the throttles and burst forward to the stricken vessel, something didn't sound right to Firehawk and he played the distress call again and again, then he switched to the private red patrol channel.

"Semjasa this is Firehawk, you remember that freighter captain you beat at pool a few weeks ago in the bar?" he asked cautiously.

"Yeah," Semjasa replied "three games to two it finished.."why."

"You remember the name of the Captain and the ship?" he asked with growing concern, what was it that was bothering him about this. Suddenly on the main channel the SS Goldrush captain reported its cargo was ready to blow and they planned to jettison it into space, control was trying to convince them to wait but it sounded like they had already stated the sequence.

"Firehawk, Semjasa, this is Angel, enough of the

chatter we have a job to do." Angel shouted audibly annoyed at the seeming pointlessness of the conversation, she was used to these sorts of conversations but this did not seem the time or the place to her, she trusted the others to do their jobs but despaired at the attitudes they shown on and off duty.

"Captain Harkness.. her ship was the SS Goldrush.. oh.. OH!" Phil said ignoring her, thats what was bothering him..the voice was distinctly male "Angel, Firehawk, better get away from there..now!"

It was too late.. it all happened so fast. The cargo bay doors blew open and, like parasites a squad of fighters burst out firing as they did, Angels ship took the brunt of the fire, the shields absorbed the first few, but the next salvo destroyed the cockpit section entirely destroying her fighter before she had time to react. Andrew just managed to avoid more than a few glancing strikes on his shields. The ships, Su-MiG 470 Vampires which were a common sight to Andrew as they were the ship of choice for most outlaws and instantly recognisable by their flying wing spaceframe that had the outer wing areas canted at a slight upward angle. These particular Vampire fighters all had markings suggesting this group of pilots belonged to the Bloodfist pirate clan. , Eight of them streaked towards the Starcore vessel, the remaining four seemed intent on finishing Andrew off, leaving the empty hulk of the SS Goldrush floating as the explosions from the jury rigged systems used to do the stunt overloaded.

"Control this is Firehawk, Angel is down, I repeat Angel is down, we have twelve pirate fighters inbound. Launch the standby patrol now..Now damn you" he screamed over the comms as he twisted and turned to avoid the enemy fire. Control answered

"Green patrol are preparing to launch, stay calm Firehawk, help is coming" not soon enough thought Andrew, the enemy ships luckily all seemed more concerned with getting the kill themselves than working as a unit which worked in his favour, he was able to keep one step ahead, his tight manoeuvrers had brought him behind one of the enemy fighters, switching to guided missiles he awaited the targeting computer to lock, suddenly the targeting lock indicator just switched off

"Damn, not now, not again" he shouted as he slapped the console in a futile gesture, there wasn't time to switch back to lasers so he just dumb fired two missiles, one harmlessly passed by, the other struck the enemy fighter dead centre, Andrew banked right one of the other ships copied while the others seemed to have other ideas, they were looping round to try and get a better shot, firing wildly in front of him, the Vampire fighters they were flying were not equipped with smart targeting and were trying to judge the lead shots themselves which was difficult to do in the heat of battle. The shots were getting more desperate, Andrew suddenly hit full reverse, the ship in pursuit shot in front of him.. into friendly fire and was cut down before anyone could react, two down only two more to go. In the distance the other members of Red Patrol seemed to be handling themselves, he could see streaks of light as Green Patrol finally launched but it would still take them too long to get out to him. Just then a single fighter with GalCorp markings suddenly jumped into the system near the chaos.

"GalCorp ship, This is Firehawk of Waypoint Security, I don't know who you are or whatever you are doing but a little help would be nice" Andrew said desperately into the comms. The Reply came swift.
"This is White Knight, rendering assistance." Eastman realised this was probably for him the worst thing to do but morally, he knew he had to do something, besides his light engines were close the meltdown so he wasn't going anywhere any time soon. Arming his weapons he flew into the fray dispatching the nearest pirate with ease and he and Andrew worked together to take out the last of that group by engaging the lone pirate and in the heat of battle the enemy pilot was so focused on the Waypoint Security fighter that he forgot about the GalCorp ship slotting in behind and raking the engines with laser fire, the debris from the resulting explosion peppering Matt's shields.
"So..White Knight that as some smooth flying, but its not over yet" Andrew said as he flew to the aid of his colleagues, Eastman tucked in just behind and to the left as they both headed to the Starcore ship and the ongoing firefight by then Green Patrol had joined them

and were making light work of it, one ship turned around and was flying out to space.

"leave it to me" Matt said pivoting his ship around and locking on with guided missiles destroying it instantly, Andrew was about to congratulate him for his help when the ships computer flashed an alert when it properly scanned Eastman's ship, saying he was a wanted man.. for murder no less. Andrew sighed and shook his head. surely not but it was his duty to bring the guy in.

"White Knight" Andrew said calmly and with a hint of sadness "Drop your shields and power down your weapons and fall in behind me, your under arrest...I'm sorry", He hoped the GalCorp pilot would listen, the guy had saved his life it would feel wrong to fight him, he saw on the scanners Easton had indeed done as asked.

"Following your lead Firehawk, Don't worry I will not try anything stupid" Matt flew in behind Andrew with Phil and Rob taking flanking positions, Green Patrol took over perimeter duties, Matt just hung his head, he didn't know what else to do.. hopefully he could explain to them the situation, that Firehawk seemed reasonable, he knew there was no way he could fight out of it, as they entered the docking bay, he was directed to a cordoned off area where some armed guards were waiting.

Andrew landed his ship and immediately got out headed over to Matt's ship, taking his helmet off as he walked, he had just got there to see Easton get out his ship and a guard to unceremoniously ram the butt of his rifle into the pilots gut, Andrew broke into a run

" That's for murdering those techs." said the guard and went to strike again only to feel Andrews HKG 170 sidearm barrel pressed against his temple, Matt suddenly noticed the guards had turned their weapons to the security pilot.

"Do it again.. I dare you," said Andrew calmly though the sweat on his face and matted down brown hair combined with his light blue eyes made him look crazed "you won't get another chance, the guy is innocent until proven guilty or don't you remember the law?" by that time Rob and Phil had reached the scene and had their weapons drawn on the guards, they didn't really have an agenda in this, they were just sticking up for their fellow pilot, just then a shot was fired in the air and everyone turned around, the administrator, Gustav was there with the Chief of Security, a large man mountain named Obasi Adeyemi who was standing with his sidearm pointed in the air.

"Everyone calm down," he bellowed "Guards get this suspect to a cell, Red Patrol come with me," the guards firmly but politely ushered Matt away and the security pilots fell into step as the chief walked to the lifts "I am sorry about Valdez, I truly am. I am also pleased about the manner in which you dealt with the pirate attack but..." he turned to face them, his face all business "...that does not excuse you for your actions just there, if you see a suspect getting treated poorly again come to me am I understood." they all nodded silently "Good, now if you do not mind I have work to do, you are stood down for the time being, Firehawk you are now the lead pilot of Red patrol." he concluded and walked away, Phil shook his head and put his hand on Andrew's shoulder

"Don't worry I'm thinking the same," he said "why would a murderer assist us and not side with the pirates?" Andrew turned round and nodded, Rob leaned against some cargo crates.

"Yeah, what Phil said, something doesn't add up," Rob mused as he ran his hands though his blonde hair and absently looked up at the docking bay ceiling "And what was with the chief trying to make out we are all over emotional, yeah I'm sad we lost Angel. She was a big part of our team but if he knew her like we do.. like we did... he'd know she wouldn't want us crying about it. She would be more concerned with did we complete the mission." Andrew nodded.

"I know Rob..I know, she always said she would rather die in her cockpit fighting than on a hospital bed. I know I will always wonder could I have done more to help her, the sad fact is I couldn't but I do know one thing, there is something not right going on with the GalCorp pilot and I'm gonna find out what." he headed to the cells.

"We will be in the bar at the usual time, to toast Angel, let us know if you find anything " Phil said as Andrew passed him.

CHAPTER 3

Matt slumped down on the bunk and looked around his cell, how could be be so stupid, him, a wanted man, helping a local security pilot when it would have been easier to just run,he punched the thin mattress in frustration.

"Well that is one way to relive stress" said a voice, Matt turned around to see the pilot he had saved, as the pilot walked closer, Matt could see for the first time that the pilots stride was awkward, as if carrying a knee injury.

"Firehawk I presume?" he guessed.

"Andrew Douglas of Waypoint Station Security, but yes some people call me by my callsign Firehawk" he said politely. Matt nodded and took a breath.

"Matt Easton, of.." he shook his head" ..formerly of Galcorp Defence Force, callsign White Knight" he said, it seemed only fair to extend the same pleasantries, getting up, Matt walked forward and leaned on the old fashioned bars, only to get a small jolt of electricity.

"Be careful, our chief is old fashioned, he thinks bars are more real, took forever to get him to install the electrical current flowing through it." Andrew said smiling. Matt rubbed his hand and lay down gazing at the ceiling, and started humming a tune to himself, Andrew stayed, thinking.

"Whats on your mind?" Matt asked curiously

"I thought it would be obvious, why were you on the run? the feed said you were some homicidal maniac but my gut tells me that's not the case... so... what's the deal?" Matt turned on his side and looked at Andrew and looked into his eyes to gauge him, he felt he could trust Andrew, so he sat back up.

"Well, after a few tours in the armed forces, I wanted a new challenge and GalCorp had a recruitment drive wanting experienced pilots for their defence fleet, I wanted to help people and there is not much of a miliary presence out here and as for law enforcement I don't think even Colonial Marshals have much to do with the outer territories" Andrew nodded with interest, for all the military and various law enforcement organisations tried, there were still a lot of systems poorly protected if at all, and especially in the outer systems so it was not uncommon for groups and companies to employ their own, albeit highly regulated, fleets to protect their assets. Matt sighed then continued

"I quickly noticed something was amiss, training

and wargames exercises seemed more offensive minded than defensive, the out and out refusal to stop pirates targeting non GalCorp ships, when I was due to take an assignment the SS Ramesses, only to find out last minute i was transferred to a lesser mission. to calm down and relax i worked on my ship and i was doing some flight checks and was retuning my comms system, it had been playing up, only to intercept a message between Director Gladstone and the Silver Blades pirate leader Remus Fox discussing payment for a mission or something, I recorded what I could before they discovered someone had tapped into the line, there was only one option for me, get in my ship and get out of there and here I am, in a cell awaiting transfer to some prison colony where I'll be conveniently out of the way or worse, allowing them to slaughter innocents.." he slumped his head in frustration.

"The Silver Blades attacked a ship bound for Astra Sanctuarium a few days ago and it was full of pilgrims, innocent people Astra Sanctuarium is a mineral rich planet, now that I think of it, we have had many reports of pirates operation in that sector and they are always targeting the planets with some commercial worth, but where the people there do not use it commercially. Now they have appeared to be genuine acts of piracy, but if what you are saying is true, it looks like GalCorp is trying to scare and intimidate the people off or offer 'protection in return for whatever rights they want, what were you hoping to do? raise an army? It sounds by the lack of military intervention there is some bribery or something going on so they won't help," he said shaking his head and smiled sadly "well unfortunately I have to go, meeting some colleagues to toast a fallen comrade, but I'll stop by the chiefs office and see what can be done for you." Andrew said as he was walking away. Matt stood and with a defiant tone said.

"Yes, I would start an army to fight for the weak out there, no one seems to care and you guys can only do so much," Matt suddenly remembered something "you said your callsign was Firehawk?" Andrew nodded. "I remember hearing of a pilot called Firehawk in the year above me in the academy, a demon in the simulators took on five ships on his own and survived, was well known for unusual flying style, but, suddenly he was gone, what happened?" Andrew looked at Matt and sighed

"they found out I had a rare knee condition that caused extreme pain under pressure, be it walking or flying, the only option beyond becoming a painkiller addict was to get a doctor to dull the pain receptors around the knees, unfortunately that made me unfit for service, but, this place had lower standards. Like you I want to protect the weak, I'd love to do something I'm a Catholic myself, I have been to Astra Sanctuarium several times, I know, the thought of anyone attacking the colony disgusts me to the bone, they are just religious pilgrims minding their own business, but what can I do?" he says with a sound of helplessness "what can I do?" Matt met his gaze.

"We could work together, help me out of here, if you are the same man I heard of, he would never back away from a challenge," he said chancing his luck "help me to help others." Andrew looked down, pinching the bridge of his nose.

"I need time to think about this, okay?" Matt nodded.

"I understand." he said solemnly, Andrew stalked out without saying a goodbye, he had to get more information.

Chief Adeyemi sat at his desk watching Andrew study the full report of the incident surrounding Easton, confusion evident on the pilot's face.

"Officer Douglas, I'd like to finish up here tonight," he said getting up and putting his jacket on "Yes, there is so many holes in the claims made you could paint it yellow and call it Swiss cheese, yes it doesn't make sense but by tomorrow when the GalCorp people come to collect him it will no longer be our problem." and he turned to head out, Andrew slapped the folder down on the table.

"Chief, if you know like I do that there is something wrong.." he trailed off just picking up on something the chief said "Galcorp collecting him? not CBI or the Marshals?, oh now I know something stinks, we should examine the flight recorder, Easton says the evidence to his claims are there." Andrew stood staring at Adeyemis back and the chiefs shoulders sagged and he turned around, defeat etched on his face.

"I know," he explained "I have been in contact with both agencies, both have decided to let GalCorp deal with this, it happened on their station, their security services have jurisdiction apparently..and we can't look at the recordings, GalCorp demanded the computers were wiped.."

"... You got to be kidding," Andrew interrupted "and you gave the order without even looking ar the data from it?"

"No, I don't like it any more than you.. The command code to delete the database on the fighter was included in the warrant they sent out. Nevland went over my head and told the guards to do it the moment he landed, I questioned his reasons for doing that, but you know what he is like, he told me that he does not want to upset Galcorp as they do send a lot of business our way" sighed the Chief, Andrew knew it wasn't the first time the two men had a falling out over the old argument of doing what is lawful and what is good for the station, Andrew shook his head

"We all know Gustav doesn't care much about but I tell you I'm inclined to believe what he told me over what these files from GalCorp say" he then relayed to the chief what Matt had told him about the recording

"Unfortunately Officer Douglas," The chief said with a defeated sigh "any evidence to back you up has been deleted.." he saw Andrew about to say something but raised a hand in warning "and yes the fact they wanted it deleted does make everything even more suspicious but without anything to back him up, we can do nothing more for him," he was about to say he hopes it will be a fair trial but they both guessed from the evidence that the chances of that were slim "They will pick him up tomorrow and we will go about our business, its all we can do." Andrew stood silent in thought then looked at the Chief with a defiant fire in his eyes he had never saw before in the pilot.

"Nothing legally anyway." Andrew said, The chief shook his head and replied.

"what you gonna do? break him out? ruin your career over this?" he pinched the bridge of his nose in frustration "I believe the rest of Red patrol are waiting for you in the station bar, go, have a few drinks get some sleep, I'll see you and the rest here tomorrow before your patrol time to discuss a replacement for Officer Valdez." Andrew calmed down when reminded of Angel. "

your probably right chief." he said in a tone that suggested he wasn't fully convinced, he sighed and walked out past the Chief, Andrew was a good pilot if a little hotheaded but the Chief wasn't worried, he wasn't going to do something stupid.

"To Angel, one of the best Pilots I ever knew." Andrew said, drink in hand held high, Phil and Rob likewise with their drinks.

"To Angel." they said in unison, then stood in silence, for a few minutes, they were joined by a friend of theirs, a station technician and shuttle pilot Gareth

Brazil, sometimes more commonly known to his friends as 'G' who listened intently as Andrew brought him up to speed with he days chaos, Gareth looked confused.

"They demanded a data wipe?! he said thinking "its not unheard of but not in something like this and that line about software..I don't buy it but what you gonna do?" Andrew ushered the group to a quiet booth in the bar and told them of Matt's offer and then the whole business with Gustav wiping the fighters data. Phil shook his head and took a large gulp of his drink, the beer wasn't the best he tasted but the quality had improved at the station recently.

"Andrew, don't tell me your considering helping this guy?" when he saw Andrew just stare, with a look he had only saw a few times before "Dammit mate you'll get us killed!" Andrew shook his head.

"No Phil," he said "not us, not asking you guys to get involved, this is something I have to do alone. I know before when Gustav has overruled the chief on things we have went along with it even if we didn't want to but not this time, if I do nothing he is as good as dead and you know it but it is my choice alone okay?" This time Rob interjected.

"Sorry, not accepting that, we are a team, besides Phil and I both agreed even before you told us the whole story that guys probably innocent and I signed up to help the innocent, not to do GalCorps dirty work." Phil nodded in agreement and added.

"We are supposed to be enforcing the law but as you pointed out out beloved administrator stops us doing our job, we've had enough."

"The three of us will break him out before GalCorp get here." Robb continued. Andrew sat upright, he shouldn't be amazed at the loyalty of his fellow pilots but he was, he never thought they would do something like this, both were risking a lot to do this, just then Gareth spoke up.

"Don't you mean four?" the others looked at him shocked "What?" he continued "whatever plan you have you will need someone with my skills, and anyway I am bored here and if you guys go? who am I going to drink with? the losers at green patrol?" he shook his head "And besides I can secure a shuttle for us to escape in without alerting suspicion, but what what is the plan once we get him off the station?" Phil gave Gareth a friendly backslap and Andrew shook his head.

"There is no way to talk any of you out of it is there?" he looked to see all three of them shake their heads, they were committed to the plan "As for once we get out of here, I have an idea, but Phil..you won't like it." Phil thought for a minute then rolled his eyes.

"No, not John Adams, anyone other than that petty crook?" Andrew took a breath and tried to reason with Phil.

"Phil, his ship stops off here tomorrow and the guy woes me a few favours, plus I hear he has apparently very recently acquired some military grade fighters, I don't know what class, but they have to be better than the crap we fly here" he saw Phil look deep in thought as he continued "and we will need decent ships if we are to do Easton's plan to help the people of the outer territories." It made sense and Phil knew it.

"Okay," he said finally, "Still don't trust the guy though," and he finished his drink in one go "so how are we going to break Easton out?" Andrew leaned close and motioned the others to do likewise.

"Well here is what we do first..."

CHAPTER 4

Even though there was no-one else in the cellblock, Matt still experienced trouble sleeping. The recent events playing over and over in his head like some sick joke in the end he decided to sit up, the lights had brightened up as the stations lighting entered day mode. Matt took to pacing his cell an nearly leaned on the barrier but remembered what the security pilot had told him, suddenly there were voices from the corridor.

"...Got clearance to take the prisoner for some last questions before GalCorp forces take him." said a familiar voice "Chief Adeyemi's orders." Another voice replied.

"This is irregular, I'll need to see your clearance."

"Here it is, right here," the first voice said followed by striking sound followed by the sound of a large weight hitting metal floor, the doors opened and

Andrew, dragging a guard by the feet came in, he wordlessly took the guards identity card and used it to open the Easton's cell before further dragging the guard into the cell, Easton stood astonished and confused, Andrew threw him the bag he had slung over his shoulder.

"Security isn't as tight as it should be, only one guard... careless, here put these on, can't you tell a jailbreak when you see one," Andrew said as he managed to, with Matt's help put the guard on the bed and covered him with a blanket "It won't fool anyone for long but it will give us the time we need," he uttered. With urgency, Matt opened the bag, in it was a Security flight jacket, a baseball cap, sunglasses and a belt with holster and standard issue pistol, Matt held the pistol up and looked at Andrew.

"You sure? you trust me enough?" he asked.

"Sure," Andrew countered rather incredulously "I don't make a habit of this you know, now hurry, G's system hack won't last much longer," Matt didn't ask who G was or anything, he hurriedly put on the items and followed Andrew out to the nearest shuttlelift neither spoke on the journey, when the lift doors opened they made their way to the hanger.

"Thank you, If I'm honest I wasn't sure you would actually help..why?" Matt finally said, he looked at Andrew's face as they walked trying to figure him out, Andrew stopped and looked at Matt intently.

"After we spoke, I went to talk to the chief, it turns out al evidence you recorded has been erased," he then went on to tell Matt the discussion he had with the Chief, Matt listened nodding, Andrew started again heading towards the docking bay "So," he added as they walked "I had enough, Gustav, the administrator who runs this station has always had dubious morals but not I think he's full on corrupt, I refuse to do his dirty work." they turned a corner, right into Rob and Matt, Matt pulled the pistol from the holster and aimed at Phil who was closest to him, Phil snorted and brushed the weapon away.

"Hey. take it easy.. you are late but luckily Gareth has secured the shuttle." Matt looked puzzled, he hadn't expected the others to be part of this but that was a question to ask later they hurriedly made their way to one of the stations utility shuttles, as they walked up, one of the pilots of Green patrol, and officer by the name of Maciej Dziekanowski, also known by his callsign Magic saw them and called out.

"hey what's Red Patrol doing on station at this time?" Andrew peeled off the group and steered Maciej away sighing,

"We have a new recruit from the reserve lists to train, I want to see what he is like in a shuttle, don't want him trashing a fighter in his first training mission do we?" Maciej shrugged it made sense, Andrew left to join the others, when he climbed in the back he noticed the back had four storage containers, Andrew pointed to them with a confused look.

"Oh," Gareth said as he looked back from the pilots seat "while you guys were away setting things up and stuff I raided your quarters and lockers and grabbed as much as I could from each, its not like we are going back," He looked at Matt and smiled "Haven't forgotten you, I'm sure that flightsuit probably is starting to get a little ripe inside, there's a bag there, various lost and found items that may fit along with some extra Waypoint Station Security gym attire I took from the quarter master, don't worry got your sizes from the file GalCorp sent the station," he said smugly "all aboard the jailbreak express." the doors closed and he eased the shuttle off the pad and casually flew out of the bay, as usual the station was a hive of activity as usual Matt looked at the others then outside.

"So? what's the plan now?" he wondered, Andrew smiled.

"We fly out to the outer edge of the stations scan range where a ship, the SS Thunderclap will take us away from here," Phil snorted smoothed his dark hair down and shook his head but Andrew continued "The captain has agreed to supply us with what we need to enact your plan, he owes me though I had to tell him why we were doing it before he agreed." he shrugged and sat in the co-pilots seat just as a large vessel jumped into the system, its sleek curves and light blue flashes of colour, it was the SS Ramesses, a shuttle was launched with a fighter escort.

"Overkill or what? if that idiot doesn't hurry up we are screwed." said Phil pointedly.

The administrators office on the station wasn't the biggest and a man of Chief Adeyemi's stature made it seem smaller as he once again tried in vain to let him investigate the Easton case more, Gustav sat emotionless, two of the stations security guards flanking him when Captain Miller and his GalCorp guards marched in.

"Captain Joseph Miller here to escort the prisoner back to Carnarvon to stand trial" he handed the appropriate papers with a flourish to Gustav who gave the papers a casual glance before saying

"Everything seems in order Captain, glad to help GalCorp, as you can see we have him safely locked up." Adeyemi took a look too and noted that they had already scheduled his execution, Officer Douglas was right he thought now more than ever he he had a feeling Easton was innocent. Gustav he flicked a switch and on the monitor behind him appeared... the guard Andrew had earlier knocked out, now awake and waving his arms to attract the attentions of the camera, he looked at Miller and smiled feebly.

"I apologise, I will sound the alarm at once, Adeyemi, alert the security forces, scramble a patrol.." he was cut off when his console exploded in sparks, everyone looked to see the Chief with his sidearm pointed at the console, and his security badge in his other hand.

"No," he said solemnly, he had realised who had broken the Galcorp pilot out, damn Officer Douglas, he should have saw it, but he sympathised with the pilot and admired him for standing up for what he believed in "I've had enough of serving you, you are corrupt, you are willing to hand over an innocent man to die, I can no longer be part of it." and he tossed his badge down, Gustav looked at him intently, anger rising.

"You!..Guards take him to the cells." he said and the guards either side of him approached the chief, one put a hand on his shoulder, he shrugged it off saying.

"I know where the cells are." and walked out of the office with the guards flanking him, Captain Miller pulled out his own commlink.

"Miller to SS Ramesses, launch second fighter group, sweep the area for suspicious vessels" he stared deep into Gustav's eyes and slammed his fist on the table and wordlessly left, his guards following close behind. Gustav walked out to the hall and stopped the nearest guard and took the man's commlink and input the frequency that would tie it into the stationwide announcement system.

"This is Administrator Nevland, all security search the station for an escaped prisoner, Green and Red Patrols, scramble your fighters and join Blue Patrol and the Galcorp forces in scanning the ships in the area, priority one." he handed the guard back his comms before running after Miller in the hop to convince them it wasn't his fault, as he turned to corner, he nearly ran into Maciej, who was heading to the docking bay too to launch.

"Sorry sir", Maciej said "Green Patrol will be ready to join Red and Blue Patrols on patrol soon."

Gustav waved him on then it hit him.

"Officer Dziekanowski, what do you mean Red Patrol are already out there? I literally just gave the order..." then it slowly hit both of them, Maicej ran with extra purpose and left Gustav standing in shock, when GalCorp hears about this...

"Well, they are on to us now." Gareth shouted back to the passenger area "a stationwide search, fighters launching, both ours and GalCorp" he looked out the viewscreen, "where is that ship, there was only so many times he could pretend to be scanning the derelict hull of the SS Goldrush for salvage when the comms beeped, Andrew hit the activation button

"Firehawk, this is Magic, look I know what you done and trust me I don't like the situation anymore than you, but if you guys follow me back, you will be treated fairly, please respond." Andrew turned to Gareth and quietly asked.

"How soon before Green patrol are in weapons range?" Gareth indicated three minutes then tapped the scanner monitor that showed some GalCorp ships seemed in a race with Green Patrol for the shuttle, just then a beat up old cargo ship jumped into the system, it was the SS Thunderclap, its side bay doors started to open.

"Well, are you guys getting in or not?" A voice came over the comms, Gareth put full power into the engines and headed to the larger vessel the GalCorp fighters, having overtook Green Patrol started to fire, Gareth took the shuttle into the cargo ship at full speed, not bothering with the landing gears, he landed it and the ship skidded to a halt just short of the bulkhead as the shots from the fighters glanced harmlessly off the bay doors closing, the SS Thunderclap then re-engaged its lightdrive engines and was gone just as Green Patrol got to the scene.

Maciej had noticed the GalGorp ships did not bother to aim for the shuttles engines or use their EMP torpedoes to disable, they were aiming to kill.

"Hey", he got on the comms to the GalCorp fighters "we were supposed to disable and detain, not destroy, report back to your ship at once, this is Waypoint Security jurisdiction." the Galcorps looked for a minute as if they wouldn't comply but they turned around and headed back to the SS Ramesses, but not before one of the pilots answered back with a chilling warning.

"Their fate has already been sealed."
Maciej sighed and rubbed his eyes and said out out to no one in particular.

"Good luck with that, rather you than me," he knew Red Patrol would be a hard group to beat he then added to himself before guiding Green Patrol back "Firehawk you are out of your mind you really are."

CHAPTER 5

The SS Thunderclap jumped out of lightspeed near the Barbeau Nebula, its blue and purple lighting a soothing sight to the fugitive pilots as they stood on the ships bridge. The ships captain, John Adams turned his chair.

"I wish you had given me more warning I could have gotten you the ships before I got you guys but as it is here we are, I only ask you tell no-one else where my supply is." The pilots looked at each other confused, Matt spoke up pointing outside.

"In the nebula?" he asked, clearly puzzled, John just smiled weakly and said.

"That's right, long story but for another time best not be waiting any longer than we need to because ..."

"... you are a scumbag who will rob us blind and throw us out an airlock first chance her gets." Phil interrupted dryly, John just rolled his eyes.

"Hi Phil, love you too, I'm not that kind of person. Yes I do indulge in odd bit of smuggling, trust me when I say most cargo ships do the same, I am just safeguarding my stock," he sighed then turned to Andrew "I had reread your message a few times, you guys seriously taking the fight to GalCorp on your own? You are brave i got to give you that, i can give you what you asked for at the bitcreds we agreed on, are you really sure you want to.." He was interrupted by the shipwide alert alarms.

"Another ship just jumped in to the system, its the SS Ramesses." said Johns weapons officer, a young man by the name of Ben Tracey "they have a weapons lock on us." suddenly the ship jolted from laser fire tot he shields, John doe the only thing he could do.

"Tessa, take us into the nebula, full speed, Ben, return fire." everyone knew the weapons systems on the ship would have little effect but they had to do something, Tessa London, an attractive if stern woman with unnaturally bright green hair was a competent helm officer and wasted no time executing the order.

"Captain Miller, we found them." said Millers first officer, a short man by the name of Ronald Cairns, the bridge of the SS Ramesses was combat ready, Miller smiled

"Good, launch fighters to ensure they don't get away, one flight should do it." He knew the smaller cargo vessel could outrun him and it had a head start and looked to be going into the nebula, smart move by the ships captain, whomever it was.

"Okay, how did they knew where we were," asked Phil to no one in particular "G, you did turn off the transponder... didn't you?" all eyes turned to Gareth who nodded.

"yeah, sure I did, unless.. oh no, don't tell me they were fitted with backups, I thought that was only station security vessels, sorry guys." now was not the time for recriminations. Ben looked up from the scanner on his terminal and announced.

"Fighters launched, four ships on a direct intercept course." Andrew went up to Johns chair.

"So," Andrew said "I assume you have a plan." more explosions rocked the ship as the GalCorp fighters targeted the helpless ship There was only one thing for it, John knew it.

"We go into the nebula, it was the plan anyway, we just have more urgency, Tessa, take power from everything except life support and dump them into the engines if you have to." he ordered, they had to make it, the fighters attacked again and again, managing to knock out the lightdrive engines.

On the SS Ramesses bridge, Captain Miller was enjoying watching the pilots pick apart and almost play with their prey, disabling various systems before going for the kill, he had saw them do it several times before.

"Captain," Commander Cairns said suddenly, "they are entering the nebula, shall we keep up the attack?", Miller pondered it a few moments before shaking his head.

"No, recall the fighters but keep close tot he nebula, keep an eye on the scanners, we'd be blind if we go in, make sure the minute it exits at any point, we will be there waiting." he said as he sat back on his captains chair smiling. they were only delaying the inevitable.

An hour passed as they went further into the nebula, the damage reports were not positive, shields weapons and lightdrive were gone, at least two decks are open to space, they were repairing what they could bu it wasn't looking good at all, the pilots were told they were following a locator beacon what would show them the source of the merchandise though Phil still maintained the crew were planning to betray them somehow, suddenly out of the main viewport something slowly came into view, it was a ship, the closer they got the better they could see it, it reminded Andrew of the old sea naval aircraft carriers he used to see in military history books, only with an enclosed and pressurised flight deck (that still ran the length of the ship) and large engine banks that were about a third of the length of and attached to the rear half of the ship.

"What the.. that's an Olympus Class, not saw one of those in years," exclaimed Rob, the Olympus Class light carrier was one of the earlier starfighter carrier designs, entirely obsolete by the time the war broke out and was relegated to training duties "The UES Hermes, yeah, it was my first posting, brings back some old memories." Phil glared at John.

"Explain.." he demanded, John sighed and stood up, walking toward the viewport.

"Well, for one you are right, its an Olympus class, the UES Hades to be exact, I had to use this nebula as cover for repairs after running afoul of the Venom Fang pirates... and yes Phil I was supplying them with equipment, no weapons before you say anything in fact my refusal to do so resulted in this little escapade... Anyway, we came across this beauty and boarded her in the hopes of finding parts, the ship is in as perfect condition as it can be, if it wasn't for the fact the engines appear to be non functioning I would have sold it but as it stands I came up with the idea of selling the fighters, shuttles and what ever else I could." he said looking at Phil daring him to react, Phil just stared back, Rob however looked deep in thought He then asked.

"The UES Hades you said?" John nodded.

"yes, why?"

"The fate of the UES Hades is a mystery that dates back to when the Olympus Class were being built," Rob said, pacing as he did "She was in the final stages of being built at the docks at Jupiter and the computer core was being installed, but one of the techs responsible was secretly a member of the group Starpeace."

"Starpeace?" Matt said confused "That group who

believe that by bringing war to the stars we are destroying some sort of cosmic balance or something?" Rob nodded.

"Yeah amongst other things but as I was saying, The tech uploaded a virus program to sabotage her, at first when it activated everything seemed fine, but systems started acting up or going offline, things soon got out of hand the self destruct suddenly activated and wouldn't deactivate no matter what they did, in the end everyone evacuated then suddenly the lightdrive started to power up and she jumped out, destroying the surrounding docks. They caught the tech years later trying the same on another ship and he was arrested but not before admitting to the loss of the UES Hades." the others stood in amazement, Phil shook his head.

"Rob, I remember you telling me this years ago, but if the self destruct activated why is it in front of us now? and why did no one look for it?" he asked.

"Well," Rob mused "They assumed it must have been destroyed by the self destruct as for why it didn't, I don't know."

"I think I do," came a voice, Tony Moss, the SS Thunderclaps engineering chief entered the bridge "The computer core is slag, the ships basically brain dead, must have been part of the program you mentioned and when it melted down it must have stopped the self destruct," he handed John a datapad "Its not good new, lightdrive and weapons are so badly damaged I'm not sure I can repair them." John just sighed.

"do your best Tony, that's all I ask, Tessa, how

long before we dock with the UES Hades?" John was wondering if helping the pilots was really worth the hassle, Tessa looked up from the helm controls.

"Five minutes, coming up to the portside docking port" she replied, John and the others left the bridge to get ready to board the carrier.

The UES Hades was like a ghost ship, devoid of the normal sounds you'd expect, Tony had explained that while the ships computer core was not working, some systems were still functioning but on low power, they made it to the large hanger deck, thebay doors fore and aft were closed but what caught their eye was the row of fighters that faced them.

the cockpit was at the very front and on the nose was a rapid firing laser cannon that could rotate on both axis to give the weapon a wide field of fire, two short wings heald brackets for missiles and on the wing tips thruster pods with both aft and fore thrusters, the main fuselage tapers at the back and ended in two large thrusters giving the ship a vaguely 'T' shape, Rob knew exactly what they were.

"FA 255 Battleaxe Class multirole fighters, man these are old, already on their way out by the time the Olympus Class ships were being built they were superseded by the FA 265 and the FA 280 after that." he said remembering his military history as he admired the closest fighter, Andrew walked around it, looking closely.

"Are they suited for our needs more to the point?" he asked Rob as he looked in the open cockpit, Rob gave a big grin.

"If G gets a look at them and says they can fly these will more than do, they were built to last, later models traded armour and shielding for manoeuvrability, and cheaper cost, they won't be the fastest and they might a little sluggish compared to what we are used to but they are better than most fighters we will come up against." They sent the next few hours examining the fighters as Gareth checked each ship out

"Turns out there is three squadrons worth with enough spares to keep them going and even build more if it was ever needed" Gareth said and pointed out that while they were low on power from being disused, they were still flightworthy.

"So what now?" asked Phil as he adjusted the seat of the fighter he had picked out for himself, Matt looked around and said.

"Andrew and I were speaking about this, we were thinking of heading to the station known as the Hub, maybe seeing if we can recruit others to the cause, then take it from there" just then John and Tony came walking to them

"Got bad news, the SS Thunderclaps lightdrive is a write off and there's no compatible parts here I guess I could always send Tony in my shuttle to get parts and come back but we don't know if the SS Ramesses is still out there and even if we could get the parts my ships in bad shape... what?" he trailed off when he noticed

Andrew smiling.

"John. the solution is right in front of you," he said and noted Johns confused expression so he stretched out his hands "The UES Hades, think on it this ship can hold at least the same amount in its cargo bays as what you have now, she's not that much larger than the SS Thunderclap, she's already legally yours by law under salvage rights plus you have the best part."

"And what would that be?" John asked curiously, Andrew looked at Matt giving him a I know what I'm doing look.

"Well," he started "our current plan while solid carries a lot of risk, basing ourselves at the Hub, a largely lawless station and limits what we can do, however, a mobile base like this? we can do so much more and safe in the knowledge we won't be betrayed by someone looking for a nice GalCorp payday," Phil snorted but Andrew continued "Plus it means you mentioned you have found it harder lately with attacks on your ship during runs, you will have us as fighter escort for your runs, think on it." John was thinking he relised Andrew was talking sense it would mutually benefit them to work together.

"I have two concerns," he said finally "One as you know or guessed I do..occasionally of course.. have done some trades that may be..illegal, for us to work you would need to turn a blind eye to the contents of the cargo bays that are designated for my use alone, agreed?" All but Phil nodded, Andrew looked at Phil imploringly.

"Okay, okay but if you ever put our lives at risk with your crap.." he said menacingly.

"I won't, trust me." John countered, Phil just stared then finally nodded, John raised his next concern.

"While the lightdrives are clearly operational, most things aren't, the main drive is not connected, the shield power regulator wasn't installed and half the weapons are not operational, the other half not even installed yet and there is various other minor issues." He looked at Tony to explain further.

"We would need a spacedock to get this ship up and running and even if the other systems were fully functioning, we can't operate this ship safely without a main computer, otherwise I may have considered taking it before now but I'm guessing if you brought the matter up you must have some idea." but Andrew just looked blankly at him, he had forgotten that part, luckily Gareth spoke up.

"Lets deal with last problem first, what computer core does the SS Thunderclap use?" he asked.

"It's a Lovett series 88 model, why do you ask?" Tony answered.

"We could disconnect the computer core of the UES Hades and replace it with the one from the SS Thunderclap." he said excitedly, Tony shook his head.

"I thought of that, its not fully compatible and the core itself is a mess, all the connections are melted." he said mournfully but Gareth was not put off.

"It is if we run bypasses to the physical core itself, sure it will mean ripping the core from the SS

Thunderclap bringing it her and patching it into the system physically but it could be done." he said hopefully, Tony thought for a minute.

"Granted it would only give us about seventy or eighty per cent of the computer capability a ship like this would usually have but its worth a try," he agreed "though what about the other issues? We could I suppose get the main drive online but would need to cannibalise parts from the SS Thunderclap to do that and to fix some of the problems this ship has, but the other issues? I'm not sure." but Gareth was already ahead of him.

"Well the weapons are not a priority right now but the engines and shields are, the engines seem the easiest part and as for the shields, it won't be ideal but the generators from the SS Thunderclap are damaged but the regulator is still working? right? why not use that?"

"You could," Tony said slowly "but we would only have at most sixty five per cent power to the shields, but we would be underpowered and outgunned in general." but Gareth explained that even then the UES Hades would still be formidable and was worth the risk, Tony nodded and greed, Andrew looked around smiling.

"Well we got a deal, we help you get this ship up and running and assist in your cargo runs if you let us make base here?" John nodded and extended his hand, Andrew took it and shook on the deal.

"Well this should be interesting." mused Phil dryly.

CHAPTER 6

Everyone, both the pilots and the crew of the SS Thunderclap worked together to transfer as much as they could from the stricken cargo vessel, upon further examination there were more problems with the UES Hades than initially thought, the starboard airlocks were all inoperable, the shipwide comms were only half connected and they needed to strip the SS Thunderclap of some of its consoles to use on the larger carrier, the most notable being the weapons console on the bridge but they fixed what they could, prioritising systems to get the ship moving as some of the repairs could be done on the move. Even then it would take several hours just to get the carrier moving, the shields and the engines were fixed first but it was the computer core that was the most difficult of the necessary tasks. Gareth and Tony were in the Core room trying to splice the new core in,

Gareth sighed as they worked.

"What have I gotten myself into." he muttered as he took great care in disconnecting the cabling and power conduits running to and from the original core, as Tony secured the housing for the SS Thunderclaps core to the floor with a few bolts just in front of the old ones housing.

"Its amazing there is still power after all this time." Gareth mused as they started to connect the the relays, Tony shrugged.

"These old military grade reactors in theory are capable of lasting hundreds of years, probably even more when it went in emergency power saving mode when the computer core failed," then he looked at the mass of cables and power conduits and sighed "Its going to be an nightmare patching all this up to work with this old thing." he said shaking his head, Gareth on the other hand was smiling.

"Tell you the truth, I'm not sure it will work either, but I enjoy a challenge." and they set to work.

On the main Hanger deck, next to the pristine fighters and the UES Hades compliment of shuttles including two large recovery shuttles for retrieving pilots who eject, was the sole shuttle from the SS Thunderclap. The Thunderclap One was a large modular shuttle designed for ferrying cargo to and from the ship. John insisted they take it, as the rest of the ships crew were busying themselves getting the ship ready, the years of floating derelict had allowed some of the systems that worked to get into disrepair, John and the pilots were going over the finer points of the partnership, Matt in particular was adamant about a few details.

"So," he said choosing his words carefully "you will allow us and anyone we recruit to live here and base and will assist in our fight with GalCorp? and all you are asking is we don't concern ourselves with your cargo? I don't see what is in it for you here." Phil nodded in agreement.

"I agree, there's gotta be something more." he said pointedly, John sighed.

"Between GalCorp and their Silver Blade lapdogs, not to mention other pirate groups, its getting way too dangerous in the outer regions, I had thought of taking a couple of fighters from here and hiring pilots but lets be honest, the best I'd get are some backwater idiots who think flying their daddy's mining shuttle a few times a week means they are a pilot at leas with you guys I know I will get decent protection," he said thinking "plus the more I think on it theres no way I could simply go back on the SS Thunderclap and continue as before, Galcorp have made it personal, if helping you guys upsets them its worth it." just then a large tabby cat ran between his legs and across the hanger, Tessa followed a few seconds later looking confused.

"Has anyone saw Nakamura?" he asked as she looked around.

"Who's Naka.."said Andrew confused"..wait the

cat? the cat's called Nakamura?" he realised, Phil smirked and shook his head.

"What kind of name is Nakamura for a cat?" his voice sounding highly amused.

"If you must know," Tessa countered with barely controlled rage "His full name is Shinsuke Nakamura actually, cats are people and deserve proper names too." she stormed off to look for the cat, John shrugged.

"I know, she is a little eccentric but she is the best helm officer I have ever had," he pleaded "Anyway, I better go and check on things." he said as he headed off to oversee the transfer of cargo and supplies from the SS Thunderclap, just then the lights in the hanger brightened and the hum of the engines were louder, over the ships comms came Gareth's voice.

"Guys, the UES.. or should I say SS Hades is operational." there was wave of cheers that swept over the hanger bay to that announcement.

The pilots and John's senior crew were in the ships pilots briefing room, a large room with a desk in front of a large screen and rows of chairs in a semi circle like an amphitheatre. They were listening as Tony told them the current status of the newly rechristened SS Hades.

"...Life support is fortunately fully functional, the only food dispensers working are in the mess hall for now, we can make do with that until we have time to fix the others. We have about forty per cent of the weapons compliment for a ship this size, we can to get one starboard airlock to function but unfortunately it would mean one of the port side airlocks would be out of commission, we had to install some consoles from the SS Thunderclap on the SS Hades bridge and other areas, our shields are functioning but only at sixty five per cent and the computer core transfer was successful but only working at seventy three per cent of what previous core would have been capable of. Everything else we can do in transit or once we have the parts needed but it will get us to the Hub at least as it is now." he said looking exhausted. "also apparently some of the storerooms are stocked up with flightsuits, crew jumpsuits, first aid kits and other items, all except weapons but I suppose it was getting ready for entering service" he concluded.

"So," said Matt "Where to first? the Hub?" John nodded.

"I'm going to need to recruit more crew, I assume you guys will want to recruit pilots plus hoping to pick up some stuff for the ship and a few jobs," he said, "I recommend once we go there you go to a bar called Lilly Pad and ask for the owner Lilly Tamzarian." Both Rob and Phil let a groan out.

"Something we should know about?" Asked Andrew confused, Phil straightened up in his chair and spoke.

"It was before you came to Waypoint Andrew, you do not want to cross her, we were convinced she was responsible for a number of attacks on cargo vessels years ago but couldn't prove it despite every time her ship, the SS Abstrakt had docked at the station, there would be attacks within twenty four hours of her leaving." he sighed and looked to the ceiling, rob continued the story.

"Eventually we captured a fighter pilot involved in one of these attacks, the guy was terrified but he was willing to gather the evidence we needed in return for immunity when we caught her the next time it happened," Rob said "So we let him go, made it look like he escaped but next time the ship visited the station nothing, we assumed he had double crossed us until we boarded a cargo ship they raided and found the poor guys dead body tied to the captains chair with his tongue cut out and a bomb strapped to him.. we barely escaped before it blew up.." Andrew and Matt looked at each other in shock.

"Guys," John interjected "As lovely as this story is, and yes I have heard many similar stories surrounding her, before we do anything there is the problem of what to do with the SS Ramesses, it will still be out there you do know that?"

"Way ahead of you John," Andrew said "Gareth has a plan, though we need the SS Thunderclap to do it." John nodded and silently gave his consent.

Captain Miller paced around the bridge of the SS Ramesses, they had been waiting hours but he knew how important it was, he had to deal with Easton before he did any real long term damage, the evidence may be deleted but Easton still saw something incriminating and they couldn't afford to have him loose and telling anyone what he witnessed

"How long has it been now?" he asked Cairns

"About five hours at least," the first officer said, checking his console "more like six, they must know they can't hide in there forever" just then Corbin Hayes marched onto the bridge.

"Let me launch a full squad and go in there after them." he said, looking at Miller intently. Miller did consider it but it would be too risky. However he could understand the pilot's frustration, this was taking entirely too long.

"Are you sure long range scanners haven't picked them up exiting the nebula from another point?" Miller asked Cairns, who nodded, he turned his attention to Corbin "I would love nothing more than to let you loose in there but you know the dangers of navigating a nebula, let alone fighting in one." suddenly Cairns stood up and shouted.

"Sir, a ship emerging from the Nebula, its the shuttle that left Waypoint." Miller went to his chair and keyed a command into the console attached and the scanner information appeared on the main screen just above the front viewport.

"Launch a flight of fighters, orders to destroy," he commanded, "Corbin I want you to stay here, let some of the other pilots handle this." Corbin looked ready to voice a protest but thought better of it and stood watching the tactical information there was something about the situation that didn't feel right, Miller could feel it. It was like this was designed to draw the SS Ramesses out of position, just as he saw the fighters streak to the shuttle out of the nebula shot out the SS Thunderclap, only the quick reflexes of the helm officer prevented a collision such was the that speed the cargo vessel exited.

"Fire all weapons on that ship." he yelled, anger evident in his voice, where they playing at?, soon the SS Thunderclap was engulfed in weapons fire.

"Sensors reading multiple hull breaches, she is going to blow."said of the the bridge officers from his console, just as he spoke the cargo vessel erupted in explosions, Miller looked out the viewscreen in silence before speaking to first officer Cairns.

"Have the fighters reported in?" Cairns nodded.

"Yes Captain, shuttle was destroyed with ease." he said smiling, "It was a clever manoeuvrer, I wonder which of them was actually the decoy.." Miller looked at Cairns thoughtful then shook his head as he stood and headed for the exit, it had been a long day.

"It doesn't matter now either way, they are dead now, Cairns you have the bridge, Once the fighters have docked engage the lightdrive, set course for our Asteroid mining operation in the outer territories and update Director Gladstone on the Easton situation." he commanded as he left, in the way to his quarters he had an uneasy feeling, but he wasn't sure why but something did not feel right, maybe after a sleep and a freshen up he would feel different.

CHAPTER 7

An Hour after the SS Ramesses left the area the SS Hades emerge from the Nebula, Andrew had joined John on the bridge.

"See John, told you the double bluff would work just thankful G was able to jury rig the autopilot systems to do the job." he said with a smile, John was mournfully looking at the floating wreckage that used to be his ship floating off to starboard, the ships name still partially visible on the charred hull. He was snapped out of his thoughts when Andrew patted his shoulder.

"Its the end of an era, she was the first ship I had you know," he turned to Andrew "but lets hope this is the start of a new era, ever been to the Hub before?" Andrew shook his head.

"No, I heard its quite a rough place from what I people have said in passing" Andrew replied, John continued

"You will love it trust me Tessa, set course for the Hub, lets see what this ship can do."

"Yes sir." Tessa said with a smile as she programmed the helm controls, the carrier jumped out the system.

It would take a few hours to get to the Hub which gave everyone a chance to relax for the first time in a while, Andrew headed to his newly assigned quarters. The pilots, appropriately chose to stay in the quarters that would have been taken up by the carriers pilots if it was a fully operational military vessel, the quarters had the added benefit of being closest to the hanger, his quarters were marked on the door by a piece of tape with his callsign on it, the room itself was compact and practical. a wide bunk set into bulkhead, a desk with chair, a screen set into the bulkhead above the desk and a built in wardrobe and drawers and a small separate room with toilet and washing facilities.

"Home sweet home." he uttered to himself and unpacked the storage container Gareth retrieved from Waypoint for him, he was halfway through unpacking with the door chimed and Matt stepped in.

"Hope I'm not disturbing," he asked, Andrew shook his head and gestured for Matt to sit on the chair, Matt's quarters were across the hall from Andrew's "I just want to thank you for.. well everything really." he said, Andrew smiled as he hung a set of rosary beads next to the bunk.

"Matt, trust me when I say this, I done what any decent person should do," he said as he stored some clothes "If I did nothing you would probably be dead by now." There was something about Andrew's reasoning and his actions that piqued Matt's curiosity.

"Why did you do it? and be honest." he asked, Andrew stopped and sat on the bunk rubbing his temples.

"Ever since I was little I was encouraged, mainly by my grandfather to be true to myself, he also instilled in me a strong sense of honour, I realised that the more I found out about your situation the more I felt something was wrong, I had to act, I couldn't simply sit back and do nothing any more." he then leaned back on the bunk and looked at the ceiling suddenly looking exhausted, Matt Pointed to Andrew's flight jacket and the military wings, which were silver ones cadets wore as opposed to the gold ones he and Rob had on their uniforms.

"I notice you still wear your cadet wings, why?" he asked curiously.

"It's a fair question," Andrew replied sitting back up to look at Matt "When the doctors discovered my knee condition and I was medically discharged I was devastated, I hadn't failed a test or done anything wrong, yet I was destined never to wear the gold wings and do my bit for my planet. I wear them as a reminder that I did my best and although ultimately is wasn't enough, I didn't let myself or others down, must sound crazy."

"No," replied Matt smiling "Its not, We're not that much different are we? we both want to do the right thing, to help others. I'm just glad to have earned your trust." Andrew shook his head and smiled.

"Matt, that moment you helped me with these pirates back at waypoint showed me everything I needed to know about you," he said getting up and resuming his unpacking, Matt stifled a yawn, prompting Andrew to ask "When is that last time you had a decent sleep?"

"Dunno," he replied "I probably should get rest I guess." Andrew gave hin a sympathetic look and said

"Well we have a few hours to kill, don't worry I'll wake you when we get to the Hub." Matt couldn't disagree and left Andrew to unpack.

Matt crossed the hall to his room, which unlike Andrew's it wasn't already littered with personal effects, all he had was the clothes provided by Gareth to unpack and he wasn't in the mood to do that yet he also decided to see what he could get at the Hub to make his quarters more homely as he took off his shoes he lay on his bed only to be disturbed with a knock on the door, It was Ben, John's weapons officer, Matt noted he was now wearing a jumpsuit from the ships stores with all the military insignia removed.

"Have you saw the cat?" he asked awkwardly, Matt looked back into this quarters and shrugged.

"No, I haven't, I take it Tessa asked you to help her." he said with a sigh, just then Tessa came up the hall.

"You found him?" she asked franticly. Ben and

Matt both shook their heads, just then a yell of pain came from one of the other rooms, the door to Phil's quarters slid open and out flew the cat, landing on the hard floor and hissing at the open doorway, Tessa ran up and scooped him in her arms as Phil, holding his left arm which was covered in scratches came out to the hall.

"That cat is a menace, we should blow him out the nearest airlock." he said angrily, Tessa stepped forward and was toe to toe with Phil

"If anything happens to Shinsuke," she said calmly and full of threat " I will come down here and castrate you with a blunt knife, go that?" and with that she kneed him in the crotch and walked off, Phil dropped to his knees in pain as Matt said to Ben.

"She really loves that cat doesn't she?" Ben nodded and headed off after her, Phil regained composure enough to go back to his quarters, Matt shook his head and closed his door and lay on his bunk, he was so tired he didn't even remember falling asleep.

Back in his quarters Andrew was finishing his unpacking, placing a framed photo of himself Angel, Phil and Rob on the desk, it was taken after one of their first missions together as Red Patrol, he remembered when he joined Waypoint security, initially he was there as a stopover before going on pilgrimage to Astra Sanctuarium but a recruitment poster for the security forces flight division caught his eye and they apparently they were so desperate they were willing to overlook his knee problem, assigned to Red patrol he bonded with them almost immediately. He wondered how Angel would have reacted to all this.

"Daydreaming are we?" he heard a voice, Andrew turned around he saw Phil and Rob standing at the doorway. Phil's arm as all scratched, but he didn't dare ask why, he heard the commotion outside the quarters and felt it best not to ask.

"Hi guys," he said as he closed the packing container, "settled in okay?" Phil and Rob both nodded, Phil then sat and spoke.

"Andrew, Rob and I have been talking, don't worry, we are still with you on all this but you do realise how dangerous recruiting others will be? We don't have much if anything to offer financially and I doubt anyone decent will sign up for free bed and board with a chance to go shoot some corporate ships once in a while, its hardly enticing is it? and will we be able to trust the ones who will join?"

"I had thought of that and more," Said Andrew wearily "We can't do it with just the four of us, well five if we can persuade G to fly too, we just need to be careful who we recruit that's all, we have flight simulators onboard so I am sure we an run people trough them to train them to our standard and I'm sure once we have a few successes more will join. As for security issues not much we can do but be vigilant and watch out for anything wrong,you guys have trusted me this far, trust me now.". Phil got up and nodded. "You are right," but then asked "How do you know John will be as vigilant about his recruitment?"

"Damn Phil," said Rob abruptly "You really don't trust the guy do you? He won't wanna do anything that will put him or his business in danger, hell the only reason he is letting us base himself here is for his own protection that and the hope by making life difficult for GalCorp our actions help his profit margins," Rob shook his head and looked at Andrew "you can take the man out of law enforcement but not law enforcement out the man," he said gesturing to Phil "Phil, you really should get those cat scratches treated, I think I saw some first aid kits in one of the storage rooms earlier." and with that they both left, Andrew just lay on his bunk, enjoying the silence, the only sound being the hum of the engines it was so relaxing, he had been fighting sleep ever since Matt had left but now he just let his eyes close and he fell into a deep and peaceful sleep.

The SS Hades came out of lightspeed just out of sensor range of the Hub, John and Andrew agreed the less people who saw the carrier the better, the pilots were all waiting on the hanger bay next to one of the shuttles, Gareth ran up to the group.

"Sorry I'm late, was just getting these." he said breathlessly, and handed out cards to everyone. Phil took one look and scowled.

"Bitcred burner cards?" he said with disdain.

"Phil, relax, before we left I managed to hack into your bank accounts and transfer the funds onto these,"

Gareth explained "I knew the minute we did this our accounts would be frozen and we need the money." it made sense, burner cards were an anonymous way to carry money and as such they were frowned upon in some places due to their association with illegal activities, Matt looked confused as he turned his over in his hands.

"But Gareth..I mean G surely my funds were seized before all this, why have I got a card?" he asked.

"Yeah," Gareth looked sheepish as he answered " I hope everyone doesn't mind but I skimmed a small amount off everyone's accounts to provide Matt some finances." No-one argued that point, it was only fair and considering a few minutes before they weren't even aware they would still have money to their names so it was more than acceptable. John walked past them, like the rest of his crew, he had taken to wearing a ships crew jumpsuit, though his had captains insignias on it ad teamed it with the black tactical vest he always wore.

"You guys coming? I'm taking the Thunderclap One." he asked as he hurried to his ship.

"Yeah, yeah," said Phil irritably "we're coming."

The Hades Three was the shuttle chosen to transport the pilots, primarily a troop transport, the interior had combat seating along the sides of the main compartment with seats at the front for a pilot and co-pilot. Gareth was the designated pilot.

"Flown anything like this?" Rob asked as he slid

into the co-pilots seat. Gareth shrugged.

"Looks simple enough" he said as he went through the startup sequence.

"Hey, how are you co-pilot?" Phil asked pointedly as he straped himself into on of the seats in the main compartment, Rob swivelled his seat round to face Phil.

"Simple Phil, I flew a few ships like these in my military days.. that and I was here first" he said with an impish grin.

"Real mature Rob." Phil retorted as Rob turned his seat to face the front again, laughing as he did so. Matt leaned close to Andrew and whispered.

"Are they always like this?" he asked.

"Not at all," Whispered Andrew "Just most of the time."

CHAPTER 8

Soon the Thunderclap One and the Hades Three shuttles had left the SS Hades and docked with the Hub, it was a station like no other Matt had saw before, it looked liek several stations cobbled together, it was the one of the largest stations in the colonies and the inside was just as large and chaotic, the main promenade area was a hive of activity, John turned to them and said.

"Well guys, the Lilly Pad is just up ahead, just ask to speak to Lilly, she will get the word out to pilots."

"Hold on." said Phil "Why are you not going with us?" but John just shrugged.

"I have business elsewhere, contracts to pick up, crew to hire, upgrades for the ship, general business." he answered and disappeared into the crowd, Leaving the five of them standing there, they all had decided to wear casual clothing as not to draw too much attention, Matt had changed into waypoint branded gym wear and the flight jacket Andrew had given him and they all done something to change their appearance a little, Andrew had started to grow a goatee, though it was growing in a slightly different shade of brown than his hair, Matt had shaven his black hair even shorter, Phil had his dark hair in a flat top and Rob was trying to grow a moustache which like the rest of his blonde hair had flecks of grey, Gareth just let his hair look messier than usual but they all looked somewhat different than they used to, Phil was the first to speak.

"So, I don't know about you but I'm getting a drink." and he walked towards the Lilly Pad bar, the others followed, The bar was unsurprisingly busy, drink and conversation flowing freely. They found a booth to occupy in quiet corner, it was decided that Andrew should go up and meet with Lilly, as Phil and Rob had met her before Gareth heard too many stories and Matt wanted to maintain a low profile, Andrew went up and spoke to one of the barstaff.

"Excuse me, Can I speak to your manager Miss Tamzarian, please." he said and flashed a smile, she didn't look impressed and shot him a glare with her striking light blue eyes.

"Who wants to know?" she sneered, he dropped the smile and stared at her.

"Okay," he said sighing "you wanna play it that way, I am looking to hire pilots and heard your manager is the best person to get the word out, now I could try elsewhere but I don't think she would be happy that you let some potential business slip past her." she stood staring at him for a few seconds before curtly nodding and walking away, she returned a minute later beaconing him to follow, he went with her behind the bar, down a short corridor and she gestured to a door and walked off, Andrew hesitantly entered, the office he entered was clad in blacks and deep reds, he stepped in fully and felt a gun press on his back.

"So," a commanding yet seductive voice said from behind "Officer Douglas, you look good for a dead man," he spun around, his security training kicking in and knocked the gun out the attackers hand and pinned them against the wall, only then did he see her, a tall athletic beauty with long straight raven hair, everything she wore, her thigh boots, the gloves, her jumpsuit all light leeching black, the matte look of the jumpsuit in contrast to the shiny look of the rest of the attire. Lilly simply laughed despite being pinned against the wall of her own office "Easy there Officer, I have to be careful who I let in." he released his hold and backed off a few paces.

"How did you know who I was and what do you mean still alive?" he asked, Lilly shrugged and walked around and sat at her desk, putting her feet on top of the desk and leaning back.

"Its my business to know everyone who walks in here, say hi to officers Marconi and Hellman will you and haven't you heard? According to reports the SS Ramesses blew you and your friends out of the stars near the Barbeau nebula," she said with a sly grin "and I see you are working with John Adams, I bet Officer Marconi..or should I call him big Phil," she winked playfully "loves that, so why are you here?", Andrew went over and sat on the chair on the other side of the desk and sighed.

"We are needing help, pilots mainly, we can't offer much except a place to sleep and food but we are offering whomever takes up our offer a chance to fight back against the various pirate groups and GalCorp." he felt honesty worked best here, Lilly got up and paced around.

"You are planning to tackle GalCorp?" she smiled "Interesting I assume the handsome young man in the flight jacket with you is Mister Easton? It will be a hard sell to people but it can be done, but what's in it for me? everything tells me you don't have much in the way of funds." Andrew nodded and decided to keep up with the honesty and explain everything to her.

"...But if you aren't willing to help I suppose I can always try other places." and he got up to leave, she stepped in front of him.

"Stop" she said softly "I didn't say I wouldn't help, like you I see what GalCorp is doing to this region but if I help you with this, If I help you get in contact with pilots and other information, you must be willing to help me," Andrew looked in her eyes long and hard, she was being sincere, her seductive bravado gone "not now, but in the future if I need something, will you help?"

"Okay, if you help us, we will help you," He got up from the chair and looked at her, something in her eyes.. "What is the real reason you are doing this? all I have heard is your a formidable force to be reckoned with and yet here you are offering to help despite any obvious benefit to you."

"You really want to know?" she said looking to the ceiling "when I was growing up my parent ran a small mining operation, GalCorp came in and undercut us, drive my father out of business died with barely a bitcred to his name thanks to them, If helping you hurts them I'd say that is a good deal." she flashed a smile tinged with sadness but composed herself.

"Thank you for being honest." Andrew said, his voice full of concern "I assume you know which table to send people to, we will be there all day, thank you again." he said as he walked out, she slumped in her chair muttering.

"Your getting soft in your old age Lilly." as she made the arrangements.

In what seemed no time at all there was a steady stream of potential pilots at the booth, all discounted. One woman leapt over the table and tried to gouge Phil's eyes out because she hated the way he looked at her. One pilot, a young pale skinned male from Mars colony kept insisting that despite being nervous he could be a valuable addition nearly jumped when Andrew accidentally dropped his drink, the politely dismissed him and suggested he consider a less stressful pursuit.

"This is hopeless." said Phil burying his face in

his hands.

"Excuse me but I heard you were hiring pilots," said a voice, they all looked up to see a young dark skinned pilot, his hair in cornrows and sporting a neatly trimmed goatee "Marcus Anthony, callsign Brutus." he said extending his hand, after a brief moment he was welcomed to the table and sat down.

"So," Rob asked "I take it you know why we are needing pilots, what could you bring to our little group?" he said smiling, it was his turn to interview.

"I grew up in this region, my dad used to fly cargo in the outer colonies. I was flying by age nine, when my dad died I tried to continue the business but pirate raids have been more and more frequent so I had no choice but to sell up. I saw this area of space get worse by the year and I want to do something to clean it up, something needs done" the others nodded finally someone sensible.

"Do you have a ship?" Andrew asked, Marcus shook his head "its okay we can supply you with one." Andrew offered, they told Marcus to be outside the bar for closing time, he left to pack, smiling as he did, unfortunately the recruitment of Marcus wasn't the turning point they had hoped, the others were just as unsuitable as before, one pilot being shocked when they said they would be fighting GalCorp and that they weren't recruiting FOR GalCorp. Matt had left to go shopping in the promenade, wanting to get some clothes and other things for his quarters, when he came back he had to pry someone off Rob, all because Rob dared question their flying ability, Matt sank into his seat and was about to ask the others how things went while he was gone when two blonde ladies approached them, one had her hair in a tight ponytail, the other had her hair messy and short.

"Good evening," said the ponytailed one "I am Suzanne Sommer and this is my sister Ellen, we hear you are recruiting pilots." she said in a heavy accent, Matt guessed they were of Germanic descent.

"We are," he said with a smile "I hope its not rude to ask why you wish join us?" he gestured for them to sit but they preferred to stand, this time Ellen spoke.

"We are from Bayern Kolonie, supply ships to and from our colony are attacked by pirates, GalCorp offer to hep but demand our council sell the planet to them, oh we would be allowed to stay..." Matt held out a hand, he could see where it was going, the colonists would be indentured to GalCorp, they had figured that was one of the many devious strategies the company was implementing.

"Say no more, welcome aboard, what are your callsigns?" Rob said.

"Callsigns? we want our enemies to know exactly who we are, no need to hide our identities." snapped Suzanne, Andrew filled them on the rendezvous place and time, when they walked away Phil shook his head.

"Wow, never mind the enemy, they terrify me." he said.

It was the end of the evening and as they left, Andrew went back up to the barstaff he had spoke to earlier.

"Hi, send Lilly my thanks and say I'll be in touch if we need any more help." he went to walk away until she waved a small datastick in her hand.

"Not without this you won't." she said mockingly, he took it rather sheepishly and joined the others. Suzanne and Ellen were outside waiting along with Marcus, who was unsuccessfully trying to indulge in small talk with the sisters, suddenly Phil patted his pockets.

"Damn I left my burner card inside, hold on." he said as he rushed inside, luckily it had fell below his seat and no-one had noticed, as he turned around a young man, stood in his path, messy dark hair, flightsuit and jacket ill fitting he threw a lazy salute.

"Craig Caldwell reporting for duty," he said "I'm here to sign up." Phil looked the guy up and down.

"How old are you," he asked.

"Seventeen," Craig said, damn thought Phil he's just a kid "but don't let that put you off, I can and will prove myself to you and the rest of the Galaxy." the kid said full of confidence, great thought Phil he's a weirdo too,

"Listen kid," he said as politely as he could "I'm going to do the best thing I could and not sign you up, I'm saving your life kid, trust me." he then walked away and didn't look back no matter how loudly the kid protested, he met up with the others and headed to docking bay where their shuttles had docked.

Docking bay seven was one of the hubs smaller bays but event then it looked large to Matt, the Hades three was were they had landed it but the next ship was the Hades five, not the Thunderclap One.

"She's on the SS Hades being unloaded, had to make several runs, new crew and cargo." John said walking to them and anticipating the question.

"So, tell us what cargo are you hauling?" said Phil suspiciously, John just shook his head.

"You know the deal Phil," John said with a touch of frustration "but relax, mainly just boring stuff you know, power cells, machine parts, general supplies." he then turned to Andrew "But I also managed to get things for the SS Hades, a couple of laser cannons and some a anti fighter guns, they aren't military grade by any means but every little helps I secured a some other parts to improve performance and effect repairs, oh also managed to get an assortment of handguns and rifles cheap, I figured there is a chance we may get boarded and before you ask Phil no I don't have plans to sell them, the guy who sold them to me was practically giving them away." He had a few crates in front of him and opened one for inspection, Rob picked up one of the carbines, looked it over and set it down.

"SIG 790B's? nice, old but reliable." it turned out the pistols were also SIG's, P526's to be exact, both weapons were obsolete but they took what they could get as the SS Hades armoury didn't get its weapons delivered before the incident at the shipyard, the crates were stored on the Hades Five. as Garth helped Marcus, Suzanne and Ellen load their stuff on the Hades Three, Andrew asked curiously.

"You just came back for the weapons?" John shook his head.

"Oh no," he said "Picking up passengers."

"Passengers? are you mad?" Matt said incredulously from behind them they heard a rather gentle voice.

"Captain Adams We wish to once again thank you for your kindness." they all turned to see a group of six nuns, in the full traditional black and white habits, the one who spoke looked to be in her late thirties, Matt noted that both Andrew and Rob had suddenly straightened up a little and looked a little self conscious, John smiled.

"Sister Theresa, welcome," he said leading the nuns to Hades Five "Where are my manners, here are the courageous pilots I spoke to you about, Sister Theresa, meet Matt Easton, Andrew Douglas, Phil Marconi and Rob Hellman, guys this it Sister Theresa, who is returning to Astra Sanctuarium," He gave the pilots a wink and a I know what I'm doing look "Her chartered passenger ship cancelled due to the heightened threat levels in the area, I said the SS Hades could get them there and safely, Now if you make your way to the shuttle we can get going." they walked to the shuttle and John made to follow them but Andrew grabbed his arm.

"You told them everything?" he asked anger

rising, John shrugged.

"I thought it was the best course of action, you want to gain a reputation don't you?" the reasoning, though flawed made some sense but Phil pulled his sidearm out and pointed it at John's head.

"I knew it, you can't be trusted can you?" he said with venom in his eyes, but Rob gently held and lowered Phil's arm.

"Easy Phil, they are nuns if we can't trust nuns who can we trust?" he said patiently and calmly, Phil just holstered his weapon and shook his head, as they headed to their shuttle Matt asked Rob.

"Rob, I have to ask, I know Andrew is but are you.." he started.

"Catholic? hell yes," he said with a smile, reaching into his shirt and showing the metal crucifix he had attached to his old dog tags "and proud of it.", they continued to the ship when something caught Robs eye, a solitary box on a gravsled next to the Hades Three, he called over to John.

"Hey, this one of yours?" but John just looked at is slightly confused before replying.

"Must be, can you guys take it onboard?" he asked, rob nodded and he and Matt loaded it on, whatever it was it was heavy, soon both ships were loaded and on their way back to the SS Hades.

Back on the SS Hades the hanger deck was alive with action, the new crew John had recruited were in a line as

Tessa and Ben took note of their names, position and handed each of them a jumpsuit, Matt could see John was taking running the carrier seriously. Rob had been tasked with showing the new pilots around and was currently showing them the fighters they would use, the Sommer sisters had fighters of their own but elected to leave them behind as they were old Starflash Comets which were poorly armoured and under powered . suddenly there was a loud noise of a container falling over and he heard Phil shout.

"what the hell!... you?" Matt and Andrew turned around to see the container they had taken onboard on its side and the lid off and Phil standing over a young man with his sidearm drawn, Andrew rushed over.

"Phil, what the hell is going on" he looked down at the kid who looked up at Phil defiantly

"Well," Phil started "This kid approached me on the station wanting to join but Andrew he's only seventeen, we can't risk putting him in a cockpit." his tone ranged from angry to pleading, Andrew held out his hand and helped the kid up, Matt lead him away as Andrew talked with Phil.

"So" he asked casually "What's your name?" the kid adjusted the backpack he wore and sighed.

"I'm Craig Caldwell, callsign Hellbringer." he looked at Matt earnestly "I just want a chance to prove myself." there was hurt in his eyes, Matt had to ask.

"This is important to you, why?" he said as he sat on a munitions crate and gestured Craig to join him.

"May dad" he said slowly "went by the callsign

Hellraiser, the fought for the Hexstar Militia and flew many missions, all successful but one day the war stops and he is told 'don't you know, you guys lost' he wanted to continue to fly but his Hexstar Militia background closed a lot of doors, labelled a murderer and hated. he took to alcohol to block out the pain of defeat," he started to well up "He would cry while looking at his medals, he was happy when I applied to be a pilot in the United Earth Military but when he saw my rejection letter he blamed himself, the drinking got worse then one night he got drunk, stole a shuttle and..well the crash.." he broke down, he didn't need to say any more about it "My father was a good man.. a great pilot." Matt put an arm around the kid, noting the jacket he wore was his fathers judging the Hexstar insignia on the sleeves, it was a familiar story, soldiers who fought on the Hexstar side vilified in certain circles, once he calmed down a bit he explained he just wanted to honour his fathers name and make him proud.

"Well Craig, you can stay onboard," he saw Craigs face light up "But as for being a pilot, not yet, but you can assist with readying the fighters, its the best I can offer.. for now." Craig looked slightly dejected but shook Matt's hand.

"thank you" he said softly.

CHAPTER 9

Later that evening in the SS Hades mess hall, a large but basic room filled with long tables and bench seating and food dispensers along one wall and monitors at regular interval around the walls. Rob, Phil, Gareth and the other pilots minus Andrew and Matt all sat at the same table eagerly looking at the doorway, They had spent the night trying out the flight simulators which were located on the same deck and were awaiting Matt and Andrew returning from their turn, everyone went one on one in simulated dogfights to get used to the fighters, Rob faced off against Phil, Suzanne against Ellen and despite Phil's protests, they allowed Craig to fly against Marcus.

"Its very obvious who will win," said Suzanne "Matthew will win with his superior training and combat experience." the others had noted the sisters never shortened peoples names, Rob and Phil chuckled to themselves.

"No, my money is on Andrew," Phil said smugly.

"No," said Ellen pointedly "Twenty bitcreds that Andrew is beaten by Matthew." before they knew it even members of the SS Hades crew were betting, most believed Matt would emerge victorious, the answer wasn't long in coming, Andrew walked past the Mess hall, knees clearly bothering him by his walk and Matt entered the room looking stunned, sitting on the empty seat at the pilots table.

"I had him.. I had him locked..how?" he looked at the others blankly.

"What happened?" asked Marcus curiously, he was one of the few who bet on Andrew.

"Well I was on his tail" Matt said "and he was pulling out every evasive manoeuvrer he could then suddenly he levelled out.. flew straight..."Rob and Phil looked at each other as if they knew what was coming next "Suddenly, he jumps to lightspeed, I lose lock and next I know my fighter is being laced with weapons fire and the simulation ends and it informs me that if it was real my ship would have blown up," he looked at Phil and Rob "what did he do?" Rob and Phil had a little mock argument over who would tell the story then Phil decided to say

"What Andrew did is a manoeuvre he calls hopping. you see all he did was over ride the safety on the lightdrive, if you input the co-ordinates you are already at in a lightdrive computer safeties stop the lightdrive activating but if you disable it, it will jump, a very short jump mind you, the minimum distance it can before deactivating again," he smiled broadly "What Andrew also discovered is the minimum jump distance takes him out of most fighters weapons range and as most if not all targeting computers just assume he's jumped out the system take a while to re-establish lock, by then he has circled around and has you in his sights." Matt scratched his head.

"You are kidding? right? he could rip his ship apart doing that, he could ram into an object at that speed and get killed instantly, there's so many reasons why doing that is a bad idea" he said full of surprise, this time Rob replied.

"Oh he knows that, that's why he's careful of when and how he does it." Rob explained, Matt just shook his head, Suzanne went over to a crate she brought onboard and pulled out a bottled beer and handed it to Matt.

"Here Matthew, this will help, made from the springs on our colony to the same Bavarian blend that has been used for centuries." she almost smiled as she twisted the cap off and handed it to him, Phil looked at his bottle of beer and sighed.

"How come he gets the good stuff and we get Econo-Beer?" he said reading the label, Suzanne just stared at him and Matt just smiled and enjoyed the drink, for the first time in a long while he was just able to relax and enjoy himself.

It was late so the corridors were quiet as Andrew headed to his quarters, even simulation flying aggravated his knees and despite the operation it still affected him, he was waiting at the shuttlelift when he heard a soothing voice behind him.

"Mister... Douglas is it?", he looked around and saw Sister Theresa.

"Call me Andrew please," he said forcing a smile "can't sleep?" she smiled and nodded.

"Sometimes I find a quiet walk helps me sleep, especially onboard a vast starship as this, the pulse of the engines the quiet calmness of the empty corridors," she had a point, even with the new crew intake the ship was still technically undermanned for its size. Tony had managed to set up some systems to be semi or fully automated due to this but even then she looked at him intently "Captain Adams told me about your mission, it sounds like you gave up a lot."

"We did but what else were we to do?" he said as the shuttle lift arrived and they both got in, he continued to explain in better detail Matt's discovery, how he was framed for a crime and the plan to take the fight to the Silver Blades and GalCorp, she got out the same floor as him and continued to listen patiently, they got to his quarters and he stopped to go in.

"I assume when we arrive you will want to talk to the Cardinal?" she asked innocently, Astra Sanctuarium was governed by one of the Catholic Churches Cardinals, Cardinal Otani, personally appointed by the Pope himself.

"That was the plan, along with the leaders of the other colonies in the region." Andrew replied, she smiled and her eyes seemed to sparkle with thought

"Well," she started "It is difficult to gain an audience with someone of the Cardinals importance but I may be able to help, after all without this ship we would not now be heading to the colony safely..if at all." she gave him a wink and walked on, Andrew laughed softly and shook his head, for a nun, Sister Theresa seemed quite an interesting person.

The next morning in the pilots briefing room Matt and Andrew stood at the main monitor at the list of names they had on it, it was decided not to put them into traditional four pilot flights, at least not until they had more recruits, no the order of today was lead and wingman assignments.

"Phil and Rob go together obviously, they have flown together for so long splitting the team up wouldn't benefit us." Andrew said as he touched the screen to group the two together.

"Agreed," Matt nodded, clearly nursing a headache judging by the way he was rubbing his temples "same for Suzanne and Ellen."

"To be honest," said Andrew shaking his head "They pretty much demanded we never separate them, okay that only leaves who do we have as wingmen." It was decided as they were saw as co-leaders of the group, one being the others wingman didn't seem right, plus

Matt freely admitted he and Andrew had such vastly different flying styles that it would be difficult to keep formation, Matt pondered hard then spoke.

"Well, why don't you take Marcus, we had a few more simulation runs last night after you left and after we had a few more beers," Matt said as he drank a glass of ready mixed aspirin "he is a bit unorthodox like you, we ran the simulation dogfights in an asteroid field, Phil couldn't find him until it was too late, turns out he landed on an asteroid and powered down and waited for Phil to get close before powering up and wiping him out." Andrew nodded, clearly impressed.

"Its an old smugglers trick, probably learned from his father, even then it takes a lot to blindside Phil like that, good call," Andrew said "but what about you? can't have Craig, you said while the kid is good for the simulator you don't feel right putting him in actual combat, plus Phil would go nuts," he went silent as if thinking then clicked his fingers "Of course..what about G?"

"G?" Said Matt surprised "The same guy who is running checks on my ship as we speak?" Andrew nodded and went on to explain.

"You see, G flew a lot of shuttles for Waypoint station and was on the reserve list for pilots for the security patrols, if you hadn't came that day Angel died, chances are I'd have wanted him in Red Patrol, his combat skills are a little rusty, our simulators were barely functional." Matt looked a little unsure but agreed to try.

Soon the other pilots along with Craig and Gareth entered and took seats, as they did, John turned up with one of his new crew members, a short rubenesque lady in her mid twenties with short dark hair and a nervous smile on her lips, she also wore her crew jumpsuit but like many others they had saw had started adding personal touches, for example she had her jumpsuit tucked into some flat knee high boots and wore a silk scarf around her neck, she gave a shy wave.

"Guys, before you begin this meeting, this is Liana Cotungo, she has volunteered to be your flight controller on the bridge, just thought you guys should get to know her," he said patting her shoulder "anyway I have a beard to trim, cargo to count and check.." he caught Phil staring at him and grinned "Phil..your not a lawman any more and its not illegal.. just not advised." he said mysteriously before leaving, Liana looked awkward at the Doorway, Andrew came and shook her hand.

"I'm Andrew but you will probably be calling me Firehawk," she looked at him slightly wide eyed as he spoke but he put it down to her nerves, he gestured everyone else to introduce themselves and give their callsigns and invited her to sit in one of the empty chairs. Matt went through the wingman assignments, Phil and Rob looked relieved, Suzanne and Ellen just nodded politely, Marcus pleased with becoming Andrews wingman, Gareth fell off his seat when he was told he'd be a pilot, Craig looked equally disappointed that he wasn't chosen, Matt walked up and up a reassuring hand on Craigs shoulder.

"You will get your chance Craig, just keep doing what your doing, helping prep the fighters and keep practising in the simulators." he had noticed that while Craig was wearing the same jumpsuit the rest of Johns crew wore, he still wore his dads flight jacket over it, Gareth eventually stood and regained enough composure to look at Andrew, the one he suspected, correctly, of making this choice.

"What are you guys trying to do to me? I'm a tech. you know that." he said with an edge of panic, rob walked over and gently pushed Gareth into his seat again.

"G, you and I both know you want to fly, you were a reservist for us back in Waypoint." he said but Gareth just looked up at Rob.

"that was years ago and I was drunk when I filled in the application, it was a few more Bitcreds in my pay a month, I was never going to get called up." he protested but This time Andrew spoke.

"G, if all..this..hadn't happened, wanna know who I would have had in mind to replace Angel?" he let it sink in a few minutes, once he saw Gareth understand Andrew was meaning him he continued "You are a better pilot than you think." Gareth looked at everyone and seeing there was no way out of it held his hands up in mock surrender.

"Alright, Alright, I'm in, but Matt just letting you

know I haven't flown anything smaller than a cargo shuttle in a long time." Matt just smiled.

"I'm sure we will be fine, we have time before we get to Astra Sanctuarium to practice." he said reassuringly as Andrew informed everyone they were arriving at the colony tomorrow and expected everyone to use the simulators to get used to fighting as a duo and get used to the ships and their wingmen against simulated opponents, as everyone left Andrew saw Matt pull Craig aside and talk reassuringly and noticed Suzanne's eyes linger on Matt ever so slightly but shook his head, it was the first time either sister seemed to show something in the way of emotion, it was probably nothing he thought as he went to grab his gear from his quarters.

CHAPTER 10

By the time the SS Hades jumped into the Astra Sanctuarium system all the pilots had logged on more than enough hours on the simulators and were as ready as they could ever be, Andrew was making his way to the hanger, he was wearing his old black Waypoint security flight suit, though with a few added details the chief would never have allowed. A Scottish flag on the sleeves, below that there was a badge with the initials A.M.D.G. on it, then the Douglas clan crest and finishing off the sleeve badges was a curious personal logo that was a downward facing Orange triangle behind a stylised hawks head in Reds and yellows, his black helmet also adorned with this logo and a strip of Douglas tartan painted on, the plan was he, Matt, Marcus and Gareth would fly escort for Johns shuttle while the other pilots were on standby, he heard someone run up behind him and turned to see Matt, back in his GalCorp uniform, though he had the Galcorp logos removed, covering the GalCorp logo on the breast with the shield shaped badge with a white background and red cross of Saint George. It was agreed that both of them would see the Cardinal along with John, Andrew felt having John there might help things as he had traded with the colony before, Matt was smiling

"Its going to feel good to be flying again, properly flying." he said They both knew what Matt ment, the simulations were good but are nothing compared to the real thing when they reached the hanger they saw the others standing, Phil and Rob were like Andrew and wearing their waypoint flightsuits, Gareth and Marcus were wearing ones taken from the ships stores and The Sommer sisters had their unique grey and black flightsuits with white and blue chequered patterned edging.

"Well, while its not a combat mission this is our first operation as a unit, lets hope it goes smoothly." Andrew said as he looked at the others, Ellen raised her hand.

"What is the units designation?" she asked before he had time to acknowledge, this was something they had spoke about, they felt it was a good idea to name their group and had been brainstorming the night before to no avail, most things just made them sound like another pirate gang, something they wanted to avoid.

"We haven't decided yet," Matt said casually "But we are still open to suggestions." just as he finished he decided to tell them something John told Him and Andrew the previous night was the SS Hades had a fake transponder installed so when any flight controllers scanned it it would come up as a cargo vessel the same model as the SS Thunderclap, John felt it best not to make it too obvious she was a military grade carrier ship just then there was activity near the shuttles, John and Tessa were escorting the Nuns to one of the shuttles, John was doing his good host bit with Sister Theresa, Andrew couldn't remember the last time he had saw John so well groomed, the guy wanted to make an impression, He was making his way to his fighter when he heard someone shout for him, it was Liana, she had something in her hand.

"excuse me, can I ask a huge favour?" she asked, still full of shyness, Andrew smiled and nodded "Can you take this to be blessed on the planet, its the only thing I have belonging to my mother left and it would mean a lot, I would have asked the others but, I feel you may understand better." her eyes looked pleading, he decided it wasn't the best time to ask her to explain and took the object, it was a small box, singed with carbon scoring, he opened it to reveal a gold chain and crucifix, the cross, although gold had intricate etching to make it appear like wood.

"I'll do my best, us Catholics gotta stick together." he said and winked with a smile, she smiled back and thanked him then headed to the bridge to start her fighter control duties, Robb came up behind Andrew and cleared his throat startling him.

"Oh!" he started "When I ask you to get something of mine blessed you tell me no but our new flight controller flutters her eyelashes at you what happens? you do it," Andrew rolled his eyes,

"Rob, your personalised beer tankard is not something I am going to present to a Cardinal to get blessed, so stop asking." Andrew said wearily as he put the box in his pocket and climbed into his cockpit.

The launch went with no hitches, the fighters took up an escort formation around the Hades Two shuttle, they entered the atmosphere and seem the colony in all its glory, was situated on a coastline in a natural formed harbour that had been build up from into the surrounding area you could also wee the cathedral and the main complex, which was patterned after the Vatican back on earth, just in a smaller scale.

"SS Hades Flight Control This is Firehawk, have we received permission to land?" asked Andrew cautiously.

"Confirmed Firehawk," said Liana all business and no hint of her previous shyness "Fighters go to pad D and shuttle pad F." the breeze fom the Ocean Galilee was a comforting sight as they left their fighters and removed helmets and made their way to meet up with John and the others, a young man, a monk by his robes had driven up in a hovercart that had benches designed for taking passengers from the docking port.

"Brother Michael as your service, I am here to

take you to the cathedral as our guests, Sister Theresa, you and your sisters will have a transport to pick you up for the convent soon. All except Sister Theresa, the Cardinal has a special request for you." an he handed her a small datapad.

The journey was interesting, on the journey to the main town they noticed the sides of the road were adorned with with life sized statues depicting the stations of the cross, Matt and the other pilots except Andrew looked around in awe,

"Andrew, what does Astra Sanctuarium mean?" asked Matt curiously.

"It's apparently latin for Star Sanctuary" Andrew replied.

"When you say sanctuary do you mean..." Marcus started to ask.

"...As in the religious kind." Andrew replied. As they reached the main colony centre John nudged Andrew.

"why a Cardinal and not the pope?" Andrew slapped johns head hard.

"The Pope is still in the Vatican back on earth, you know that." the others laughed, when they pulled up outside the Cathedral, they got off, thanked Brother Michael and entered though the main doors, the place was beautiful, the shape and interior design was very modern and sleep, but the stainglass windows which had a traditional look instead of looking out of place complimented it they all sat down, the others looking bewildered when Andrew bowed and made a sign of the cross as he did so, soon a priest came out from the side door and announced.

"The Cardinal will see you now." Andrew, Matt and John stood and followed the priest to a large office room just off the main sanctuary, Cardinal Otani sat at a large desk , he asked them to sit and they did, out of politeness.

"Greetings gentlemen," He said with a light smile on his lips "Sister Theresa was good enough to fill me in on what you propose to do. We have had some offers on the colony by GalCorp, and as you know more of our pilgrimage ships are getting through, what exactly are you offering that we have not heard from any other mercenaries so you are not this first to offer protection and other services." he looked at each of them in turn.

"Well," Matt "spoke up "we are doing this to help you and other colonies first and foremost, not for our own gain." Otani nodded then pointed to Andrew's A.M.D.G. patch.

"Ad Majorem Dei Gloriam, very apt if what you are saying is true," he noted dryly "either you are a Jesuit or.."

"..actually its a nod to my old school and church, Saint Ignatius, though I see what you mean." interrupted Andrew then he saw Matt's confused look "It means for the greater glory in latin" then addressed the Cardinal "things have been getting worse and worse in these territories, someone has to take a stand'"

"Ah yes, your hunger to see justice brought to these parts, the power of your convictions was so much you both left your professions to do so, you come across less like bandit pirates and more like Ronin, masterless Samurai." Otani explained "In my spare time have a hobby of studying ancestral culture, You understand the Catholic church can not and will not condone violence so we can not publicly endorse or support you in your crusade," The pilots went to stand but Otani gestured them to remain seated and he addressed John

"Captain Adams, it is my understanding you were able to make this run with no problems, how regular could you make such runs from here to The Hub?" he said, John looks at him after a few minute of thought.

"I'd say once every two weeks maybe every week depending how other deals go." he answered rather bemused, Otani handed him a datapad.

"Captain, we would like to offer you a contract to regularly bring pilgrims to and from Astra Sanctuarium, take your time to read it over" John did, he noticed something seemed odd, if he didn't know better he'd say some of the supplies they would receive for this job would benefit the pilots more, he showed it to the other two, it was obvious, officially Otani couldn't help but was unofficially by giving John a shipping contract that seemed to benefit them a little too much, "John put his thumbprint on the pad to formalise the deal, Otani stood and shook Johns hand to finalise it.

"I do apologise but I have other things to attend to but Thank you again Captain Adams, and good luck with your crusade gentlemen." he said, but as he turned to leave Andrew rounded the table and pulled out the box

Liana gave him.

"Your Eminence," he said giving Otani his formal title "could you please bless this as for a friend." Otani took the box and made a sign of the cross over it while softly uttering a blessing on it before handing it back Andrew thanked him and went to join the others as they left the Cathedral, Matt was confused.

"So what exactly went on in there?" he said.

"well," Andrew answered "Otani wants to help but is forbidden from outwardly showing support by the Church so he is unofficially helping under the pretence of just helping John shuttle pilgrims back and forth." John nodded in agreement.

"One clause in the contract was assistance with keeping the ships defences in top condition to ensure safe travel by the pilgrims, I assume that's you guys," he added "anyway we have a few hours before we need to leave, there may be more jobs at the landing bays." he headed back to the shuttle which the pilots decided to enjoy the sights.

By the time they had returned to the landing bays, John had managed to load some new cargo, compliments of his new deal with the colony and he had one more surprise, out of the shuttles bay door stepped Sister Theresa, sporting a loose fitting black jumpsuit with patches identifying her as a member of the Catholic church and, interestingly enough there were patches showing she was medically trained too, she had a simplified headdress or coif on, it was a simple white headband with black fabric that was attached to the back and went down to just past her shoulders. It showed off her wavy back hair slightly, Sister Theresa also had a large case with her.

"Hello again gentlemen, Cardinal Otani has granted me special dispensation to join Captain Adams crew as a spiritual wellbeing officer and to take care of your medical needs as I understand you have no medical officer onboard."

"None of the ones at the Hub looked trustworthy." John agreed as she went back into the shuttle, the pilots went to their pad and boarded their fighters, Marcus pointed to the small bag Andrew had in his hands.

"What's that you got there?" he said curiously.

"Nothing, just a little gift for someone." he replied mysteriously, Marcus just shrugged and went to his ship.

On the flight up Matt had an idea and contacted Andrew.

"Firehawk, this is White Knight, "Been thinking about what Otani said and I think we have a name for our Unit, Ronin Flight." Andrew thought about it for a few minutes, yes, Ronin flight sounded apt.

"White Knight, that sounds like a great idea." he said as they flew back up to the SS Hades.

CHAPTER 11

After they made the jump from Astra Sanctuarium to Bayern Kolonie, apparently to deliver industrial grade generators, Matt saw them get loaded into the Thunderclap One. It was the only shuttle that could take them, he was on the deck with the two sisters after they had taken a run around the hanger and were now talking about what he could expect from the colony and suzanne in particular was more than willing to tell him, from what he understood it would not be easy to convince the elders and that despite being from there, taking them down could do more harm than good due to circumstances they wouldn't get into, when Matt went to get more water Ellen punched Suzanne's arm.

"You like him don't you?" she said teasingly.

"No!" Suzanne protested "I am only being..." suddenly an announcement came over the shipwide comms.

"Distress call received, Pirates attacking a cargo vessel in a nearby sector, dropping out of lightspeed." it was decided that they would hold off having the SS Hades actually brought into combat for as long as they could, the idea was it would jump to a nearby sector and then the fighters would jump the rest, the sisters, ran to their ships, as they clumsily put their flightsuits back on.

Soon the Hanger bay was pandemonium, the pilots getting into their fighters, Gareth was the last to arrive as he had fell asleep and it took Phil throwing a mug of water in his face to waken him up, the tech who took over servicing the fighters, red haired man by the name of Gordon McKay commented to Andrew as he gestured to Gareth.

"I hope he flies them as good as he fixes them." Andrew just laughed and prepared his ship for launch, as he went through the checks he contacted Liana through his helmet comms.

"So, what are we dealing with exactly?" he asked.

"Pirate raider attack on a cargo vessel," she replied "SS Kingfisher is being attacked by ten fighters, possibly Sliver Blades" she went quiet then the comms switched as if it was a private between Andrew and her "Good luck," she said softly, he got everyone to check in and confirm they were ready and for the techs and ground crew to clear the area before launching by twos.

"Everyone prepare to jump on my mark," he said

once they were all clear "Ronin Flight, activate lightdrives... Now!", he activated the lightdrive and jumped out the system.

John watched from the SS Hades bridge front viewport as the last fighter jumped out, he saw Liana get up from her console and head out off the bridge.

"Something wrong?" he said curiously.

"No, nothing, just forgot to.. you see.. "she trailed off once he turned to talk to Tessa about the next planet on the route, she made her way to the Chapel Sister Theresa had set up in one of the disused multi purpose rooms, it was christened Saint Joseph of Cupertino by Rob but most just called it Saint Joe's, Sister Theresa was already there organising the place when Liana came in.

"Sister, I need to talk to someone and I don't know who else to turn to." she said barely holding back tears, Sister Theresa guided her to a sea and put a comforting arm round her.

"Of course, what is the matter?" she said soothingly and with that Liana told her everything that was on her mind the past few days...

The pirate fighters were swarming around the SS Kingfisher like angry wasps, it looked like they were using Vampire fighters and old Stellar Engineering VFA670 Darts, fairly common fighters in civilian, pirate and mercenary hands, the slender fuselage that houses the cockpit, engines mounted the third of the way down wings that pointed slightly forward from the rear. They were laying waste to the boxy larger ship which was trying to lay down defensive fire, which was becoming more sporadic and desperate as newly named Ronin Flight jumped into the system.

"Attacking fighters this is White Knight of Ronin Flight, break off your attack or we will engage." Matt waited a few moments to see how they would respond. Some of the pirates broke off the assault and headed to face off against the new arrivals, Matt noticed the Pirates had sent the Darts to intercept and the Vampires to continue the assault.

"White Knight this is Firehawk, I think you just got your answer."

"I had to try. I count ten enemies just like we were told, four have broken off to confront us,Suzanne, Ellen, G and I will head to the cargo ship to assist its defence, the rest, keep the oncoming ships busy." Andrew grinned and instructed Marcus, Phil and Rob to follow his lead as they streaked ahead of Matt's group and opened fire on the enemy, destroying the lead fighter, as they got closer he issued another command.

"Semjasa, this is Firehawk when I break right you break left..now!" Phil and Rob went left and Andrew and Marcus when right, two of the pursuing fighters followed Andrew and the remaining one Phil, the same they had just created allowed Matt and the others to fly onward to the cargo ship unopposed.

"Semjasa this is Pollock, what now? this guy is tight on us." Marcus said as the enemy fighter laced the space around them with laser fire, clearly not bothering to aim properly, Phil had an idea.

"Pollock what do you say we go oldschool this time?"

"The hatch weave? Oldie but a goldie, lets do it"

"Good I'll break right and see which one he follows, break now." The pirate stuck to Rob, following him on his loop still firing wild and failed to see that he was being set up as Phil's turn brought the pirate into weapons range but the pirate was too focused on Rob, Phil fired two quick bursts, the first collapsed the ships shields, the next struck the cockpit killing the pilot instantly.

Andrew and Marcus were having a difficult time, their pursuers were able to work as a team too.

"Firehawk this is Brutus, these guys are really starting to get to me." Phil said dryly he evaded laser fire, He then looked over at Robs ship and saw Rob give a thumbs up.

"Oh come on Brutus, this is where the fun starts, besides, I got an idea" Andrew suddenly cut engines but let his momentum carry him along at the speed he had been going and pivoted around using the vectoring thrusters before reigniting the engines at full power towards the pursuing pirate ships. The lead Dart peppered his shields with fire, at the last minute, Andrew sent volley after voley of shots aiming at one of those big wing mounted engines, the ships shields failed after the first few blasts and the rest tore into the engine itself, Andrew taking advantage of the main gun tracking ability to sustain fire. The resulting explsion ripped off the wing and sent the rest of the ship in a dangerous spin, hitting the other Dart and causing it to spin out of control. This allowed Brutus, who had executed a tight banked turn and gunned down the helpless enemy fighter.

"Firehawk this is Brutus, did you mean for that to happen? The ships colliding that is?" Marcus asked

"Well there was always the danger they wouldn't, that the second one would move out the road on the debris but luck was on our side" Andrew replied. Being Andrew's wingman was going to be more interesting than Marcus thought. They regrouped with Phil and Rob

"Firehawk this is Semjasa, what kept you?"

"Hey, you only had one to deal with"

"True but..."

"Semjasa this is Pollock, it's obvious he wanted to show off to his new wingman, now if you are finished gossiping can we go help the others?"

"Pollock this is Firehawk, yeah we probably should." and they headed toward the SS Kingfisher at top speed, afterburners on.

Matt could see the SS Kingfisher had taken a lot of punishment, its comms must be down as they were getting no replies from their enquiries.

"G, ready for your first taste of combat?" he said in a forced cheerful tone.

"I doubt I'll ever be ready for that Ma... I mean White Knight" Gareth's voice was filled with nervous energy, he was about to give orders when Suzanne and Ellen thrust forward, blazing continuous fire, took out a pair of enemy fighters and mercilessly obliterated another with their combined fire.

"Whoa, Easy there leave some for the rest of us." Gareth said half jokingly as the Bavarian duo chased after one of the remaining fighters leaving Matt and Gareth with just two, Matt had worked a lot with Gareth in the simulators, the pirate fighters separated in the hope to isolate their pursuers.

"Stay on the lead G, don't let the other one distract you" he reminding Gareth, Matt then lined up the ship in his crosshairs and gave a few bursts of fire, the pilot dodged to evade but in the heat of the moment, or in a second of stupidity forgot Gareth was there and brought himself right in Gareth's field of fire, shredding the engines and blowing the pirates vessel up instantly. Matt smiled, Gareth will do just fine.

"Lets get the other one shall we?" Matt said as they looped back, but the other ship was nowhere to be saw, the scanners were not showing him, suddenly..

"White Knight, this is Firehawk, got one on your tail." came over his comms, he checked his scanners again, sure enough there he was, the other pilot must have looped behind them and flew close to their engine wash, it was a known blindspot but a very hard thing to maintain. He also saw the other four ships of Ronin flight head to the cargo vessel, the lone ship fired a few shots at Matt's ship before heading for open space at full power, followed by the ship the sisters were pursuing, on the same exit vector, Ellen's ship nearly collided with Matt's as she flew furiously to maintain weapons range once again they both focused fire on the one ship, destroying it completely, the other ship was able to activate its lightdrive and escape.

"White Knight this is Suzanne, we are going to pursue the enemy.." she said. anger obvious in her voice, was cut off by Matt.

"Negative, we did our job, besides maybe he will tell the others it won't be so easy to attack helpless ships any more." Matt said wearily, Both sisters seemed to have a lot of anger when they flew, it was something to keep an eye on. A message came over the comms, it was from the cargo vessel

"This is Captain Asad of the SS Kingfisher, thank you for your assistance, how can I repay you?"

"No Problem Captain," Matt replied "Ronin Flight are here to help, just get word out that we will help anyone in peril, the Pirate gangs gave rules these stars for far too long."

"I will." Asad replied, a little bit of hope creeping in his voice and the ship jumped out the system.

"Well I don't know about you guys but that was a successful first mission," said Andrew "time to go home."

Things were quiet on the bridge of the SS Hades, Liana had returned to her post, John was pacing everyone else trying to busy themselves.

"Fighters jumping in, they're ours." said Ben from his tactical console, Liana looked at him and asked.

"How many?" trying to sound unconcerned.

"looks like all of them." Ben answered, Just then Sister Theresa walked in.

"Captain Adams, how are you." she said in that serene way she said things, John looked at her curiously, she never ventured near the bridge before.

"Oh Andrew and the others have just returned from their mission." he said.

"Good good, all of them?" he nodded and she turned to Liana and smiled, Liana gave a small smile back, John saw it and wondered what that meant but instead decided to ask questions another time.

"Liana, get in contact with the pilots and lets get then in the hanger." he ordered with a smile, she turned to her console all smiles and started procedures.

CHAPTER 12

The fighters of Ronin Flight were greeted with enthusiastic applause as they landed in the hanger, most of the ships crew were there, as they got out the fighters Andrew looked at Matt, he could see Matt sporting a big smile, they both knew that while they had only just begun, it was still a terrific start. Rob took his helmet off and seeing the large crowd shouted.

"Everyone, a celebration of the first successful mission of Ronin flight will take place in the mess hall in two hours," he then then led a chant of "Ronin! Ronin!"

"Sounds good to me." said Marcus as he walked put Andrew and Matt, Matt nodded.

"Yes," he said "yes it does." and headed for a shower.

Andrew was walking to the mess hall to join the celebration when he turned a corner and literally bumped into Liana

"Sorry," he said quickly Then remembered something "wait there, please, I have something for you at my quarters" he said but she smiled and made to follow him

"It's okay I'll come with you." she said, he detected a hint of nervousness but dismissed it.

"Sure, come on, its not that far away anyway." They reached his quarters and Andrew invited her in as he searched the pockets of his flight jacket and found what he was looking for. Andrew handed her the box with the crucifix necklace she gave him to take to Astra Sanctuarium "I managed to get it blessed for you, and I got you this," he handed her the bag he bought at the colony, she put her hand inside and pulled out a nice light blue silk scarf with golden trim and a border design that looked like gold crosses on stain glass windows of varying shades of blue, she was in awe of it and looked at him confused.

"Thank you! but why?" she said as she admired the scarf, Andrew sighed and looked at her intently.

"I've noticed ever since you have come onboard it seem you have been showing signs of nervousness, I can understand, you probably took this job thinking it was just another cargo ship doing normal cargo runs, then you find yourself caught up in this." she nodded, she genuinely wasn't expecting this at all "I'm just trying to make you feel welcome."

"Thank you, I guess you want to know the full story?" she asked, Andrew looked at her and nodded.

"Only if you want to" he said sitting down on the edge of his bed, she said next to him "but you don't need to explain yourself if you don't want to" but he could tell that she had been looking to tell someone, and that someone happened to be him.

"I do, it's okay. My family are originally from Pescara back on Earth and I had been attending Mars University studying communications technology when I heard my parents had been involved in an shuttle accident returning from a trip to Milan, the crash killed them almost instantly. I couldn't concentrate on my studies so I took a year out to explore the colonies by the time I got out here my funds were drying up and spent the last few months working at one of the cafes on the station saving what I could, a few days before Captain Adams came to recruit I tried to charter a ship back to Earth but the ships captain just cut and run with most of my bitcreds, I was alone..scared.." she started crying, Andrew just held her, recent events hadn't been kind to her.

"Well, Sounds like it was a good job John was needing a communications expert." he smiled at her, she looked up tears still in her eyes

"I would have done anything to get off that station." she said with her voice quivering "I was getting desperate..."

"Liana, calm down, you can always talk to me, okay?" Andrew said soothingly and he brushed away her tears and inched closer before giving her a reassuring hug. He then, on pure impulse added "Look, your beautiful and intelligent, well at least I think so anyway.. don't ever think for a second you are alone in all this" their eyes locked and in that moment, even though he knew he'd be missed at the celebration, there was only one person he wanted to be with right now, and he could sense she felt the same, he had noticed he was still holding her close and noted she had not let go of their embrace either. She looked like she wanted tell him more, something she believed to be important to her.

"Andrew, I really should tell you something. It won't be the first time you have been there for me," she said slowly and softly, he looked at her confused but she continued "You see, the ship that brought me out to this region was the SS Bohemian Star, about six months ago, we had a stop over at Waypoint and were attacked, I left behind a...", suddenly Andrew realised and reached for the chain on his neck.

"You mean this? I remember that incident nearly killed me. When I woke up in hospital, I was told someone had left me something, they didn't give me a name, only that she was travelling on the SS Bohemian Star.",he pulled his chain, revealing his academy dog tags and a Catholic medallion, whereas Rob had added a cross to his tags, Andrew had a small silver oval medal, one side depicting the Virgin Mary and the other a cross with an M intersecting it, it was what is known as a miraculous medal, the closest Catholics get to a good luck charm. Lianas eyes lit up.

"You still have it..I.." she stopped talking and just kissed him, the kiss seemed to last for hours, when they stopped Andrew was about to say something but she just smiled at him, put a finger to his lips went back in for another kiss.

The pilots were toasting their first success together, the Mess hall was alive with celebration, Tony and Craig were talking to Gareth, Tony especially interested in the fighters handling because Gareth unlike the other pilots could describe it from a techs perspective and was already thinking of improvements, Marcus had a group of hanger deck crew mesmerised as he retold the story of the battle using his hands to try and show the different manoeuvrers, Phil and Rob were telling the Sommer sisters about life of Waypoint station and the various missions they flew and Mat was sitting nursing a beer, suddenly Rob came over and sat with him.

"what's wrong? We got a great start today." he said in an effort to get some cheer from Matt, Matt looked and smiled.

"I am happy believe me, Rob you probably know better than anyone else after all you served in the military and with the law, you ever felt this.. good after a mission before?" Matt asked, Rob looked at Matt intently as if working out if Matt was being serious.

"Now that you mention it, it does feel.. different." he admitted, Matt continued

"I have flown many combat missions during and

after the war but today it was like was doing it because I wanted to and because I knew it was right, no one ordered me to, there was no doubt in my mind, it was liberating." Robb nodded in agreement, he knew what Matt was driving at, when your part of a larger organisation like the military there are times you are called to do things that don't always sit right with your own ethic but for the most part have to do them anyway.

"I know that" Rob started "that's partly why Phil and I joined Andrew in freeing you, because we think on the other end of that scale, don't like doing things simply because we were being ordered to do so even if it seems wrong, something had to give and in the end we just snapped I guess, speaking of which where is Andrew?" they both looked around but then Rob shrugged "his knees must be really bothering in tonight, come join us," he said getting up "I'm sure you have some great academy stories, say do they still do the aggressor flights in the simulators?"

"what's that?" said Craig wandering over to them.

"They still do yeah," Matt said answering Rob, then he turned to Craig "As you can imagine while simulators are great for training, computer opponents can only do so much so what they did was when one set of pilots were in one simulator room some instructor and selected other cadets were in another connected to the first and were randomly assigned enemy fighters." Rob continued.

"Of course of course the pilots didn't know at the start which enemies were computer and which were human and the it was totally anonymous, of course you can sometimes tell individuals by their flying techniques and quirks or some actually broke the rules completely and just plain told people it was them, very few kept the secret."

"So," Craig said intrigued "did either of you do this aggressor stuff?" Matt shook his head.

"No, I was asked a few times but refused, just wasn't my thing I guess and besides as Rob said people would find out and it created problems."

"I did a few times," Rob said "And I remember Andrew saying he did as well but he never told anyone while he was at the academy though, he liked the mystique of it and before you ask unfortunately when I was there I was some who bragged about it and got into a few fights for my troubles," he shrugged "was worth it though." Phil and the Sommer sisters joined them,

"Was anyone part of the battle of Eden Prime? What was it like?" asked Craig suddenly, the battle that ended the war over the Hexstar capital planet was a long battle that claimed so many lives

"I arrived quite late," replied Matt "I was part of the reinforcements but I saw enough, it was a huge melee. I'm glad it didn't get to the stage of troops landing on the planet as that would have gotten really messy." everyone nodded with interest.

"At least back then you had ships that were well maintained," said Phil ""I remember one time fighting a huge pirate attack at Waypoint when my ships left thruster wasn't working, my landing gear was stuck down..."

The party and the stories continued through the night, Andrew of course did not join them though no-one noticed Liana was missing too.

At GalCorps asteroid mining operation in the Avari system the SS Ramesses stopped to offload supplies, Captain Miller was relaxing in his quarters, it had been a quiet run this time much to the displeasure of the fighter pilots, he was thinking of taking a trip to see the leader of the mining operation, a rather frustrating man by the name of Jose Rojas, well what he really was planning to do was meet Jose's wife, the idiot was too into his work to notice Salma. Miller made sure every time they came to the system to... show her some quality attention, he was just about to go to his personal shuttle when an urgent comms message flashed up, the screen in his quarters activated showing a very frustrated Director Gladstone.

"Miller! I thought you had dealt with our recent problem!" he snapped, Miller looked confused.

"What do you mean?" he said putting his jacket on the chair. Gladstone pushed a button off screen.

"This was an intercepted transmission I received from one of our.. allies." Miller knew he was meaning the Silver Blades then suddenly over the audio came a recorded transmission, it sounded like the type you would hear combat pilots have, a lot of callsigns used, none familiar until l he heard.

".. White Knight, this is Firehawk, got one on your tail.." Gladstone switched it off and glared at Miller, Miller for his part looked genuinely bewildered.

"I am sure we killed him, and the people who helped him, they tried to outwit us with a decoy.." his voice trailed off.

"Miller, our allies had ten ships when they started their mission, the one bringing this message was the only survivor," Gladstone said steadily getting angrier "They had to abort, I can not express to you enough how bad this would be if they suffered more failures like this, SS Ramesses is to stay out in the outer colonies until you have dealt with this problem for once and for all, got that?" and the transmission ended abruptly, Miller grabbed an ornament from his desk and threw it at the screen, watching it bounce off harmlessly, he activated the the comms to contact the bridge.

"Cairns, the minute we finish offloading supplies get ready to leave, order Hayes to step up combat drills, we will need them soon." he said commandingly. Cairns voice came back, barely hiding the joy, he knew what the captain meant, they were going to see some action.

"Yes sir." Miller then headed for the bridge, he was sure Salma would understand.

CHAPTER 13

The next morning, the SS Hades had taken orbit around Bayern Kolonie. The Mess hall was quiet as Phil walked in nursing an hangover, Rob was sitting at a table with Marcus and Andrew, and with the sole exception of Andrew the others looked as if they were suffering the same as him, Marcus even more so, using his meal tray as a pillow. Andrew however looked alert and happy.

"Hi Phil," he said a little too loud for Phil's fragile head "Matt as already went down to the planet with G, John and the sisters," Andrew finished the last of his mess hall dispensed breakfast wrap and got up to leave patting Marcus on the head "Come on, we are on alert standby." Marcus sat up and went to get out his seat as Andrew left Liana walked into the room, he held her by the waist as she kissed him tenderly and whispered something to him before he left while she went to the food dispensers. Phil and Rob looked at each other in shock, Marcus seeing Andrew leave just rested his head on the table again.

"What the hell?" Phil uttered, as he did Sister Theresa slid into the recently vacated seat.

"What is so surprising Mister Marconi?" she said clearly amused "didn't he save her life? back when you were still security at that station? she was onboard.. oh what was the name.. The SS Bohemian star?" Rob stopped what he was doing and slapped Phil's arm.

"She's the one you told me about?" he said confused. Phil looked just as confused.

"Her? Really?" then thought for a moment "Oh yeah."

"Can someone explain all this before my head explodes, not that it will take much doing the way I'm feeling." Marcus said, suddenly alert again.

"Six months ago," Rob started "one of the pirate groups, the Screaming Skulls mounted a huge assault on Waypoint Station, one of the main targets was a passenger ship named the SS Bohemian Star. The Screaming Skulls were notorious for extorting and ransoming so its not a surprise and they came prepared, even had managed to convert a cargo vessel into a gunship, we launched every ship the security forces had and we lost some good pilots that day, the pirates were sending boarding shuttles to the SS Bohemian Star. Andrew took it upon himself to shoot them down he got the first four, but the fifth was harder and he had two fighters on him but he refused to give up, just as he turned the last shuttle to slag his ship was hit bad, Phil knows what happened next" Rob finished and let Phil continue.

"He obviously survived but was in a bad way, it took several operations to remove shrapnel from his body, amongst other things, he was in intensive care for nearly a month. Angel, our old flight leader and Rob were in for minor treatment so I was in seeing them and one of the doctors told me one of the surviving passengers from the SS Bohemian Star, which had sustained a lot of casualties, had been waiting outside the intensive care ward, eating, sleeping, everything, refusing to leave and asking for updates on him from the doctors. After two weeks the ship was repaired enough to continue on its way so she reluctantly left, but not before asking the doctors to put something next to his bed, it was a.. Rob what was it called?"

"A Miraculous Medal." Rob answered.

"Yeah, one of those," Phil said clicking his fingers, he then leaned forward to Sister Theresa "are you saying that was Liana?" The Nun merely nodded smiling.

"Yes, she told me everything, she thought after it she would probably not see him again and she had no idea when she came onboard here he was part of this It was only when she met him on here and heard his callsign she realised it who he was but was afraid to tell him in case he thought she was crazy. After all they had never actually met before she came onboard but he had been on her mind all that time and when you went out on that mission she panicked, worried for his well being and came to me for advice." Rob let out a slow whistle

"Lucky they found each other again," Said Marcus as he went back to nursing his headache "and that he has such a good wingman watching his back." He added absently but Sister Theresa shook her head.

"Hardly, luck has nothing to do with it, the Lord works in mysterious ways Mister Anthony, and shouldn't you be somewhere else, being a good wingman?" she said with a sly smile as Marcus grabbed his helmet and dashed for the door to the hanger.

It was a beautiful evening, Matt took a stroll down the main boulevard of Bayern Kolonie, he and Gareth had been seeing the sights for a few hours now, Suzanne and Ellen were talking to the colony elders trying to convince them to help them in their battle but from what they had said in the past he wasn't confident.

"Did you notice something about those two in the battle?" said Gareth thinking out loud "its the way that if they are going after one target they both fire at it at the same time, its a bit..overkill." he said showing he was nervous about voicing his opinion, Matt was glad he brought it up though and gestured Gareth to sit on one of the wooden benches.

"I know, and the way they attacked way before I gave any orders, they showed a little of this in the simulators and I put it down to them wanting to prove themselves, now I'm not so sure," he said thoughtfully "I doubt they will tell us anytime soon." there was a commotion outside the council building, Matt and Gareth went to investigate, it was Suzanne and Ellen being forcibly ejected from the door. Suzanne broke free of her guard and struck the guy hard in the face, Ellen pulled out her sidearm, Matt jumped in between the sisters and guards.

"Calm down! what the hell is going on?" he said desperately, the sisters just stared at him

"They refuse to listen, they even said if we don't leave orbit in twenty four hours they will tell GalCorp about us." said Suzanne spitting on the downed guard, Matt turned to the remaining standing guards.

"Don't worry I promise we will go." he said calmly

"Just take them with you, please." the lead guard said as he knelt to tend to the guard Suzanne punched, Matt lead the others to the landing bays and once they were out of sight of the council building.

"What the hell," he said more confused than furious "we are trying to make friends not enemies." he shook his head when Suzanne spoke.

"They are not interested in outside help."

"It is believed that if they resist and use violence things will just get worse," Ellen added "Its always been the way of the Elders council." just then a young blonde haired man approached and asked.

"Are you the courageous pilots who defeated the Silver Blades? the landing bay is buzzing with the news," he said softly, Matt could tell from the accent he was a local "Sorry forgive me I am Ulrich-Matthaus Moller-Altmann, my friends call me Umma," he held out his hand and Matt shook it "where do I sign up?" Matt looked confused.

"I thought the people here were not for taking on Galcorp and the Silver Blades?"

"And are you even a pilot?" Ellen asked pointedly, Umma looked disappointed.

"I am a pilot, I fly supply shuttles to and from the cargo vessels, I don't believe you don't remember me, I was there when you first campaigned the council, most of the others left soon after you did." Now Matt was confused but Suzanne anticipated his question.

"A group of us were going to buy fighters and train as a defence force but when we presented our ideas to the council they, like now refused and we were threatened with banishment, so we decided to leave and continue the fight ourselves, but the others, I have no idea," Matt nodded and another pilot would be useful.

"Welcome aboard Ulrich.." Matt started to say.

"Just call me Umma, most do." Umma countered and they headed to the landing bays.

After landing back on the SS Hades and Matt introduced Umma to the others, Matt motioned for Andrew to follow him as he worked on his ship, he trusted the techs but as ever he found solace in working on his own ship himself.

"what's wrong?" said Andrew, Matt sighed as he

opened an access panel.

"Well," he started "Its the Sommer sisters, their actions during our last engagement were a little extreme, they didn't wait for orders to fire, they pursued every ship like a pair of wild predators, they just seem very aggressive, I've tried to get to know them, work out with them but I'm just worried that they come across as bloodthirsty." he said as he checked systems.

"Well I would say that its possible that they are more aggressive because they have a stake in this, their home is out here but I don't think that's all it is, we just need to keep an eye on things and make sure it doesn't get out of hand." Andrew said thoughtfully,just then Rob came over with John and they had concerned looks on their faces, Andrew and Matt looked at each other and realised this can't be good news, Rob handed Matt a datapad.

"what's this?" Matt said confused but as he read it it became obvious, Andrew looked at him confused.

"Okay, what's going on?" he asked eventually, Rob answered as Matt read on.

"Its a GalCorp news bulletin," he sighed "Apparently due to what they are calling an increase in pirate raids and the emergence of a new and extremely dangerous pirate group the SS Ramesses is to be on constant tour of the outer regions and will be resupplied in transit, this will continue until the area is deemed safe."

"In other words the pilot that got away during our last battle told his bosses who in turn told Director

Gladstone and now the SS Ramesses has a new mission.." Matt said looking up.

"...to hunt us down, right" Andrew finished, Matt Nodded.

"We picked it up after Matt suggested we monitor any GalCorp channels," Said John as he tried to explain "of course we are not going to receive any encoded transmissions but stuff like this is easy to intercept, I'm beginning to see what you mean, ethers something big going on." Matt just sat the pad down, shut the access panel and walked off in silence, he entered his quarters and just let out an anguished scream before sinking to his knees, he knew this would have happened eventually but not now, not yet there was no way they were ready.

"Hey, whatever it is it can't be that bad," said a voice, as Matt looked up he saw Phil standing at the doorway with a bemused look on his face "I take it you heard the news that GalCorp as released its hound after us?" Matt nodded, Phil helped him up.

"Phil, we aren't ready, we need more time.." Matt started to ramble but Phil just stared at him.

"We will just have to be ready, Matt we all knew it wouldn't be easy." he tried to tell Matt but Matt just sighed.

"Phil," he said "its not just a matter of tackling some poorly skilled pirates flying antique ships any more, we will be going up against GalCorp pilots, most are ex military and with the best equipment..."

"...I know," Phil interrupted "We will just need to train harder then, you have went through their tests, you could come up with schedules and stuff for us." Matt nodded, Phil was right.

"Yeah, I can do that," He said "Sorry just the past while have been an emotional roller coaster, I guess I didn't realise how badly it was affecting me," he said as he got up and went to splash water on his face "Plus I guess after the deception at the nebula I thought it would at least be a while longer before I would have to face GalCorp again, can I ask something Phil, why did you agree to help? loyalty to Andrew or something else?" he asked.

"Well," Phil laughed "that had something to do with it, he wouldn't have done what he did without just cause but no, you see my family have always upheld the law but the more I tried to continue that tradition the more i realised something, the Law and justice, two things that should come hand in hand are nothing of the kind. I saw the the law prevent justice too many times to feel comfortable wearing the badge any more. What happened in your case was the last straw," he said thoughtfully "I probably would have quit long before now but, when all you know is law enforcement and you are expected to carry on the family tradition, its pretty hard to imagine being anything else." he said thoughtfully as Matt dried his face.

"I can understand that," he said finally "and Rob?" he asked curiously.

"Oh, he has his reasons." said Phil anticipating the question "but he hasn't even told me what they are, he's kinda secretive that way but I do know he was fed up of the Waypoint security politics too," He smiled at Matt "I'm going to get something to eat, you coming?" Matt shook his head and sat on his bunk.

"I'll get something later" he said finally as Phil left the room, he then reached for a datapad and started planning, he would have one of the techs create GalCorp enemies to face in the simulator and try and program them with the tactics he was shown, might not be ideal but it would be a start.

CHAPTER 14

Captain Miller sat behind his desk in his ready room just off the bridge when Corbin Hayes, the ships lead pilot came in with two datapads

"You wanted me to study these files Captain?" He asked, Miller nodded, he had requested the files of Easton and the pilots who aided his escape from Waypoint and had asked Corbin to look at and give his thoughts as a pilot on each, he handed Miller one of the pads.

"The first one as we know is Matt Easton, Callsign White Knight. aged twenty seven, flew in later years of the war, you know the rest." Yes, they both knew, and looking at his record again he could see why GalCorp would go for a pilot like him but he could also see why he wouldn't have went along with the SS Ramesses..secondary mission, Corbin pressed a button on his pad that change the file on both pads

"Now this is Philip Marconi, callsign Semjasa, aged Thirty three, been in law enforcement all his adult life as well as his family, it seems in his mid twenties he left the police force on earth to go and take up a position at Waypoint, apparently he needed a new challenge, from what I can understand his piloting skill is decent but not spectacularb." Corbin said.

"This one I don't understand," Miller said tapping his pad "The guy sounds like he lives and breaths law yet he helped break sone one out a prison cell." Corbin agreed, it was odd and tapped the screen of his pad again causing both to change.

"This one is Robert Hellman, callsign Pollock, aged Thirty six, this guys military career is interesting, medals and citations along with numerous reports of flying and heroism then suddenly after some time on leave he came back and his performance dropped so bad he was saw by a psychologist who deemed him no longer fit for duty, he was invalided out and wound up on Waypoint as part of the security detail. He's one to watch, we can't discount his experience." they both agreed and Corbin moved to the next file.

"This one," he began "is one that interested me most, Andrew Douglas, callsign Firehawk, aged twenty eight and seemingly the one who was the ringleader behind the breakout. I have heard of this guy when I was in the academy, some, myself included were convinced he had tampered with the simulators he was too hard to kill, there were rumours that he'd disappear from weapons lock, no countermeasures or any normal means of doing so, yet deal deadly blows to opponents, his tactics were unusual and in my opinion made him more dangerous, he was discharged, No-one knew why."

"I think I do, look further down, when he left our recruiters approached him but he was rejected when a medical found out his knee nerve endings were dulled due to an existing condition." Miller sighed.

"I'd say he and Easton would be the top priorities to eliminate," Corbin said thinking, "the other two files, a Gareth Brazil, a thirty two year old tech and John Adams, a twenty seven six year old known smuggler whom apparently would turn informant for Waypoint security from time to time. Neither are not big threats, but rest assured none of the pilots are anything I can't handle." he sounded confident.

"Apparently they were heard over the comm channels refer to themselves as 'Ronin Flight', strange choice of name." Cairns said as he read his datapad and shaking his head.

"Doesn't matter what they call themselves, I will defeat them" Corbin said with a sneer Miller smiled too, he had every confidence in him to get the job done.

Onboard the SS Hades it was business as usual, Phil marched into the mess hall holding Nakamura the cat in one hand dumping the feline in front of Tessa.

"Tell that thing my quarters are out of bounds." he said visibly annoyed, Tessa calmly stood and picked the cat up, handing him to Liana who was at the other side of the table.

"That thing as you put it has a name and he will go where he pleases." she said furiously she squared up to him standing toe to toe just as Andrew walked in with Rob and Marcus, Matt was sitting at the unofficial pilots table finishing his breakfast and observing the scene.

"Nakamura got into Phil's quarters again." he said when he saw Andrews bemused face, it seemed to be a running joke that the cat almost always apparently wanted to be in Phil's quarters despite his open hostility towards it, Rob smirked and shouted to Phil.

"Aww come on Phil, hes so cute." Phil just rolled his eyes and walked to the pilots table.

"I better not find him in my quarters again." he said pointedly at Tessa, just then alert klaxons were sounding, Johns voice came over the comms.

"Battle stations everyone, its not a drill, repeat not a drill, Ronin flight, you may want to launch asap", everyone suddenly stood and ran to their respective areas, Liana ran to Andrew and kissed him quickly whispering it was for luck before heading to the bridge, as they headed to the hanger he noticed Matt was looking at him with a bemused look. Andrew shrugged.

"Its a long story." he said.

"Look forward to hearing it.. after we deal with this emergency" Matt replied.

The pilot's locker room attached to the hanger was a hive

of activity Matt reached into his locker and retrieved his helmet, while zipping up his flightsuit, Andrew almost always wore his flight suit so he was one of he first to be ready. Looking over at Umma, who was slipping on his flightsuit, Matt realised something.

"Andrew, Umma will have to fly on his own, we have no-one to be his wingman," he said, he saw Phil tense.

"And we aren't asking the kid, before anyone suggests anything." he said abruptly, Andrew thought about it.

"He can fly as a third with Suzanne and Ellen, for now anyway." the sisters looked like they were going to say something but thought better of it, they all managed to get to their fighters, Matt got on the comms to Liana on the bridge.

"What's the alert for? I thought we were near a colony?" he said, Liana relied.

"We are. The colony is called Midgard, and it appears to be under attack, hard to tell how many from this range as we dropped out of lightspeed at the systems edge." Matt sat silent as he prepared the ship for launch, Andrew and Marcus had already launched and he and Gareth were next, he slowly built up power then when it had reached a satisfactory level, he engaged the afterburners, no matter how many times he did it it was always an exhilarating experience, as each pair launched they flew straight to the colonies defence, Midgard was founded and named by an explorer by the name of Morten Bjornstad who named it after the old Norse name for Earth as he felt it reminded him of his homeland of Norway, it was known as a comparatively low tech colony though the orbital defences looked very new.

"This is Firehawk to the rest of Ronin Flight, we have an update on our aggressors, one light refitted cargo ship and six fighters, White Knight may I suggest you and G go with Semjasa and Pollock and take on the fighters while the rest of us tackle the cargo ship, it seems to be running as a gunboat support." Matt agreed but he took a mental note to ask why he didn't assign the sisters to fighter clean up, did Andrew notice the same thing as he did? Matt kicked in the afterburners, the pirate identifications were coming up showing them as part of the Screaming Skulls and the fighters were early model AS88 dual purpose fighters also known as Starflares. The long fuselage and variable geometry wings of the craft made them just as effective in atmosphere as in space but they were very outdated. The fighters were already in a battle with the orbital defences, Matt targeted the closest fighter and instantly destroyed it, the other ships turned their attention to the new threat

"This should be fun" he head Phil say over comms, three of the remaining ships had targeted Hm and Rob, the two that went after Matt and Gareth, suddenly his ship rocked with weapons fire, not from the fighters but the orbital defences

"SS Hades this is White Knight, can you tell the colony we are friendly? please?" he said as he brought down another fighter, Lianas voice replied

"Johns trying his best but they are sceptical" he replied sorrowfully, Matt cursed their luck, Gareth made short work of the last pursuing fighter, making full use of the main cannons field of fire he had looped back and gunned the enemy down before the enemy had even expected him to be able to, the pilot thinking he still had time to target Matt first, they were just in time to see Andrew's group make short work of the cargo gunship, like Gareth they had made good use of the field of fire to rain down sustained fire on fragile jury rigged power convertors, Phil and Rob had a novel approach, they actually lead the pirates back into the orbital defences field of fire, the Battleaxes were able to soak up the weapons fire from them.. the pirates weren't so lucky.

"White Knight this is Firehawk, all hostiles have been eliminated, another successful mission don't you think?"

"Indeed it is" was Matt's reply "Lets see if the good people at Midgard will talk to us now"

The battle was over before it really had time to start, Matt had to admit he was impressed with how they performed but was shaken out of his thoughts by another comms Message from Liana

"Distress call coming from just outside the system, a lone fighter being pursued by pirates, lightdrive down needs assistance, oh and the colonies defences are now set not to attack , John just managed to convince them we are genuine" she said it was a tricky one, it could be a trap, he had heard stories from Phil and Rob about such things, luring defenders away from targets with bogus distress calls

"No need to send every one, Brutus, Suzanne and Ellen can come with me to help, you guys stay on alert in case its a trap" Andrew said quickly "Keep Umma here with you guys, just in case" Umma's simulator performances against other fighters were not quite as good as they could be which is why Matt felt Andrew was leaving him behind.

"Okay Firehawk, good luck" he said as the fighters jumped into lightspeed, the SS Hades was just taking up orbit and getting ready to deploy Thunderclap One "This is White Knight, I'm going to the surface as escort to Thunderclap One, Umma you take up position as G's wingman, Semjasa, your in charge until myself or Firehawk return" a string of affirmative responses came back to him as he flew to take position on point of the lumbering shuttle, he knew it was a risk but they had just helps protect the colony, now for some hearts and minds work, he hoped Andrew wasn't heading to a trap but he put that thought to the back of his mind for the moment.

CHAPTER 15

The four Ronin flight ships dropped out of lightspeed at the co-ordinates given in the distress call, the scene that was laid out before them was an old battle scarred fighter trying to hold its own against two other fighters, Darts by the looks of them and an armed shuttle bearing the markings of the Silver Blades.

"Wait a minute" Andrew said in shock "Brutus, scan that fighter for me, that is an old Vanguard fighter right?" he shook his head in disbelief.

"Firehawk this is Brutus, yeah, once pride of the Dynamic Astrospace line, hey its registered to Waypoint Station, isn't that where you came from?"

"It is," Andrew answered as he switched comm channels "This is Firehawk of Ronin Flight to Waypoint Security starfighter, identify yourself." he looked at his instruments, they'd soon be in weapons range.

"Firehawk? that really you? its Astro Ace of Green flight, help me out and I'll explain everything." came the reply, Andrew thought carefully, the call sign was familiar, of course now he remembered. Nicolae Petrescu, the new pilot who only joined a few months ago, he remembered Phil shaking his head at the younger pilots callsign, even though he explained it was a childhood nickname given to him by his parents, what was he doing out here.

"Suzanne, Ellen, this is Firehawk. I assume you can take care of the pursuing fighters?" the only answer he got was the two of them kicking in the afterburners hard and vectoring their Battleaxes sharply to intercept the pirate fighters "Well, Brutus, that leaves us with the shuttle, we will come up either side of it, see who it decides to trace." Marcus sighed.

"Knowing my luck it will be me." he said half jokingly as they flew towards the Shuttle, which had turned to face the new threat. Andrew had an idea.

"Brutus, start shooting the moment you get to weapons range and do not stop." at that range these lasers were not the most accurate but he knew what he was doing, within seconds both ships were lacing the shuttle with weapons fire, the larger ship didn't even try to lock its own weapons, instead firing a few wild shots of its own as it tried to flee.

"Just as I thought." muttered Andrew, the pilot of the shuttle was not willing to risk such a vessel in this battle, armed shuttles were essential to any pirate group, the early shots were designed to panic the pilot into thinking more about preservation than attack but by running they presented the fighters with a golden opportunity, it only took a few more hits to collapse the shield and one direct hit to the engine manifold was enough to blow the shuttle up, they swung round back to the waypoint fighter, only to see Suzanne and Ellen had already destroyed their fighters and were flying in protective formation, the poor ship looked in bad condition, a surprise that it got this far out.

"Astro Ace this is Firehawk, can you make a jump to the Midgard system?" he asked, his eyes alert for any more ships.

"This is Astro Ace, if I divert most of my remaining power maybe but she's falling apart as is, but anything beats floating out here." came the reply, so Andrew and Marcus took up positions either side of the stricken ship and they all jumped together.

The ship did manage the jump but not much else, it barely made a landing in the SS Hades hanger and it was clear Nicolae was beat up pretty bad himself, he had a nasty cut above his eye and had several bandages, one in particular on his abdomen was bleeding out, he was rushed to the medbay where Sister Theresa looked him over.

"Its lucky they got you here when they did," she said as she used the dermal repair device to seal the wound, the original attempt looked sloppy "any later and I'm not sure we'd be talking." The young pilot smiled groggily and looked at Andrew who was sitting next to the bed

"Andrew," he started "you won't believe what has been going on since you left, the Chief was arrested, apparently he tried to stall Gustav from ordering us to pursue you guys, after you left Dziekanowski started asking questions to Gustav who has taken direct control of security now about the whole affair too but the next day on a normal patrol the Silver Blades launched a raid..."

"Odd, the Silver Blades have not tried to raid Waypoint for years." Andrew said disbelievingly, he let Nicolae continue

"Yeah, I know right? but they didn't try for any cargo vessels or anything, just went straight after Dziekanowski, when they got him they targeted the rest of Green Patrol. I barely survived but something just didn't sit right with me so I discharged myself from the medbay, I tried to find the files on the database about the recent events but nothing, they were seemingly erased so I went to talk to the chief in the cells. I knew one of the guards and he let me see him, he told me he suspected you were going to help Easton in some crusade in the outer regions so I decided screw it. I have to get out of here." he saw Andrew look at him in disbelief.

"how did you know where to find us?" he asked.

"Well, I made my way to the Hub, figured it was a good place to start, I got into a fight with some locals who noticed the Waypoint security badges on my uniform, I woke up in the office of a woman called..

Lilly?" Andrew nodded "She said she got her people to save me from getting a worse beating and that I was the fifth Waypoint lawman to pass by here in so many days and gave me what she was sure was the schedule of the ship you were on," Andrew went to ask how she'd know but figured she probably has her own ways so kept quiet "I had to stretch the lightdrive to the limit, after one jump I ran into my.. friends that you gladly eliminated, however it looked like they were laying in wait for something else, I took out three fighters before I jumped again but as you saw they followed.." he winced in pain as he tried to reach for a drink.

"Easy there," Sister Theresa commanded softly, handing him the glass "You have to stay here for a day or two for observation." just then Phil and then Rob came in.

"Damn Petrescu, you look like you been through the wars." said Phil ruffling the young pilots hair, Rob waited for The nun to look away and slipped Nicolae a bottle of beer, winking.

"You'll be needing one of these I bet. Good to see you again man." it was good to see him again. For one thing, it meant once he was fully fit they would have another properly trained pilot in their ranks, Andrew took it on himself to explain Nicolae's journey to the others as Sister Theresa administered a strong painkiller to him, she spotted the beer bottle but said nothing, just shook her head at Rob. Phil couldn't believe what he was hearing.

"sounds like Gustav's well in the pocket of

GalCorp now, he must have told them Maciej was snooping and they used the silver blades to silence him, damn, Between that and the chief being arrested, I want to make him pay." he then punched a bulkhead in frustration.

"Enough gentlemen, my patient needs rest, out!" Sister Theresa shouted as they left Rob turned back and said.

"We managed to retrieve your stuff from your fighters storage compartment and put it in quarters for you, we put you next to a mean Bavarian lady who likes to snore." he then turned to Phil and whispered "Don't tell Ellen I said that, she scares me", Nicolae just smiled and gave a thumbs up letting the painkiller take effect.

Andrew was just walking to his quarters when Matt came out of his.

"Hey, just spoke to the leaders of the council on Midgard, they can't, obviously publicly endorse us but they aren't going to exactly run off to GalCorp either." Andrew nodded in approval.

"Well its to be expected I guess, Have they had much dealings with Galcorp?" he asked. Matt outlined it as best he could, it seemed like Galcorp have a minor interest in the planet that's nothing compared to the aggressiveness they have shown other colonies, something about turning it into some executive retreat or something.

"Naturally they aren't interested in selling," Matt

admitted "but here's the curious thing, they don't believe that is all GalCorp wants." Of course Andrew thought dryly, from what he had saw of the photos Midgard was a paradise of conifer trees, clean springs and starry nights, GalCorp would gladly strip mine the place for the wood alone.

"Sounds like a result for us, not ideal but I suppose there is an element of general distrust, your getting the hang of this diplomacy business." he said with a smile, out of three planets visited so far only one had outright turned them down completely, there was hope.

"So, hows your pilot?" Matt asked curiously.

"Well," Andrew said "he's a little shook up but otherwise he will pull through," Andrew said stifling the urge to flinch in pain, his knees were really sore, while the operation to dull the nerve endings did make it more bearable, it still hurt "Excuse me." he said walking stiffly to his quarters, Matt looked on in sympathy. As he headed to the mess hall Matt bumped into Liana who was holding a tube of analgesic gel.

"Oh, Hi Matt, erm, is Andrew in his quarters?" she stammered, he noticed she was wearing a new scarf, blue, similar to one he saw Andrew buy back on Astra Sanctuarium.

"Yeah," he replied "And by the looks of it he will be needing that." he said pointing to the tube, Liana looked down shyly.

"I know," she said quietly "he doesn't let on but the strain of flying.." she looked at Matt her eyes full of concern. Matt had noticed that after every flight, even in simulators, Andrew did seem to be in pain with his knees, he was now beginning to see not only why he was discharged from the academy, but also just how much Andrews own determination to continue to fight through the pain truly was. He looked at Liana and gave a comforting smile.

"Well it looks like he has you to care for him." he didn't want to pry, he had heard rumours but felt it best not to indulge in the gossip, she looked at him and smiled

"Yes, yes he does, I know there are whispers but the truth is I do care about him," she looked down shyly "I know I sound crazy but there is a connection there. I can't explain it." she said as she headed down to the pilots quarters and he resumed his way to the mess hall.

CHAPTER 16

The next three planets on The SS Hades stopover list went by relatively uneventful. Camp Cornette, a small colony world that hosted professional wrestling events and broadcast them to other colonies and they seemed pleased that someone was actually doing something about the pirate menace. For reasons Matt couldn't fathom, the leader of the colony did present him with the gift of a tennis racquet as a sign of respect for taking such a stand.

"Planning to take up Tennis?" Phil quipped with Matt returned. Andrew, who was a wrestling fan himself had to explain that the colony was named after a well respected wrestling personality from the late twentieth century called Jim Cornette, who was known to carry a racquet around with him, Matt hung it up for display in the mess hall. Then there was Pacific Colony, a planet with most of its landmass under water and the colony itself on stilted platforms just above the waterline, Matt admitted he could have stood and listened to the calming sound of the water for hours. The administrators there proved interesting as they were contemplating putting together their own fighter defence force. The leaders of the Dutch colony of Voorbeeld were hadn't had many dealings with pirates but were intruiged by the Ronin's efforts. All three planets, like the others they encountered couldn't give official support but agreed to give whatever surplus supplies to aid the Ronin, unofficially of course, though they did mention if if the Ronin gained a good enough reputation they may consider endorsing them officially which was a step in the right direction.

Matt walked into the mess hall which seemed to be the unofficial hub, Andrew Gareth and Marcus were there with Umma mulling over the choices at the dispenser, being a military one it originally had a very bland if functional menu (the devices reconstituted proteins and and nutrients into identifiable facsimile of food that depending on who you ask is either a good enough taste or barely any taste at all) Johns crew had added a few more selections from the old SS Thunderclap, mainly junk food though.

"Well, I'm finally cleared to leave medbay," said Nicolae, who came in still walking a little stiff, he has his Waypoint flight suit lower part on and the arms of the suit tied around his waist and was wearing a t-shirt from the SS Hades equipment storage "Hows the dispensers here?" Umma turned and said.

"Well its not the best but beggars can't be choosers", Nicolae went over and chose a chicken tikka dish before sitting with the other pilots.

"Its good to see you up and about mate," Andrew said, and he meant it, the few times he had saw the young Romanian in action he had been impressed "Hey Umma, with Nicolae flying with us you get to be a wingman as opposed to some spare." he said smiling at Umma, the two young pilots politely introduced themselves and shook hands and then Andrew gave him an abridged list of the events so far.

"So," Nicolae said trying to take it all in "you guys are basicly out here trying to disrupt GalCorps attempts to oust colonists from their planets? of course I'm in." suddenly Craig burst into the Mess hall and tried to speak but was out of breath.

"Trouble in the simulator room." he managed to say once he composed himself.

The pilots ran to the simulator room to see Suzanne, sidearm drawn and pointed at Phil's head while Rob had Ellen pinned on simulation station canopy.

"What is going on here!?"shouted Andrew, clearly angry. Suzanne, without taking her eyes off Phil, answered.

"They started it." Phil shook his head.

"We were having simulated dogfights to train up and they called us cowards because we apparently are not bloodthirsty enough." the last part was said as he looked at Suzanne intensely. Matt groaned and put his head in his hands, they needed to sort this thing with Ellen and Suzanne out, he stepped forward.

"Suzanne, Ellen come with me, the rest of you, just stay calm" he gave a look at Andrew suggesting he have a word with the others, once Matt and the sisters left Andrew turned to Phil and Rob.

"Well?" Andrew asked

"As I said, it was just a regular simulation dogfight but as it got on, the more intense they got, Rob just asked them to calm down a little but that just made things worse..." Phil started.

"...before I knew it the simulation was ended and my canopy was pulled open and Ellen started punching me," Rob added, rubbing the side of his face "She has a mean right hook." Andrew sighed and stared at the ceiling. The Sommer sisters were getting out of hand but what could he do?

"Guys, I'll talk to Matt about this. I've noticed this myself. This hyper aggressive approach is going to get one or more of us killed." he said eventually.

"We get that they are local here and it is probably more personal for them but they do realise we have given up a lot to help these people?" Phil countered.

"I know that, you know that.. hopefully in time they will too, lets go to the mess hall. You look like you could do with a drink." Andrew said with a sigh.

Matt took the two Bavarian pilots to the briefing room where they both sat down sullenly.

"Okay what's going on, your aggression is getting out of control. Could someone please explain" he said half pleadingly, Suzanne looked up, her blue eyes burning into him.

"You understand our mission you understand the stakes involved, but to some of them, they treat it like it was some game." she said with barely contained anger.

"This is our home," Ellen continued "we were raised here. When this is over, you will all probably go back to your lives elsewhere, we will always be here, we want to make sure future generations are safe." there was a tone to her voice that suggested this had been on their minds for a while, Matt pinched the bridge of his nose.

"We aren't just some mercenary band and as for what happens if we ever finally expose GalCorp? I do not know for sure, but for now we are all devoted to the cause, and you have to trust me, I have saw most of these guys in action, they are not taking this lightly, okay?" he said, so that was it, they felt they had to do more, be more ruthless to show everyone just how important the mission is to them, he did his best to explain they didn't need to and that it might help if they integrated better to the group.

"We will try." Suzanne said eventually. Ellen nodded in agreement.

Matt got them to follow him back to the mess hall where the sisters apologised to Phil and Rob and shook hands on the understanding they put it all behind them.

"Its okay," said Phil half smiling "It was a pretty awesome kill actually, i was just shocked you got me so quick. please take a seat and meet the new guy, he's an Ace don't you know?" he said winking at Nicolae who rolled his eyes.

"Damn Phil, when are you going to stop making fun of my callsign,"

"Me?" Phil said with a look of exaggerated shock "No, I would never do anything like that."

"Yeah," said Rob with the same tone of voice "You would never do such a nasty thing, Nicolae, how could you think that of Phil" then they laughed. Nicolae turned to the sisters and explained "Astro Ace is what my parents called me when I was younger." both Suzanne and Ellen gave somewhat sympathetic smiles and sat at the table, they still appeared awkward around the others but not as much as they used to be, it was a start in the right direction.

Later on when the ship was getting ready to break orbit, John was on the bridge checking the cargo manifest on a datapad when Marcus walked in, John looked up and Marcus replied to the unsaid question.

"Just observing, used to love being on the bridge of my dads ship when he would leave orbit." John smiled, he too admitted it was a sight he never tired of either.

"Yeah," he said "I know what you mean, I could just stand here and stare at the stars for hours. Wasn't your dad was Cassius Anthony wasn't he? flew the SS Caesars Chariot right?" Marcus nodded then asked.

"So what routes are we using?" John shrugged and explained just the normal trade routes then looked at him curiously, Marcus pulled out a data stick.

"You may find this more useful, its a copy of my dads old smuggling routes, will benefit you more than they would me right now." John took it shaking his head.

"You realise," he said, looking at the data stick intently "That everyone always wondered how the Caesars Chariot always was able to deliver quicker than anyone else and avoid pirates and bandits, hell I think even they would want this information too, thanks," he beacons Tessa over and asked her "can you program these routes into the navigation computers?"

"I'll help" said Marcus flashing Tessa a sly grin and rushed to the main navigation console to help, she looked at him cautiously as he squatted down next to her but he felt something move against his leg, his smile grew wider

"So," she said coldly "why have you kept this to yourself until now." she started the file transfer and integration into the lightdrive computers. Marcus just looked at her, her green hair, the light skin, the darkly gothic makeup made her look equally severe and beautiful, he felt something at his leg again, was she rubbing her foot there? was her coldness just a public front, he thought he'd test the waters.

"Well," he said lightly putting her hand on her thigh "you see I wanted to wait until I was sure of things, sure that we'd be able to make a difference and not just some glorified mercenary or pirate group, now I'm sure we are doing the right thing and that we can make a difference." he winked at her, she leaned closer.

"The only reason that I'm not tearing that hand off you and beating you to a pulp with it is that you are a good pilot and will need that hand, but I may forget this fact if you do not remove it now." she said in a quite yet menacing tone, he quickly moved his hand.

"Hey," he said "you were stroking my leg with your foot, I'm sure of it.." he trailed off and looked down, there was Nakamura the cat, he looked at her and gave a weak smile "I'm sorry, I really am." her stare showed she was not impressed, he got up and walked off "well Tessa, I can see you have things well in hand, when your finished can i have my data stick back?" without looking and in a very frosty tone she replied.

"yes, when i am fully finished." she then scooped the cat up and held him close stroking his head as she awaited the upload to finish, Marcus left the bridge clearly embarrassed.

"There there." she said to the bewildered cat as she placed a kiss on its head as John looked on.

"you are terrible sometimes Tessa, you know that?" he said stifling a laugh, a cold grin was the only reply he got from her.

CHAPTER 17

Like a fearsome predator the SS Ramesses entered the Luxor system, one of the few GalCorp funded colony planets in the region to meet a resupply ship, the frigate SS Seti.

"Getting a distress call from the SS Seti." said the communications officer, the smaller ship was under attack.

"Bloodfists," Miller cursed when he saw the attackers swarming the SS Seti, the Bloodfists were rivals of the Silver Baldes and by extension, in Millers eyes anyway, made them enemies of GalCorp.

"we have issued warnings but the pirates have not responded" said the communications officer. Miller shook his head, of course they wouldn't.

"Issue the statement that we have no other choice but to use deadly force." Miller stated. A glance at the tactical screen on the bridge showed him that the Frigates few fighter escorts were already destroyed, he could have the SS Ramesses swoop in and make a big statement but he had another idea, he hit the comms panel of the captains chair "Hayes, get your pilots ready, we have a problem to deal with."

In the SS Ramesses pilots locker room, Corbin, halfway into putting on his flightsuit stopped to run his hand over tattoos on his right arm, every tally mark tattooed onto him represented a confirmed kill. Corbin then looked at his left arm where two X's had been tattooed on the inside of the wrist, they represented the two times he was bested in combat and to served as a painful reminder of failure, the first was as a result of an encounter when he was still a cadet in the simulators, a pilot flying as an aggressor bested him after a long duel and the other was a Hexstar fighter ace who took out most of his squadron back in the war, he managed to defeat and kill the Hexstar pilot but never found out who was the simulator aggressor, he was snapped out of his thoughts by his wingman, Austin Downs, a young pilot who used the callsign Snap Shot.

"Ready?" he asked, Corbin just looked at him and a cold smile formed on his lips.

"Oh I'm ready, just a pity these backwater pilots playing pirate are not really much of a challenge these days.. but Target practice is always welcome."

"I know what you mean, it seems that these days

we no sooner launch than we are back in the hanger and heading for a debriefing" Austin said absently "What I wouldn't give for a real challenge." Corbin nodded in agreement then turned round to the other pilots.

"Okay you guys know the drill, we have an opportunity to once again show the locals out here the price of meddling in GalCorp affairs, time to show them the error of their ways," he then smiled "Showtime gentlemen." there were cheers among the pilots as they ran to their ships as he made his way to his own personal ship, it was an Apophis class interceptor like the others but on its curved wings had large black omega symbols painted and there were tally marks painted on the hull like the tattoos on his right arm marking every kill, both from his military days and GalCorp, Corbin did a quick check to make sure the missiles were secure in their holdings and everything was safe before donning his helmet and climbing in the cockpit.

"Flight Control this is Omega, are we good for launch." he said calmly.

"Omega, you are good for launch, good luck." came the reply, Corbin had decided they only needed four fighters to take on the pirates,who apparently had nine fighters, secretly Omega was confident he could take them all on himself but he knew Miller wouldn't approve, he readied himself and fired up the engines and exited the hanger.

"Fighters launched" said Cairns looking up from

his console, Miller smiled, he had grown to enjoy watching his pilots perform.

The pirate fighters broke off their attack on the frigate, The pirate ships were an assortment of Darts, Vampires and one Starflare. The frigate at this point was badly damaged, Corbin shook his head, they were flying in a tight formation out to the GalCorp fighters.

"Too easy," he muttered before activating his comms "all fighters prepare your burst torpedoes, fire." each fighter fired the large missile that hung below its centreline, the effect looked impressive, the missiles were not guided but had a different purpose, Corbin like the other GalCorp pilots keyed a code into their missile control consoles and waited to hit the send code. just as the missiles were about to fly past the pirates Corbin hit the send command, as did the others, the missiles detonated and when they did sent a wave of explosive fragments that struck and destroyed five of the oncoming fighters.

"Gentlemen this is Omega," Corbin said smugly "I make it four against four, pick a target and engage, good hunting." the target he selected veered off wildly with Corbin's ship in hot pursuit, the pirate was decent, his evasive flying was giving Corbin a tough time but, he thought, decent wasn't good enough, he was the best, suddenly through the comms came a voice, it was the pirate.

"I take it I am addressing the great pilot Omega?"

came the voice mockingly.

"You are." he replied, why not entertain this fool, for now

"Good, any last words before you die GalCorp scum?" followed by manic laughter Corbin would have replied but the other pilot had turned his comms off and violently put his ship into a tight loop round to face Corbin dead on, weapons blazing, he knew the shields could take it so just stayed on course selected guided missiles and the minute he got a lock the pirate veered off in an attempt to shake the lock but, Corbin just fired two missiles, one missed the other shredded the doomed pilots ship. Idiot, Corbin thought, if he had ignored the target lock and stayed on target he might have had a chance of penetrating the GalCorps ships shields. He hoped when he finally comes up against Easton and the others they are more of a challenge, well at its one more mark to add to his ship.

"This is Omega scratch one pirate, status updates?" everyone replied with conformed kills "well lets head home and get the beer in, I'm buying."

He was just leaving the hanger bay to get a shower when Corbin heard raised voices so he went to investigate. It was two of the pilots, David Abrams, a rather brash and arrogant pilot who answered to the callsign Supernova and Jack Reid who used the callsign Agent Orange, were having a heated exchange.

"Hey, I had that ship in my sights, another second

and I would have got him, you stole my bloody kill." Jack shouted.

"Oh I'm sorry but you were way too slow," said David, his voice oozing sarcasm and he kissed his right wrist "my reflexes are simply way faster than yours."

"Oh yeah?" Jack growled menacingly, balling his hands into fists "You are one arrogant little prick you know that? I ought to teach you a lesson in teamwork.." and he went to swing at David when Corbin intervened, putting his body between them.

"Hey!" he shouted "What the hell is going on?.."

"...He stole my kill" Jack said, pointing at David, who was smiling smugly.

"Jack, I have told you time and again. Stop waiting for the perfect shot, just shoot when they are in your sights then crap like this won't happen, will it?" Corbin said, it was true, Jack did usually wait too long trying to line up a shot. He was a good pilot, just pedantic. Corbin turned to David.

"And you can wipe that stupid smirk off your face, you are a great pilot kid... However stunts like this are not gong to endear you to squadmates," he then looked at both of them in turn and spoke loud enough for everyone to hear "The next pilots I see arguing will be sent back to Carnarvon station for redeployment, am I understood?" There was a chorus of affirmatives "Good, just what I like to hear." he said and walked off towards the locker room.

"You will need to keep an eye on that guy Abrams" said Downs "he is after your job, you know that don't you?" Corbin nodded, he was aware of the younger pilot and his ambitions and knew that Downs coveted that position but Downs was a solid pilot and a good wingman but a leader? No, the kid didn't have an original thought in his head but as long as he believed there was some chance of succeeding Corbin he remained totally loyal.

"I know, pity for him I have no plans to retire for a long, long time," Corbin smirked, if he was honest, Abrams would probably be the one to replace him if and when the time came based on performance alone, he was just rough around the edges and arrogant but experience would temper that "But he is right Jack is too much of a perfectionist at times, anyway that is a problem for another time." he said and entered the locker room, already unzipping his flightsuit.

Now the threat was gone the supplies could be transferred though due to the damage, the SS Ramesses sent some damage control teams over to help the Frigate get up to fighting strength enough to reach a friendly shipyard for proper repairs.

"Captain Miller, a call from Mister Vulpine." said the communications officer of the SS Ramesses, Miller rolled his eyes, he knew that was Remus Fox of the Silver Blades wanting to talk, he knew the pirates were doing important work for GalCorp but Miller on a personal level didn't like working direct with him.

"I'll take in in my office." he said exiting the

bridge, he reached his office and took his time to pour a drink, sit and take a sip before keying the command to transfer the incoming call, on the screen appeared Remus Fox.

"I hope your having fun while my Silver Blades get torn apart, that's twice your..problem.. has bested us and they easily defeated a Screaming Skulls raiding party, what are you going to do about it." You could hear the annoyance in his voice, Miller just calmly sat and mused a while before responding.

"Remus, my dear fellow, we are doing our best but we are only one ship." he then shrugged as if he sympathised with the Silver Blades leader.

"Director Gladstone assures me I would have your full co-operation, we are awaiting the arrival of something big that will help our cause but we would be grateful if your beautiful ship would render assistance when we finalise our plans." Remus said smugly, he knew Miller would have to help, of course Miller knew that what he was wanting was once they figured out the next place Easton's little band would be, the Silver Blades will send the co-ordinates for an ambush.

"Agreed, send me the co-ordinates when you are ready." and with that he had ended the communication, Remus was shaken, Miller could tell, He wondered what the pirate meant by something big, it had to be a ship, probably a heavily modified cargo ship or something, though he remembered a pirate group known as the Shadow Demons used an old Hexstar frigate, that is until The SS Ramesses reduced it to scrap metal, one thing that was bothering him was were was this Ronin Flight Easton and his friends were calling themselves now based? that should be the top priority not chasing shadows with a scumbag like Remus Fox, they had already checked out a few abandoned mining stations that could be used as a base of operations but had concluded its probably a cargo ship ran by John Adams to replace the one Miller destroyed, its definitely a mobile base, Easton was not foolish judging by his records.

"Sir," came a call through the comms "The SS Seti has completed the supply transfer and its not ready to leave the system." miller sighed,, back to the hunt, at least until Fox sends the co-ordinates of the ambush.

"Good, when it leaves get ready to search the next system, we will find them, with or without the help of Mister Vulpine." he sat back and took another sip of his drink, he wished Gladstone wouldn't meddle with things and just let miller handle it, Gladstone was getting too nervous, afraid his acts will be exposed, not if Miller could help it, he will track them down and kill them once and for all.

CHAPTER 18

Andrew entered the simulator room of the SS Hades ready for the first test of Matt's program to train them how to defeat GalCorp vessels, Craig was already getting things ready though that didn't surprise him, Craig seemed to the unofficial simulator tech and he was talking to Matt, Gareth and Marcus who were all already there.

"Hey there Andrew," said Marcus cheerfully "Apparently G and Matt are going to be GalCorp pilots in the test, Craig has hooked some machine up to Matt's pod so it can learn GalCorp techniques from his flying." Andrew nodded, it seemed the logical option as there is only so much they could learn from Matt's notes.

Matt shrugged "Got the idea from the old academy aggressor training, it was no big deal." but they could see Craig had a question before they started.

"Andrew, about that aggressor training, Rob told us you would do it from time to time, what was it like, I mean sure Rob told us his exploits but mentioned you had a real good one to tell, also what fighters were the aggressors using?" It was obvious it wasn't just Craig wanting to know so Andrew smiled slightly and started.

"Well first, now Craig bear in mind the war was going on at the time so we flew Hexstar Aerospace In60c's, decent controls but too lightly armoured for my liking" Craig Nodded.

"My dad used to say that too" Andrew took a moment to remember that Craigs father was a Hexstar militia pilot during the, he then continued.

"My last aggressor flight was the day before I was given the medical that caused my discharge. The simulation was the asteroid ambush scenario," Matt nodded it was one of the more challenging simulator scenarios but said nothing allowing Andrew to continue "anyway its a pretty even battle and it gets down to just two of us and this pilot is flying close to me like a shadow but I'm using the asteroids to avoid being targeted and any attempts to get behind him or at least get my weapons to bear are countered just as quick so I get to this big asteroid and hug it tight, skimming its surface and I arm all my missiles and when the asteroids curvature takes me out of his sight I just release the missiles to float freely behind me, he flies right into them.. game over." Matt shook his head, he knew it had to be an unusual tactic.

"Do you remember the pilots name?" but before he could

answer Craig countered.

"I thought no-one knew who was flying aggressor ships." he asked.

"That's half true," Andrew said patiently "Pilots flying aggressor would know who was taking the simulation run, but they wouldn't know who we were and I do remember his callsign."

"Who?" said Matt suddenly intrigued, he and Andrew were at the academy at a similar time maybe he knew the pilot.

"Some cocky guy called Omega, claimed no pilot could ever defeat him and because I left soon after he never found out it was me, apparently he went on to be some war hero or something..." Andrew trailed off seeing Matts shocked expression "...what?"

"Okay," Matt said "Two things, you defeated Omega? and secondly, you want to guess who is the lead pilot on the SS Ramesses?" Andrew didn't need to but did anyway.

"I'm going to go out on a limb here and say Omega." Matt nodded, Andrew just rolled his eyes "Oh terrific, yes he is a great pilot but has a huge ego, trust me we can deal with him." He said confidently Matt wasn't so sure but Marcus suddenly spoke.

"well I don't know about you guys but I came here to fly not to chat about old times." Andrew and Matt smiled and got ready to start the simulation, Matt turned to Craig and said.

"Can you load scenario Ronin versus Galcorp zero zero one into the simulation." he then pulled on his helmet and climbed in the simulator pod, he was curious as to how it would work...

As the simulator test was happening, in the mess hall Liana was sitting talking to Tessa who was feeding Nakamura when Nicolae walked in.

"Have you saw Andrew or Matt?" he asked as he eyed the cat with curiosity .

"They are in the simulators testing a new program." Tessa said as she stroked Nakamura's back eliciting a loud purr from the feline.

"Ah," he said, not taking his eyes off Nakamura "Okay, was just wondering if I as getting added to the pilot list yet and who my wingman would be, sooner I know the sooner we can train together, thanks for your help." he smiled and left, as he left Suzanne and Ellen walked in.

"May we sit?" Suzanne asked politely, Tessa nodded smiling and immediately asked a question.

"So mind if I ask? how come you two don't have interesting sounding callsigns." she said curiously, Liana looked interested too.

"It's easy," Ellen said matter of factly "As we told the other pilots we are not interested in hiding our names, we want everyone to know exactly who we are and what we are doing and also we don't believe in giving ourselves fancy nicknames. We are happy with what our parents chose for us." Tessa and Liana just looked at each other with eyebrows raised.

"We were just asking, though you have to ask how some of them come about their names." Tessa mused.

"Matthews is easy" said Suzanne suddenly "He is an honourable man who stands for what is right and good, white Knight is perfect for him." Ellen nodded in agreement.

"There is an interesting story behind Andrews," added Liana, the others looked at her, she shrugged and continued "in his first run in a real fighter in the academy his ship developed an engine problem, he had to land it with engines cutting out and half the ship on fire, he managed to land safely but ever since that the commanding officer referred to him as the Firehawk and it stuck." Tessa shook her head, of course Liana would know.

"Marcus's seems to be an ironic take on his name, from what I hear, his dad was big on Ancient Roman history," Tessa added, as the conversation continued they realised they worked out why the others chose the names they did, all except Phil.

"What is a Semjasa anyway?" was Ellen's retort, just then Matt came into the mess hall with Gareth and absently said hi before sitting at the pilots table.

"I should really stop duelling with Andrew in the simulators." he said rubbing his temples. Gareth laughed and sat next to him slapping his shoulder.

"At least you got the data you needed." Matt nodded then smiled.

"Your right, we will start training simulations

tomorrow," he then turned to the table the ladies were sitting at and said to Suzanne and Ellen "fancy being the first two to give it a run through?", Suzanne jumped up out her seat smiling with an affirmative on her lips, Matt had noticed Liana slipped away, no need to ask where she was going.

"Can we run through tonight." Ellen said eagerly, matt shrugged and smiled.

"Well," he said "Craig will still be there, what the hell, I'm up for it, c'mon Gareth, us four against some GalCorp fighters?" the truth was Matt was tired, it took a lot out him coming up with the tests and helping with the simulation but he admitted the eagerness of the Sommers sisters was infectious, he promised himself one run and he will get some much needed sleep, yes just one run and bed, that sounded like a plan.

Matt jolted awake to find himself in one of the simulator pods with a blanket over him and a datapad next to it resting on the data input console, he looked up to see the lights were in night mode and as such were on a low setting, the datapad had a message reading.

"Hey Matt, you fell asleep halfway during the second run through. The blanket belongs to Suzanne, she didn't want to wake you, signed G." Matt read out loud then groggily he climbed out the pod and hastily folded the blanket, he'd give it to Suzanne in the morning. He headed to his quarters, the hallways were quiet and he could hear every step he made, as he walked past the mess hall he saw Sister Theresa sitting herself, curious, he went over to her.

"A bit late for you surely Mister Easton?" she said suddenly "something on your mind?" Matt was caught off guard by the question but felt it only polite to answer, he took the seat across from her and sat down.

"I'm worried," he started "I'm worried that by starting this crusade I'm not just dooming myself but everyone on board, when I first deserted GalCorp I didn't have time to think, I just acted, from then on I had been going on my guts and adrenaline but the report that the SS Ramesses is on our case,it shook me up, snapped me out of my bubble, I try to put a brave face on it but its hard. I know I'm dong the right thing, its just I guess I fear I will ultimately fail." he looked down with his shoulders sagging, Sister Theresa just smiled sadly.

"That's only normal Mister Easton," she said reaching over and taking his hand to reassure him "have you ever been in command before?" he shook his head "what you are going through is what any good leader goes through, in fact, the day you stop caring about the lives of of the others is the day you should truly be worried about. You are a good man Mister Easton, trust your instincts and the skill of your fellow pilots and you will succeed now, let us pray together, let us pray that you receive the strength and fortitude needed for the upcoming troubles we will face."

"I'd like to, but I'm tired, also, I'm not Catholic and barely a Christian." he said starting to rise but she didn't let go of his hand.

"No-one is perfect," she said in that serene voice of hers "and besides it will be a short prayer." so he sat back down and together, in the empty mess hall, they prayed.

It was afternoon the next day before Matt woke up in his quarters to the sound of his door chime, it was Andrew.

"Good morning, or should I say afternoon" he said cheerily, holding out a cup of coffee, Matt accepted the cup and took a sip, not too hot just as he liked it "You look a lot better today, you must have needed that sleep" Andrew noted. Matt sat on his bunk and sighed.

"Yeah, I had let everything get on top of me, blaming myself for dragging people into my private battle with GalCorp, that sort of thing but I will admit Sister Theresa is one hell of a woman, I'm not saying I'm one hundred per cent over it all but i feel a lot better than I have these past few days." he said taking another drink of coffee, Andrew sat in the chair next to the bunk.

"Yeah, our resident nun has that effect on people. Can I ask you something that may sound a bit personal?" Andrew said carefully, Matt nodded, curious as to what Andrew would think is a bit personal "Well, when we are all together and sharing stories of dogfights and battles you tend not to say much, either you didn't see much action... or did you see too much?" Andrew said hoping he wasn't offending.

"Well," Matt started slowly "at first I was serving on space stations as part of fighter defence but after a few months i did get moved to the front lines and saw a lot of combat, even took part in the battle over Vista Prime," Andrew let out a slow whistle, that was on of the deciding battles in the war, Matt continued, staring into his coffee mug "I don't talk about it because I guess I don't see it as me doing anything special, just my duty, all i ever wanted to do is protect people." there was a long pause then Andrew stood up.

"I can understand that," he said thoughtfully as he headed for the door "I'd probably be the same if I had made it to the end of training. One thing I didn't miss when I was discharged was the blood thirsty machismo a lot of other pilots had." Matt looked up and smiled, it was amazing how like minded they could be and he had noticed, with the exception of the simulator aggressor stuff Andrew didn't talk much about his exploits either, in fact it was mainly others who told people about them instead, then Matt suddenly remembered something.

"Can I ask something probably a lot more personal than your question." he said with a wry smile.

"Sure, Andrew said slightly confused.

"What is the deal with you and our flight controller Miss Cotugno? if its okay to ask that is." Matt said almost reluctantly like he wasn't sure it was his place to ask, Andrew gave a soft sigh.

"I've been waiting for someone to ask, I take it someone had told you about the SS Bohemian Star incident," Matt nodded, ever since Phil and Rob told Sister Theresa the story had spread around the ship "Well you now she was the one who waited outside the intensive care ward waiting for news of me. She had to leave with the ship before I woke, even then the doctors had reassure her seveal times I would pull through and all I ever had was her Miraculous Medal and a vague description of her from Phil, no name or nothing. As I was heading to the party to celebrate our first victory we bumped into each other and she reveals she was that girl from the SS Bohemian star"

"Oh," said Matt finally working it out "That's why you weren't there" Andrew nodded

"Matt," Andrew continued softly with a hint emotional pain in his voice "You know what it feels like as a pilot? Its an ultimately thankless task. We are expected to go out time after time and fight until we die or too broken down to continue, medals and citations are nice trinkets but it feels empty. My near fatal attempts to keep Liana and the others onboard that ship had a profound effect on her, she waited as long as she could to see if I was okay, she actually cared what happened to me. Then one thing lead to another and we have been seeing each other whenever we can ever since. I don't know what it is but there is a connection there. Matt, I have never been a success with the ladies. I remember when I recovered enough to be back on active duty a small part of me kept wondering if she would return. I never told the others in case they thought I was crazy but there is a good reason I wear that miraculous medal."

"You hoped that maybe she would come and get it back or something?" Matt asked curiously, Andrew nodded

"It turns out she was hoping to actually come back and see me someday, but one thing lead to another and she ended up here of all places. However neither of us expected to hit it off as quickly as we have." he had a contented look in his eyes, Matt could tell that at least to Andrew this was no casual fling.

"I'm happy for you, I really am," Matt said and got up "I suppose I better get some food, care to join me?"

"Of course," Andrew smiled, "Besides I think we are nearing the next stop of Johns cargo run, some asteroid mining Barons space station or something. could be interesting."

In the hanger Nicolae was checking out the Battleaxe assigned to him by the ground crew, he was adjusting the cockpit seat and controls to his personal preference when Umma came up to him.

"Hey, Andrew told me this morning I'm your wingman, I'm Umma." he climbed up the boarding ladder and offered his hand, Nicolae took it and shook his hand.

"Nicolae, though when flying call me Astro Ace," flew a fighter before, i mean a real one not simulators." he said, might as well get to know his new wingman.

"No," Umma said "Just shuttles mainly, my first taste of action was my first outing as part of Ronin flight." Nicolae could see why he was assigned as someone's wingman and not the other way around, just then from nowhere something jumped seemingly from nowhere onto the fighters cockpit canopy, it was Nakamura.

"The cat gets everywhere." said Nicolae, who tried to shoo Nakamura off in a futile gesture when Tessa approached them.

"Shinsuke, you naughty cat, come here," she said in a mock angry tone and with that the grey feline just lept off the ship into her waiting arms "I told you not to go near those dangerous ships didn't I." she said cuddling him.

"How does she do that." Nicolae wondered out loud, Umma had no answer.

CHAPTER 19

For an independent asteroid mining operation it was well equipped, Matt just marvelled at it as he and Andrew observed from the bridge of the SS Hades.

"Baron Chopra doesn't believe in doing anything small does he?" said John from behind them "His Barony is the biggest non company owned business out here which is good for us as with an operation as big as this lots of things break down which means guys like me get big paydays binging in spares and other things"he smiled slyly, Andrew knew what he meant, there were a few of these operations with self titled barons running their own mining businesses and their territories were their own domains where they could do virtually anything.

"Are those Tsunamis?" Matt asked as he pointed to the small group of five fighters patrolling the area, their flanks emblazoned with Baron Chopra's insignia, the Kawaguchi F89 Tsumani was a highly expensive fighter for its size and weapons loadout and were saw as status symbols as much as combat vessels, John nodded.

"yeah, that reminds me, Liana, best inform the Baron who we are, last time he saw me I was still commanding the SS Thunderclap, i don't want him to thinking we are pirates or something." just as he said that the weapons officer Ben Tracey looked to from his console.

"Ships coming out of lightspeed the other side of the field, a modified passenger liner and eight fighters identifying as Silver Blades, they are too far away to detect us. Looks like they are flying Vampires according to out scanners" one of the few fully intact systems on the SS Hades was its military grade sensor package, it gave them almost twice the range of the best civilian equipment. Matt looked at Andrew as he saw the Barons ships vector toward the incoming threat.

"We should launch too to help" he said while heading out the bridge, Andrew followed suit, giving a glance to Liana as he did.

They were soon launched and catching up with the other defending ships, the Tsunamis might be newer models compared to the Battleaxe but the Ronin ships were quicker.

"This is Ghost of Katar Squadron, identify yourself." the pilot sounded as if he was under a lot of stress.

"This is Firehawk of Ronin flight, we are with the SS Hades and offering assistance," said Andrew before switching his comms channel to the Ronin flight channel "Okay White Knight, how do you want to play this out?"

"Its a tough one, looks like they are going to focus on the fighters so we should focus on the passenger liner, it seems bristling with weaponry," Matt thoughtfully "You take Brutus, Suzanne and Ellen and assist Katar Squadron, if the liner gets closer its weapons could do alot of damage." Andrew acknowledged and his group banked away to join the defending fighters, The liner was large and looked formidable but Matt's scans were showing the ships weapons were badly fitted

"This is White Knight, focus on the weapons, first," and they started swarming the liner firing into it relentlessly, it was clear that the weapons were not designed to target fighters but a lucky shot hit Gareth's ship in a glancing blow and wiped out his shields but he otherwise reported he was okay it was becoming clear that their weapons were not doing enough damage "Damn, Firehawk, this is White Knight we can't seem to make too much impact on this ship on our own."

"White Knight, this is Firehawk, bad time to call.. wait, might be able to help you there." Matt looked confused until out of nowhere streaked Andrew's fighter... followed by a pirate fighter, he flew right to the liner and just pulled up at the last minute, Matt could see the shields briefly impact on each other, the other pilot was too slow to change course and slammed into the shields, the impact fully collapsed them and caused damage to the larger ship. Matt checked his scanners, the shields were down, oddly the ship continued on course to the Barons space station.

"Firehawk, this is White Knight, thanks for the assist, White Knight to the rest of you, continue the attack." this time they were able to inflict a lot of damage, they must have paid a lot for a shield that strong he thought.

"White Knight, this is Firehawk, Hope that worked." Matt once again wondered how the hell Andrew developed such unconventional tactics as he swooped in for another run, taking out two turrets, he had noticed Gareth seemed a little tentative ever since he lost his shields, he could see the dogfight that Andrew had rejoined, the Pilots of Katar Squadron were surprisingly good, he took a note to himself meet them after this, suddenly, while Nicolae and Umma were starting their own swooping run on the liner, the larger ships crew must have been too busy fighting them to notice a large asteroid floated closer and slammed into the side causing multiple explosions before lazily drifting off.

"White Knight, this is Suzanne, the fighters are retreating, heading your way." came the call through the comms, five fighters few towards them, not even bothering to evade, The four ships of Andrews group in pursuit with the Barons fighters preferring to hang back, Ellen eliminated one with concentrated fire, the one Marcus followed suddenly veered off for no apparent reason and hit an asteroid, destroying it immediately, Nicolae took one down flying headlong into it, firing his weapons at the last minute.

"Yes!, I love these fighters!" he exclaimed over the comms, one of the pirates decided to loop back as if trying to let the other get a better chance of escape, Matt decided to ignore it and fly past to try and get the fleeing ship, the rearguard fighter got a few glancing blows to his shield before fire from Suzanne's Battleaxe cored the cockpit.

"come on, come on." Matt said impatiently as his main gun tracked the pirate, they had just about cleared the asteroid field when weapons lock was conformed, a few short bursts of fire were all that was needed to destroy the already damaged ship.

"This is White Knight, area free of enemies, return to base." he said, just then Johns voice came over the comms.

"Guys, great job out there, just been speaking with Baron Chopra himself and he's impressed enough he has granted us access to his repair docks, was thinking finally get to upgrade the SS Hades with the weapons and materials I got from the Hub." Matt realised it would take a few days but it was much needed work, in its current state the SS Hades was not going to be much use in a battle and the area was well defended so there were few safer places to be at this moment. might ease some nerves some of the pilots had been showing lately just to relax for a few days.

The SS Hades just barely fit into Baron Chopra's repair dock, Matt had went over with John to get a chance to speak with the Baron face to face, meanwhile Andrew was called up to the bridge by Liana who had an urgent comms message for him, he went to her communications console and Liana put the signal on the monitor, it was Lilly.

"Ah, Officer Douglas, I know, I know. You are not an officer any more but old habits die hard." she said winking slyly.

Andrew rolled his eyes a little "Hi Lilly, hows things at the hub and what has made you contact me? we already know GalCorp are aware of us."

"Well," she started "it seems your successes are all people are talking about here. To anyone who is not a pirate or hoping to be one, you guys are heroes, in fact a few pilots even enquired around how they would join you and after background checks, you can't be too careful, and after I weeded out the GalCorp spy and the below par pilots I got them to rendezvous with you at your next stop which will be Baron Chopra's station, right?" Liana looked at Andrew wondering how she would have known the schedule but remembered Andrew saying that's how Nicolae knew where to find them and that he thought it was probably from accessing Johns cargo lists for the SS Hades that got her the information, as for what happened to the spy, Andrew had a look that suggested to Liana he wasn't sure he wanted to know.

"Actually Lilly, we are already there." he said smiling. She looked confused."

How? what, of course, one of the the pilots you recruited was Cassius Anthony's kid right?" Andrew nodded his smile growing, she looked at him as if she didn't know if she should be pleased or angry "Anyway I've already told the Baron not to blow the ship I sent them in out of the stars when it appears, which should be in the next few hours, Lilly out." and the screen went blank, no mention of who they were or how many, he figured she was using an encrypted transmission and wanted to end it quick before anyone could hack it, he looked at the flight control board, they had decided to have two ships patrolling around the SS Hades at all times just in case the Barony had any more unwanted guests.

"Who is out there right now?" he asked curiously as she checked the board.

"Phil and Rob," she replied "they haven't been out long." she had just finished saying that when over the comms.

"SS Hades this is Semjasa, there seems to be something up with my..." they heard a loud shriek. "..What the..? Get this cat out of here, seriously?" everyone on the bridge turned round and looked at around to see if Tessa was there, thankfully she wasn't.

"I think she's helping co-ordinate repairs with the Baron's engineers" Ben said, anticipating Andrew's question. Phil would need to land and Andrew guessed he wouldn't be happy..

"Liana, Tell Phil to land and take a break once he has landed, get in touch with Craig and tell him to suit up and take one of the unused fighters and continue the patrol as Robs wingman." Liana smiled, she had heard Andrew and the other pilots talk about Craig and knew his love of flying.

"He will like that." she said. Andrew smiled and went to greet Phil and diffuse any potential situation but before he went Andrew told Liana.

"But remind Craig its just a one off, he's not a regular pilot yet, okay?" She smiled in response as she started giving the instructions over the comms.

As expected Craig was excited with the news if the smile on his face was anything to go by. Andrew was waiting for Phil to land shouted over to Craig

"Good luck." and give him a thumbs up as the younger pilot climbed into his cockpit. Andrew had noted it had been the Battleaxe he had been working on in his spare time. Gordon McKay, the senior tech did the final checks on the fighter before preparing it for launch. Craig sat with his fighter in the ready position for a while, presumably awaiting for Liana to give the go ahead. Suddenly the alert klaxons indicated imminent launch and for all personnel to retreat to a safe area (which were marked on the floor with yellow diagonal lines). Andrew tossed Craig a lazy salute as he prepared to fly out of the hanger, the kid returned the salute with a smile and gunned the throttle and flew out the hanger.

"Enjoy it kid" Andrew said to himself

Phil landed just as Craig took off and didn't look happy as his fighter canopy opened and he threw Nakamura out. One of the techs caught the furball deftly and set the cat down gently

"Something needs done with that cat," Phil said as he took his helmet off before climbing out the cockpit "I'm going to have a word with Tessa about this.." he then had a thought "Who is out there taking my place? Nicolae? Marcus? One of the sisters?" Andrew shook his head.

"No" he replied, being careful with what he said next "I thought this would be a good opportunity to see what Craig can do..."

"..Dammit Andrew, I know you mean well and I'm not saying he isn't a good kid but what if he gets ideas and thinks he can now fly combat missions" Phil interrupted.

"For all we know he might be a natural. Phil, he has wanted to fly ever since he got here, at least with this we get to evaluate him outwith the simulators and anyway it's a one off for now." Andrew reasoned.

"I guess you're right," Phil sighed and walked off, Nakaumra jumped up on a crate next to Andrew. He went up to the cat and scratched behind its ear, saying.

"You really like annoying Phil don't you?" the cat just purred in response.

CHAPTER 20

Matt was in awe of the Barons office on the space station, it had the feel of a planetside Mansion than a functioning space station, the floors looked more like marble than metal, the walls and ceiling bright and gave illusions of space, even the lighting would wash the walls with a different hue depending on the time of day and all the seats well upholstered, the tables made of what looked like real wood. It seemed like Baron Chopra was very eager for Matt to tell him everything they had been doing since they came to the outer colonies.

"Mister Easton, you are a brave man to take on GalCorp and the pirate gangs, as you can see we have our own issues with them but thanks to my son Yohul and his pilots as well as our various other defences we manage to do well out here," The Baron was a short man wearing a black military cut suit with golden detailing on the sleeve and down the front seams, dark skinned with short greying hair but had a fire in his eyes Matt had not expected to see "Ever since taking over this operation I have tried to get the other colonies and Barons to do something about the raid and attacks, be it hire protectors or even campaign for have some Colonial Marshals assigned to the area, something. that is why I am keen to help however i could." Matt noticed the Baron had military wings on his chest, would explain a lot then. John produced a datapad.

"here is what we have delivered to you and here is a list of supplies we may find useful if you are willing to help with supplies." he handed the pad to the Baron who looked at it intently.

"We have some of what you need and I thank you for transporting my cargo, i have waited too long, some cargo captains are unwilling to brave the pirates these days, my daughter Richa will help you with the supplies you need." as he spoke a beautiful lady in her late twenties wearing a black flightsuit paired with a flowing black and gold scarf draped over her neck came over and took the pad and looked through it before guiding John away.

"Now I know you are asking what I want in return as it looks like I am giving you more than you are giving me." he was right, all they done is deliver some cargo, sure they helped repeal invading pirates but that was just lucky timing, Baron Chopra pointed to his military wings.

"Yes, I served many years ago, rose to the rank of

Admiral. This Barony is part of my retirement and if I am honest, my forces are enough to defend here but nothing more, I want you to succeed because it will make this region safe again and more prosperous."

"I understand." Matt nodded, it was clear the Baron was a proud military man who was pleased to see someone try and restore order to the area of space he called home.

"Good," the Baron smiled, "My station and repair yard are always open to you and your people my friends and honoured guests anytime, i understand the work you need will require a few days to complete and I believe my daughter will be some time with Captain Adams, are you vegetarian?" Matt shook his head "Good," he activated a button on his desk and behind them a small dining table and chairs rose from trapdoors in the floor he had not saw before and spoke into his comms "My usual chef, plus one more for my guest" he looked up "Chicken okay?"

"Yes, thank you," he replied "You don't need to do this you know."

"Nonsense, a proper meal will seal our deal and you are a guest, it would be rude not to show you hospitality." Matt shrugged and took a seat as did the Baron, who proceeded to regale Matt with tales of the military back in his time.

Later on the shuttle trip back to the John couldn't believe what he was hearing.

"Let me get this straight" Said John slowly "While I was dealing and haggling with the Barons daughter, who I may add is an evil genius when it comes to cutting a deal, you are in the Barons office being wined, dined and entertained?" Matt said nothing but did notice some sauce on the corner of his mouth in his reflection on the viewport window and wiped it quick, john just shook his head "I hope it was worth it." he muttered.

They landed soon after and Matt was greeted by a smiling Craig as he exited his fighter just behind Robs own ship.

"What happened?" He asked slightly confused but Craig explained that he had to sub for Phil who had an unfortunate incident and it was okay as Andrew authorised it, mentioning Andrew made Matt suddenly remember something and he chased after Rob.

"Rob, can I ask you a strange question?" he said once he caught up Rob looked at Matt curiously and finally replied.

"Sure, but just so you know I didn't do it." he raised an eyebrow at Matt as if he had guessed the question

"What?" said Matt suddenly caught off guard "No.. No, I was just going to ask, do you know why Andrew is so, how to put it..." Matt started, but it seemed Rob actually guessed what Matt was going to say.

"..Why he likes to employ, oh let's just call them

unconventional, tactics?" right Matt nodded "Well not sure its my place to say, however as long as I have known him he has been diabolical with his creativity, he once told me that he knows he's not the best by a long shot and he knew that its not enough to be lucky either, a lot of his moves like the lightspeed hop, using enemies to destroy each other are things he initially came up with on the fly. Between you and I he is a good friend and someone you want flying with you but I'd hate to find out what's going on in that head of his, I mean think on it the fact that he even thinks of doing half these things is crazy." Matt laughed and headed to his quarters, he was feeling quite full, maybe a lie down then hitting the gym might be in order.

The mess hall was quiet, that is until Tessa stormed in.

"You tossed Nakamura out of your ship" she shouted at Phil, who was getting something to eat.

"Listen, Tessa," Phil said with some restraint, "You need to keep a closer eye on that cat. What if I had crashed into an asteroid out there because of that cat?" Tessa pondered this for a few moments then gave an answer.

"I can't make any promises, he is a free spirit and I won't curtail his movements but I will make sure the techs keep the cockpit canopies closed when not being used. Hopefully that will stop him getting in the fighters, okay?" she said with a tone that suggested he should accept her compromise.

"It's better than nothing" Phil conceded as he watched her leave as Nicolae walked in.

"What was that all about?" he asked.

"Oh, Just Tessa and that damn cat," Phil replied as he sat down, stabbing at his food with a fork. "The bloody thing got into my cockpit."

"Not good, is that why you are back from patrol early?" Nicolae sat across from Phil.

"Yeah, now Craig is out theredoing the rest of the patrol with Rob in my place" Phil had a sullen tone to his voice.

"Maybe this will be a good experience for him" the Romanian pilot countered.

"Not you too" Phil said shaking his head. Marcus came in and sat down with a look like he had some news.

"We are getting more pilots" he said with a smile "Andrew just told me."

"How, why, who? Come on, tell us." asked Phil but Marcus shook his head.

"I don't have too much details but things could get interesting around here." Phil and Nicolae just looked at each other,

" Oh yeah? Interesting?" Phil asked "but interesting in a good way.. or a bad way?"

"Not sure, only one way to find out," Nicolae replied "We wait and see."

Liana was walking hand in hand with Andrew to his

quarters after her shift on the bridge was over and they were idly chatting about what to do with their free time when a voice from behind

"Hey," it was Matt "I not long back from the Baron's station and I had a very interesting conversation with the man." Andrew and Liana listened intently as Matt explained everything.

"Seems like you have your first proper ally here." Liana said, still cuddled into Andrew.

"It Does," Matt admitted "By the way what was going on in the hanger and why was Craig flying with Rob?" both Andrew and Liana laughed then explained about Phil finding the cat in his cockpit and having to send Craig out to continue the patrol "How was he." Matt asked.

"He is good, I think Rob must have been seeing what Craig was capable of, encouraging him to do the reporting in, getting him to do asteroid scans, that sort of thing and, from my perspective anyway, did well." Liana answered, she had been monitoring them the whole time.

"She's right," added Andrew "I think all that time in the simulators and observing our simulations has helped, I don't know about combat missions yet but hes getting there... oh before I forget Lilly has sent a few pilots our way, don't ask how she knows we are here and don't worry she has weeded out any GalCorp spies." Matt was going to ask what that meant but could tell from their expressions it was better not asking.

"Do you know who they are?" Matt asked.

"No, Lilly wouldn't say but they had heard of our

exploits and wanted to sign up," Andrew said "Though I get the feeling Lilly is still not sure what to make of us, we are not quite mercenaries or pirates but we are not quite the law either, I think she wants to trust us but needs more time and proof." Matt agreed, if she knew their schedule she could have sold that to the Silver Blades of Galcorp but she didn't.

"Anyway guys, I'm off to my quarters to rest then maybe hit the gym." He half smiled.

"Night Matt, we won't be too loud." Andrew said slyly and when Matt turned round Liana gave a cheeky wink, Matt just shook his head and laughed.

CHAPTER 21

The pilots were gathered in the hanger to greet the new arrivals, their shuttle just had jumped into the system, John had told them he was surprised it even got there when he saw it from the bridge and they saw why when it landed on the main deck, Sister Theresa appeared next to the pilots, curious about the newcomers.

"The only thing keeping it together is the rust." commented Gareth as the doors opened on it, first to exit was a young man, clean shaven, short brown hair and Matt noted was wearing military wings on his flight jacket and Matt noticed that the flightsuit was standard military issue so clearly Matt had a lot of questions for this one, the second was a very formidable looking lady, tall with dark skin which contrasted with her rather bright flightsuit which was mainly grey with white and bright orange trimming, her hair in braids that were mainly black with every third braid being the same eye hurting orange as her flightsuit trim but had seemed a rather cheerful pilot who was wearing a plain grey baggy flightsuit, he was sorting a baseball cap backwards and was looking around with a smile what turned out to be the last pilot exited the shuttle and seemed a little nervous, her black flightsuit was teamed with black boots that went to her knees, had platform soles and had buckles up the sides, her metal studded belt had a buckle in the shape of a stylised cats head, her white coloured hair had purple tips and she wore old flight goggles as a hairband, all four of them just stood near the shuttle as if not sure what to do now, Matt and Andrew went over to greet them.

"Hi," said Matt smiling widely "I am Matt Easton, callsign White Knight and this is Andrew Douglas, callsign Firehawk. I assume Lilly told you everything." the first pilot nodded and spoke.

"She did, and also supplied us with this, erm, transport," he said gesturing to the shuttle "at a large discount of course," he extended his hand "Nathan Jones, callsign Nate Dawg, thats D-A-W-G, as opposed to D-O-G." Matt could hear someone smirk, sounded like Phil, The next pilot stepped forward and looked at Matt intently.

"Tamika Henley, callsign Quinque, I hope we can get out there and bring order to this area of space" she said with a joyless smile, she had deadly intent, Matt gave an involuntary shudder then he looked at the third pilot who tossed a lazy salute.

"Alan Allford, callsign Pyrus," Matt had heard of lots of odd and interesting callsigns but this one was odd by any standards, as it was the scientific name for pears but he shrugged as Alan continued "I would have came in my own ship, unfortunately I crashed when landing at the Hub, you see the struts wouldn't deploy but I suppose it was an old Ingram Industries D65 Wildstar that was barely functioning anyway but here I am." he said with a carefree air. Matt and Andrew turned to the last pilot.

"Kate Dale, callsign Kitten," she said with a rather confident air "I had the misfortune of flying this rust heap." she gestured to the shuttle, Matt nodded, there was something about her general attitude that suggested she was going to be an interesting addition to the group, Matt then gave them a little welcome speech he had prepared, showing them the ships they would be assigned before taking them to their newly assigned quarters.

"After such a flight a rest and freshen u will be needed, the food dispensers are only working in the Mess hall at the moment. We will all meet at the pilots briefing room in two hours." he said as he lead the new recruits off, Andrew walked up to the other pilots.

"So," he asked, "what do you think?" as he scanned everyone to gauge reactions, The Sommer sisters immediately happily noted it was good for more female pilots to be in the team, Phil felt there something about Nathan, a bit too uptight he thought. Nicolae disagreed and pointed out the military wings.

"If he's academy trained that can only be a good

thing right?" was Nicolaes reasoning Phil still wasn't convinced. Rob was curious about some of the callsigns and how he has found usually you can tell a lot from a persons callsign.

"in that case me what is a Quinque?" everyone looked confused until sister Theresa spoke up.

"Quinque is latin for the number five, for whatever reason this number must hold some importance for her." she shrugged, everyone noted Marcus hadn't spoke yet, he was oddly quiet and thoughtful.

"He is probably wondering which one he will flirt with first." Phil said half jokingly at which point Marcus snapped out of his daydream

"What?" he said confused "No, I didn't flirt with you two," he said gesturing to the sisters "and not to Liana or any of the other crew on here guys, the Tessa incident was a one off, besides, that Tamika girl looks like another headcase, no offence ladies." the last comment directed at Suzanne and Ellen

"None taken." Ellen said while glaring at him, Andrew shook his head.

"Listen guys, you heard Matt be in the pilots briefing room in two hours, don't be late." he said while shooing them off the hanger deck.

Every pilot was in the briefing room on time, the next pilots for the most part sat separate but Matt hoped that would change after a mission or two, but first he thought something to break the ice and after he had informed that he would pair up Kate as Nathan's wing and paired Alan and Tamika together, with Tamika as the lead pilot of the two.

"Now to get you used to our fighters I think its best to have you face off against some of our more experienced pilots." he scanned the other pilots to see who he could have them fight, he already figured having them face Andrew is not the best choice as he would probably frustrate and demoralise them and to be honest Marcus was getting just as crazy, "Kate and Nate I'd like you to work with Nicolae and Umma, Alan and Tamika, you can work with Phil and Rob, any questions?" there were mutterings but no-one asked anything.

"Okay everyone dismissed," Matt said as everyone filed out, he slumped on the podium and said with a sigh "This should be interesting." to Andrew who stayed behind to talk to him.

"Did our new recruits tell you much about them when you showed them about?" Matt looked up and nodded.

"Yeah," he said as he rubbed his neck "Nathan was in the military as you could probably guess but won't say why he left," Andrew raised an eyebrow but said nothing, Nathan looked lie a poster boy for the military as well "Alan is a strange one, he comes from the outer regions its self, a colony we haven't been to called Amaethon Colony which is an agricultural planet and he used to dust the crops for his family's farm but convinced them to let him leave to find himself when he came across our call for pilots." Andrew seemed surprised.

"That colony isn't one GalCorp have bothered too much with from the reports we have saw," Andrew noted "still its interesting and good to know yet another local."

"Yeah," Matt admitted "makes us seem less like invading mercenaries, Tamika is a very curious case she comes from the old Hexstar territories, wanted to be a pilot but their forces never let her join for reasons she wouldn't say and has since been a pilot for hire but decided to join us after Lilly told her about us, our aim has struck a chord with her so she signed up." Andrew nodded, sounds like she has something to prove and sees the Ronin as the best way to do so.

"And Kate?" Andrew asked "What's her deal?"

"Well," Matt said thinking "you see she is the daughter of one Thomas Dale, callsign Lynx." Andrew looked shocked, walked over and said.

"I remember hearing about Thomas Dale, he was a hero in the early days of the war it took an entire squadron of Hexstar ships to take him down, that's his daughter?" Matt nodded "Okay, well I don't know about you but I am going to the bridge to talk to John, find out what going on." Matt picked up his own bag.

"Yeah, I'm thinking of getting some time in the gym, say Hi to Liana for me will you?" Andrew smiled widely, Matt knew the real reason he was going up.

"Yeah mate, I will"

Above Nepri Colony the SS Ramesses orbited as they

resupplied, Captain Miller was in his office when he was informed by his comms officer there was another message from Mister Vulpine, Miller rolled his eyes, he hated that stupid codename, everyone onboard knew it was Remus Fox.

"Patch it through." he said wearily, on the screen was Remus Fox, his dyed red trimmed short Mohawk and red tinted goggles made him look stupid to Miller.

"Ah, Captain Miller I have some news for you, my special big surprise will be here in the next day or so, you know the old Jericho Barony?" Miller nodded, it was abandoned a few years ago by the the owner, a Quentin Jericho. rumour had it he was conned into buying what turned out to be an Asteroid Barony that had been stripped nearly bare of any useful minerals, after efforts to make something of it he gave up and just abandoned it. the station itself lay in lockdown, borderline derelict.

"I remember of course," he said "I'm surprised you haven't taken it as a base for yourselves, after all no-one else is using it."

"The thought had crossed my mind but its a little too central to things, too much casual traffic, you understand," Remus leaned forward "Will meet you there in a few days time, we can discuss in person the best idea for an ambush." Miller shook his head why did he get the feeling this was just as about showing off some new toy as it was actually coming up with a plan and hovered his finger above the end communication button.

"I'll be there." he said quickly hitting the button, he did not want to listen to another word that moron had to say and sat back in his chair, he was getting increasingly frustrated with the Silver Blades and Gladstone's insistence that they work together, he remembered his own suggestion he made when Gladstone first approached him with the idea was to take some trustworthy people from the security forces and create a mock pirate unit that would do the same job only be more dependable. Gladstone ruled it out as he believed only genuine pirates would work, he shook his head and decided to wait until they had resupplied before ordering them to the rendezvous.

CHAPTER 22

After enjoying some rest at Baron Chopra's facilities the SS Hades had made its way to the colony world of Novaya Sibir, the surface was covered in ice and snow so the Colony was mainly underground with only a large dome visible from the surface. Matt as unofficial diplomat and spokesman for the Ronin went down with John to speak to the colonists while Andrew and Marcus went to the simulator room to get some flight time in. As they came in Kate was just leaving with Nathan still checking out his performance on a monitor.

"Hi" Andrew said warmly to Kate "Matt told me your Thomas Dales kid?" she looked a little shocked and lowered her head into her hands before nodding Marcus looked at Andrew perplexed "Is everything okay?" Andrew said with a hint of concern, she looked up the and her eyes were close to tears.

"I'm sorry... I just... okay... every time someone hears my name, I'm always compared to my father or asked how great he is and I know you mean well but I am not him nor will I ever be" they could tell from her words how big a toll the expectations must have been over the years "and then there are some of my life choices some of my family do not approve of."

"Hey," said Marcus in a sympathetic tone "Its hard, I should know, have you ever heard of Cassius Anthony?" she looked thoughtful for a few minutes and nodded "Well I'm his son and heir, for years I was expected to take over and carry on the family business but as you can see, things haven't turned out that way. I can still see the look of disappointment on my mothers face when I told her I had to sell up."

"Yeah, just be yourself, no-one will judge you or compare you to your dad or anyone else."Andrew added as Kate relented a soft smile.

"Thank you," she said "it means a lot." and she headed down the corridor.

"You know," said Nathan from behind them "personally speaking she has nothing to worry about. She's better than a lot of pilots at the academy." Marcus turned and snorted.

"Yeah and unfortunately I fear she'd be expected to be better than all the pilots not just a few on her name alone, what's your story anyway?" he said gesturing at the military wings, Nathan sighed.

"During the war I flew troop transport gunships mainly but after the war there less opportunities except the odd planetside manoeuvrers training and if I'm honest I signed up to fly starfighters and was transferred to ground support not by choice," he shrugged "I just want to fly in space." Andrew nodded, he can imagine the frustration Nathan felt.

"What scenario were you running" Marcus asked, Nathan went over to the console and called it up, Marcus smiled "Hey, Andrew fancy a one versus one?" Andrew rolled his eyes.

"Its asteroid chaos isn't it?"he said wearily, it was one Marcus loved, the asteroids were fast moving and the map was designed up make trainee pilots aware of their surroundings in combat more "if you insist" Marcus keyed it in and almost lept into his simulator pod.

Matt had a productive meeting with the colony administrator, while the colony wasn't targeted much if at all by pirates, Administrator Andropov understood what Ronin flight were hoping to achieve but admitted all he could offer is a friendly port and use of facilities du to the fact that the colony kept to itself mostly. Matt could see why, It was a snowstorm on the surface but in the colony itself it was a bustling community. John had admitted earlier the colony is one of his biggest customers.

"Hey Matt over here," shouted Liana, who volunteered to travel down with them as it was the one colony she was always curious about seeing, Matt looked to see if he could find her and quickly noticed her looking up at the large dome, her now almost trademark look of scarf and tall boots with her jumpsuit were now complimented with a thick quilted coat that had a fur trimmed hood and leather gloves, he walked over "Its amazing isn't it?" she said looking at Matt.

"It is." he admitted, wondering why she called him over but they stood in silence for a few minutes.

"I love him," she said suddenly "You must think I'm crazy, we haven't known each other that long but these past weeks have been so intense for everyone, not knowing from one day to the next what will happen. It has made me think a bit more clearly about what I want from life.. and I never felt this way before about anyone.. ever. I'm worried though that if I tell him he may not feel the same yet. You know him as much as anyone, what do you think?" she looked at him hopefully. Matt considered this and looked at her.

"Well, Phil, Rob and Gareth have known him longer," butt the look she gave him suggested that asking one of them would be a terrible idea, so Matt continued "He hasn't said these words exactly but it seems pretty obvious he feels the same way, look at his actions, you are the first person he wants to see after every mission and before it he always wants to see you before he goes. I'm not expert on relationships. I really am hopeless if I am honest but he loves you, I'm sure of it." she looked at him thoughtfully.

"You are probably right about Andrew... and about yourself, you aren't an expert otherwise you would have noticed." she gave a sly smile at the last comment.

"Noticed what?" he said but was distracted by Gareth running up to them.

"Hi guys we are ready to go, Johns waiting on the pad." he said as he gasped for breath, Matt and Liana laughed.

"Well let us not keep the captain waiting." he said as they made their way to the surface landing pads.

Marcus had finished his simulator time with Andrew and while Andrew went back to his quarters, he walked into the mess hall and saw Kate talk to Tamika, Alan, Nicolae and Phil so decided to join them.

"Are the simulators free?" said Tamika with an air of authority, Marcus was slightly taken aback.

"Uhh yeah sure." he said "Andrew and I just finished" Tamika grabbed her helmet from the table and jabbed Alan in the arm.

"Easy," said the laid back pilot, who was wearing his baseball cap the proper way this time, Marcus noticed it had two pears on the front and that he had a bottle of pear cider in his hand "someone is keen." Alan muttered as he rose downing his drink in a few gulps before taking his jacket from the back of the chair. Tamika stepped closer to Alan, she was taller and looked down at him.

"No, but I believe in regular practice and as my wingman it is important we work together, if you do not agree I am sure we can get new assignments, is that what you want?" she said low and menacingly, Alan backed off hands raised in surrender.

"Hey I'm sorry... " he began to say when Phil spoke up.

"Tamika.. We appreciate your determination but you don't need to prove yourselves to us, okay?" he said preparing to stand just in case.

"Sorry," she said with a sigh "I am used to working alone," she then looked at Alan "Its nothing personal, having a partner to rely on and work with, well its been a while." Alan held out his hand and Tamika shook it and smiled slightly.

"Well what are we waiting for." he said sounding more enthusiastic and they both headed to the simulation room, Marcus let out a slow whistle.

"Wow and I though the Sommer sisters were severe," he said then took a seat "So what were you all talking about?"

"Hey Marcus," said Phil "was just telling the newbies about how we broke Matt out of the cells back on waypoint." Marcus rolled his eyes.

"Really that old tale, what about the exploits of your units best pilot?" he said smiling as widely as he could but Nicolae shot that down by quipping.

"Neither Matt or Andrew are here" Kate laughed so hard her drink came out her nose as Marcus looked crestfallen, just then Tessa walked in holding Nakamura looking strict as usual but when she saw Kate seemed to let a smile escape her lips and she sat next to the young pilot.

"Hi there," she said cheerfully "I'm Tessa London

and this little fellow is Shinsuke Nakamura." Kate immediately tentatively reached out to the cat, Tessa's smile grew wider and she wordlessly urged the pilot to stroke the cat so she did nervously at first but then Nakamura moved from Tessa to Kate so she could stroke him better. Tessa smiled.

"His fur is so soft" Kate said as the cat purred.

"You should feel honoured, he doesn't got go many other people and even if he does they don't appreciate it." Tessa said, her last words were dripping with venom and she was staring at Phil. Kate was just lost in the moment stroking the cat then she looked at Tessa.

"Oh, I'm Kate," she said "I love your hair, nice colour," Tessa blushed and smiled shyly then turned to the guys, her expression changed to all business.

"Anyway, I came down with a message to whomever is feeding Nakamura laxatives better stop," everyone noticed she never took her eyes off Phil who looked unconvincingly innocent but turned to Kate smiling "If you ever want someone intelligent to talk to, my quarters are always open." and she walked away with an extra spring in her step, Nakamura jumping down from Kate to follow her.

"Okay that was weird," Marcus said looking at every one else "surely i didn't imagine that, I'm not the only one, Nicolae you saw it too right?" Nicolae nodded.

"Yeah, she knew it was Phil." Phil nodded in admission but Marcus just narrowed his eyes and stared at the Romanian pilot for a few minutes.

"you know its hard to tell if your just messing with me or being serious, hell we all know you did it Phil but that's not what I'm talking about, never saw Tessa like this before, she was ..nice." Kate just smiled.

"She's just being polite, what so wrong about that?" she said "Maybe she appreciates someone who actually knows the difference between a human and a cat touching you." Marcus just looked at her then Phil.

"You told her about that?" he said accusingly.

"What? she was bound to hear about your little misunderstanding with Tessa at some point." Marcus just shook his head and walked out muttering, Kate looked at him as he left shaking her head.

"Poor guy," she said "easy mistake to make, anyway I want to check out my fighter maybe customise it a little." and she got up and walked out.

"I will say one thing," Nicolae said wryly "This is way more interesting than Waypoint station that is for sure."

"You can say that again" said Phil as he went to the food dispensers.

CHAPTER 23

The SS Hades left orbit and made a quick jump to a place of interest John felt Matt and Andrew would want to see, Matt said he would come after he had checked a few things on his ship.

"What am I looking at?" said Andrew what he was seeing on the viewscreen was something similar to the Chopra Barony but a smaller scale and devoid of activity, John smiled sadly.

"This" he started "was home to Baron Jericho, now its abandoned, the guy bought it off the previous Baron without realising all that could be mined from the surrounding asteroids pretty much had been taken so it lays vacant after many ideas to revitalise the Barony failed but it provided the best place and opportunity to do a weapons test now we have everything fitted and connected," he turned to Ben "Target the nearest asteroid with the cannons and fire," he then looked to Andrew "These were the ones already fitted but weren't connected and if I am honest we don't have as many of these as we should but we knew that already." the large cannons bombarded the asteroid into oblivion, Andrew nodded.

"Very efficient." he said simply. John turned to Ben again

"target some of the smaller asteroids with the new radid fire laser batteries and fire." as the batteries poured out laser fire on the asteroids John explained "These are ones we had some trouble fitting at first, they aren't military grade like the cannons but are the best I could get, we had to modify the battery hardpoints but as you can see they work" Andrew nodded.

"So the SS Hades can fight if need be," he said with a slow smile developing "Good, no missiles?" he asked, John shook his head.

"Its not so much we don't have launchers" he said in an apologetic tone "its more in order to have enough on board to be viable in combat would simply cost us way too much so I prefer to spend it on energy weapons like the laser batteries" Andrew nodded it did make sense

"Ship coming out of lightspeed," Ben announced "Its..its the SS Ramesses!"

When the SS Ramesses jumped into the system, Captain Miller was not prepared for what he saw.

"Is that what I think it is? an Olympus Class Carrier?" said Commander Cairns "I know you said They had something big in store but i didn't expect this." Miller rolled his eyes, It would seem the Silver Blades leader was not exaggerating when he said he had a big surprise.

"It fits his ego that's for sure," Miller observed, "Better contact him and find out what his big plan is," he turned to the communications officer "Get them on the comms, we need to get organised."

"We are getting a communication from the SS Ramesses, they.. they want to know if Remus fox is here?" said Liana looking perplexed. Andrew and John looked at each other.

"No, they don't think this is a Silver blades vessel? do they?" John said disbelievingly but already he could see Andrews eyes sparkle with an idea, he looked around and gestured for Tessa to come closer, John could see what he was thinking, with her Green hair and makeup she would look like the sort of person who would serve on a pirate ship.

"Tessa, got some of your makeup nearby?" he said innocently, Tessa was about to protest but then sighed.

"Yes, hold on." and pulled a small box out of one of her pockets, Andrew then told her do something to look more like a pirate, so she took some of her red lip gloss and painted three streaks from her forehead to her right cheek, going over her eye and she put her hair in a top knot ponytail except for a couple of strands at each temple

"They are getting impatient." Liana said starting to stress, Andrew walked over looked into her eyes,

"Calm down Liana, first put them through to Tessa's console and get the order to the pilots to get to the fighters ready to launch and get Matt up here now," Tessa turned round and asked what does she say if they want to talk to the leader of the Sliver Blades, Andrew looked perplexed but then thought "Say he's preparing his personal fighter for battle and doesn't want to be disturbed from his ritual or something, and remember your a pirate, be nasty, imagine.. imagine Phil had just shot Nakamura.", he could see the anger in her eyes just then Captain Miller appeared on the small screen.

"Remus.. hey who are you?" he ordered.

"I am...You know what all you need to know is I am second in command of this Vessel, Our glorious leader Remus Fox is busy and can not be disturbed." Miller wasn't giving up easily.

"I need to talk to him now," then more to himself than anyone "Then we can get this over and done with." Matt walked into the bridge and Andrew beaconed hm close but gestured for him to be quiet, when Matt saw the SS Ramesses out the viewport he nearly swore until Andrew brought him up to speed. They went over to Bens security console and brought up the scan of the SS Ramesses. Ben pointed to the connection between the main rear engine and the main hull of the ship.

.

"That part there seems to be the best place to hit, a lot of system conduits are clustered there, one good unshielded hit could render that whole side of the ship disabled" Ben pointed out. From behind them they could hear Tessa doing a great job in her role.

"...Now? you want to talk to him now? listen to me you jumped up corporate sleazeball its all easy for you to demand I get him but Captain Fox is looking over his new fighter, making sure it suits his requirements and I will not pull him away from that just so you can ask the stupid questions and ever thought how he would react, is it you he will fire out a bloody airlock? no its me..."

"Hit there and you will disable just about everything on that side of the vessel, weapons, hanger doors, that sort of thing its a good thing we hit it on the starboard side" Matt agreed with Ben.

"Why starboard?" asked Andrew looking confused about it. Matt just shrugged.

"For some reason GalCorp protocol is the Starboard side hanger on any of their ships is for fighters and maintenance ships, the Port is kept clean for shuttles and for dignitaries to land on, we stop or at least delay their fighters we have a chance of getting away with minimal damage. Be prepared to lock on but didn't give the final command into the console as Matt said the minute they detected it it would be game over if they did it too soon." Ben nodded in understanding. Tessa was doing really well as the frustrating pirate.

"...so listen here Captain whoever you are not that I care about your damn name you can sit on your over upholstered comfortable fancy captains chair and wait, got that?"

"Can't you just patch it through to him? Please." Miller said growing weary and a little scared of the green haired terror. Tessa shook her head and let her mock temper rise a few more notches.

"Patch him through? he told me not to disturb him for anything, haven't you been listening or are you secretly wanting me to be a short term tester of this ships airlock system? and we can't anyway, you may have noticed this ship is not new or in the best condition." her expression turned from one of disgust to one of mock lustfulness "Or can you brave men spare some parts and techs for us poor bandits and pirates?" she pulled the zip on her jumpsuit down just enough, "Just a few parts, pretty please," and she winked "I think you will find there would be some of us over here who would be very.. very grateful, if you know what I mean"

"Nearly there." said Matt, Andrew indicated to Tessa to keep going, she was very convincing as a pirate, Miller looked flustered. as the SS Ramesses flew nearer, still shields down the vulnerable section near the main engines were exposed, just then the scans detected another ship coming in.

"An old Hexstar Gunship, its the Silverblades, its identifying as the SS Foxblade," Ben announced nervously. John looked flustered as he seen the slender ex military ship come into view, heavy weapons dominating the front of the vessel. he could only utter.

"We are so screwed." and slumped in his chair.

Andrew acted fast.

"Ben fire now, Tessa wrap up the conversation, Liana tell everyone to launch, Matt, we better get ready." Matt nodded and followed Andrew out of the bridge but John asked.

"Surely we should just try and outrun them in the SS Hades?"

"No," said Andrew "Even with the new weapon systems and the SS Ramesses partially disabled those two ships together could still wipe us out, if we launch we can create a fighter screen for them to focus on while you escape, you will stand a better chance of getting out of here" he caught Liana looking at him worried "Liana, it will be okay, trust me." he then kissed her and left with Matt.

Their ships were ready for launch by the time the two of them got to the hanger bay, the place looked almost empty as the others had just launched.

"Good luck out there" Matt said to Andrew, they both knew this would be their biggest challenge so far

"You too." Andrew replied as he climbed in his cockpit and did the quickest preflight check of his life, eased his helmet on and flew his fighter out to join the others. Matt flying close beside him until they caught up with the others.

On the SS Ramesses, Captain Miller was getting

frustrated.

"Look, I just want to talk to your captain, please tell me is there any way at all I can get a message to Captain Fox now, any at all," he said through his gritted teeth "I will even ask about spare parts if I could just speak to him" this woman was impossible, worse than some of the admin back at GalCorp, suddenly his tactical officer caught his attention.

"Sir another ship has entered the system, an old Hexstar gunship by the looks of it, a gunship and it has the marking of the Silver Blades." Miller looked confused if that was the Silver Blades arriving who was he talking to? The lady on the screen suddenly picked up a grey cat.

"Sorry for the deception and I have to go, things to do but here is Nakamura to say goodbye," and she had its paw in her hand and was making the cat wave at them, another call came from the Tactical console.

"weapons lock, brace for impact."

"Shields up!" Miller ordered but they knew the reality, Cairns just verbalised it.

"Too late." the ship lurched hard with the blast Miller looked out the viewport to see the Carrier launch fighters.

"Well played Easton, Well played" he muttered as he stood up ready to engage the new threat

CHAPTER 24

All the ships of Ronin flight launched just as the Silver Blades were launching their own fighters, the SS Ramesses was a ship in trouble.

"John," said Andrew through the comms "Stay on the Starboard side of the SS Ramesses and jump out the system while you can to a safe system," there was only one sure fire place they would be remotely safe and that was Baron Chopras territory "we will follow once you have jumped," he switched channels to the Ronin flight channel "Okay, I count twenty enemy fighters defend the SS Hades till she jumps then make your way to the Chopra Barony, okay?" everyone gave an affirmative, the two opposing fighter groups raced to each other.

It wasn't looking good for Captain Miller, not only were

they unable to fire at the enemy but they couldn't launch their fighters.

"Hayes is getting irate down there Captain," Cairns said mournfully, Miller knew that feeling, how had things gone so wrong? how did they know the SS Ramesses would be there? these were questions for another time,

"Contact engineering see if they can find a way to patch around the problem, we need to join this battle and now,"

Matt had just took out a Silver Blades Vampire fighter and was about to take out the wingman when the pirate ship exploded and another Battleaxe flew thought the explosion,

"White Knight this is Astro Ace, sorry but he was in my sights" Matt smiled and shook his head, unlike alot of pilots Matt never obsessed about number of kills and he noticed Nicolae was very surgical in his technique, it was only two shots he needed to destroy the ship, Matt could see the SS Hades power away from the SS Ramesses at full speed but he head a shriek on the comms,

"This is Ellen, I'm hit... and sustained an injury," Matt could see her ship fly past, there was a jagged scar of carbon scoring on the side and she looked pained, the more he looked the more he realised she had been hit with a glancing blow from the SS Foxblade. What were they thinking openly engaging a ship that size, she was a military vessel not some jury rigged junk heap, he shook his head despite himself.

"Ellen this is White Knight, just jump out as soon as you can," he saw her ship jump out the system then he got back on the Comms " Guys steer clear of the enemy cruisers, understood? Ellen was lucky." he said as he swung back into the fray.

In the SS Ramesses hanger bay, Corbin was all suited up and ready. One of the other pilots, David Abrams marched over.

"What's taking so long?" he demanded, Corbin held up a hand.

"If you give me a moment I will find out," he said, his tone suggested frustration as the techs were explaining for the hundredth time the problem, but one looked pensive so Corbin demanded he speak up.

"There is a way," the tech said then shook his head slowly "But it would jam the hanger bay door open and we wouldn't have the atmospheric shield."

"Okay, do that, and hurry" Corbin said.

!I can do it from the control room but will take time." the the explained, Corbin nodded.

"Get everything stowed away and evacuate everyone from the deck, prepare the Port hanger for when we land," he turned and told Abrams "Tell everyone to get into their fighters and get ready to launch." Abrams nodded and ran off to tell the others as Downs approached.

"They knew exactly were to hit us didn't they?" he mused, Corbin turned to him and said.

"Oh they did all right. Just remember Easton, however briefly, was one of us," he got ready to climb into his fighter "Let's make sure he pays for the damage.. if you get my meaning" and a malicious grin appeared on Corbins face.

The pirate fighter pilot was probably regretting targeting Andrew as he pulled out manoeuvrers the poor pirate as barely able to match, the battle had descended into a melee with everyone going one on one, Andrew was enjoying toying with him so decided to see how he'd react to one of Andrews more unusual moves, suddenly he just cut power to the engines, going forward purely on forward momentum and turned the ship to face his opponent but still moving away, halfway through the move the comms sprung to life.

"We are nearly there." he heard Liana through the comms and without bothering to switch to a private channel just said "Andrew.. I mean Firehawk I know this isn't the best time but.." and at that point he was able to bring his weapon to bear.

"..I love you too" he said knowing what she was going to say and at the same time fired, destroying the pursuing fighter and reactivated the engines "see you soon I promise."

"Firehawk this is Brutus, your just an old fashioned romantic aren't you?" Marcus said and

Andrew saw Marcus take out an enemy fighter by shooting the cockpit, killing the pilot instantly.

"Brutus this is Semjasa, you jealous much?" he noted Marcus didn't respond, but suddenly over the comms was the shout.

"This is Kitten, the SS Ramesses has opened its hanger doors." damn thought Andrew just then the SS Hades jumped out the system.

Corbin saw the carrier jump out and swore to himself

"Oh well lets make this victory costly, all fighters launch."

"This is White Knight, all fighters jump out as soon as you can, that is an order." shouted Matt as his heart sunk, he saw that Omega was leading the charge, of course he would, almost immediately two Ronin had jumped out, Gareth and Marcus, most of the others who weren't actively engaging pirate fighters were heading out ready to jump, Rob was next to go to lightspeed.

"The is Astro Ace, see you on the other side" Nicolae said as he jumped followed by Phil and Kate. Nate destroyed a pirate fighter just before jumping himself and Alan shot one on Tamikas tail.

"Quinque this is Pyrus, I got your back, lets go" and both jumped out, the GalCorp ships were getting closer and it was only Matt, Andrew, Suzanne and Umma with the SS Foxblade coming closer too to cut them off, suddenly Suzanne just looped around and headed for the GalCorp ships, Umma seems to hesitate and went after her, Matt noticed Omega had hit his afterbutrners and surged forward from his pack, Andrew went after them, reluctantly Matt did too.

"Suzanne this is White Knight what the hell are you doing?" he said with a mix of shock and anger in his voice.

"White Knight this is Suzanne, if we kill Omega the others will be easy, cut the serpent off at its head no?" Matt shook his head.

"Suzanne this is Firehawk," Andrew sounded like he was trying to talk down a child "It won't work, trust me on this" turn around and jump out the system now."

"Umma this is Suzanne are you with me? just follow my lead when I pull away you continue firing." Matt thought he knew what she had planned it was bold, using the Battleaxes stronger shields to do a one two punch, her shots weaken his shields and when her shields are weak too she pulls off and Umma is free to deliver the killing blow, if he goes along with it and the timings right it could work but was risky and after too long a silence.

"Suzanne this is Umma, yeah, sure I'll try," Matt tried to get hold of Suzanne but she had cut comms and Matt wasn't close enough to intervene and neither was Andrew, Suzanne opened fire at the same time Omega did, he could see Umma following her from behind ready to strike..then it hit him, GalCorp fighter have missiles, she wasn't used to that and in the heat of the moment had forgot, he tried getting hold of her but nothing as she pulled away to let Umma deal the potential killing blow he fired two missiles, both locked onto Umma, the first collapsed the shield the second hit his ship head on destroying it.

"Damn it Suzanne Jump now," Matt screamed losing all patience, Omega was about to pursue Suzanne untill Andrew started to fire on him, once he got Omegas attention he flew the other way with the GalCorp pilot in hot pursuit, the other GalCorp and remaining pirate ships had went after Matt and Suzanne.

"This pilot is good" said Corbin to himself, he still couldn't get over the two opilots just there that honestly thought such a simple tactic like that would work against him but this pilot was something else, his evasive flying was bizarre yet familiar.

"That's right," Andrew thought, "follow me," he said looking at the approaching SS Foxblade, his plan was risky but it had to work, it may not kill Omega but t least give him a fright, he saw Matt and Suzanne jump, just then an alert came on, the bigger ship had targeted him and started firing "Time for me to go." he said to himself and jumped out the system...

"What the..?" Corbin had to think fast and pull

out of the pursuit as he was nearly destroyed by the barrage the SS Foxblade was firing to destroy the fleeing enemy fighter which had suddenly jumped out the system.

Captain Miller slumped to his captains chair in defeat when the comms officer announced.

"The SS Foxblade is contacting us sir."

"Lets hear it." Miller said he knew this was not going to be good, on the communications screen as an angry Remus Fox.

"Is this how we are doing things now Miller? you sit back as my men are slaughtered by people you should have dealt with long before now and you only sent fighters in once mine are depleted, I demand answers now" Miller just looked up at the bright ceiling, where to start...

CHAPTER 25

The Hanger deck of the SS Hades was awash with activity as Matt Suzanne and Andrew landed Matt hurried out his ship and ran to Suzanne's waiting for her to come out as he saw Phil, Rob and Nicolae head to Andrew the others were standing not sure what to do but he saw Marcus whisper to Gareth, he was sure Marcus had worked out they were one short, Suzanne was finally out and climbing down the entrance ladder and he was about to speak when he heard a voice, it was Phil.

"What the hell were you playing at?" he said grabbing her as she jumped off the ladder "you cost a man his life and early cost others theirs too." she pushed him back hard.

"This is not a game," she said all anger "I saw an opportunity to take out a target that would have made our mission easier and it didn't work, My sister nearly

died today. we can't afford to mess around any more."
Phil, still on the ground looked at her.

"Tell that to Ummas parents," he said coldly,
Suzanne lost all composure and leapt on him, throwing
punches and elbows at the former lawman.

"Don't you dare, he was one of us, one of my
people, we are defending our homes.." she said as he
assaulted him, she felt herself get pulled off him and
pinned against her ship, it was Rob, who was angrier
than anyone had ever saw him.

"You think you have a monopoly on loss and
pai,n" he said in a way that shocked even Phil "you
never had to watch a comms feed to a loved one cut
short because her ship was destroyed as you were
speaking to them, you never had to suffer watching your
best friend die of oxygen starvation as your ships float
powerless in the middle of space while a rescue ship
shows up just too latte, I understand its your home but
snap out of that deluded little bubble your living in and
get with the program, we are a family we win together
lose together get that through your thick skull will you?"
he released his grip, his anger fading as he turned to the
others "We will raise a glass in honour of Umma later
tonight at the mess hall," then he turned to Suzanne
"And no I"m not drinking to forget him, its in honour of
him, its a pilots tradition and you are welcome to come,
if you want." and he walked off.

"Okay shows over, we all got somewhere to be."
said Andrew aware everyone was standing around
unsure what to do but with some prompting left the

hanger bay, Andrew and Phil went up to Rob while Matt stayed with Suzanne who looked in shock.

"Suzanne," he said as softly has he could,, the last thing she needed was yet someone else shouting at her "Rob is right, we are a family on this ship, granted a bit dysfunctional but we are here for each other." he stood hoping for some sign she heard him, she just looked at him tears welling up.

"I'm sorry about Umma," she said softly before pulling Matt close and crying on his shoulder, unsure what to do, Matt just held her until she stopped, she looked at him, her eyes red and puffy with crying as if not sure what to say or do.

"Well, Ellen is probably in the medbay worried why you haven't came to see her yet." he said leading her off the hanger bay, she nodded silently.

"Wanna talk about it?" asked Phil as Rob stood looking at the floor, he looked up at Andrew and Phil.

"Well I suppose I should tell you," Rob sighed "during the war my actions had merited a promotion to major and head of my own specialised squad so I thought I'd tell my fiancee, she served as a nurse on one of our hospital ships but as we spoke, some Hexstar cruisers jumped into the system and cut her ship and its escorts down, the last thing I heard was her anguished scream, then a few days later as my squad were jumping out of a hotspot when my ship and the ship of one of my squadmates was hit, we jumped but our lightengines failed before we got to our destination, his ship was more damaged than mine, I watched him die slowly..I couldn't do a thing.." Phil pulled his close friend in and hugged him.

"Rob, why didn't you tell us." Phil asked, Rob just looked at him apologeticly.

"It took me a long time to get over it, was discharged from the military, I just wanted to forget about it, you know focus on the future." it explained alot, Rob always had this almost zen like attitude to things, it wasn't that he didn't care, he was worried he'd start caring too much. Of course he had been there when other pilots had died, like Angel but Suzanne's apparent attitude must have made him snap.

"Come on mate as you said, we are family." Andrew said hopefully, Rob relented a sad smile and walked off, Phil went to follow but Andrew stopped him.

"I think he needs to be alone for a while." he whispered to Phil.

Later in the mess hall it was still and quiet as Matt and Andrew stood in front of the gathered pilots and ships crew, Ellen had joined them against Sister Theresa's wishes but was sitting on a seat with a crutch beside her, her flightsuit pulled down to her waist and the arms tied in a knot,, you could see the bandages under her tank top, Matt raised his bottle of beer and said.

"We are here in celebration of a victory over GalCorp and their pirate allies but to also mourn the loss of Ulrich-Matthaus Moller-Altmann, or as most of us known him as, Umma. he was a brave pilot who had only served with us in a few short engagements but his courage and heart was there for all to see and Ronin Flight is a sadder place now he is gone, to Umma." he said finally.

"To Umma!" said everyone raising their glasses and taking a drink and everyone broke off into groups and the room was filled with the chatter of conversation again, he could see Liana weave her way through the crowd and to Andrews side slipping her arm around his waist she looked beautiful in a dress Matt was sure he saw her buy on Novaya Sibir, he pulled her closer and they wandered off to talk to the others, Matt took the opportunity to slip away from the gathering, suddenly he heard footsteps behind him, it was Suzanne.

"I just want to thank you for your support," she said meekly "You are a good leader and an honourable man."

"Thank you," he smiled "I'm glad Ellens injuries weren't too severe, just a few days rest and she should be fine, you should probably get back to her." She nodded but hovered as if she wanted to say something but in the end chose not to say anything and just headed back, Matt shrugged and went to his quarters, he wasn't in the mood to mingle tonight.

Andrew and Liana had slipped away from the party shortly after Matt did and went to his quarters.

"You did everything you could from what I heard." she said as they stepped inside. he nodded sadly.

"Yeah, I know but that;s not what;s bothering me, I've lost people before, important people." she knew he meant Angel, his old squad leader from Waypoint Station, amongst others "Its more that there was a moment, when I saw the SS Foxblade jump into the system and they figured we weren't who we said we were I genuinely thought we are not getting out of this alive." She held him close.

" I know." she said softly, Andrew looked down at her.

"You want to know what got me through it all? the thought of seeing you again, I meant what I said earlier, I love you Liana." and he kissed her, Liana melted into his arms.

"I love you too." she whispered. They stood holding each other in the middle of the room for a while then he took a step back but still holding her hands to admire her look, she still wore her blue scarf and the dress which was a sleeveless number that started blue at the top and faded to black at the bottom which ended just below her knees just above the tops of her boots.

"You like it?" she said biting her lip and looking up he nodded and said.

"You always look beautiful to me." He looked at her lovingly and intently as if he had something to ask "Liana, I have been thinking, why not just move in to my quarters, I mean you have said that yours are too big and your hardly there these days, what do you say?" She smiled and said.

"Its a big step."

"But one I'm willing to make, what do you say?" He said hopefully. She replied.

"Yes, in fact I was hoping that was what you would ask" and she winked, whispered something into his ear then took his hand and lead him to the bunk.

"My first mission and someone dies," said Kate mournfully as she sat with Tessa, Nicolae, Tamika, Craig and Marcus "Umma was a nice guy, he and Nicolae helped me with some of my technique.. In the cockpit," she added the last part because she was aware Marcus was staring "are you always this childish?" he was about to answer when Phil walked past.

"Oh no, only when he's drunk, sober, asleep, awake, hungry or well fed." he said swatting Marcus in the back of the head and sat with them, everyone else laughed but Kate looked at Phil as if wanting to ask something.

"Something on your mind?" he asked.

"Well," She said carefully "If I am out of line please say but you all seem a bit too relaxed by all this, I mean someone just died, you know?" she looked as if she was regretting asking but Phil just nodded and smiled.

"Its okay, the truth is you never get over watching friends and comrades die and in fact the day it doesn't at least bother you is the day you should stop but you can't let it overwhelm you either, Umma was a great kid, good pilot and I know I won't forget him or what we been through together," he took a drink and shook his head "but life goes on and I admit there is a little thing called revenge too, whatever works best for you really." Craig nodded.

"My dad used to say the same, he didn't know what was worse, pilots who were too cold about their emotions or ones that let their emotions overwhelm them." the others nodded in agreement. Looking to change the subject Nicolae asked Tamika.

"What's it like being a mercenary pilot for hire?" the whole table suddenly seemed interested.

"Yeah," said Marcus "I mean I can imagine what some of the jobs are you get hired to do but has there ever been any unusual ones?" Tamika looked thoughtful for a minute then set her drink down.

"Good question," she mused "The strangest job I ever had was during the war actually having to pretend to be a Hexstar pilot and stage a bitched hijack my own client I'm sure you heard of him, Governor Jaime Cortez."

"No! you did that?" Phil said surprised, Kate, Marcus and Craig looked shocked so she explained "Cortez was governor of the colony New Iberia and was a strong supporter of the Earth Government but was unpopular with his people until an attempted kidnapping by Hexstar forces." Tamika looked a little embarrassed.

"Well, trust me, those Hexstar forces were just me in a stolen ship and uniform and it was not one of my proudest moments, to deliberately fail but it paid well." she shrugged "I will confess I did rough him up a bit, make it look good... for free of course." and she smiled "another round?" she asked to a chorus of affirmatives, no-one, except for Phil, noticed that Rob wasn't in the mess hall with everyone and Phil was glad no-one noticed as he figured Rob probably just wanted some time alone.

CHAPTER 26

It took a while but the engineers of the SS Ramesses finally managed to repair the damage to the relays and couplings enough or at least bypss the ones that are too damaged so the ship could to continue the hunt at more or less full strength. The chief engineer told them a journey back to Carnarvon was needed for proper repairs but they could not afford to lose time doing so Captain Miller asked Commander Cairns and Corbin Hayes to his office, he poured himself a drink, something he had noted he'd been doing more and more these days.

"It was a lucky shot," Cairns said as he refused Millers offer of a drink himself "Though there is one thing we know for sure," Miller said nothing, just looked at him to explain "With a carrier like that, they have no need for a base." the others nodded in agreement, Miller drained his glass in one mouthful and slammed it down hard.

"Between Gladstone trying to micromanage this operation and Remus Fox acting like we are there for him and not the other way around I just know this whole thing is in danger of blowing up in our faces." Miller sighed " if it was just us we could have hunted them down and dealt with it swiftly and effectively"

"Yeah," Corbin said pointedly "but what do we do?" Miller thought carefully.

"For now? we continue our mission, do our job and find these guys but who knows what the future will hold. I want readiness drills doubled and we run with shields and weapons active at all times, we will not be fooled again, dismissed." Miller said as the others left he sat back and sighed, they needed to end this and fast.

First thing in the morning Andrew woke up to find Liana coming into his quarters with an equipment crate, he didn't know if she was just keen to move in or felt that it would serve to distract him from Ummas death despite him reassuring her he was fine but he couldn't blame her for trying. She opened it up and started to take things out as he pulled his flightsuit on.

"Good Morning." he said as he helped her unpack her crate, she just smiled and kissed his cheek, he pulled out two identical pairs of boots to the ones she was wearing and looked puzzled.

"How many of these do you have? I thought you only had the one pair?" she laughed and looked at him playfully.

"Three including the ones I have on, what can I say, I like the style and I don't wear anything else," she saw him grin and realised what she said and added "on my feet I mean." Andrew shook his head and reached in to the crate and pulled out a handful of scarves.

"I think you'll need a whole drawer just for these alone," just then the door chime sounded and Andrew shook his head and kissed her cheek "I wonder who that could be." It was Matt, Andrew invited him in.

"Liana, glad you are here too actually." Liana stopped and stood next to Andrew as they both looked at him with interest.

"What do you mean?" Andrew asked a little confused.

"Well," Matt started "was it just me or did either of you detect a sense of hostility when Captain Miller thought he was talking to the Silver Blades?" Liana nodded.

"Yeah, even the first message gave me the feeling he just wanted to get things over with, are you sure they are working together." Andrew nodded in agreement with her, he picked up on it too, Matt thought carefully.

"Its entirely possible that the whole Silver Blades partnership is all Gladstone's idea and Miller feels he has to go along with it, I believe he is a willing accomplice to Gladstone but either doesn't like working with the Silver Blades or may even believe they don't need the pirates at all." He said finally.

"That could prove interesting." agreed Andrew

"Though I think avoiding any more direct confrontations with the SS Ramesses might be a good thing."

"Why?" asked Liana looking a bit confused, Matt answered.

"I'm guessing its the same reason Andrew told John not to engage the SS Hades against the SS Ramesses beyond that one shot, kill them and not only will they just send another ship and make out we are just an evil pirate gang who cost a crew of GalCorp employees their lives and all that whereas its hard to be the bad guy if all you do is take out a pirate gang" Andrew nodded in agreement, if they pursued and attacked the SS Ramesses they could make it sound like the Ronin are just another pirate gang preying on corporate interests. Matt looked as if there was something he he wanted to say but seemed unsure.

"Matt," Andrew said as reassuringly as he could "If you want to say something you can tell me."

"Andrew I know it may seem a bit soon but Nicolae will need a new wingman, I think its time to give Craig a chance" Matt prepared himself for Andrew to say no but was surprised when he said.

"Sounds reasonable, he did well covering for Phil during that patrol and has been working a lot on simulators not to mention he has been very mature about everything, other people would have been pestering us every time we went out. I'm sure its not the under the circumstances he would have wanted to gain a place as a pilot but I think he will seize the opportunity to prove his worth" Matt gave a sigh of relief and stood.

"Thanks, replacing someone is never a situation I was comfortable with, I better go to the gym, with Ellen healing from her injuries Suzanne needs someone to workout with."

"How Is Ellen?" Andrew asked "the techs are still repairing her ship, she really was hit bad." Matt stood and stretched a little.

"She's healing well, a few days and she should be fit enough to fly but in the meantime she has been instructed to rest. If any good has came out of it is that hopefully Suzanne and Ellen may calm things down a bit in battle and not take crazy risks any more." he left to grab gymwear from his room, Liana just looked at Andrew and asked.

"You think he knows?", Andrew looked at her in bewilderment "Come on, you haven't noticed. I think Suzanne is keen on him." Andrew just laughed.

"Suzanne? neither of the Sommers seem to show much emotional range in general. are you sure?" she nodded her head and cited various incidents where she has been vocal on Matt;s virtues as a man and pilot but Andrew was unconvinced "Could just mean she has some sort of professional respect for him." Liana sighed.

"If it was anyone else I'd agree but with her it just seems more than that, trust me." Andrew said nothing just pulled her close and kissed her then eventually answered.

"If you say so, anyway, you have to finish unpacking," though he didn't let her go and for her part she wasn't keen to get away "though it could wait a little longer." and they kissed again.

Rob was exiting a simulation pod just as Tamika and Alan were entering the room.

"You are early," Tamika said "I didn't see you in the mess hall last night" she said as she opened a pod and started to configure the settings "Everything okay?" she asked as she watched Rob ease his helmet off.

"Yeah, it wasn't so much Ummas death a Suzanne's response to it that got me. It did affect me, I won't lie about that, every death I've witnessed does but you get one with things.. you have to", he set the helmet down "I'm thirty Six, been a combat pilot most of my adult life. Being a combat pilot is what I love and you have to take the good with the bad, people will die. If it gets too much I either go for a spin in my fighter or a simulator run or two, flying has always helps calm me down." he said looking like he was glad to finally just say it.

"Thirty Six?" Tamika countered, "I'm Thirty eight and I understand, I had to track down and kill my own husband," Rob looked shocked "He was Hexstar intelligence and he was planning to defect with vital information to the Hexstar war effort. I figured if I didn't someone else will," even Alan looked shocked at her but she added "He were already separated and well, it was cheaper than divorce." she smiled at them Rob just shook his head.

"Okay that.. I have to hand it to you would have

taken some guts, wow I'm glad your on our side," he said looking a little more like his old self "For one means I'm not the old one of the group any more," He turned to Alan and saw that Alan's cap, helmet and flightsuit all had badges with pears on them "Care to explain the pears? Please?" he asked, Tamika looked at Alan too with newfound curiosity.

"Hey, you know where I'm from right? well I family have one of the biggest pear orchards in the colonies and I'm sure you have heard of Allford and Sons Pear Cider? well I'm the grandson," Rob nodded and Tamika just shrugged "anyway," Alan continued "I'm the youngest of four and had nothing more to look forward to than maybe getting a job flying shuttles to ferry our produce to the cargo ships and didn't want to join the military so I left and as I love flying took up a few jobs until I bought my own fighter and wanted to become a mercenary when I heard about you guys." Tamika just shook her head.

"You wouldn't have gotten much with that old ship you had, whoever sold it to you ripped you off but still, why the Pear motifs." Alan just smiled and explained.

"You may notice I don't take myself serious and there's so many pilots with crazy and macho names, I wanted to be different and as pears are my background, I thought why not?" Rob then turned to Tamika and looked her up and down.

"I'm going to guess your either the fifth child in your family or.."

"... On your first mission you killed five people" said Phil who just walked in "Been trying to find you, everything okay?" rob nodded?

"Yeah, just went for a simulator run to clear my head, was just asking Tamika here about her callsign." he answered Tamika sat in a simulator pod and started to strap in while Alan set up his pod.

"Well gentlemen, some things just have to remain a mystery," she said with a wink "Maybe you will find out someday but not today." and she pulled the canopy down, Alan shrugged as he got in his pod too.

"Don't ask me, I'm just her wingman," he said before closing his canopy too, Phil lead rob out to the hallway.

"Was trying to find you all morning, was worried about you after last night." Phil said, all concern.

"I'm fine, really, That Tamika though, that is someone you don't want to cross, did you know she killed her own husband to fulfil a contract" Phil looked shocked.

"Your kidding?" and when he saw Rob wasn't kidding, He leaned against the bulkhead and sighed.

"Terrific, its times like this I long for the days of long boring patrols then mission report writeups at Waypoint I really do." he said as they walked to the mess hall.

Matt was on the bridge, in the seat usually occupied by Lianna as he answered a comms chat with Baron.Chopra

"I hope you and your men are okay." Chopra asked, voice full of concern.

"We lost a man" Matt said with a tinge of sadness to his voice "but it could have been worse, thank you again for letting us return so soon." Matt could see the Baron pace before replying.

"As I said, you are welcome any time, in fact I daresay your crusade has gave me an idea" he said with a smile.

"Oh? What sort of idea?" Matt asked curiously.

"You will just have to wait and see, I have a lot of things to sort out first. But I will say is it will be mutually beneficial. If you don't mind I need to go, a Barons work is never done" Chopra shrugged and ended to call. Matt shook his head, what did the Baron mean? Hopefully he would find out sooner rather than later.

CHAPTER 27

After a few days, once again the SS Hades set off from Baron Chopras territory, the Baron gave them extra supplies free of charge over his daughters protests and had his fighters give an honour guard as the carrier left.

"He really wants to show how supportive of us doesn't he?" said John to Matt and Andrew whom he had asked to the bridge "Guys, I know our arrangement has been very much we fly to our destinations and you guys are just passengers who get to use the hanger bay for your ships but between the confrontation with the SS Ramesses and the fact we seem to work well and are integrating and mixing well, I asked the crew earlier about this and they agree we are all in with you, yes we will still need tot do cargo runs but when it comes to getting involved in your side of stuff, we are all in." Andrew wasn't too surprised.

"You were keen to be part f it from the moment we started, you were just wanting to see if we'd do well or not," John shrugged but didn't deny it "Welcome onboard..officially now." he said as John went over to the navigation console, it was the relief navigator, a young guy he only knew as MacIntyre and not Tessa on duty.

"Set co-ordinates for Bendis Colony and engage lightdrive," he said as he turned to Matt and Andrew saying "never been to this one in a while.. should be interesting." he said as the lightdrive engaged.

"Hey, simulator time " said Nathan outside Kate's door, he gave up on the door chime and just banged on the door itself,just then Marcus and Nicolae were returning from the gym.

"She might already be there." Marcus offered, Nathan shook his head and told them he already looked when the door behind him opened and revealed that Kate was only half ready.

"Give me a few minutes." she said flustered then turned around and finished pulling her flightsuit on, just then Tessa pushed past Nicolae and walked into Kate's quarters smiling sheepishly.

"Hey, I can't find my.." she started Kate pulled out a bracelet from her flightsuit pocket.

"You left it on the floor when you left this morning." Tessa slipped it on and kissed Kate on the cheek before heading out the quarters, Kate just looked at the three pilots and rolled her eyes.

"Okay, what is it?" she said the realised "Yes she spent the night here, anything else you want to know?" she said visibly annoyed. Marcus put his hands up in surrender.

"Hey, take it easy no-ones saying anything, I'm just surprised."

"What about?" she said confused "That I like other women as well as guys? Marcus you must have lead a really sheltered life."

"No, its not that," Marcus said looking visibly annoyed as if insulted she'd insinuate what he thought she was insinuating "Its more the fact that the green haired crazy cat lady really likes anyone, apart from Nakamura of course."

"Are you and Tessa serious like Andrew and Liana or what?" said Nicolae rather abruptly, earning a punch in the arm from Marcus.

"what type of question is that to ask someone?" Marcus said shaking his head "..So..are you?" he asked suddenly himself.

"It's okay," said Kate sighing "If your going to spread gossip you might as well know the facts, that night we had drinks in the mess hall to honour Umma, well I didn't wanna be alone so she said she would sleep at my quarters if it would help. We started talking and one thing lead to another, now I wouldn't say we are serious but I think she's really cute and we do enjoy each others company so who knows?"

"Well one thing I do know is we need to be in the

simulator room." Said Nathan dryly, as he made his way down the hall with Kate running behind him fastening her flightsuit as she did.

"I don't know about you but I'm going to have a shower." Nicolae said, Marcus shook his head.

"I might get something to eat first, worked up an appetite in the gym.. catch you later." he said as he headed down the hallway, stopping to dump his gym bag in his quarters.

The hanger bay was quiet when Matt walked through, all the fighters motionless quiet yet still looking as deadly as ever, we saw Craig tinker with one of the ships, he noted it was the same one Craig had flew when Andrew let him patrol with Rob.

"Hi, is this a good time or should I come back later?" he said as he saw Craig work on the engine manifolds, he looked up from his work, closed the hatch and climbed down.

"Hey, something wrong? I double checked Ellen's ship and the replacement parts will hold but you won't believe the amount of work it took." He said as Matt looked over at Ellen's ship, with fresh armour plates and some other work it was hard to see where the damage had been but then he remembered why he was looking for Craig.

"No no," he started "nothing like that, Andrew and I have noticed your dedication to your work, Gareth, Tony and the other techs sing your praises too," Craig smiled shyly "plus we have noticed your time in the simulation room, now I know its not the way you'd want it to happen but, how to say this, Nicolae will need a new wingman and.." before he finished Craig let out a shut in celebration and gave Matt a hug.

"Thank you, you won't regret it I promise." and he ran off down the hanger, nearly bowling over Gareth.

"Someone's happy," he commented to Matt when Lianas voice came over the comms "Matt, Andrew you might want to get up to the bridge, you may want to see this."

Matt got to the bridge and out of the viewport was Bendis Colony, or rather what was left of it, Bendis colony was not on the planet, the planet being Semele a gas giant, Bendis was its moon and had three large habitat domes, though one had been completely cored and the others badly damaged, Andrew turned round and acknowledged Matt.

"We can't say who attacked for sure, just that it was recent." was all he said.

"Are there survivors?" Matt asked "if there is we have to do something, why would anyone do this?", John stepped over to answer.

"Bendis colony has large metal deposits and were fiercely independent, notice the orbital batteries and the fighter wreckages? these guys could put up a fight and were rarely hassled by pirates but GalCorp must want it badly."

"Any survivors?" Matt asked again, John told Ben to scan the colony.

"Dome two is completely wiped out, dome one definitely no lifesigns and has been venting atmosphere.. hold one, reading lifesigns in dome three."

"Right, I'll need three shuttles." Matt said snapping into action, but Andrew held out a hand.

"Easy, you don't know who it is, could be survivors, could be pirates looking for something and are awaiting pickup, anything possible, think logicically here/" Matt stared at Andrew but relented/

"What do you suggest?" he said finally.

"First," he turned to Liana, "have the other pilots and any volunteers to meet us in the hanger as soon as possible," he turned to Matt "we can discuss the rest on the way." he said as they headed out of the bridge.

Everyone was gathered in the hanger in front of the shuttles, the Ronin pilots and some assorted crew and techs as Andrew told them what happened to Bendis colony the shock and the urge to do something about it grew amongst the crowd, he then stepped back and let Matt continue.

"Okay, I will be flying Hades One with our volunteers, Alan, you will be flying Hades Two which will be used for any survivors we hope to find, also Sister Theresa will be flying with you, as for Hades Three, Kate, you will be flying that" he then looked at the pilots "Andrew and I have talked and as we believe there's no telling who is down there we will need armed support and we looked at everyone and decided the best people to send over are," He paused briefly " Phil with your law enforcement training, Rob, Nathan, while you trained as pilots you were both given full weapons training so you two are going over as well, Tamika, your skills could come in useful too, Gareth we will need your knowledge of electronics, we don't know what state things will be when we get there." he opened the crate he had brought to the hanger with him and called the pilots he had named over and handed each of them the SIG 790B carbines they had in storage and a P526 sidearm to everyone bar Phil and Rob who had theirs from their Waypoint Security days and Tamika who had her own custom pistol, Phil checked the sights on his carbine as Tamika dumped her carbine back in the crate and left to the locker room.

"Not shot one of these in a while, could get interesting." he said, Tamika returned while Phil was still examining his carbine and dumped a weapons case on an equipment box, the case was in her customary black and orange colour scheme.

"These carbines are okay but this time I'm going in with old faithful here." and she opened the case and brought out a very well worn but well maintained New Armalite NAR 94 with interchangable sights, custom pistol and forward grips made of a memory plastic that conforms to the handlers touch, a flashlight attachment and a custom orange and grey camouflage paint pattern. She took it out the box and started checking it was still in decent condition, Nathan and Rob stopped their weapons inspections too and were eyeing up the rifle with interest.

"Impressive," Nathan said "what is she capable of?" Tamika was holding it in a ready position as if checking the sights were still true

"Well it has selective one shot, five shot bursts and full automatic," she said as she pulled out a pair of goggles with orange polarised lenses "The scopes have an option to broadcast to this fashion accessory here, there are other bells and whistles but you don't need to concern yourself with any of that." Rob shook his head, smiled and said.

"You are something you know that? every time I find out something more about you I get a little more scared."

Once things had calmed down a little, Andrew stepped forward.

"Okay, Marcus, Suzanne, Ellen, Nicolae and Craig," Phil's head snapped up when he heard Craig;s name but said nothing "You guys are with me, we will launch fighters and be ready to attack if anyone returns to try and finish the job, Good luck everyone." he said as everyone ran to their assigned task, Andrew caught up with Ellen.

"You sure you'll be okay?" He said, he was well aware he was down half his pilots for this and that of the ones he had available, Craig was untested in real combat and Ellen was just coming off an injury.

"I'm sure." she said trying to reassure him, Suzanne came over.

"Do not worry I'll look after my little sister, I promise." she said, Andrew noted her voice had lost some of its harshness, he shrugged and ran to his fighter to launch.

"

CHAPTER 28

As the shuttles headed to Bendis colony, Phil and the other pilots who were designated as the armed support were preparing, putting on body armour found in the ships stores and doing weapons checks.

"So, how good a shot are you?" Kate asked Phil as she piloted the shuttle to the landing bays for the third atmosphere dome.

"Well, when I was in the police back on earth I was one of the best in my precinct" He said as he adjusted the straps of his body armour" but since then I have let it slide a little and its been a long time since I used one of these" he held up his carbine, Rob looked over.

"Yeah, at Waypoint us pilots didn't get to play with the big toys" he said with a smile, but they all looked at the back when they heard Tamika.

"It never leaves you, trust me." she had put her braids in a ponytail, had her flightsuit pulled down to her waist and the arms tied around like a belt, her sleeveless top under the body armour revealed numerous tattoos on her arms as she expertly reassembled her Armalite after stripping it down soon after they had got in the shuttle, Nathan looked at the others and whispered to Gareth. "I feel sorry for any pirates she runs into." Gareth nodded in silent agreement.

The fighters flew a holding pattern over the colony, Andrew keeping an eye on his scanners just in case anything happened.

"Firehawk, this is Brutus, you are weapons trained from your time at the military right?, why aren't you down there?" Andrew smiled and gave a slight chuckle.

"Brutus, this is Firehawk, probably but who would be here keeping an eye on things up here? you?"

"Firehawk this is Brutus, hell yeah I could." there was a chorus of laughter over the comms.

"Brutus, this is Firehawk, the people have spoken." there was a sudden message through the comms, it was Matt.

"Firehawk this is gound team, we have just landed and there's some bad news, pirates are here."

Next to the Hades shuttles were two badly maintained

fighters and an armed shuttle, all bearing the Bloodfist logo, Matt gripped his carbine a little tighter.

"Okay, we need to be on alert, the lifesigns were situated in two main areas marked Alpha and Beta on your hand scanners, I'll take one group to Alpha and Phil, you take Beta." they divided the crew volunteers into two groups of four each and issued them with sidearms, additionally Phil took Tamika and Rob while Matt took Nathan and Gareth while Kate and Alan guarded the shuttles being the least experienced with firearms, as the others left the hanger, Alan turned to Kate and gave a silly smile.

"Well aren't we quite the 'Pear', don't you think?" he said as he slung his carbine over his shoulder and sat on the shuttle ramp, despite herself she let out a chuckle.

"that pun was terrible." she said between fits of giggles.

The colony under the dome should have been thriving with activity but looked like a ghost town,the walkways littered with bodies. site Alpha looked like a security building that had been locked down, Gareth was trying to hotwire the door while the others look for anything amiss, Sister Theresa went with his group.

"There you go." said Gareth as the door opened and Nathan and Matt moved in weapon in hand but not raised, what they were met with was few groups and families huddled around and one security officer pointing his sidearm at Matt nervously.

"I'm Officer Chevalier ,Colony security, who are you and are you here to save us?" he looked scared out his wits, Matt eased forward.

"I'm Matt Easton of Ronin Flight, we are part of the SS Hades crew, what happened?" he said putting his carbine down and letting it hang from its strap on his shoulder.

"The Silver blades showed up in a big ship, one we never saw before, in the past we have turned them away but they came in huge numbers this time and took out communications in the first volley, a volley which also disabled the orbital turret control, we were totally defenceless and our small fighter force was no match for them they even landed to slaughter people they hadn't killed from space, I managed to get these people to safety here, they tried to get in but they suddenly left, as if they were satisfied with what they had done or something." Officer Chevalier said franticly. Matt had noticed blast marks on the building, this was extreme even for them, Sister Theresa ran to Matt's side.

"Anyone needing treatment?" she asked, Officer Chevalier let her examine the obviously scared colonists.

"How long have you been like this, kept in here?" Matt asked with genuine concern.

"About a week, maybe more, did you manage to find any more survivors?" Chevalier said hoping to hear some good news but Matt gave him the bad news but told him he had hoped the other team would find more, Matt also realised this attack happened before the SS Foxblade joined the SS Ramesses at the old Jericho

Barony. This was as much a weapons test for their new gunboat as it was an act of piracy especially if this place was known as a tough place to raid the this would be the best test bed for the SS Foxblade and it could smash this places defences then other colonies will be a lot easier in comparison, suddenly he heard weapons fire in the distance.

"Beta team this is Alpha team, everything okay do you need assistance?" Matt said into his comms.

"Negative Alpha Team, engaging the enemy but we can cope for now." With a sigh, Matt looked at Nathan.

"Lets get these people to the shuttles"he said then to Officer Chevalier "what's the fastest way over there?..."

Beta team were near the main food court area when out came a Bloodfist pirate, who upon seeing them started to fire before Tamika cut him down but the rest of the Bloodfists showed and they were soon engaged in a firefight, Phil and Rob were pinned down behind a low wall and Tamika was using a shot up transporter as cover.

"Well this is fun," Rob said "Makes a change from flying." one of the ships volunteers took a hit on the shoulder.

"Get back," Phil shouted to the volunteers, as they dragged their colleague back from the action, the Pirates took that as a sign to advance when suddenly Tamika sprinted from her cover and shot three of the pirates who were more focused on the other two pilots while Phil took down the remaining one.

"Well that was easy." Tamika said with a smirk, when Rob looked up and on the upper walkway was a pirate ready to take a shot at Tamika, he brought his weapon up to bear and shot, he missed the pirate but hit a sign behind which fell down nearly hitting the enemy if they hadn't leapt off but the pirate fell awkwardly and screamed in pain, Rob ran over, it was bad fall but the person looked alive, he eased off the helmet to reveal a young woman in her mid twenties with black and red streaked hair, Phil ran over too and kicked her weapon out of reach.

"My leg, I think its broken," she said clearly in severe pain "who the hell are you people and why are you here?" Rob motioned for a volunteer to give him a first aid kit as Phil knelt next to her.

"Hey, it was who you attacked the colony." he said accusingly but she looked bewildered.

"Wait? You actually think we did this?" she said disbelievingly, Phil saw Tamika on the comms, she went up to Phil.

"Apparently," she said "It was the Silver Blades, not Bloodfist who attacked here and they used the SS Foxblade, Matt has a security officer from the colony and he doesn't know why the Bloodfist pirates are here either."

"Well, only one pirate now," Rob added as he found what he was looking for, single use pain killing syringes and injected two into her, he could see that it wasn't just her leg, she was nursing some burns on her arm too, he helped her up, taking the weight of her bad leg "I don't know about you but we better go," he saw Phil's look as he eyed the pirate with suspicion "Hey I know it might not make sense right now Phil but we are taking her with us, there's something not right here and she can tell us once she is stabilised." she looked a little drowsy as the pain killers took effect, Phil shrugged and picked up her helmet, which was black and had the name Redpunk stencilled in red on it. Phil shook his head as he saw Rob headed back to the hanger bay then supervise Tamika and the others to check the area out just to be sure.

Andrew listened as Matt informed him of the events.

"Hold on," he said over the comms "Are you saying that the Silver Blades attacked but Bloodfist prates were found there? can't be, those two groups are sworn enemies." Matt nodded as he looked at the survivors who were settling into the shuttles.

"I know, it doesn't make sense does it? I'm thinking of going back out for another look for survivors." Matt replied.

"Uh, bad Idea, we did a flyby of the dome and that thing isn't safe and looks like the structure could go any time, best getting whoever's still out there back to the bay." Andrew advised.

When Matt commed Phil about the structure problem, there was no need to repeat it, he rounded up his volunteer group and he and Tamika kept the group together as they made their way back, suddenly there was a series of loud creaks, Phil looked up, then looked at his fellow pilot.

"That does not sound good," he said, a little bit of fear escaping his voice "We better run for it I think." Tamika nodded and shouted.

"Everyone move, now." and she lead everyone as they sprinted for the Hanger deck, It was a winding route they had to take and the creaks and groans of the metal above them was growing more and more ominous, Phil couldn't help glancing up and could swear he saw cracks develop but there it was, the Hanger entrance airlock, Phil slammed the switch to close it behind him, it wouldn't close.

"Oh come on," he said hitting it repeatedly, Tamika brushed him aside and shot the control panel and reached in to the mess of wires "Tamika whatever your going to do, do it fast, he could see some warping of some of the structure, it could go at any point, Tamika stabbed the circuit board with a knife and down came the airlock door just in time as there was a loud noise, the sort you'd only here when something large suddenly loses all its air.

"This is Firehawk, I hope no-one in that dome, its just collapsed." Phil laughed and spoke into his comm.

"Don't worry mate, we are all safe, barely." he said as he got to his feet and headed to the colony main hanger deck, Tamika slapped him on the back.

"Your okay for an ex lawman." and they both laughed loudly..with a touch of nervousness.

CHAPTER 29

They managed to get the survivors safely to the SS Hades with no further incident, Nathan had taken a look at the Bloodfist shuttle and discovered it was a Hexstar assault shuttle and was worth salvaging, he was looking over it with Gareth in the Hanger, with its side entry doors and stubby wings bristling with weapons Matt could see why it could be useful.

"John's people are setting up temporary bunks in cargo bay three for everyone, its one of the bigger bays." said Andrew to Matt as he climbed out his fighter "So, we captured a Bloodfist?", Matt nodded/

"She is in the Medbay right now,I was about to go talk to her if you wanted to come." he offered "You are right though. Something doesn't make sense here", as they left, Andrew noted that Phil, Rob and Gareth were chatting happily away to Tamika on the way to the mess hall, was good to see the new pilots mixing well, he may join them after he talked to the pirate in medbay.

There were some colony survivors in the medbay too, but none as bad as the female pirate who identified herself as Redpunk, her leg was a rigid support and her burn wounds to her side and arm treated.

"I have gave her some bone repair stimulant injections to heal the leg quicker," Sister Theresa told Matt and Andrew "But even then it will be a few days before she can attempt to walk and even then she will need a crutch and definitely a knee brace for a while."

"Can we talk to her?" Andrew asked, The nun nodded but asked them not to cause her too much stress. As they walked in she attempted to sit up a little better but Matt let her know it wasn't needed.

"So, Redpunk is it?" started Andrew "Why were you there on the colony? the colonists said it was Silverblades who attacked them." she looked at him intently as if working out if she should trust him she shifted her weight slightly and sighed.

"We were escaping, The Galcorp ship the SS Ramesses launched a massive offensive of our stronghold yesterday, myself and the others who were in the ships you found at the colony, we managed to escape, we realised there was no way we would win, he had nothing that could match that ship." she looked down distraught "Our ships were too damaged to travel far so we stopped here thinking it was still an active colony, maybe they would show us mercy hell even a prison cell and prison food would be a good alternative to death, I've heard of storied about how GalCorp treat prisoners and it seemed better to give ourselves over to an independent colony but we saw what you did and we went scavenging for food and parts to fix our ships when you came along." she put her head in her hands in despair.

"So, your the last Bloodfist" Matt said wondering out loud "or at least one of the last, others may have gotten out, but I don't get it, Why would they attack a pirate group if they are already working with one." suddenly Andrew leaped to his feet as if he had an idea.

"Erm.. Redpunk can you remember some of the last colonies you have raided?" just had a thought." he said his mind racing. She took a minute to think.

"Well I remember going on a raid to Nepri colony and one at Mendes colony, wait I heard about a raid gone wrong at Luxor colony, why?" Matt had realised what he was getting at and checked his datapad.

"All Galcorp colonies" he conformed. Redpunk nodded slowly.

"We figured that is seemed the Silverblades were leaving them alone they would be fair game for us." she started feeling sleepy as Sister Theresa brushed past them.

"Her medication is working, best letting her rest for now." she said softly but firmly, as they left, the pirate just looked over weakly and said.

"Red, everyone just calls me Red outside the

cockpit." Sister Theresa gave her another dose of painkillers and quietly lead them out as the girl drifted off to sleep, as they walked down the corridor Matt seemed to be going over something in his head.

"There's something not quite right here, something feels wrong." he said more to himself than anything, just then Liana came running up behind them with a datapad in hand.

"There you are," she said, as she stopped to take a breath "You might be interested in this." and she handed the datapad over to Matt who read it with a growing sense of anger.

"What is it?" asked Andrew, Matt sighed.

"Its another GalCorp news bulletin. They are saying that the SS Ramesses attack on the Bloodfist headquarters was as a direct result of the destruction of Bendis colony, they claim they answered a distress call but got there too late but hunted down the Pirates back to their base and eliminated them, Director Gladstone has went on record saying that they are aware it was not a GalCorp colony and they didn't need to do what they did but in these 'hard times, we should all help each other to ensure the safety of one another' and he is funding a rebuild of the colony that will be administered by Galcorp." Liana looked puzzled at both of them.

"I don't get it, I thought you said it was a Silver Blades attack?"

"Well," Andrew said "Put it this way the Silver Blades attack on the colony was brutal and once word got out there would be widespread condemnation of the event, Galcorp are using it to their advantage, they find and take out one of the biggest pirate groups and one that was targeting mainly GalCorp colonies... who just happen to be the rivals to the pirates they are working with.. and claim they have done it in retribution for Bendis Colony, makes them look like the good guys, makes GalCorp look good and make it harder for us to convince them they are not." Matt nodded in agreement

"And its a win win situation, GalCorp get a nice mineral rich colony to mine and the Silver Blades don't need to worry about their biggest rivals any more."

"But surely the survivors.."began Liana.

"...They could claim initial scans picked up no survivors and if any of the survivors challenge them with the truth. GalCorp bribes the one that can be bribed and discredits or silences the ones that can't." said Matt dryly.

"Trust me, they will have every angle covered, I'm going to my quarters, I really need to lie down I think." and he walked off looking like he had a huge weight on his shoulders, Liana just looked at Andrew concerned.

"Will he be okay?" she said leaning into Andrew for comfort

"Yeah," he said with an air of uncertianty "I hope so."

The question of where to take the Bendis colony survivors was difficult, they had contacted the colonies hat had been on friendly terms with them and then asked the survivors themselves which on of the colonies that offered to take them in was the one they wanted to go to, after much deliberation the colony of Midgard, was chosen by them to move to, at least until they decided what they wanted to do with themselves, soon the SS Hades was in orbit and preparations were in place to send them down planetside, Matt was waiting to see them off when Officer Chevalier walked up to him.

"I guess this is goodbye officer." Matt said shaking the security officers hand.

"Please call me Remy," he said "Actually I was going to ask you about that, I want to stay onboard, I have flight training, I can be useful on future ground operations," he then looked at Matt earnestly "My home was destroyed, I think I'm entitled to some payback." Matt nodded and agreed to let him stay but told him for now as his flight skills were rusty he would have to practice in the simulators a lot first and if he wanted he could work with Tamika and Phil could take the pilots not experienced in firearms and give them weapons training "I can do that, and what about the Bloodfist pirate?" Matt thought about it.

"She's still in the medbay but I'll be honest with you it is a hard one."

"Doesn't this colony have some sort of security force?" Remy asked curiously but Matt shook his head.

"Nothing much, just a few ground based officers" Matt said to Remys disappointment "The truth is to me it feels like she's as much a victim of all this as anyone else." he realised something needed to be done, but what? just then Andrew and Marcus had returned from the surface, having spoke with the colony's leaders, usually it was Matt's job but Andrew was curious about about what the colony looked like, as he got out his ship Matt beaconed him over.

"Andrew, we need to talk about what to do about Red," he said "I think we need to call a meeting in the pilots briefing room." Andrew nodded.

"Yeah, I been thinking of that myself, I'll alert the pilots." and he headed off to arrange things.

Later the Pilots plus Remy, Sister Theresa, John and most of the bridge crew were assembled in the briefing room.

"Okay," Started Andrew "We have a situation, as you know in our medbay lies one of the surviving members of the Bloodfist pirates, I know some of us have history with them," no-one needed to ask, it was a Bloodfist attack that caused the death of Andrew, Phil and Robs flight leader Angel back at Waypoint "But she is as much a victim of GalCorp as the rest of us, do we give her a chance to join us or do we send her on her way in some way once she is fully healed?" he then open up the floor for discussion, Phil stood up.

"I say we stick her in that junk pile that Kate flew herself and the others in and send her on her way, I assume the security at Midgard won't take her?" but Rob stood and walked to Phil

"No," he said surprising everyone "Phil, we have been friends for a long time and we usually agree but no, she deserves a chance, she lost everything just like us, I know they killed Angel but she wasn't one of those pilots, we killed them, remember so that means she wasn't there, I say give her the option to stay." there was fierce debate, Nathan, Gareth, Suzanne, Ellen and Nicolae were on Phil's side with Marcus, Kate, Alan, Craig, Tamika and the bridge crew on Robs, Matt had a thought.

"Sister Theresa," he said as he stepped forward "You been tending to her these past few days and talking to her, what can you tell us about her, maybe it may help with the decision. The Nun gave a small smile and stepped up.

"Well, at first she wasn't talkative but as I gained her trust she told me a lot, she grew up and orphan in the Hub, No idea who her parents may have been and she only has vague memories of them so I am guessing they died when she was at and early age, she lived in the ventilation system and took to stealing food and clothes to stay alive and warm."

"How did she end up a Bloodfist?" asked Nicolae.

"I was getting to that, a few Bloodfist's visited the Hub and she was caught trying to pick picket one, he took pity on her and raised her as his own," Sister Theresa "continued the name Redpunk was his nickname for her and it stuck, she can't remember what her original name might have been. Only that either her first or second name began with R." Phil looked sheepish.

"The Bloodfists were the only family she ever knew," he said quietly almost to himself "Dammit Sister, okay, I'm not totally sure this is the right idea but if the majority agree then okay, she can stay if she wants." John looked at him.

"Well, congratulations Phil you joined the human race." Johns comments to Phil usually had an undertone of loathing hidden by humour but Andrew saw that John was genuinely surprised by Phil's U-turn, Andrew could see Remy wasn't too convinced, understandable all things considered, he followed Matt or the briefing room to give Red the news.

"Hows the Leg?" Andrew asked Red as they entered the medbay ward, she tried to sit up and winced in pain.

"I feel better than I look trust me, but I have been told I should be okay to walk tomorrow, will need a leg brace or something for a while, I dunno, never really had much to do with doctors, or nuns," she said with a weak smile "This is where you tell me that once I'm up and running you want me off the ship, right?" she said immediately losing her smiled and looking down.

"Actually," Matt said sitting on the edge of her bed "We'd like to offer you a chance to get revenge," she looked surprised "I take it Sister Theresa told you aout our fight with GalCorp?" she nodded "Well, we could always use another pilot, if you want that is, if not we can supply you with a ship and supplies to go wherever you wish." Red looked shocked and stared into the distance for a while taking it all in.

"I have nowhere else to go, are you really serious?" she said finally as she looked at Matt, then Andrew "about letting me stay that is?" they both confirmed they were serious, she broke into tears, only stopping to say "thank you." once she calmed down and confirmed for sure she would join them Matt And Andrew left her to rest.

"We do have one problem," Matt said "Remy wants to fly for us too and well, you know..." Andrew saw what he meant, they would have to put Red and Remy together and they both saw Remy's reaction to them agreeing to let her stay.

"I know," Andrew said thinking "What about Remy can be Tamikas wingman and we move Alan to work with Red, he was one of the ones completely in favour of her staying, I can tell them if you want" Matt nodded, it made more sense Tamika could also help Remy with his flying like she was doing with Alan and they'd already be working on firearms training together.

"Well I'll inform the crew," Matt said "I think Liana wanted to see you anyway." he smiled and gave Andrew a knowing look. Andrew answered.

"Well can't keep her waiting, can I?" and he went off to find her.

Nathan was with Gareth and Craig on the hanger fixing the assault shuttle they had salvaged. the main thing was to replace the power couplings to the light drive.

"So Craig," said Nathan " Your dad flew for Hexstar? what was his callsign?"

"Hellraiser, why? did you ever fly against him?" Craig asked as he pulled out the damaged parts and placed them carefully down, Nathan looked thoughtful for a minute then replied.

"Just curious, unfortunately I was usually flying shuttles filled with troops dodging enemy batteries and trying to land while the same troops would blame me for the bumpy ride."

"Ah," Craig said absently "I take it that wasn't your preferred assignment then?" Nathan shook his head laughing.

"No, I joined to be a fighter pilot so you can imagine my disappointment when I was transferred but I made the best of it I guess, only served about six months active duty before the war ended anyway," he said with a hint of regret "It was never a good feeling seeing the fighters fly out a hanger knowing you could be up there with them, y'know."

"I don't know," said Gareth "back when I was a tech at Waypoint there were times I was glad not to be going out there too," he then flashed a smile "But here I am one of you guys, a hot shot pilot."

"Well a pilot anyway," said Andrew from behind him "So you guys really can get this thing back up and running? I can see why you'd think its useful Nathan, good call." he said admiring the vessel.

"So," said Craig hopefully "what's our next move?"

"Well I been thinking about that, still to run it past Matt," Andrew said while absently checking out one of the wing guns "but I got a few ideas."

"I bet you have." said Gareth.

The state of the art gym facilities on the SS Ramesses were second to none in Corbin Hays opinion as he went for his afternoon training, David Abrams passed him as he was getting ready in the changing area, having just finished a gym session himself.

"Hey, Abrams," He said with a tone of authority "I hope you sorted out things with Reid, I heard you two had another difference of opinion in the mess hall" the younger pilot rolled his eyes and sat on the nearest bench.

"Yeah, I was wondering when you were going to bring that up." he ran his fingers through his heavily styled black hair "I have apologised but I stand by what I say. The guy takes too much time with a kill, he is going to be a liability"

"Kid, let me be totally honest with you. You are good, very good" Corbin looked at David intently "Hell I could see you as future flight leader.. easy I'm not thinking of retiring yet... but at least try to act like a team player"

"I came to make money and do my job" David said with a surprising intensity "Reid and his crap is getting in the way of that..."

"...I get that, but just.. Look, after this mission is

over I will review pilot performances. If reid isn't performing as well like you say I will look into getting him transferred." He hoped that would stop the bickering between the pilots, at least for a while.

"Okay" David said with a tone that suggested it would have to do "Thanks for listening anyway." he got up and left just as Captain Miller came in.

"Anthing I should know about?" Miller said as he got ready for a session in the gym.

"Just pilot stuff. its all sorted for now anyway," Hayes said before changing the subject "I saw the latest news bulletin," Hayes started as he finished getting ready "Gladstone knows how to spin a good tale. If I hadn't been out there myself wasting some of those bloodfists myself I would have swore it was completely true." he flashed an evil grin at Miller who shrugged.

"He's good for something I guess," he quipped "The lunatic Remus Fox should not have attacked Bendis colony like he did, luckily for once Gladstone used his head and seized on a golden opportunity, was good fortune that we knew the base location thanks to an informant," he smiled sinisterly "he was.. compensated.. for his troubles, after all, can't have any loose ends can we?" and they laughed.

"You know," Hayes said deep in thought "You are right, we were lucky. Remus Fox is becoming more of a liablity, something needs done about him." Miller got up and headed to the gym.

"Patience," he said "That time will come, sooner than you think."

CHAPTER 30

The next day Sister Theresa confirmed that Red could now leave the medbay but she would need to wear a leg brace, luckily it was the type with a hinge at the knee joint so she was able to walk with just a slight need to limp, she refused a crutch as in her words didn't want any pity, Rob, who felt obliged to help her as he did fire the shot that injured her and Kate who just wanted to help out the new female pilot showed her to her new quarters, all she had was her flight helmet as her flightsuit was badly damaged so one from the ships stores was given to her, it hung a little loose but it would do.

"oh, I recovered these for you," said Rob handing her the patches she had on her old flightsuit and he left as he was on alert standby with Phil, as he left Alan dropped by.

"Hi wingmate," he said happily, Red looked confused for a minute then remembered Andrew stopping by the Medbay earlier to tell her the arrangements "Alan Allford, callsign Pyrus, I think we will make quite a pear." despite themselves Kate and Red laughed.

"I told you stop the bad pear puns." Kate said once she calmed down, Red looked at her curiously.

"He's like this all the time?" she said.

"Pretty much," then Kate explained Alan's family history, to which Alan took a bow.

"Its all true, my family grow more pears than anyone and proud that not one of our crops have been hijacked." Red rolled her eyes.

"There's good reason for that," she said in a droll tone "What is a pirate gang going to do with a shipment of pears." Kate let out a giggle, she could see Alan already forming an answer in his head.

"Eat them, make pear cider or take up farming themselves maybe." he shrugged with a playful glint in his eye, they could see Red noticeably relax knowing that her wingman didn't seem bothered about her past, there was a knock on the door frame of the open door, it was Marcus carrying a small box filled with two beer bottles, a Mug, and a few trinkets from the ships stores.

"A welcome basket for our new pilot." he said but saw Kate and Alan there and suddenly looked awkward, Kate went over took it off him and handed it to Red, who looked through it, there was in addition to the mug, there was a t-shirt, a towel, a brush and a handwritten welcome note, Kate raised an eyebrow.

"how come we never got anything like this, has Remy got one?" she quizzed Marcus who was looking nervous, Alan noticed too.

"And anyway I thought you preferred four legs and fur." Marcus shot him a look then left muttering to himself.

"What was that about?" Red asked, so Kate explained about the incident with Marcus, Tessa and the cat.

"So hes something of a ladies man?" Red asked.

"He wishes," Kate snorted, "come on lets get something to eat." Red looked up suddenly a little worried.

"I'm not sure." she said meekly but Kate took her arm and helped her up and walked her out her quarters followed by Alan.

"I'm still not sure you have done the right thing," Remy said as he sat with Matt, Andrew and the Sommer sisters in the mess hall "Its not that I feel sorry for her, I do, its just she was raised by pirates and would still be one if things had worked out different, just saying." Ever since the decision to let her stay most of the pilots had accepted the choice but Remy remained sceptical and Ellen shook her head.

"As much as I was against it at first there could be some benefits."

"Like what?" Remy said looking unconvinced,

Suzanne decided to answer.

"I would have thought it would be obvious, she knows information about the pirate underworld. I admit I am personally not fully convinced it is a good idea but maybe we should give her a chance." before Remy could answer a flight helmet and flightsuit that looked taken from the ships stores were dumped in front of Remy, he looked up to see Tamika staring down at him.

"I hear you are my new wingman and that your piloting skills are rusty," she said matter of factly, he nodded meekly, clearly taken aback by her bluntness "Well," she continued "The simulators are free, lets move." she walked off, her helmet in one hand, Remy gathered up his flightsuit and helmet and headed off after her, as he was leaving, Red entered and he looked at her suspiciously and she nearly headed straight back out but Kate and Alan guided her to sit with the others.

"Do not worry about him Redpunk, he needs time, a lot has happened." said Suzanne, the Sommer sisters habit of using the other pilots full first names was quickly whispered to Red by Matt when she sat down.

"Don't worry, I'm not going to kill, rob, blackmail or enslave anyone," Red responded "but I suppose not every day your home gets destroyed by one set of pirates, then anther bunch of pirates try to scavenge the place and who knows what else."

"Not to mention most people see all the pirate groups as one in the same." added Matt nodding, Andrew looked deep in thought though, as if something Red said got his attention, he got up and left still deep in thought, Nakamura suddenly ran into the mess hall and into Kate's arms.

"Hey Shinsuke, who you running from?" she soon got her answer when Phil came in, just finished from being on alert as the SS Hades was leaving orbit "Oh." she said finally.

"Give me that cat Kate, the crazy thing leapt into my cockpit the minute I opened the canopy, if Tessa can't control that cat then it has to go, simple as that and by go I mean out the airlock into space, make sure you tell her that seeing as you two are close friends after all." and he stormed out, Red turned to Kate.

"He really hates your cat." she said as she tentatively stroked Nakamura who purred approvingly, Kate went to explain the cat belonged to Tessa and how Phil hated the cat and how Kate and Tessa were close. "how close?" Red asked, Kate whispered into Red's ear and they both giggled.

"So, yeah you could say we are pretty close." Kate eventually said.

That night Matt was wakened from his sleep by a loud banging on the door, he got up and opened it to see Andrew looking like a man possessed.

"I got it Matt, I think I know how we can clear your name and finally solve all this, we need to call a meeting first thing in the morning to plan this." Matt looked at the man whom he had grown to consider a close friend and struggled to work out why this sudden revelation.

"Andrew, mate, have you been awake all night with this?" he said a little bit concerned "Is Liana awake too?"

"No," Andrew countered "She sleeps like a log and don't worry, I am fine, I do have one word to say to you though." he flashed a devilish grin.

"What is that?" Matt asked wearily, just wanting to sleep.

"Blackmail." Andrew said and suddenly headed back to his quarters, Matt shook his head and closed his door, maybe the pressure was getting to Andrew, who knew for sure, but what did he mean by blackmail?

Early the next morning in the pilots briefing room, Matt and Andrew had all the Ronin assembled, not all were exactly fully awake yet, Marcus had a cup of coffee in front of him Alan looked still half asleep and Rob hadn't shaved yet, Andrew started the meeting by asking Red a question.

"Red, you mentioned yesterday that the Bloodfist used to deal in blackmail, amongst other things? right?" she looked uncomfortable but answered.

"Well, yeah record every communication, find dirt on opponents and stuff like that, why?" she looked reluctant to talk about it.

"Well," Andrew said putting a reassuring hand on her shoulder as he walked past her "One of the first problems we faced was Matt's copy of the vital recording proving the Silver Blades and GalCorp ... partnership... was erased but there must be copies." but Matt shook his head.

"there's no way Gladstone would record it, he wouldn't want any evidence." he said, disappointed but then Tamika spoke up.

"No, but the Silver Blades might, I know I always recorded any contact with anyone who hired me." suddenly the other pilots started to work it out.

"Yeah, of course", said Phil thinking hard "they are not stupid, they must know that at some point GalCorp will screw them over and leave them out to dry so if they have real hard proof of GalCorps illegal deals..."

"...Its like an insurance policy," finished Nicolae "You don't enter a deal like that without planning a way out".

"Blackmail," Red nodded now realised why Andrew had looked thoughtful after she mentioned it the day before "But only one problem, any recordings would be at their base and no-one knows where it is, not even me and believe me when I say we hunted for that base for years." but Marcus wasn't phased by that.

"Oh we will find a way, I don't know how, a tracker on a ship, recover a navigational computer from one of their ships," he turned to the Sommer sisters "that means no destroying them all ladies, sorry". Suzanne rolled her eyes as Ellen just pretended not to hear.

"You'd probably need to board the station, I can't see them letting you remote uplink," said Remy who turned to Red and asked "what do you know about their base?" Red thought for a minute.

"Not much as I said we tried to locate it for years but we did find out one thing, you won't get a Silver Blade to give you the location, they would rather die than risk the wrath of Remus Fox, there's a legend that went that when one of his men compromised their previous base he let the man live, for a while anyway."

"What happened." said Craig, who seemed to regret asking the moment he spoke Red looked at them, her eyes showing genuine fear.

"He had defected to the Screaming Skulls, they protected him for a while but the rumour goes that, on a visit to the Hub but his ship doesn't even make it there instead they captured him, put him in a sealed flightsuit and helmet, strapped him to Remus Foxes personal fighter, after a few manoeuvrers, Remus went to lightspeed and with only the suit to protect the defector.. well you can imagine." Craig suddenly looked ill, a sealed flightsut could keep you safe in space for a few minutes, enough to be rescued by a shuttle but n its own could not withstand to forces on it going to lightspeed would cause. after a few awkward minutes Nathan said.

"Well if we are going to do it we should prepare, the assault shuttle refit is nearly finished but we would need to choose and drill a group of us who are going to actually do the mission."

"We could set up cargo bay four as a killhouse to practice, I noticed the carbines we have can fire non lethal rounds, which will be ideal." Remy added. Matt thought about it.

"How many are needed to crew the shuttle Nathan?" he asked.

"one can fly it but ideally you want two." Nathan replied.

"Okay" Matt said "You and Kate will crew the shuttle, myself, Rob, Gareth, Phil, Remy and Tamika wil form the group assault team, I want Remy and Tamika to come up with a regime to get us working as a cohesive unit" they both nodded and Tamika gave a predatory smile. Andrew then spoke.

"Well it looks like it will be myself, Marcus, Suzanne, Ellen, Nicolae, Craig, Red and Alan will be your support team as well as taking out any base defenses, seeing as we don't know its location or what it even is, Craig can you and Gareth work on a selection of base attack programs, Space stations, mining platforms, set then in asteroid belts, nebulas, anything, I want us prepared as if and when this opportunity prepares itself we won't have much time to do it, everyone dismissed" as they filed out, Matt stayed and went up to Andrew, for the first time in a while he could see Matt's eyes have a twinkle of true hope.

"Thank you." he said.

"Why thank me," Andrew said with an innocent look on his face "All I did was realise something we should have thought about a long time ago, the hard part is still to come." Matt didn't know if he was being modest or genuinely didn't see it as a big deal he realised just to leave it at that.

"It's okay, I'm off to talk with Tamika and Remy about their plans." and he walked out, suddenly full of newfound hope.

Later on, in the mess hall and Phil, Rob, Marcus, Gareth and Alan were having lunch, Remy and Tamika were the other side of the table, going over datapads, clearly deep into their work, Marcus looked around and called Remy over.

"Yes?" Remy said, slightly annoyed to be taken away from his work.

"Remy my dear man," Marcus started "have you thought about a pilot callsign? just curious and please don't just use your name, your not one of those who prefer to go by their real names are you?" Remy looked a touch confused.

"Never gave it much thought to be honest, I suppose nobody goes by their real names?" he asked, Phil told him Suzanne and Ellen did and that they see callsigns as a strange sign of weakness, Remy shook his head "Well, I won't be doing that, any suggestions?" The other pilots started to think just as Kate came in, Phil explained to her the dilemma Remy had so she sat down to help, unfortunately most names were rejected, though no-one thought Phil's idea of Bendisman was particularly good, as was any variations on anglicising his surname to Knight as they already had Matt using the Knight moniker.

"I got it," Said Alan who jumped up off his seat

"I'm guessing you have French heritage," Remy nodded in agreement so Alan continued "what about, Victoire? sounds good, and represents your urge to be victorious over your enemy." Remy repeated it to himself a few times before nodding with a smile.

"Victoire it is, thank you."

"Just happy to help, how is my old slave driver of an ex-wingmate?" Alan said as Tamika rolled her eyes.

"I can hear you." She said shaking her head as Remy hastily explained that she was an amazing wingmate and had helped him a lot but gave Alan a look to suggest whatever Alan had went through with her, he was now enduring, a call came over the comms.

"Can I get the other pilots to come to the hanger, the assault shuttle is finished." it was Nathan and he sounded pleased with himself.

Not too long ago the ship in front of them was a barely functioning wreck, now it was gleaming, a fresh coat of paint the same grey as the fighters, Nathan looked tired but pleased with himself as he explained what he had done.

"The first issue was replacing the damaged parts as we had to modify the spares we have onboard to work with Hexstar equipment but Gareth helped me with that, she now has full lightdrive capabilities and can reach top speed with the normal drive." he walked over to the wing mounted weapons "As you see I've replaced the Hexstar tri-lasers with regular target tracking laser batteries like the ones on our fighters and.." he added tapping the bulky attachment to the mid wing mounting strut "..Is the original Hexstar light cannon, she can pack quite a punch, Inside I had to replace the pilot and gunner seats with more comfortable ones from our fighter spares, what do you think?" Matt walked around it and grinned

"very good work, confident you could fly her in battle? shes not like United Earth forces ones you are used to." Nathan nodded enthusiasticly.

"Of course," he said with confidence "just give the word and she's ready, as am I." matt smiled at Nathan's attitude, they still had a long way to go but it was good to see spirits high.

CHAPTER 31

It didn't matter how he argued Captain Miller was losing the battle with Director Gladstone, his latest suggestion was to supply the Silver Blades with missiles and other weapons, including GalCorps own Burst torpedoes which were expensive to say the least.

"Director, this, is a bad idea, I think we are giving those pirates far too much help and despite all our help they are not getting the job done." He said passionately.

"Bendis Colony would disagree with you there," The Director said, his face looming large on the comms screen "But have no fear they will be getting the missiles that don't get past quality control, they will work but be of a lesser quality, you worry too much Joseph, remember they are our allies." Gladstone said condescendingly and signed off, Miller stared at the blank screen for a few minutes, Commander Cairns entered the office and reported in.

"We are to guide an unmarked cargo ship to these co-ordinates where our.. ally will take it off our hands, I assume this is Gladstone's work," miller nodded not saying a word, he didn't need to, his face told the whole story "Captain, you should know that most of the crew share your frustration." Miller looked up at him as if noticing him for the first time

"oh, thank you Cairns, yes lets rendezvous with this ship, lets play Gladstone's game.. for now."

The world known as Colonial Samoa loomed large in the orbiting SS Hades viewports as John flew down to conduct business with Matt and Gareth as fighter escort and as ambassadors for the Ronin, landing at the spaceport of the Capital, Anoa'i City.

"I didn't expect something like this." Gareth said as he climbed out of his fighter.

"I know," Matt agreed, staring at all the tall buildings, parks filled with all sorts of greenery and the general infrastructure "apparently it is one of the oldest colonies out here" he said as they exited the spaceport and decided to admire the scenery for a while before their meeting the colony administration. The main roads in the city were lined with statues of famous people of Samoan decent.

"This would make for a great vacation spot.. if it wasn't for the pirate raids" Gareth said, wondering out loud.

"Well, lets see if we can get them to understand that when we put our case to them" Matt replied.

Andrew was in the briefing room working with Red and Craig on the simulator program they would need to practice assaulting the Silver Blade base with by using the defences and size of the Bloodfist base as a baseline, relying on Reds knowledge of her old home.

"The only problem is our base was an abandoned research station" she said cautiously.

"Its okay Red, its more the firepower and defensive capabilities we need as opposed to the physical shapes and designs." Craig reassured her "It sounds like both pirate gangs were comparable in size which will make this program somewhat useful, trust me on this." he smiled warmly in the hopes of convincing her that she was being useful, Marcus walked in holding four cups of handing them out to the others.

"Thanks Marcus" said Andrew as he looked at his datapad as Marcus looked over the plans himself.

"Hmm, very nice, of course all this will account for nothing unless we find its location, how will we do that by the way?" he asked the question everyone else was thinking, it was the one part of the plan that hadn't appeared to have been given as much thought as the rest, Andrew shook his head.

"I don't know," Andrew said with a sigh "I've still to figure that out, its the most difficult part of this operation, we need to find out in such a way that they won't suspect a thing until its too late, the best way would be some sort of tracer program or bug but how do we get it there? Of course there's capturing a ship and pilot but from what we have heard, the pilots won't talk and we don't know how much is stored on their fighter computers if any, for all we know they probably purge them." Red nodded.

"They do, always have done as far as I know. The Bloodfists have tried that technique, several times" she shrugged "of course it doesn't help that half their ships are very old and the computers barely work as is anyway." they noticed she looked awkward when discussing her past life Marcus moved closer and looked at her intently.

"Red, we are not judging you, well maybe Remy is and to be honest I'm not sure Phil is too happy with it either but the majority of us, we want and need someone like you." he said then realised he was holding her hands only to let go in embarrassment and stepped back unsure of what to do, Andrew spoke up.

"He's right, plus bear in mind most of us are wanted in some way, we have all had to make adjustments and given time you will too, guys like Phil and Remy may give you a hard time but they have their reasons, doesn't make them right, just don't let it worry you. Anyway, we been at this all afternoon, what do you say we call it a day and resume in the morning." he said as he saw the tiredness creeping into Craigs eyes, he was a good kid and was eager to please but the program wouldn't be of any use if he was half asleep when making it, they left the briefing room but Marcus hung back to speak to Andrew.

"I hope Remy loosens up around her, every time he walks past her, he glares at her." Marcus sighed, Andrew nodded in sympapthy.

"I know and we keep telling him, look, I don't know the guy all that well but unfortunately i know the type, he won't let up until she does something that proves she has changed in his eyes, its the whole actions speak louder than words thing." Andrew explained, Marcus just rolled his eyes and walked out, Andrew didn't ask what he was going to do and wasn't sure he wanted to know, suddenly the alert alarms sounded.

As they escorted their shuttle from the spaceport Matt thought to himself about the meeting with the ruling council, they seemed very positive especially after hearing of some of their exploits, they offered help by way of general hospitality and aid should the Ronin need it, he was snapped out of his thoughts by a comm message from the shuttle.

"White Knight, once the ship is shuttle is docked can you and G stay out? Liana has just reported to me that there's something on the edge of the sensors here so we are going to check it out and if its hostile then we will need you, the others are getting ready to launch." said John, Matt could see the logic, no point in landing and causing chaos if they need to immediately relaunch.

"G this is White Knight, escort formation with the

SS Hades, don't land yet, repeat don't land yet."

"White Knight this is G, what's wrong? pirates maybe?" Matt didn't answer but tried to link his scanners to the SS Hades for a closer look, the only thing he could think of is that we were waiting for them to leave whomever it was before advancing, either way it wasn't good.

The hanger was busy as the techs taxied the incoming shuttle out the way in preparation to launch fighters, Andrew was already by his ship, helmet in hand ready to launch as he watched the others get ready, Suzanne and Ellen were first to come through, running in perfect step to their ships, Nathan and Kate were next, he noticed the platforms on Kate's boots made her look just as tall as Nathan and he noted they were in deep conversation followed by Phil, Rob and Marcus, though Marcus looked a little distracted.

"What is it with Marcus today" Nicolae said from behind Andrew, making him jump slightly "he has been acting like a caged wolf." Andrew just shrugged as behind Nicolae Craig was trying to mime that it was Red that was on Marcus's mind though Andrews confused look just made Craig do more elaborate gestures until Nicolae noticed him and shot him a look as if toget him to stop. Just then Remy and Tamika walked into the Hanger, Tamika went straight to her ship but Remy waited at the entrance and when Red and Alan walked in, Remy grabbed Reds arm and Andrew heard him say.

"I will be watching you, any betrayal and.." he didn't finish it, Marcus had came over, turned Remy around and punched him in the face.

"Leave her alone," he hissed as the other pilots ran over Phil and Rob were holding Marcus back and Tamika was at Remy's side "she's a Ronin now just like you, your not the only one Pirates have targeted, it wasn't even her clan that attacked you and you know it, you know yet you still.."

"Enough." shouted Andrew "Lets not fight amongst ourselves, especially if we have others out there to fight against, now get to your ships" as Marcus walked up to his fighter, flexing the hand he punched with, Red ran up to him and stopped him, he noticed she was wearing a flightsuit from the ships stores but had put her old badges on it.

"Thanks, really, she said looking at him warmly "I appreciate you trying to help me fit in, I really do, friends?" she held her hand out, he shook it and smiled.

"Friends." he replied.

John was on the bridge pacing up and down as the SS Hades broke orbit.

"Course set for the scanner blips." Tessa said with a sigh, she wasn't convinced it would turn out to be much, the planet had many moons and could be something about one of them affecting systems, it wouldn't be the first time, but John wasn't so sure, there was something oddly familiar about it.

"hold on, Liana, can you contact that new pilot, Red or something, tell her what we know and see if it fits anything." Liana looked doubtful but still contacted Red.

"Shall I arm weapons?" Said Ben cautiously, John gave him a nod.

"Yeah, no harm in being careful"

Red was in her ship but the canopy was still up, Andrew and Phil had came over to her to hear first hand what her answer would be, she looked at Andrew who had climbed the entrance ladder.

"What Liana described is slightly curious. There is one pirate gang that would do something like this, wait for a ship to leave then target the planet or get the ship when it heads out the system, i'ts a tactic of the Screaming Skulls but never heard of them targeting here before." she turned and activated her comms "Liana, sounds like it could be a Screaming Skulls tactic, they are waiting for us to leave." Andrew leaned over and asked.

"Is John still broadcasting a fake transponder?" after a few minutes Liana confirmed that John was still using it "Okay lets launch." he said climbing down and running to his own ship, Phil stayed and shouted up a question.

"You had many run ins with these guys?"

"A few, even amongst the pirate gangs they are hated" she answered looking down at him "They would kidnap and ransom and we didn't agree with that method of piracy so we were especially at odds." Phil seemed satisfied with that answer and went to prep his fighter.

Matt had been listening in to the conversation via the comms.

"White Knight this is G, It's looking more and more like a good decision to keep Red around" Gareth was right, she was already proving to be a valuable asset to the team

"It is, isn't it" he replied "And from what I have seen of her in the simulators, she is quite the pilot."

"Yeah so I have heard, I'm just glad she is on our side now" Gareth said in response.

CHAPTER 32

By the time they others launched and linked with Matt and Gareth they were close enough for a detailed scan, an old refitted cruiseliner with the Screaming Skulls emblems visible on the sides was launching fighters from both its hangers.

"White Knight, this is Firehawk, looks like they were planning a surface raid, best keeping that ship away from planetside" Matt agreed, such a big ship to attack a colony and it wasn't like they knew the SS Hades was there.

"SS Hades, this is White Knight, care to deal with the cruiseliner?"

"This is SS Hades, already moving into position." said Liana, The SS Hades turned so it would bring its broadside to the enemy ship in order to bring more weapons on it

"This is Firehawk, engage enemy fighters at will." The SS Hades opened up on the larger vessel as the fighters locked in combat, almost immediately two of the pirate vessels were destroyed unsurprisingly those kills were by the Sommer sisters, Andrew was pleased to see they were more measured and not as angry in their flying but that it hadn't affected their flying.

Tamika had locked onto the nearest ship and fired a few shots causing it to engage tight evasive manoeuvrers, but she took a breath and calmly angled her fighter to intercept it, knowing her ship couldn't directly match he move and using her years of knowledge to outsmart the other pilot, she had just regained weapons lock when she heard.

"Quinque. this is Victoire, out of position, need help", she squeezes the trigger and the targeted fighter exploded with little effort and then she looked around, Remy had tried to match the enemy fighter and his inexperience was showing, he didn't realise his ship wasn't as manoeuvrable and as such was out of position and now two pirate fighters were targeting him, she swore as she relised she couldn't get into a good position, his voice as getting more panicked with each message, suddenly both ships were hit by a hail of weapons fire, one ship exploded and its debris tore up its wingman followed by Red and Alan's fighters flying past.

"Victoire this is Redpunk, you should be okay now." Tamika was suprised at the ex-pirate, she was expecting some nasty quip in light of Remy's attitude, she was glad that wasn't the case/

"Redpunk this is Quinque, good save there, Pyrus I hope you are learning." she smiled despite herself

"Quinque this is Pyrus, of course, Redpunk and I make quite the pear you know."

It was times like this Nathan missed flying dropships and shuttles, he had a particularly good set of pilots on him and Kate and there was nothing he could do.

"This is Nate Dawg calling anyone who can help," the fighting had drifted over to above the SS Hades, the Carrier had the upper hand over the Screaming Skull ship, its return fire getting more sporadic, over the comms came a message.

"Nate Dawg this is Firehawk, I want you and Kitten to manoeuvrer as if you are going to land but when i give the order, pick a direction and break for it, got that?" Nathan looked confused but shrugged and acknowledged.

"Nate Dawg this is Kitten, did he say land?"

Andrew got on the comms to the SS Hades and told them to clear the hanger deck and open the aft doors.

"Firehawk, this is Brutus, I hope your not doing what I think you are going to do, cause I'm not going to follow." Andrew smiled, Marcus had been his wingman long enough to know one of Andrews crazy ideas when he saw one, Andrew kicked into full speed and made for the aft entrance, Marcus broke off at the last minute and flew over the carrier, Andrew simply flew the full lengh of the hanger bay...

..the enemy fighters scans sensed Marcus's ship but stayed on target, lining up the two fighters heading for the hanger...

"This is Firehawk, Break off! Break off!" Nathan and Kate flew hard to the left...

...As Andrew had been flying inside the SS Hades and thus his ship transponder was being masked by the SS Hades own they did not see his fighter flying towards them guns firing until it was too late.

Some of the pirate ships were trying to flee but as Matt flew after them, a large explosion filled one side of his field of vision, the Cruiserliner had been destroyed

"This is Pollock, the SS Hades didn't destroy that ship, its own munitions have ripped it apart" Matt shook his head he was noticing a trend with these badly refitted ships, no wonder the Silver Blades went with a proper warship, some of he fighters managed to get to lightspeed but there were a couple of stragglers, Matt assumed lightdrives were damaged, he was about to target one when Craig flew in targeting the fleeing fighter, making use of the main guns tracking stayed on course for the second ship, one the first was destroyed he bore he weapons on the second dispatching it too, impressive, all the time in the simulators was paying off big time.

"White Knight this is Hellbringer, are we going to pursue the surviving ships?" he could hear the excitement in the kids voice.

"Hellbringer this is Semjasa, easy there kid, don't get too cocky." he forgot that Phil was initially against Craig having any involvement

"Hellbringer this is Pollock, ignore Semjasa, hes just grumpy, you did good kid but let them go then they can tell stories of terror about the great Hellbringer." he said with a laugh.

"This is White Knight, good job out there everyone. Ronin, lets go home." he said as he headed to the hanger.

As he got out of his fighter, Matt saw Remy head over to Red's fighter, taking his helmet off as he moved and he stood almost imperiously as she got out her ship and took her helmet off, shaking her scarlet red hair loose.

"Can I help you?" she said with an air or defeat as if expecting another assault on her character, Matt saw Andrew subtly tell Marcus not to interfere.

"Yes" said Remy swallowing hard. A black eye

was developing where Marcus had punched him "I am sorry I doubted your honour, you were amazing out there, I am pleased we are on the same side." he said, stumbling over his words a little and held out his hand, she grabbed his wrist pulled him in for a hug.

"Apology accepted," she said "Though next time follow your wingmate not the target, trust me it works out better." Matt smiled as he headed off to the locker room it was good to see the new pilots getting along.

Phil was storing his helmet away when he saw Nathan looking confused on the locker room bench, Gareth was there too as was Kate who was putting her hair in high pigtails in the mirror.

"What's with him?" he asked Kate, she looked at Phil then Nathan.

"Oh, he's trying to work out Andrews tactics," she smiled "He flew into the hanger to hide his transponder so the ships pursuing us wouldn't see him, seemed a bit dangerous if you ask me." Nathan looked at Phil as if to confirm that as his thinking too, he just laughed as Andrew himself walked in, his stride stiff as it usually is after flying, he looked around bewildered.

"Did I miss something?" he said in a confused tone.

"Oh, he kids are confused about your tactics." Gareth said with a cheeky smile.

"oh, I see," Andrew sat on the bench across from Nathan "Nathan, Kate, look at it this way, you are both still alive, that's the important thing" He then stopped a moment and thought "ask yourself, if you weren't expecting it, they sure as hell weren't and that's why it worked so well. Unpredictability is a powerful strategy, keeps everyone on their toes,"Andrew smiled and then got up and pointed to a photo that had been hanging on the changing room since the Ronin came onboard. By the looks of the attire Nathan guessed it was a early nineteen forties era pilot, probably during World War Two. "Know who that is?" Andrew asked.

"I had been meaning to ask about that" Nathan admitted

"Yeah, Rob and I put it up there to inspire us, we had it up on our locker room wall back at Waypoint Station. It is World War Two American naval pilot Captain Stanley Winfield 'Swede' Vejtasa," he saw the blank looks on Nathan and Kate so he continued "He was a prolific fighter pilot but one of his most notable engagements was before he was a fighter pilot. You see he managed to take down three of the best Japanese fighter craft with battle hardened pilots... "he paused for effect "A dive bomber and for over seventeen minutes he outmanoeuvred them by using the plane's ability to pull out of divebombing runs to make turns that is impossible for his opponents to match and after over seventeen gruelling minutes he managed to down all three Japanese planes." Andrew smiled "its not the fighter craft but the pilot that makes the difference. Remember that" he said and walked out, Nathan looked especially impressed. Tessa was walking in she whispered to Andrew.

"Lianna is waiting for you in your quarters." and gave him a wink, she then walked up to Kate and smiled.

"Looking good," she said glancing at the female pilot admiringly "Would you like to come over to my quarters later, don't want feel up for socialising in the mess tonight and could still do with good company." Kate blushed and looked down at her flightsuit.

"Sounds good to me, I'll change into something more.." but Tessa stopped her.

"Oh your fine as you are, trust me." just then, Marcus came in and opened his locker to store his helmet, a large grey furball flew at him.

"what the.." he shouted dodging out the way as Nakamura landed on the floor on his feet, Phil laughed and shook his head.

"But Marcus, I thought he was your type?" he said with a playful smile as he dodged an attempted back hand slap from Tessa and ran out the room laughing, Tessa then picked up the cat and held him protectively, Marcus looked up at the ladies and pointed to Tessa.

"I've said it before and I'll say it again I thought it was you." he said accusingly as Kate walked out shaking her head, Tessa walked up to Marcus and said playfully.

"Only in your dreams flyboy." and walked off with Nakamura purring in her arms, Marcus just shook his head, dusted himself off and stored his helmet and extra vehicular equipment they carried in case of ejection.

"I'm guessing that jokes getting pretty old," came a voice behind him, he turned to see Red standing with her helmet in one hand a four pack of what looked like cider bottles in the other "Now don't get any ideas, we are just friends after all. I'm just wanting to thank you again for sticking up for me."

"Where did you got the cider from?" Marcus noted, pointing to the bottles. Red looked down and giggled

"Yeah, gift from Alan for a first successful mission together as wingmates, apparently we make a great..." she shook her head "..pear" she looked as if she felt foolish even uttering it.

"The kid sure loves his pear puns" Marcus agreed.

"He does, anyway I was thinking... only if you want that is, we could go to my quarters and chat a while," she smiled warmly "We both grew up out in this region and I bet you have some crazy stories."

"A few. And I am willing to wager that you have had some interesting and unusual experiences in your time as a pirate." he countered.

"That is one way to put it" she said handing him a bottle, Marcus took it and smiled then followed her to her quarters.

CHAPTER 33

"So you are aware of the plan?" Said Director Gladstone over the comms, Captain Miller stood in his office onboard the SS Ramesses trying to maintain a neutral expression despite his misgivings.

"Of course, if I hear a distress call from the supply ship SS RenenetI will ignore it as the attack is merely cover for the weapons delivery, but why not use one of our frigates? we have never just used our cargo vessels out here, without escort anyway" Miller started to pace as the strain of standing was beginning to hurt.

"Because" said Gladstone with an air of impatience "imagine what the Silver Blades could do with a ship like the SS Seti or one of her sister ships, it would be chaos and at least this way if they capture the ship itself and they probably will its just a lowly cargo vessel, no big deal, as for protection, I think a few token fighters will do, a few pilots were due to wash out of our training program, I think they have earned a special duty" Gladstone's smile worried Miller, the man played a dangerous game "I hope we are in agreement here?" Miller sighed in frustration.

"of course sir" he looked at the man on the screen and not for the first or last time he had to stop himself saying something that would lose him his job.

Later that night as the majority of the pilots met up in the mess hall of the SS Hades and were, as expected, discussing the latest battle. Phil was convinced the SS Hades on laser batteries nearly took him out.

"Phil," Rob said shaking his head "I told you to pull up, it was you who insisted in following that ship into the field of fire." Phil just looked at his wingman intently.

"Yeah, well I still say Tessa slipped Ben some Bitcreds, its that cat, she'll do anything for it." Phil said, trying his best to convince Rob but his wingman was distracted by something. He noticed Kate hadn't joined the others for drinks.

"Where is Kate?" he asked.

"Last I saw she was with Tessa..." Phil answered.

"Tessa?... really? Okay." Rob replied shaking his head.

"Ah cupid's arrow finds another target." said Alan smiling "Mind you it's not like they are the first couple we have onboard the ship, just look at Andrew and

Liana."

"I'm not sure they are that serious.. well not yet anyway" Nathan commented "but Kate has seemed more.. relaxed lately so whatever is going on between them is having a positive effect on her."

"Fair play to them," Nicolae added "First it was Andrew and Liana, looks like now we have Kate and Tessa, Marcus and Red..." Nicolae was stopped by a slap to the back of his head from Marcus who had just walked in.

"Nothings happening between me and Red, we just talked and it has just as much chance of happening as Matt and Suzanne." He said pointedly as everyone looked at Suzanne. Matt wasn't there, he was on the bridge talking to John Suzanne stood up sharply.

"I will not engage in idle gossip." and she marched off followed by Ellen.

"Touchy subject," remarked Craig casually "All I used to get when I worked the simulator room when she wasn't running down others for not taking the whole thing serious was she was telling me," he slipped into a close approximation of her voice and accent "how honourable and great Matthew is," he then just shook his head "i don't know if its in a romantic way but she is kinda fixated on him." they were jolted when some carbines reconfigured for training were slammed on the table by Tamika who stood with Remy looking serious.

"Gareth, Phil, Rob, Nathan? I hope I'm not disturbing anything?" she said in a falsely pleasant tone.

"Well.." started Rob.

"Good," she said before he could continue " So you won't mind joining us in the kill house for practice runs will you? Good." she said before they could say a word, the pilots grabbed a carbine each and got up, Phil just looked at Tamika.

"Remember, this time no aiming below the waistline, okay? I don't care if the enemy may hit me down there, they are not hitting me there today." Tamkia muttered something about not being able to promise anything as they filed out the mess hall, Marcus took one of the vacated seats and sighed.

"That's why I'm glad I am just a pilot." he said to a chorus of laughter, after some pushing from the others Marcus, told them about a little about his discussion with Red, how despite her being a pirate and he the some of a cargo hauler they had similar experiences and how she is nice once people got to know her, Alan agreed.

"Yeah," he said "also she is a great combat pilot, you should have saw her rescue Remy's ass out there it was great.. it really was."

"To be fair" Nicolae said carefully "If she has been a pirate for as long as she says, it shouldn't be much or a surprise that she is as good as she is."

"I suppose you're right, if she wasn't she wouldn't have lasted too long" Marcus shrugged as Craig made his way over to the food dispensers

"You guys want anything?" he asked but was interrupted by Matt's voice echoed over the comms. Matt's voice echoing over the comms.

"Andrew can you and Liana come to the bridge?

its important."

"I wonder what that's about." Craig wondered aloud.

The bridge was quiet when Andrew entered, Matt and John both looked at him as Liana took up her position at the comms console.

"A communication from an old friend." Matt said dryly as the comm screen activated, there was Lilly looking very pleased with herself.

"There you are, and you have your rather charming GalGorp rebel with you," she said while playfully running her tongue over her lips "I have some useful information for you, the SS RenenetI will be docking here in a day or so before it continues on its supply run.. to the SS Ramesses" Matt looked confused.

"Are you sure that's a GalCorp ship? they only use one of their frigates to resupply out here, usually the SS Seti, I remember reading up on it, apparently they deem it too dangerous to send unarmed cargo ships this far out." he said as Lilly gave a sarcastic slow clap.

"Well done, you are an intelligent boy as well as attractive, very good and of course the SS Ramesses has already been resupplied recently but judging by the manifest, which by the way I am sending you a copy as we speak." Matt went to look at it, various missiles, countermeasures, burst torpedoes.. as he read on it was clear this was to supply a small army or a pirate group.

"You don't think..." Matt started "this is for the

Silver Blades? they wouldn't be so blatant about it surely?" Lilly just laughed and waved her finger at him like she was telling him off.

"Now, now, my little GalCorp runaway of course not, however if, say it was hijacked before it got to the SS Ramesses, what would be just.. one of those things, right?" Matt finally understood, Lilly continued "Now I'm sure you would be very interested in its ultimate destination and get rid of at least one enemy, as for me, one less pirate gang means that the area is a little safer and as such more people travelling through this lovely station."

"Can you put a tracer on the.." Matt started to say.

"...No, I'm just a messenger, I'm totally neutral, shame on you! however if you should come to the bar, ask for Cobalt" she said with a knowing wink and suddenly ended the transmission, Matt looked at Andrew intently.

"We need to get a tracker on that ship, we can't waste this opportunity." he said pleadingly, Andrew motioned for him to calm down.

"I have a plan," he said "lets gather the Ronin together, we have a mission to organise."

The pilots briefing room was soon busy with the pilots filing in, Matt explained the situation and the plan to place a tracker on the cargo ship.

"A tracker program should be easy to construct," said Gareth "could rig it to sit in the ships databanks dormant until activated by a signal we send, the Silver Blades won't know its there." but Nathan shook his head.

"What if they simply empty the cargo holds?" he asked.

"They won't, it would take too long and they would be sitting ducks to attack from us or other pirate gangs like the Screaming Skulls, no they will take it to their base and empty it there and either refit the cargo ship for their own fleet or destroy it but they won't simply leave it." Red said knowingly.

"I'm sure we could stage a token attempt at attack so they get spooked and fly off with it." said Rob thoughtfully.

"Only one problem though," said Phil "while the Hubs patrons probably won't notice or care, you can bet the GalCorp crew will be told who we are." he said gesturing to himself, Gareth, Matt Rob and Andrew "So can't be any of us" Andrew was already way ahead of him.

"I know that why I have came up with a small team to do this mission, if they accept of course," he turned to Red "You know the Hub better than anyone, any mission there could benefit from your knowledge," she looked surprised but accepted a spot on the team, he then turned to Craig "After G, you are the best technical minded person in the group, I get the feeling that will come in handy," Craig just grinned, Andrew paced up and down, "as it is a small team on a dangerous mission, I feel there are only two others I could trust who aren't known to GalCorp, Marcus, you know the area better than most so can pass as local trader and Tamika, we need your maturity and experience to lead the group plus you would just be seen as just another mercenary." Marcus looked at her as if he was going to protest and state he was a Ronin long before her but Tamika's cold stare silenced any complaint before he had a chance.

"what's our timeframe?" she asked, Andrew told her the ship was due to dock in the next day.

Marcus shrugged "Most ships stay at least another day or two just to allow the crew to.. enjoy the facilities, also who the hell is this Cobalt we have to ask for?" Andrew thought a while then answered.

"If I were to assume, I'd say it was an operative of sorts who may be of help, but its Lilly so who knows?" he said with a sigh "as for transport, that old shuttle Kate flew here has been repaired by Tony and the ships engineering team, they figured another shuttle could be useful and as its not associated with us it won't raise suspicion, you have twelve hours to prepare, dismissed." as they filed out Andrew glanced at Matt who looked deep in thought.

"I sure hope this plan works." Matt said before walking out, his mind racing.

The Chapel in the SS Hades was quiet as usual, Sister Theresa was praying quietly when Andrew walked in and sat next to her.

"Troubled Mister Douglas?" she said serenely without turning to look, Andrew sighed and looked up.

"It's this upcoming mission," Andrew said wearily "I Just hope everything works out I guess, I trust you'll keep an eye out on the others. especially Matt, If this mission is successful it is the first step in clearing his name." he then looked around the chapel, it was amazing what she did to the empty room, a few rows of seats, simulation candles and a simple crucifix, a few lengths of material draped around distracted people from the bareness of the walls, just the day before Rob helped build a small alter at the front.

"I always do, its why I came here and joined this crew." she said as Andrew stood up but its what she saw beyond him that made her smile.

"What?" he said then looked round, a few seats down all on his own, sitting perfectly still looking up at the crucifix as if in prayer was the one person no-one expected, Nakamura, the ships cat "Well it has to succeed now, disappoint Nakamura and you upset Tessa and I don't think even God wants to do that." They both laughed to the cats bewilderment

CHAPTER 34

Twelve hours later they were in the hanger bay making the final preparations for the mission.

"All you need to do is insert the docking pins into any access point on the ship, wait for the light to turn green and that should be the program in place," said Gareth as he handed Craig the datastick, "hopefully you won't need to adjust things on the fly but I trust you will know what to do if you have to." Craig shook his hand and climbed aboard the shuttle, all four were dressed casual as to blend in, Marcus wore the clothes he first joined the Ronin in, Tamika wore a black top and a camouflage outfit in greys and oranges Craig wore his fathers flight jacket and gymwear from the ships stores in dark grey, Red was given some clothes by Kate in the form of her spare boots, which thankfully didn't have as big a platform as the ones Kate flew in and a many pocketed sleeveless jumpsuit. Ellen donated something to Red for her to wear, synthetic leather flight jacket she had that was black with trim in red and yellow with five red stars down the sleeves, as Ellen told her it was a gift from a friend that she was too polite to say she didn't like it and Suzanne had refused to take it off her several times. Red wasn't bothered and put it on eagerly and saw it as a sign that the Sisters had finally accepted her into the group.

"It suits you more than it ever did my sister." Said Suzanne to Red as she made her way to the hanger, Tamika was standing on the ramp way of the shuttle ushering her in, Marcus had been nominated as pilot.

"Control this is.. erm.. Shuttle Tracker One.. hey!" Tamika swatted his head "Permission to take off" he glared at Tamika.

"Permission granted Tracker One, good luck." said Liana over the comms, Marcus eased the shuttle off the deck and out the hanger.

"Tracker One?" really?" Tamika said pointedly.

"Hey," Marcus countered "its all I could come up with."

Matt and Andrew watched from the bridge as the shuttle went to lightspeed, John stepped closer to them.

"Now all you gotta do is wait," John shrugged "Personally I think it could work but then again, I'm not the one having to do the hard part."

"I'd be there in that shuttle with them if I could."

said Matt softly.

"I know," said Andrew, "You'd be first into every situation, unfortunately this is one of those times you will need to do something I think may be very difficult, just trust them to do the job." Matt nodded with a sigh and just stared out at the stars.

It was business as usual in the chaotic atmosphere in the Hub, the Lilly Pad was doing great business as usual. Mercenaries, cargo ships crews, everyone came to to the infamous bar for downtime.

"I never liked this place," said Tamika wrinkling her nose in disgust "too many distractions and drinks diluted and not to mention the stench." the four of them were seated at a booth in the bar.

"Well there's the GalCorp crew over there and that looks like the pilot escorts over near the bar itself," Red noted "So, who is going to ask at the bar for Cobalt?" Red, Tamika and Craig all looked at Marcus, he opened his mouth to protest but thought better of it so he slid out the booth and made his way to the busy bar and tried to get the attention of one of the barstaff.

"excuse me," he shouted above the noise "I'm looking for a.. Cobalt?" the lady behind the bar rolled her eyes and gestured he follow her to a private room on the upper deck, the room was dark and apparently soundproofed, he felt the muzzle of a pistol on his back.

"Try and be discreet next time moron, shouting my codename in the middle of the bar wasn't a smart move, turn around with your hands in the air." he did as she said and when he saw her he remembered, it was the woman behind the bar who, when he was being recruited by The Ronin was very icy with Andrew, her petite athletic body and poker straight brunette hair framed piercing blue eyes.

"Why Cobalt?" he asked and she put the gun under his jaw.

"My eyes.. idiot" she said menacingly "okay? Any more stupid questions? I have a score to settle with the Silver Blades, more than anyone else, Lilly knows, I have to be on this mission and I don't want someone like you messing this up.."

"We all have issues with the Silver Blades what's makes you so different?" Marcus demanded, fed up of her attitude "family die? business destroyed, colony harassed, guess what? join the club," he said not caring about her weapon "Just shoot me and get on with it." she looked at him sternly then lowered her weapon

"My name is Elaine Longton. two years ago, the Silver Blades captured my ship Remus Fox personally executed my husband as I watched helplessly. If I hadn't broke free and jumped in an escape pod.. well you can imagine what might have happened." Marcus put his hands up in an attempt to calm things down.

"Okay, I can imagine, I don't want to but I am, why did Lilly ask us to meet with you anyway?" he said calmly while slowly sitting at the table in the centre of the room, for once her cold expression melted.

"She knows I want to help you but that I am not a

pilot, this mission is a chance for me to do something, also," she said with a small smile "I have the access codes for the cargo vessel, meet me at cargo bay five in two hours and bring your friends." She then shot out the small lamp that was the only light in the room, by the time Marcus opened the door she had left.

Later in cargo bay five the pilots and Elaine met up, Elaine had a datapad with all the codes they would need and Craig had already started to add the details to his own pad and to the tracker program.

"So, what's the plan? I assume you have one?" she said pointedly as she looked them all over, Tamika stepped forward and gave her a stern look of her own.

"We haven't ironed out all the details but it is best to wait until tomorrow. then Red here will take Craig as close to the ship as possible using the various conduits and ducts, the problem is it will no doubt be guarded so we need a distraction and what to do once he's ready to leave." Elaine nodded then tossed a bag she had carrying at Craig, it contained a GalCorp uniform.

"You'll need this, as for the rest of the plan I have an idea," she gave a predatory smile at Marcus "but you won't like it."

The shuttle they travelled in was secured in cargo bay five and as they had discovered that it was actually an old converted medical shuttle and had four simple bunks that consisted of frames and some webbing with a thin mattress. Tamika made the executive decision that they would sleep there that night as not to get too distracted by the sights of the station and had sent Red and Craig out to get some supplies for the night.

"We have enough bitcreds to get a decent room on the station." Marcus mentioned for about the tenth time.

"And as I keep saying, Apart from the obvious point of us not leaving much of a trace of ourselves on the station, there are too many distractions. I don't want anyone getting drunk before the mission." Tamika replied with the patience of a parent trying to explain to a child but knowing she may need to say it all over again. Marcus slumped on his bunk as Red and Craig returned.

"We managed to get some simple bedding and rations" said Red as Craig dumped the bags down.

"Are you sure we can't.."Craig started to say.

"..No, Marcus has already asked.. several times," Tamika snapped at Craig then shook her head "It's like working with children at times it really is." she said as Red made up the bunk she had chosen, the bottom one under Tamika and quickly lay on top it.

"There were some GalCorp people around," she said absently "They have no clue that this is all a set up."

"Yeah," Craig agreed "One guy was telling Red that he believes if they do well, the RenenetI may be asked to do more supply runs out here... "

"..the guy was delusional, his friend wasn't much better, he was one of the pilots. He said his callsign was...Bunnyman or something. He said that he hoped to engage some pirates in this run" Red added and shook her head as she propped herself on her side to see the others sort out their bunks.

"How's your leg healing?" Marcus asked her

"Oh" she looked surprised "To be honest I think your Nun did a really good job. I almost totally forgot about it" she flexed her leg to demonstrate. The ration packs were not the most appealing to the palette."

"I wish we had some beers" Marcus said mournfully "to take the horrible taste out my mouth" but he was silenced by a harsh look from Tamika who stood and leapt up elegantly to her bunk.

"Lights out, we have an important mission tomorrow and I want everyone rested."

"yes mother." Marcus said in a way that caused Craig to giggle involuntarily, he tried to hide his face in his hands but was only partialy successful in stifling the laugh. Tamika just shot them a disapproving look and lay down facing away from them.

Marcus woke up and found himself on the floor, looking around confused he heard a voice from the cockpit area.

"You rolled out of your bunk" he looked around to to see Red sitting on the pilots seat, he got up and went to the copilots seat.

"Can't sleep?" he asked and noticed she had a bottle in her hand, Red reached down to the floor and opened a small compartment where there was another bottle, she took it out and handed it to Marcus.

"One of Alan's cider bottles?" he asked and she nodded "What's wrong?" Red took drink out of her bottle and sighed.

"Being here, it just brought back some bad memories," she wiped a tear from her eye "even after I became a Bloodfist I hated coming back here. I just can't relax until we are far away from this place."

"I can understand that, some of the things you told me.." Marcus said as he opened his bottle and took a deep drink from it "... I can understand why comeone back here would not be a happy moment for you but the fact you did come back says a lot about your character and it means a lot to me..us.. the ..Ronin I mean" Marcus started to fluster which made Red laugh as she drained off the rest of her bottle.

"Thanks, I appreciate it I really do, I suppose we better get back to bed before Mother..." he gestured to Tamika who was sound asleep snoring in her bunk "...wakes up and catches us." she said and headed to the back, followed by Marcus who finished his bottle in one go

"Night Red" he whispered as he put his bedding back in the bunk.

"Night Marcus" she whispered back.

he

CHAPTER 35

It was afternoon the next day before the plan was put into action, Red had found a suitable access point for the air conditioning ducts and her and Craig made their way to the bay that that had the docking port which housed the SS RenenetI.

"You grew up in all this?" said Craig as he and Red crawled through the ducts, she just looked over her shoulder and smiled, noting his discomfort and picking up her pace, it had been a long time they had been crawling around for, they had reached the hanger bay that the GalCorp ships shuttles and cargo were kept, there were guards jut walking around the bay and some ships crew prepping stuff for the shuttles.

"Well here we are, the SS RenenetI, looks bigger than it did from when we saw it in the shuttle." she said as she looked at his datapad that showed a schematic,

Craig shrugged.

"Matt did mention these things take supplies all over the colonies to GalCorp colonies and ships plus there is a certain amount of ego, look at the SS Ramesses, big for a ship of its firepower and purpose, similar strength Hexstar and Earth military ships are more compact, they go for style over practicality," he said tugging on his GalCorp uniform "Man this itches." suddenly they saw Marcus and Tamika walk up to the guards.

The guards stepped forward to ask the two pilots for clearance when Tamika suddenly hit Marcus on the shoulder.

"You idiot, I told you this was the wrong bay." she said with disgust and anger, Marcus just looked surprised for a minute, mainly as the force to which she hit him and shouted back.

"Hey its not my fault, you picked that company, you said they deliver on time and where you want it to go..." he didn't finish as she hit his arm again, the guards looked confused, one lowered his weapon and raised a hand to intervene.

"What seems to be the problem?" he asked as cordially as he could, only to get glared at by Tamika.

"No-one asked you to interfere," he snapped and she drew out her sidearm, pointing it at Marcus "I've had it with you.." the guards moved to restrain them as they continued to hurl fake insults (and at least on Marcus's end some real) that no-one noticed the Galcorp shuttle gained an extra crewman as it lifted off for the ship, the guards frustratedly escorted the two out of the bay.

The interior of the SS RenenetI was quiet as most of the crew were on the station so Craig was able to move quite freely, though he procured a cap on the shuttle and wore it in an effort to further hide his identity. Luckily he managed to find an unmanned terminal in one of the unassigned crew quarters, thanks to the codes given to him by Elaine accessing the ships main computer from such a low level terminal was made easy. Once the program copied itself into the main core, Craig made sure the door was closed and settled himself in one of the bunks and tried to act natural. His plan was to pretend to be asleep if anyone came to the door, it wasn't the most foolproof idea but he didn't know how long the program would take.

"Let me go!" Shouted Tamika as she struggled from the grip of the two GalCorp guards holding her.

"Sorry Ma'am" one of them said with restrained politeness "we can't let you fire a weapon like that."

"Sensitive cargo" the other grunted. The other guards holding Marcus back weren't having much more joy.

"Oh, you hear that guys? See, I have witnesses this time," he turned to one of the guards "See what I have to put up with?" he turned back to face her "Just wait until the lawyers hear about this" he switched back to talking to the guard "been trying to divorce her for years, wouldn't you say death threats were grounds for it?"

"Sure buddy" said the guard who was completely disinterested in the petty squabble and just wanting the whole thing over and done with. This back and fourth between them went on until an officer showed up.

"What is going on here?" he demanded, taking off his cap and running his hand through what was left of his dark hair. The guard who was standing in between the fighting couple spoke up.

"Well sir, these two civilians entered the cargo bay and are apparently lost.."

"… Apparently, what the hell is that supposed to mean?.." interjected Tamika angrily., the guard ignored her and kept going.

"… an argument between them has gotten out of control." The officer looked at the warring couple carefully for a few seconds.

"I am Lieutenant Commander Renfrew and while it is regretful to see such a.. wonderful couple.. fight, unfortunately we have rues and regulations to follow and we can not allow unauthorised personnel in this cargo bay..."

"...She started it..." Marcus started but was stopped by the officers raised hand.

"Please, You could continue your discussion in another part of this station or you can test our brig, it has been a while since we had to use it and this would be a fine opportunity.."

"Okay..okay" said Tamika, feigning compliance "Come on, we will try the next cargo bay, that guy in the hall didn't give the best directions" she winked at Marcus indicating for him to just go with it"

"yeah," he sighed "sorry guys" the guards looked at the officer who nodded to them and Tamika and Marcus were let go.

"Wise choice" the officer said with a tone of false pleasantness as he watched them leave.

They waited until they were down the hall and round a corner before relaxing.

"I hope Craig is okay" Marcus said then looked intent at Tamika "You wouldn't have really shot me would you?"

"I would have to maintain the pretence" she said matter of factly "Don't worry, I would have only wounded you ans from what I hear Sister Theresa is a fine doctor as well as a woman of God" Marcus was about to say something when an air.vent panel was kicked out of its housing.

"What the.." Marcus started then he saw Red leap out "..Don't do that! Give me warning next time." he said, clutching his chest dramaticly. Tamika was too busy laughing to offer comment, Red waited then reported.

"Craig managed to get onboard okay, he was a

little nervous but he should be fine. What now?"

"The only thing we can do," Tamika said "go back to cargo bay five and wait." and she walked down the corridor with Marcus and Red following but walking at a more casual pace.

"Do you think he will be okay?" Red asked curiously.

"Yeah," replied Marcus "He is a tough kid, what do you know about him?"

"Not much, only that his dad was a pilot for the Hexstar forces and what happened to him after the war but to be honest haven't really had a chance to talk to him properly." Red admitted with a shrug. Tamika came back around the corner.

"Come on, will you two hurry up?" she said in an exasperated tone.

"Yes Mother." Marcus quipped and winked at Red who just laughed, Tamika just put her hand on he pistol.

"The guards aren't here to save you this time." she said with menace.

"Okay okay we are coming." he relented.

"What was that all about?" Red whispered.

"Will tell you later" he replied and they followed Tamika, with a bit more urgency in their step.

After what seemed like an eternity a little green light flashed, it was done,. Now all he needed to do was get out, he got up, straightened the uniform and exited the room.

"Hey, were you going?" said a voice, he spun around ready to attack even though he left his weapon with Red only to see Elaine dressed in a manner he could only describe as seductive "Don't stare kid, this is your way out."

"How?" he said puzzled.

"Well I came onboard shortly before you as I figured you may need extra help. I convinced a junior officer to take me to see the ship, unfortunately.. for him anyway.. he's so drunk, he's sleeping it off in his quarters.", they made their way to the airlock, Elaine acting like some trophy girlfriend to Craig, just then a tech stopped him..

"You got clearance to board the shuttle for the station?" he said gruffly, Craig handed the appropriate access codes but the tech stared at him intently "I don't recall seeing you before?"

"Oh," said Craig thinking on his feet "erm.. I was brought in for this supply run, didn't Lieutenant what's his face with the dark hair.."

"you mean Lieutenant Hanson? " the tech said rolling his eyes "Not again..." Elaine leaned over and smiled seductively.

"Now now, I don't think anyone needs to know, he is just taking me back to the station, he won't be long, no need to log it in is there?" she said pressing a few bitcreds in his hand, he looked flustered only saying.

"Sure ma'am no reason at all, hope you enjoyed

your time here." he said as they walked past through the airlock and into the station cargo bay.

It was easier to get past the guards, Elaine just pretended to be intimate with Craig as they walked out the hanger and made their way to cargo bay five.

"Its done, we did it." Craig announced a little louder than Elaine liked judging by her facial expression but he didn't care, the plan worked, the others congratulated Craig on doing a great job though Red teased him that he still had a smell about him from the ducts.

"That was the easy part," Tamika said with a smirk "The hard part is still to come," she then stood up "Time to go, the sooner the others know the better."

Marcus guided the shuttle in the SS Hades hanger as it orbited Astra Sanctuarium, The colony was the best place to rendevouz as it was the closest to the Hub. both Andrew and Matt were waiting for them when they landed.

"Well we did It" said Marcus to Andrew "thanks to help from that weird woman behind the bar who didn't like you." Craig shook his head.

"Marcus! she's not weird and besides she helped us a lot with access codes and stuff." he then went on to detail everything that happened though he noticeably blushed when talking about his Elaine pretended to be his date when they were getting off the ship.

"So all we need to do is wait I guess," Matt said. Red Marcus and Craig left, probably for a hot shower and change, Tamika stayed behind to talk to Matt and Andrew.

"they did a good job, you'd be proud of them.. even Marcus." she said with a sly smile.

CHAPTER 36

Over the next day they stayed in orbit, getting supplies and allowing some crew and pilots to visit the planet, Rob especially was interested as he hadn't been down the first time, still no word on the SS RenenetI and Matt was increasingly looking nervous and wondering had the effort been for nothing.

"We really should have heard something by now surely." he wondered out loud, Red, who was walking past shrugged.

"Don't count on it." she said knowingly "No pirate clan ever attacks ships in the same system as the Hub, its considered neutral ground and some tend not to even go after ships in the immediate surrounding area, think on it." she was making sense, all attacks seem to happen away from the Hub.

"Never thought of it like that." he admitted and

Red walked away with a smile.

"I knew she'd be useful," said a voice from behind, Matt turned around to see Rob who was just back from the surface "Get some rest and stop worrying, it will all work out, it always does," she smiled optimisticly "come, lets join the guys in the mess hall." Matt nodded and followed Rob to the mess hall.

It was late into the night when a distress call from the SS RenenetI , or rather one of the escort pilots, Liana played the recording to Andrew and Matt as they sat in their fighters awaiting launch, it was deemed that only Andrew, Marcus, Matt, Gareth, Nicolae, Craig, Phil and Rob would fly out, they were only to spook them not actually defeat them.

"This is GalCorp pilot Uno to any ships in the area, we need assistance.. dammit the weapons won't fire... what the.." then it was static.

"White Knight, this is Semjasa, they didn't just send those guys out in sabotaged ships did they?" Phil didn't get a response, not that one was needed, they could see from the hanger entrance the SS Hades had exited lightspeed and had started firing, Andrew had told John to stay at just beyond maximum range and fire, they got the all clear to launch, and didn't need telling twice, they were just in time to see the SS Foxblade jump out the system, the remaining pirate fighters adopting a defensive posture over the cargo vessel.

"Firehawk, this is White Knight, lets make this

look good" Matt said as he uncharacteristicly opened fire wildly on the nearest fighter, Gareth followed suit, another fighter blew up to Andrews other side, Nicolae had cut one down. he noted that no-one made an effort to attack the SS RenenetI, good. suddenly the cargo vessel jumped to lightspeed and the fighters decided to run too, but Andrew cut two down before they got a chance to jump.

"White Knight this is Firehawk, lets hope this works." the GalCorp fighters were floating dead in space, suddenly they heard an announcement on the comms.

"White Knight, this is Pollock we got a live one in this ship"

They brought in the lone surviving fighter and helped the stricken pilot, as Sister Theresa examined him Matt checked his uniform for any identification.

"Seems like we have one Elijah Maxwell, callsign Duo," he then looked closer at the card and shrugged "It says that his piloting certificate is under review, Andrew he shouldn't have been out there." Andrew shook his head as he looked on, Craig and Gareth came in.

"Well," said Garth, "we have examined his fighter and it seems all the weapons relays were non functional and I don't mean damaged, they were actually marked as defective on the casing, they didn't want these guys getting lucky and actually scaring the Silver Blades off, there was also another worrying thing, we had to disable an automatic self destruct activated the minute they left the hanger."

"From the information we can get from the ships computer the other pilots were Noah Maxwell, callsign Uno. Dan Torvill, callsign Bunnyman and Jonathon Dexter callsign Fallingstar. none of them made it." Andrew walked up to Sister Theresa concerned.

"How is he?" he said hoping for good news.

"Its hard to say. He has been deprived of oxygen, burns all over his left side of his body ribs broken, cracks in his spine, I can do all I can but he needs rest, I have gave hom a powerful sedative."

"He was a like a lamb being lead to the slaughter Sister, it was horrible," Andrew said looking at the stricken pilot "Tell us if his condition changes." she nodded and the pilots left.

"GalCorp really don't value their own employees much do they?" Andrew quipped. Matt found it hard to disagree.

Captain Miller couldn't believe the report.

"Gladstone actually sent them out there with no working weapons? just to appease Remus Fox?" he stared at the report of the SS RenenetI situation, Cairns looked as shocked "The time is coming where we may need to take control of things ourselves."

"Sir?" Cairns said slightly confused, he knew Miller was unhappy but surely he wasn't talking about what he thought he was talking about? "I know you have been unhappy with things, none of us are? but what are we going to do? its not like we can go rogue ourselves?" Miller didn't answer, he just walked off the bridge to his when he bumped into Corbin

"Ah, just the man, I have a proposal for you, if you are interested of course?" he said, opening the office door and beaconing him in "I call it Operation Corsair" Corbin smiled slyly.

"After you sir." and they both stepped inside and locked the door.

"So," Miller started, "Here's what I think we should do.."

The ground attack group, who were now stepping up training were in the main armoury getting weapons prepared for when the time came, they had decided to use some old combat fatigues found in the ships stores with the body armour. Phil, Rob and Tamika were already there getting ready when Remy and Gareth came in with a crate containing more equipment including Helmets, gloves, flashlights and backpacks plus some other extras.

"Phil? Nathan? did I hear right you both have some first aid experience?" said Remy curiously as he prepared for training, Phil acknowledged he had training in it back when he was in law enforcement and Nathan in the academy, apparently it was mandatory for all ground support pilots, Remy then handed them medical backpacks "Just in case." he said nonchalantly, Kate who realised that not only was she just there to be co-pilot and was not really experienced sighed as she sat on one of the benches.

"Guys," she said in a bored tone "I think the stuff works, is there any need to do this check every day?" Phil rolled his eyes and stepped forward.

"Kate, trust me you don't want to go over there with..what the.." suddenly from the crate near him jumped Nakamura, the ships cat staring at Phil "okay, Kate, if you want something else to do.. take that stupid animal to its owner.. please," Kate grinned and scooped the cat up leaving quickly "I hate that thing." Phil said as they left.

The peace in Matt's quarters was disturbed by knocking on the door, Andrew was standing there with a look of concern on his face.

"What is it," Matt asked "Is the Tracker not working?" Andrew came in and sat down.

"No, Liana is sending out the message now, we should have a hit soon, I'm just worried we jump in at a time where the SS Foxblade is still there, we know it goes out regular, I only hope we attack when its not there." he sighed.

"Even if its not, we'd be working against the clock to get things done before it comes back, though it just means we drill everyone harder, hows flight group handling things on their end?" Andrew stood up and paced.

"Well the Sommers have calmed down which has helped," he stated "Red and Alan are actually developing to be a good team, I think Red gives him more room to have fun which Tamika didn't, Marcus and Nicolae are helping Craig with extra flight lessons too, he won't admit it but I think he's the most nervous of us all. He sees it as his big chance." Matt nodded in agreement and replied.

"Such pressure can cripple a man if he's not careful, keep an eye on it," he sighed as if bracing himself for the next topic "I've been thinking of the best way to get the data to the authorities, as it seems GalCorp has made sure we will be seen as criminals and would surely be shot down before we got a chance to send anything and transmitting it from here would be risky as we don't know if they'd monitor relays and then theres' the issue of who to send it to." Andrew looked as if he was thinking the same.

"I see what you mean," he said carefully "We can't be totally certain that GalCorp haven't thought about this and have people in place."

"Won't Phil still have connections in law enforcement?" Matt said hopefully but Andrew shook his head.

"I thought about that too but Phil told me he lost all contact with most of his old colleagues, the ones he does know who are still there he can trust as far as he can throw them... lets be honest what we need is a miracle.. wait, of course" he said suddenly smiling "Cardinal Otani, he could get the information to Earth,

Astra Sanctuarium has a powerful transmitter used for communication with the Vatican. The law enforcement there could pass it on to the appropriate authorities."

"What?" said Matt looking unconvinced "The Swiss Guard?"

"No" countered Andrew "they are the Popes bodyguard, I'm talking about the Gendarmerie Corps of Vatican City, also with Astra Sanctuarium being in frequent touch with Earth its not going to seem too unusual" Matt nodded, it made sense when Andrew put it that way.

"I'll ask Sister Theresa if she can arrange something." Matt said heading for the door followed by Andrew, Liana ran up excitedly.

"I didn't just want to announce this over the comms but we have a hit, we found them." Matt and Andrew looked at each other , Matt had a sly smile.

"Call a pilot meeting, lets do this."

"Our target location, the old abandoned Starcore mining station in the Hyams system" said Andrew to the assembled pilots in the briefing room "Apparently it was assumed deserted ever since Starcore mined the area dry years ago" the fact it was a remote station helped of course as the Hyams system was well out of the way of the more well travelled routes, Matt stood forward.

"As we speak the SS Hades is heading to the system at lightspeed, we should be there in the next forty five minutes" He then paced the floor "First Fighter group, commanded by Andrew will take care of any fighters and other defences, when there is a clear path to the station Ground Attack Group will fly in by attack shuttle and find a way to gain access and copy the information we need to stop GalCorp, any questions?" Nathan put his hand up.

"What about the SS Foxblade?" others nodded in agreement, John, who was waiting at the doorway spoke up.

"Well in the case the SS Hades will just have to distract her, we should have more than enough firepower to do the job, don't worry about us." he smiled and walked out the room, Andrew dismissed everyone to prepare for the mission ahead.

The quietness of the medical bay was driving Elijah crazy, Sister Theresa had explained his situation and filled him in on not just the Ronin's true missions as opposed to the GalCorp propaganda and what happened with his own mission, we was feeling well enough to sit up on his sickbed, Matt walked in, his combat gear on and his carbine in one hand.

"I take it our resident nun has filled you in on everything so far then? she likes to talk, I'm Matt Easton, I'm sure you have heard of me." he gave a slight smile, Elijah nodded in agreement.

"Yeah," he said "Though if it wasn't for your rescue and hospitality I wouldn't have believed a word she said, GalCorp have everyone convinced you are some mad killer and you are all just a new pirate group but what kind of person sends their own people out the way they did, we had no weapons to fight back," he looked down "I watched on as they turned my brothers ship into shrapnel, you guys are really trying to get evidence that they are working with the Silver Blades, if you find evidence of what they did to us too I'd be grateful, take them down," he calmed down a little and looked down "I talked my brother into this, he wanted us to join the military but i convinced him GalCorp would be better, more pay and prospects but after a few months training he was worried we would be washed out until we were asked to do this.. special mission.. succeed and we could get a posting on the Amenhotep, it wasn't the SS Ramesses but we'd be fully contracted and paid pilots of GalCorp security living the dream.. now he's dead."

"Its not your fault, GalCorp did this" said Matt "I joined thinking I'd be helping people, all they wanted was a killer." Elijah looked at Matt and nodded slowly.

"Sounds like we both signed up for the wrong company," he smiled slightly "Your doctor, for a nun knows her stuff. The leg is healing okay, arm too, its the ribs and the burns that seem to be the problem." Matt smiled at him and reassured him things will be okay before leaving to prepare for the mission.

If there was any nerves amongst the fighter group it wasn't showing in the locker room, Alan took out a bottle of his family's pear cider from his locker and put it in his flightsuit thigh pocket.

"What the... Alan!, aren't you worried that thing will break?" said Marcus who was lying on one of the benches in the middle.

"First, the bottle is a special plastic designed not to warp or break" Alan said matter of factly with a smile "and its a tradition I have. After a mission, I crack one open before I get out my ship, can't mess with tradition can you?" he closed his locker door and picked his helmet up but Nicolae looked a little confused and asked.

"You have flew only a couple of missions with us and didn't you say you were only starting out as a fighter pilot before you joined?" he said in his usual deadpan way.

"So? No tradition like a new tradition," Alan countered with a shrug, Craig let off an involuntary snigger and turned away before letting out a loud laugh although Suzanne and Ellen did not look impressed at all and headed to the hanger shaking their heads, Red just smiled at her wingman.

"Alan you are crazy, you do now that?" she said as he nodded before heading to the hanger herself, he just grinned and looked at the others.

"You do realise she spent many years with bloodthirsty pirates and maniacs and she thinks you are crazy? I'd be worried." Craig said only half seriously, Alan just shrugged and followed Red out to the hanger.

Ground Assault team were all in body armor and with

the exception of Nathan and Kate who were wearing their flightsuits under it, the others had battle fatigues. Tamika cradling her rifle like a child. Phil grumbled.

"I would rather be in my fighter," he said with a sigh.

"Yeah, but unfortunately for you, there is very few others here who have better marksmanship." Rob reasoned as he adjusted the sights on his weapon

"Don't remind me" Phil said as he watched the flight group assemble to their left as Matt and Andrew walked up to them with John just behind.

"Okay," said Andrew as loud as he could "soon we will be at what we can only assume is the home base for the Silver Blades, we all know our assignments, Flight group will launch first and blaze a trail for ground assault and ensure they can fly back safe." he stepped back to let Matt say a few words.

"Guys, we have been preparing for this but as we know not everything will go to plan," he started as he paced up and down "this is our most complex and dangerous mission yet, all I an say is, stay safe, we can do this, just trust your team mates and we can get through this, John has told us if the SS Foxblade is here, he will try and draw it away from the base, if on the off chance its not.." John stepped forward to continue.

"We try and keep them at bay until you get out, if you are unable to land, just make your way to Astra Sanctuarium at best speed, its on the maximum range of the fighters lightdrives. We will rendezvous there."

"So if there's no questions..." Andrew added

"Good luck out there an hopefully we will all be celebrating at the end of all this." a cheer went up as the flight group headed to their fighters and ground assault to the shuttle, Andrew turned to Matt and shook his hand.

"Good luck." he said, Matt unexpectedly pulled him in for a hug, when he released the hug he simply said.

"Good luck to you too." and hurried to join the rest of his group, Marcus grumbled about the prospect of a long lightspeed flight in a fighter but Alan, grinning reminded him.

"It won't be so bad, for me anyway, I'll be enjoying a nice cool refreshing Pear Cider on the long journey." and he patted the pocket with the bottle in it and laughed, Marcus stared at Red who just shrugged.

"He's my wingman, not my child." she shouted back as she climbed into her fighter, it was good to see such high spirits Andrew thought to himself as he put his helmet on.

CHAPTER 37

To everyone's surprise when the SS Hades exited lightspeed the SS Foxblade was not there, flight group launched quickly.

"Flight group this is Firehawk, we don't know how long we have until the ship comes back, so lets see what we can do, Ground assault, launch after we engage the enemy we have to take advantage of this" the Silver Blades fighters from the base scrambled into action, Suzanne and Ellen held back slightly in accordance with the plan, Andrew needed them to escort the shuttle, it seemed that most of the fighting force had went with the SS Foxblade but it didn't matter to the Ronin Pilots, Andrew took down the closest pirate fighter quickly as he and Marcus swung round to find another target, Red had already took two out herself.

"Firehawk, the is Nate Dawg, ground assault are

inbound, escort fighters holding position" Darrren looked to see the assault shuttle flanked by Suzanne and Ellen.

"Brutus, this is Firehawk, lets blaze a trail for them shall we?"

It felt strange to Matt just watching a battle as a spectator but that's how he felt, the small viewports on the side doors gave everyone inside small glimpses of the action.

"Wow, that was close," said Nathan as he expected a sudden tight manoeuvrer "Who was that anyway? Marcus? Alan?"

"Neither, looks like Nicolae, its obvious as he always tilts his ship to one side before heading the other way" answered Rob, Kate looked back from the co-pilots seat and rolled her eyes unimpressed, everyone in the passenger area was doing some final checks of their weapons. Matt notices Rob had entwined rosary beads around the loop for shoulder straps of his carbine, Gareth was checking his tech equipment just as they heard the shuttle fire its own weapons.

"its okay, we have set the weapons to autofire on any nearby ships with hostile transponder ID." shouted back Kate, Matt noted how easy it was to spot the individual pilots flying styles, Nicolae's aforementioned quirk when turning, the sisters had a very distinctly deliberate style of being aggressive yet focused. Craig reminded him of the many Hexstar pilots he went up against, likewise Red had a seemingly reckless style reminiscent of most pirates. Alan was very textbook in his flying but shooting was more erratic. Marcus and Andrew were their usual crazy selves, All in all they were doing a great job of keeping the pirates at bay, another ship exploded and it looked like Suzanne who got the kill.

"You want to be out there with them don't you?" said Tamika smiling knowingly "in your heart of hearts you are a pilot, its only natural." Matt nodded.

"Of course, even n the heat of battle I always feel oddly at peace with myself." he said.

"Suzanne this is Nate Dawg, You want to do what?" said Nathan with an edge of panic, Matt made his way to the cockpit.

"What's the situation here?" he ordered, Kate turned around.

"Oh Suzanne wants to fly ahead into the hanger and.. secure it," she said "she urges us not to worry as Ellen will still be escorting us in," sarcasm evident in the young pilots voice, suddenly Suzanne's ship activated its afterburners and flew straight for the landing bat of the asteroid base "I'd suggest everyone get ready," added Kate "we are nearly there." Matt came back and passed on the news and when he returned to the cockpit all he could see in the looming hanger was weapons fire and explosions followed by Suzanne's fighter flying out unscathed.

"Well, Suzanne has just told us the hanger is clear... apparently." said Nathan as he flew in, they saw what she meant. A fighters weapons are designed to penetrate other ships armour and until then none of the shuttles inhabitants had ever wondered nor saw what happens if one such weapon discharge hit an un-armoured human body at close range.

"I think I'm going to be sick." uttered Kate, Matt went back and addressed the others.

"We are about to land so you know the drill, we disembark and find the nearest terminal, find out where the computer core is and extract the data we need and get out hopefully before the SS Foxblade shows up, okay?" a chorus of affirmatives went up, there was a slight shudder as they landed and the doors at either side opened, it was game time.

Andrew saw the shuttle fly into the landing bay

"Suzanne, Ellen, this is Firehawk, keep the area around the landing bay clear, we don't want any uninvited guests." he ordered, where were most of the Silver Blades anyway? he thought as he shredded the cockpit of a pirate fighter that was pursuing Alan.

The SS Foxblade fired a few more shots into the stricken cargo vessel, the convoy was on its way to Bayern Kolonie and Remus Fox was more than willing to help out Director Gladstone again, two converted cargo vessels of the Silver Blades flanked the Gunship and he was in a good mood, first the illicit weapons shipment from GalCorp now this haul from the cargo convoy and all without the help of Captain Miller and the SS Ramesses, he knew Miller didn't respect or even like him, not that he cared. Miller wasn't calling the shots, the missiles that were so kindly supplied to him made this attack a lot easier. One of his lieutenants who was manning the communications console approached him and spoke.

"Captain, we need to go back to Silverbase immediately." Remus shot him a glare and had one hand on his sidearm.

"Why?" he asked, visibly angry.

"Sir," the man said in a panic "Its under attack." Remus looked ready to kill the man right there but he calmed himself.

"Recall the fighters, set course back to base," he said "hurry! also, signal the SS Ramesses," he noted the look in his Lieutenants face "I know its a risk telling them the bases location but this is an emergency, understood?" and in a moment of sheer fury hit his lieutenant with a backhanded strike so forceful it knocked the man off his feet, It would take at least thirty minutes to get back , who was attacking and why? he would have his answers soon enough, someone would pay for this.

The Ronin ground assault group exited the shuttle quickly and readied weapons although they didn't need to, the full scale of the carnage Suzanne left looked worse once they exited, the walls darkened with carbon scoring from the shots, cargo containers burned out and dead bodies.. or rather what was left of the bodies scattered throughout.

"There's a terminal Suzanne didn't hit" said Gareth, I should be able to get some access there" Matt nodded and turned to Phil.

"Phil, take Rob, Tamika and Remy and watch the hanger entrance, Kate and Nathan guard the shuttle and I'll cover G while he finds out the computer core location." they all ran to their assignments, Gareth took out his custom technical datapad and plugged it into the terminal, after a few minutes he gave a thumbs up, he was in, it was too quiet, surely the pirates know they are there.

"Got it" shouted Gareth "Theres a terminal with computer core access near the hanger, it won't be as easy or as quick as accessing the core direct but it will be easier to escape from." Matt thought about it.

"Makes sense, lets go," he said as Gareth packed the datapad away and lifted his carbine, Matt shouted to the others "Okay we have a location, lets go, Remy, stay with Nathan and Kate to keep the hanger secure." Remy nodded and took up a vantage point near the hanger door behind some charred crates as the others followed Matt and Gareth.

The base was unusually quiet, Tamika was on point scanning the area ahead with Rob taking up the flank.

"Maybe with all the chaos they haven't detected

our landing." Phil mused, Gareth consulted a mini datapad he had secured with straps on his arm.

"Possibly," Gareth said as he zoomed in on the map he called up "We take the first left and its the second door on the right should contain a terminal we can use" just then three pirates came around the corner, stopped in their tracks with a look of shock then just as quickly fell dead, Tamika had quickly shot all three in the head, the loud screech of an alarm went off.

"Well," she said "if they didn't know we were here before they do now." they picked up the pace.

In the hanger Kate was exploring the area.

"Suzanne really did a number on this place," she said stepping over what she assumed was the remains of a silver Blade pirate as she walked over to a shuttle that seemed relatively unscathed "Hey, this is a GalCorp cargo shuttle," she sad pointing at it's markings "probably from that cargo ship."

"Be careful." said Nathan cautiously as he followed behind as she opened the rear door.

"Oh I doubt there's anything to worry about..hey!" she shouted as Nathan fired two shots past her head "What did you do that for?" He gestured behind her to two dead pirates who had just jumped out the ship the moment she opened it.

"I told you be careful," he said with a sigh "I don't want to have to train up a new wingmate Do I?" Kate just laughed and entered the shuttle a minute later she ran out and beaconed him in, he followed and what he saw were crates all piled up, all with GalCorp logs, Kate was reading the label on one.

"These ones are guided missiles," she said "and the bigger ones behind me are something called burst torpedoes, any idea what they are?" Nathan shrugged.

"Matt might know, why?" he asked as Kate grinned.

"We take this ship and its cargo, its only a small amount of what would have been aboard the cargo ship but I bet they were just supplying the ships involved in whatever the SS Foxblade is doing, think of it as evidence if nothing else." she said already checking the systems, Nathan just shook his head. Suddenly there was weapons fire over at the hanger entrance.

"You go help Remy, I'll get this started." Kate said with unusual authority and with that Nathan ran across, carbine ready and took up a position near Remy.

"Was just one pirate," Remy said "But heard the alarm so you can be assured that more will come, what have you found back there anyway?" Nathan explained that there was a cargo shuttle with missile crates probably were supposed to be offloaded "If thats what is in one shuttle, imagine how many the cargo ship itself had." Remy mused as he fired off a few shots at some more pirates trying to rush to the hanger.

"Got it going." shouted Kate from the cargo ship.

"Take off now, might as well get it back now in case a stray shot hits it." Remy shouted back. Kate ran in, executed a quick start up sequence and put on a headset.

"Ellen, this is Kitten, there is a shuttle with a GalCorp logo on it coming out the hanger, its me, I require escort."

"Acknowledged, I await your ship." Kate smiled and eased the shuttle out the hanger

The battle in space was going well for the Ronin, Red and Alan had took out the base defences and it was mainly a mopping up operation on the fighters, it was clear that there were just the reserves, He saw Ellen fly back to the SS Hades with a cargo ship.

"Kitten this is Firehawk, what's going on here" he asked confused.

"Sorry, will take too much time to explain." he shrugged and chased down a Silver Blade dart fighter that make the mistake of flying to close to him.

CHAPTER 38

The route to the terminal was relatively uneventful, t looked like it was an old office room but had since been used by the stations alert pilots as a sleeping quarters with some crudely fashioned beds out of containers and various padding. Gareth activated the console then sat searching the databanks.

"We should try and close blast doors on the corridors that lead to here. Hopefully it will buy us time." Tamika said thoughtfully, Matt gave her a nod in agreement, she signalled Phil to follow her and for Rob to stay and guard the door.

"Shouldn't be too long to find what we are looking for." Gareth said cheerfully but Rob just stared.

"Yeah G, but how long to download?" all he got in reply was a shrug.

Phil and Tamika had managed to close and lock off two of the blastdoors to the hanger area with a few shots into the control panels, now there was only the one near the office they were using.

"Well this mission is going easier than.." Phil started but was interrupted by weapons fire, there was a group of Silver Blades running up the corridor, it seemed they had figured out what they were trying to do. Phil slapped the control panel, only for the door to only half close, Tamika fired a few shots as Phil repeatedly slapped the button to no avail.

"Okay," Tamika declared "now we retreat." she said as they ran for the cover of the office doorway, Rob covered them with some well placed shots of his own before a shot hit him on the body armour knocking him backwards to the ground.

"That's gonna leave a bruise," he said gingerly as he tried to get back up. He noted the others worried expressions "I'm fine guys, really." meanwhile Gareth had found the blackmail recordings.

"Well, its hard to see which ones are relevant without going through all." he said shaking his head.

"Just download them all." Matt said running over to help Rob to his feet, Gareth just shrugged and started the process.

"Firehawk, this is Astro Ace, new contacts coming in, Silverblade fighters, its a good chance if they are here, the SS Foxblade will be close behind." Andrew cursed to himself then replied.

"Acknowledged. Astro Ace, Hellbringer you two guard the Gound Assault squads exit, the rest of us will slow down the incoming fighters." He felt it best to pull the sisters off guard duty as he would need their decisive shooting in this as these pilots would be the hardened raiding ones, not the ones stuck on defence duty, he only hoped Matt would hurry up.

"Just a few more files." shouted Gareth over the weapons fire, the pirates were bottlenecked by the half closed blast door and were generally pinned down but it was only a matter of time "and we are done, I do hope they like my parting gift, there's a virus in their system deleting every file they have." he said pulling the cable out of the uplink.

"Time to go." shouted Matt, at that Tamika pulled something out of her belt, was a crude device that was roughly disc shaped.

"Run." she said with an evil grin as she slid it across the ground, Gareth helped Rob who was still sore from the hit he took, Tamika covered them as they ran round the corner suddenly a huge explosion erupted and the ground shook.

"what the hell was in that?" said Phil in shock.

"Oh nothing special, just something my dad taught me how to make." she said, as she did the blastdoor down the hall exploded and Silver Blades came out shooting through the smoke, Tamika and Phil covered the others.

"Now you see why I switched to piloting?" said Phil with a sigh.

Nathan and Remy were waiting in the cargo bay when they saw a group run to them, Nathan let off one shot before Remy stopped him.

"Relax." he said cautiously, but it was too late.

"You shot me!" shouted Gareth as he held his arm "what the hell?" Matt looked at Gareth's arm.

"Its just a scratch." he said but before Gareth could reply Phil and Tamika ran up urging everyone to get a move on and with a well placed shot to the locking mechanism, the Hanger door closed over with a loud clank.

"Where's Kate?" asked Matt, looking around.

"She's on the SS Hades, trust me it will take too long to explain." said Nathan running over to the assault shuttle, as they got in and the doors closed Matt took the co-pilots seat.

"Firehawk this is White Knight," he said excitedly "Mission accomplished."

Andrew looked out of his cockpit to see the Assault shuttle fly out flanked by Nicolae and Craig as the SS Hades manoeuvring to collect them and jump out the system.

"This is Firehawk, have your lightdrives ready to jump as a moments notice." he ordered as he shot down yet another fighter, he saw more ships jump into the system then on the other side of the base the SS Ramesses jumped in.

"Firehawk this is SS Hades," Johns voice came over the comms "We have the shuttle and its escorts on board, what the hell is the SS Ramesses doing here?"

"This is Firehawk, no idea, just jump, now." said Andrew and it seemed John didn't need told twice as they jumped before the SS Ramesses got into weapons range he then ordered the fighters to jump the moment they could.

"Brutus this is Pyrus, looks like I'll be enjoying a relaxing drink in here after all." Alan said before he jumped followed by Red and Ellen. Suzanne took out two enemy fighters before jumping.

"Firehawk this is Brutus, new contact coming in, its the SS Foxblade." he said as the frigate jumped in looming large before them.

"No heroics, jump now." Andrew shouted as Brutus jumped, once he was satisfied everyone was accounted for, he hit the lightdrive activation switch and jumped out of the system breathing a sigh of relief, they had done it.

Thing were not looking good on the SS Ramesses.

"He had what?!" shouted Director Gladstone, the screen in Captain Millers office was filled with the angry

GalCorp directors face "Are you sure they were copied?"

"Why else would they come here?" said Miller condescendingly "Nothing else was destroyed, its clear what they were after the data." he paced back and forth, this was a disaster, once it gets out, he and Gladstone would be arrested, there was only one thing to do.

"Miller! we need to make this right, you need to stop them find them before they transit the data, you hear me?" Miller just looked at the screen and sneered.

"No! I'm tired of you, this is your fault, you had to get the Silver Blades involved and ignored all my recommendations, you have appeased them at every turn, hampering our efforts, well I have had it taking orders from you." Gladstone took a minute before he realised what Miller was saying.

"No..You can't.. Miller, Miller!..." was all he got before Miller cut the transmission, he then hit the internal comms button.

"Mister Hayes, begin Operation Corsair." and with that he checked the safety on his sidearm and headed for the bridge.

Over Astra Sanctuarium, the SS Hades was alive with activity as the fighters that had to jump to lightspeed themselves landed, Andrew eased his helmet off and made his way down the ladder to see Gareth and Matt awaiting him both smiling, Gareth had a bandage on his upper arm but he thought best not ask what happened with that.

"We got it," said Gareth excitedly "The recording Matt had, the framing of him for murders, the plan to ambush the Galcorp cargo ship and alot more, its all here." he held up a datastick, Andrew nodded impressed.

"So now what?" He said.

"Well," said Matt "we are going down to the planet, Cardinal Otani is waiting for us, I just wanted to wait on.."

"..me" said a voice behind Andrew, he turned to see Sister Theresa with Liana not far behind. Liana ran up and kissed Andrew and held him close, relief evident on her face. They walked to the shuttles where Nathan stood by with Kate at the assault shuttle, it seemed the best one to take given what they were transporting, Phil and Rob were in their fighters to escort it down, Andrew pointed out the GalCorp cargo shuttle sitting next to Thunderclap One

"Oh..That" said Kate with a wicked grin "I can explain" she said as Matt, Gareth and Sister Theresa boarded the shuttle.

"I'm sure you can" said Andrew dryly.

"Not coming?" Matt said, slightly confused.

"No" Andrew said as Liana put her arm around Andrew's waist "But give my best to the Cardinal."

"As he walked onto the bridge Captain Miller was greeted by four armed security officers.

"Corbin Hayes sent us sir." the lead one said noting Miller suddenly tense when he saw them.

"Good, you two, guard the exits, the other two, follow me." he said as he once again checked his own weapon, Commander Cairns stood up expectantly and vacated the captains chair took position behind it, Miller signaled to his comms officer.

"What is going on?" said Cairns, Miller ignored him.

"Put me on internal comms," and he waited for the officer to signal he was on "Crew of the SS Ramesses, we have served together for a few years now and I believe that we could and should have achieved all GalCorps objectives in this area, however due to incompetence on behalf of the higher ups we have not been allowed to show our true capabilities, to make matters worse we have had to play second fiddle to outlaws and I for one have had enough, which is why I am now taking the SS Ramesses out of GalCorp service, let us show these people what true power is." some of the crew cheered, others looked on in horror, Cairns looked shocked.

"Sir," he said "I know things have been bad, but this is GalCorp property, we can't simply take the ship, I can't let.." before he finished Miller Andrew his weapon and fired four shots into Cairns who stumbled back crashing into the glass decoration that displayed the GalCorp logo. He was dead before he hit the ground.

"How fitting," Miller said with a sigh "Cairns was a good man and I had hoped he would see things my way.. oh well," he straightened his uniform and continued "Any crew not willing to join can go to the shuttlebay where I will grant you passage back home," two of his crew, the weapons and the science officers got up from their posts and headed out, Miller beaconed a security officer to him "Once they are all gathered in there.. vent the atmosphere." the officer nodded and headed down to give the order personally.

"Sir," said the comms officer "Message from the base, it is Remus Fox." Miller motioned for him to put him through, on the main screen Remus loomed large, behind him was the computer core with several Silver Blades trying to recover any data they could.

"This is your fault Miller, you should have dealt with our problem sooner now look at what's happened.." he saw Miller walk to his weapons console "What are you doing?" he said suddenly confused. Miller said nothing, instead targeting weapons at the bases hanger entrance, the rest of the base was buried deep in the asteroid, enough of an explosion in the hanger bay however..

"I'm doing what I should have done at the start." he then fired his cannons, batteries and missiles at the base the screen showing Remus went blank as the Asteroid itself blew apart into several large pieces, the Comms officer spoke up again.

"Sir, the SS Foxblade is contacting us." Miller asked for it to be put on the monitor.

"This is Victor Chang of the SS Foxblade, you are supposed to be our allies," the man was obviously unsure what to do and a little afraid "You killed Remus Fox."

"This is Captain... no.. Admiral... Miller and yes I

did, he has been a poor leader for you, and as I killed the man it looks like I replace him as leader of the Silver Blades am I correct?" Chang nodded "good," He saw Chang bark orders to others behind him and noted on his weapons monitor that the ships that had went battle ready when he attacked the base had stood down.. smart move "Are the rest of the Silver Blades in agreement?"

"They are Admiral," Chang said "What is your first order?"

"Well" Miller said thinking "the people who invaded this base have been a thorn in our sides, time to removed it, we draw them out by attacking the Hub, it has apparently been neutral all this time but the people need to know there is no place safe for our enemies and these people like to help others, they can't resist helping a full station of vulnerable people, but before we do that, we need to pay a visit to the Avari system, I have something to pick up there" he smiled sadisticly, time to liberate Salma Rojas from her dull life on that station with her uninterested husband, he saw Chang smile widely.

"Yes sir." he said tossing a loose yet genuine salute.

"Helm," Miller said "plot a course for the Avari system," he went to his command chair and sat down, he felt good, like a weight lifted off him, he should have done this long before now. Pity Cairns wasn't part of it he thought gazing back at the corpse , he beaconed to the nearest security guard "Please take that body to the nearest airlock for disposal." he said calmly.

CHAPTER 39

The trip back up from Astra Sanctuarium as uneventful as going down.

"The message was sent" Matt said to Andrew as met in the mess hall "I've probably said this before but Otani is not what I expected a cardinal to be." Andrew shook his head.

"Thats because he's not a just a regular cardinal, he belongs the the Jesuit order." he said knowingly.

"I was meaning to ask that, what is a Jesuit?" Matt said confused.

"Jesuits are hardline Catholics to the point where some even refer to them as the Warriors of Christ, Their founder was Saint Ignatius of Loyola, an ex soldier. In recent centuries they have became a sort of Vatican intelligence agency, unofficial of course. That's why he's so keen to help us now. I knew because he immediately knew what this patch means, and it's importance to the order" he pointed to his A.M.D.G. badge "Ad Majorem Dei Gloriam, its Saint Ignatius's motto and effectively the motto of the Jesuit order itself. Everything they do..is for the greater glory of god, at least that is the theory anyway."

"Well.. anyway we need to just wait for the reply, apparently they will inform us immediately but it could take a while, maybe days to hear back" Matt sighed "maybe in the meantime let everyone relax, maybe go planetside?" just then the shipwide Comms went, it was Liana.

"We have an urgent distress call.. from the mining operation on the Avari system" Andrew noted Matt's confused look.

"But that's a Galcorp system, something's very wrong," he explained "We have to do something."

"Well, we should go respond to it anyway, it's the least we can do," Andrew said with a sigh "Otani's people can still send us a message long range."

Soon the SS Hades was in hyperspace, Matt and Andrew on the bridge with John.

"Out of all the places to be attacked this is a strange one," said John "maybe its to blame you for it so it lessens your credibility." Tessa snorted from her position and turned around.

"Galcorp is a big corporation, they are not going to waste money wrecking a station just to blame a few flyboys, it has to be real." they soon found out when they dropped out of hyperspace and there was the installation, its defences were wiped out, wrecked fighters drifting aimlessly.

"They done a real number on this place," Andrew said absently as he stared out "any survivors?" Ben checked the scanners and gave a mournful shake of the head, further scans proved to confirm, they even sent Rob and Phil out to get a closer look in their fighters.

"This is Semjasa," Phil's voice came over the comms "I will tell you one thing, this was not a pirate raid, by the looks of the damage and where they hit there was only one objective and that was to destroy," he took a deep breath and sighed "wait, one of the automated turrets isn't too damaged, might get to access its gun camera footage." Matt nodded and looked at the others before answering.

"Good going Semjasa, stay out a little while longer, just in case whomever did this returns." he then headed to the communications station where Liana was already hard as work, she managed to access the turrets onboard computer and soon enough the main screen on the console played the last few minutes.

"Okay," said Andrew analysing it "So there is the SS Ramesses there, a supply shuttle docks." Matt shook his head and raised a hand.

"Actually that's an executive shuttle, probably Millers personal shuttle, must have been down to the station and this is just him returning..." as soon as the ship entered the hanger.. The SS Ramesses opened fire

Matt just stood, mouth open in shock, Liana looked up to Andrew for an explanation but he couldn't, just then she noticed something.

"There's a probe that has just activated and emitting a signal," said Liana as franticly worked her control until she brought it up, it was Miller, his uniform now missing its Galcorp branding "It seems to be a recording." she noted.

"Ah, Easton, I hope you and your little Ronin flight buddies get this little message, like my handy work? what can I say it was getting very tiresome being a GalCorp lackey, so I decided to make a new.. investment, say hello to the new Admiral of the Silver Blades, but before I start my new endeavour properly I need to take care of some unfinished business... you!" he said pointing at the screen "you have been a thorn in my side long enough and I could hunt you and try and take you down but we both know that has not worked so far and I know how you like to be the hero, how you want to help people, well here's your chance, myself and my new fleet are in the Hub system in for the next twenty hour hours. There is a problem you see, people want to leave and I don't want them to so if you and your merry band of pilots are not there in the next day, I will have no choice but to destroy that old rust heap of a station to pieces.. your choice." as he leaned forward with a menacing leer and the signal ended, there was silence on the bridge and Matt calmly sighed and asked.

"how long ago was that message recorded?" his voice betraying a slight tremor, Lianna brought up the timestamp on the message which read it had been recorded three hours ago, only twenty one left in Millers countdown, Matt wordless left the bridge, Andrew followed him.

"Where the hell are you going?" Andrew said as he caught up to him.

"Well," said Matt as he spun round to face Andrew "Maybe if I give myself up all this can end, its me he wants.." he looked lost "I thought .. " he trailed off.

"You thought finding the evidence would be the end of it, Galcorp answer for their crimes, we are cleared and we go back to normal?" Andrew said staring at Matt pointedly.

"Something like that." Matt conceded, Andrew shook his head and put his arm around Matts shoulders.

"Matt my friend." he started "Even if you did give yourself up, it won't make a difference, hes no longer Galcorp. Miller has went rogue with the most powerful ship in the region and its personal now." Matt fell silent for a few moments, looked at him and slightly nodded.

"your right, looks like we still have a job to do," he said finally "But if we fight it won't be like before, just going up against small squads and then jumping out, we are going up against the main force and I don't think we will be able to back down once we start." Andrew agreed.

"Its the one conflict we all wanted to avoid, but we have no real choice. We can not wait on the proper authorities." he said thoughtfully Matt nodded and said.

"This could be the last thing we can do," they looked at each other in silent understanding "get the pilots together, we have alot to talk about."

soon the pilots were gathered in the briefing area being told about Millers plan.

"laying siege to the Hub? that's bold! said Phil thoughtfully "of course there's no guarantee even if we did give ourselves up that they would not just attack the station regardless," there were lots of nods on agreement "I say we fight, we have battled them and won before we can do it again." as he said that the others one at a time spoke up to say they too would indeed fight, Gareth held up a hand and spoke.

"we do have an extra trick or two, for one we can equip the fighters with the missiles Kate was good enough to.. confiscate," he gave a wry smile "and we have five burst torpedoes." that made the other pilots sit up and take notice, the devastating effects of them was legendry.

"Oh," jumped in Craig "and we can neutralise their burst torpedoes," Andrew looked curiously at him and Matt scratched his head before urging him to explain "Well the torpedoes are remotely detonated and its a particular frequency, which, as you can imagine is in the operating manual, if we jam that frequency when they fire them.. they won't detonate, or they will detonate prematurely, its not really clear which happens." Craig shrugged, "looks like we have a lot to prepare," Andrew said, "We leave in an hour and will take a few more to get there so whatever you need to do, I suggest doing it now." he didn't need to say it, they were thinking it, before their strikes were more or less hit and run, this was a whole different animal and who knows if they will make it out alive, Matt stood over the console as the others filed out, Kate looked like she was making her way to find Tessa and it didn't take a genius to know Andrew was going to see Liana, he looked up from his console to see Suzanne stare at him.

"Matthew," she started "You are a good and honourable man, I have said as much before, however there is more,you are a kind and caring persona and.." it was obvious she was struggling for word so she grabbed him by the shoulders and pulled him close kissing him deep his initial surprise gave way to passion, after it seemed like eternity they broke the kiss "How long do we have?" she said with twinkle in her eye he never saw before, looking into her eyes Matt knew that while he still had a job to do and that it was the most dangerous thing he had done so far but looking at her, thinking of her attitude towards him, she had been waiting for the right moment and this was possibly her last chance to express them, and if he was honest, not that he would admit to the others but he could think of no other person I wanted to spent what possibly could be his last few hours alive with.

"I think we have enough time," and she took his hand and lead him out the room.

"Hey.. Rob" came a voice as he was returning to his quarters, he turned round to see Tamika run up to him "Wait up" she stopped and regained her breath "everything okay?" she looked like she had something on her mind, he leaned on the doorway and just gave her a pained look,

"You really wanna know? we are about to go into a battle, a proper large scale battle, half these guys.. these kids have no real experience in it," he hung his head "I dunno, I guess I saw too many good people die over the years... " he was distracted by the sight of Alan wandering past heading to the hanger with a large crate being pushed in front of him, he and Tamika looked at each other in surprise.

"Do I really want to know?" she asked, he shook his head "Anyway, Rob its up to us old hands to make sure guys like our little pear obsessed friend there come out of this alive, anyway you once asked why my callsign is Quinque?..well.." and she leaned up and whispered in his ear, rob just laughed in response.

Rob then went into his quarters and retrieved his rosary beads "I was actually planning to to pray before everything," he said with a weak smile "we need all the help we can get.. you can join me if you like." he looked at her earnestly, she in return looked sceptical.

"I'm not a religious person but what the hell, worth a try, lead on." she said with a rare smile.

Liana seemed in a good mood as Andrew lead her down to their quarters, he didn't say much just got her to stand in the middle of the floor while he fished round under the mattress.

"Okay Andrew" she said "what's so important you brought me here when we should be preparing for.." he went up to her and put a finger softly on her lips

"There's something I want to do and I couldn't wait another minute, Liana Cotugno.." he opened the small box revealing a gold ring with two white diamonds and a sapphire in between them "will you marry me? I realise I may never get another chance to say this." she looked slightly shocked and played nervously with her scarf and bit her lip, she looked at him before nodding and giving a soft reply he barely heard.

"yes." and she embraced him tight, smiling but with some tears, he broke the hug and slipped the ring on her finger.

"its a family heirloom and I can't think of anyone I'd rather give it to. Miss Cotugno, I love you and I want us to spend the rest of our lives together no matter where or for how long that is." and he pulled her back in and kissed her deeply...

Some of the pilots congregated in the mess hall for a 'team bonding' meal as Marcus put it, Nicolae absently stabbed at his plate with his fork before looking at the others and sighed, the room was eerily silent.

"Hey surely this sort of thing is what guys like you did regular," said Marcus to Nicolae and Phil "You know? as part of your station defence duties in the day."

"Well" Phil said thoughtfully "we only had to deal with raiding parties for the most part this would be more like a full on battle." Nicolae nodded in agreement

"Phil is right, fighting opportunistic pirates just not the same." Ellen, Red, Nathan and Remy all listened with interest, Nathan looked thoughtful then added.

"The main problem I see," he started slowly "is not the fighters, a dogfight is a dogfight, its that monster of a cruiser, we were lucky to disable it last time, I don't think we will get another opportunity..."

"My main worry is Omega." interrupted Remy "I have heard a lot about him and his prowess." Phil snorted and shook his head.

"Its easy to look good shooting down pirates in rundown ships who have don't have much training or discipline." Phil stopped and looked at Red "No offence.. but I have to believe years of combat against such opposition has made him complacent, I hope." Marcus thought for a minute.

"Yeah, I just hope I don't have to fly against him," but saw everyone ;look at him "What?" he said with a sense of fear creeping in.

"You forget who you are the wingman for," said Nicolae, deadpan "you know Andrew will end up engaging Omega." Marcus hid his head in his hands.

"Ah hell," was his only response, Nathan nodded

"Yeah, its going to be either him or Matt from

what I have heard,I don't wish it on anyone."

"All pilots to the hanger, all pilots to the hanger," came Johns voice over the comms, Phil figured Liana must be busy elsewhere "We are fifteen minutes from the Hub, game time everyone."

As they got up to prepare, Red sought out Marcus and asked him to hang back a moment.

"Whats wrong Red?" he said curiously and she suddenly kissed him, much to his surprise and then she looked down slightly embarrassed.

"Sorry.. I just.. I been wanting to do that for a while and.." she was nervous, Marcus held her by the shoulders and looked at her intently.

"Don't be sorry, okay?" she relented a smile and he continued "Once this mission is over, we can talk about this.. okay?", it was his way of reassuring her they will both make it through this alive.

"Okay." she said and took his hand as they caught up with the others.

CHAPTER 40

The hanger was a mass of bodies as the techs struggled to get all the ships ready in time, Andrew gave Liana a kiss before heading over to the others, no noticed Matt wasn't there, and strangely neither was Suzanne, which was unusual, Ellen looked almost lost without her sister but a sly grin by Marcus made him turn round to see Matt emerge from the hanger entrance hand in had with Suzanne and her looking at him with more than just admiration, he released her had to join Andrew as she joined the others.

"I wondered when one of you two would make a move," Andrew said with a smile , Matt shot him a look "hey, it was obvious, everyone else could see it. So what happened?" Andrew continued.

"Well," Matt shrugged " A Gentleman never tells, now if you will excuse me," he stepped forward and surveyed the pilots in front of him, he could see that they were all looking to him and Andrew for inspiration "I have said before, I didn't plan for any of this, for you pilots to get involved, but I for one am honoured to be flying with you all once again, yes this will be harder than any battle we have faced before, we will be outgunned and outmanned but the alterative is the loss of every life onboard the Hub.. I know I couldn't let that happen..I know you couldn't let that happen, that's probably why they are doing this but let us go out there and show them the error of their ways..who is with me?" A cheer came up from everyone, Suzanne even added a sly wink to Matt that had him momentary flustered.

"Remember," Andrew said when the pilots quietened down "These are highly trained opponents, remember your simulation training, we don't have the same manoeuvrability they do, but their ships are more vulnerable to sustained fire, remember that, stay safe out there."

"Wasn't planning on dying anytime soon," said Marcus, whom Matt noticed was holding hands with Red, interesting, that may explain his wide smile. They all dispersed to their fighters, Craig and Gareth approached Matt and Andrew

"Well We have distributed the missiles amongst the ships as evenly as we could," said Gareth "but the burst missiles, well we figured they may try and use the frequency they are on to remote detonate them so we had to reprogram them with different frequency codes which is harder than it sounds and we haven't had time to test all five so be careful. We mounted them to Tamika's, Rob's, Phil's and both of your ships, its not ideal but its what we have." Andrew shrugged.

"you still did a good job guys," they both tossed a lazy salute and ran to their fighters, Andrew then turned around to Matt in time to see the sight of Elijah, in a flight suit and carrying a helmet from the ships stores and moving rather gingerly.

"I thought you may need another pilot," he said with a weak grin and saw the doubt on their faces "Its okay the good sister as cleared me to fly, just.. I have to do this, you guys saved my life.. maybe I can repay you." Matt signed.

"Only if you are sure, but you are just recovering from major injuries and you won't be with a wingman..."

"..He will be.. he has me," came a voice, they all turned around to see Tessa in a flight suit and helmet all black with a scorpion motif throughout "This isn't going to be a regular thing, I am only doing this because you will need everyone help out there, got that?" Matt went to ask a question only for her to respond with "John himself will be flying the ship, apparently he used to do it before he hired me and if you doubt my fighter piloting credentials..I can assure you I can be a fighter pilot.. I just choose not to, got that?" Andrew noted she wore Hexstar military wings but said nothing, she strutted over to one of the spare fighters that were being prepared as she did she shouted back "My callsign is Sting." Matt suppressed a whistle.

"You heard of her?" said Andrew shaking his

head.

"Oh yes.." Matt said thoughtfully "I heard about a pilot called Sting from a pilot I was assigned wingman too after the loss at battle of Colonie Du Quebec." he sighed and looked up "Tessa..Sting on her own took out half of his squadron before they realised what was happening.. in the end only two remained, as you know a lot of Hexstar records were destroyed, would have been easy for someone like her to simply slip into the background, the alternative as we heard from Craig about his dad was was to be vilified for actions during the war,"

"Yeah, it seems to have worked out for her staying under this radar this long," Andrew remarked "she had always been cagey about her past, now we know why, pity we could have really used her." he fiddled with the chinstrap of his helmet, as an announcement came over the comms.

"Dropping out of lightspeed in five minutes." Lianas tone sounded a little shaky "prepare to launch." Andrew looked at Matt smiled.

"its almost time, Good luck." and he held out his hand, Matt shook his hand and smiled back.

"thank you.. for everything." and ran over to his ship, Andrew turned around to see Sister Theresa flicking drips of holy water on his fighter.

"Mister Douglas your ship is now ready," she said with a sly smile "your ship has been blessed as your Fiancee requested." Andrew was getting in the cockpit and looked down.

"I see word travels fast." he went to sit down but felt something hard on the seat, reaching down he pulled out a bottle of cider that had a note written by Alan saying 'victory drink, no tradition like a new tradition', he looked around and saw quite a few other mystified pilots finding bottles on their seats. he felt a slight shudder as the SS Hades lightspeed drives slowed, this was it.

Miller surveyed the scene, the SS Ramesses and the SS Foxblade along with two converted cargo vessels belonging to the Sliver Blades which in comparison to the two warships were just glorified carriers for the many fighters they had brought, they had others but they would have needed overhauled before Miller would let them be used in any combat. seeing the SS Hades enter the system was fortunate as he had already decided regardless of if they did he was going to destroy the Hub anyway, this just made things neater destroying Easton's merry band at the same time, he looked to his side where Salma Rojas, the former wife if the commander of the Avari system mining operation who gladly jumped at the chance to join her lover, in fact he had even let her give for order to fire on the colony, she really hated it there.

"Looks like your plan worked my love." she purred, that's what attracted him to her, she was a stunningly beautiful woman, her dark hair short but still overtly feminine. It was her eyes that was her best feature equally mesmerising yet malevolent at the same time, she was a kindred spirit for Miller.

"Yes, yes it does." he signalled the comms officer to put him through to to the SS Hades, a soft spoken female voice replied and he demanded to be put through to Easton, he took a moment and thought that it didn't sound like the argumentative officer he had spoke to the last time.

"Admiral Miller wishing to speak to you." said Liana through Matts helmet comms.

"Admiral? Transfer him through." he said with a sigh.

"Easton," Said Miller with mock joy "So good of you to come and safe the day, I just thought I'd give you the chance to do the right thing, hand yourself over to me and I promise I will spare the station, one time offer." Matt thought about it, It would be easier but he had no guarantee Miller would honour that offer and not attack then he thought of the other pilots, of Suzanne..

"Miller," he said finally, I started something and I intend to finish it." he switched comm channel to the squad channel "Ronin flight.. prepare to launch."

It wasn't much of a surprise to see fighters pouring out of the SS Hades hanger, in fact Miller was glad, he turned to his comms officer again.

"Tell Hayes to launch then inform the other ships in the fleet to launch their fighters too," then almost to himself "and so it begins."

The sight of all the fighters launching from the SS Ramesses and the other ships was a daunting image but Matt kept his ship on course, the Ronin were in their flight pairs and were heading to the ever growing number of enemy fighters and on his scanners he could see the SS Hades moving to prepare to engage the larger Galcorp ship.

"White Knight, the is Firehawk," Andrews voice sounded oddly calm all things considered "whatever happens.. its been an honour." Matt was about to respond when his sensors flashed a warning.

"This is White Knight, burst torpedoes incoming," he said as the GalCorp fighters heading the enemy group opened fire "G, I hope your plan works."

"White Knight this is G, it should..I hope."

Hayes smiled as he watched his torpedo join the others streaking away.

"This is Omega, prepare to detonate torpedoes in five, four, three, two," and as the torpedoes shot between the ranks of the incoming enemy fighters he continued "One..now!" and he pressed the detonation switch.. nothing, he pressed again and again...

"Omega this is Snap shot, my burst torpedo won't detonate" came a message through the comms, it was his wingman Austin Downs. Soon more messages flooded the comms.

"This is Supernova, Mine won't work either."

"This is Wild Boy, what gives? The whole batch can't be faulty surely?"

"This is Agent Orange, nothing happening, what's going on?"

"This is Saint.."

"...Enough chatter" Corbin shouted "It's obvious they are using some sort of jamming, just means we will need to kill them the hard way."If he was honest, Corbin actually preferred that. It looked like he would get that challenge he craved at long last. This was going to be an interesting battle indeed.

"White Knight, this is G, told you disrupting their frequency would work," as the torpedoes sailed past harmlessly out of range "watch what happens when I stop broadcasting" suddenly the torpedoes exploded well behind the Ronin ships." Matt marvelled at the skill of his more technical minded pilots but still he looked at the amount of enemy fighters bearing down, he closed his eyes briefly took a sigh and spoke.

"This is White Knight, move in and engage, John, keep the SS Ramesses busy if you can." Johns voice came over Matt's comms.

"Already on it." Matt put his engines into full throttle

"Well, here goes nothing." he said to himself.

From his captains chair on the SS Ramesses, Admiral Miller surveyed the scene, he was a little concerned that his men's usual tactic of a burst torpedo volley didn't work, he got up and stood closer to the main screen, but his weapons officer Andrew his attention.

"The carrier is moving toward us, weapons ready." Miller thought for a minute, its main cannon did major damage last time and he wasn't willing to risk it again.

"Order the SS Foxblade to engage the carrier," he said trying to sound confident "We have better things to do."

CHAPTER 41

As the Ronin ships vectored towards the enemy fleet Andrew's comms suddenly came alive.

"..Hey, can you hear me." said a voice, it was Lilly.

"Yeah, its Firehawk," he paused then said "Officer Douglas I mean, you guys okay?"

"Well," she said in a tone of frustration "when they came they took our long range comms out," Andrew nodded, that explains why they hadn't heard anything from the station itself "the administrator tried to run off but was shot down by that GalCorp bastards ship, anyway tell your men to fly to the station."

"Why?"..Andrew started.

"Now!" she shouted in an authoritative tone.

"Ronin flight this is Firehawk, vector towards the Hub, everyone..now." he said as he switched to the frequency the others were using and heard some words of protest, especially from Phil.

"Firehawk this is Semjasa..what the hell.." but Andrew just turned his ship and trusted the Hub.

Hayes was getting ready to engage the first ship that came to him and was surprised to see the lead ship veer off to the station and the others follow in a rather disjointed way, he sighed and rolled his eyes.

"Everyone this is Omega, pursue the enemy fighters, when we get within weapons range.. fire at will." he said as he pushed his ship into full throttle and started the chase.

From the bridge of the SS Ramesses Miller seen the Ronin vector off towards the station with Hayes and the rest of the Apophis class fighters belonging to the former GalCorp ship in hot pursuit with the other pirate fighters following, the pirates were flying a combination of Vampires, Darts, even some Starflares and Wildstars plus some he had never seen before.

"What are you up to Easton" he muttered.

"Firehawk, this is White Knight, what's going on? is this some new plan?" Andrew smirked, one thing he had always noticed about Matt was he always needed to know everything.

"White Knight this is Firehawk, Lilly contacted me and requested we do this, don't ask because she hasn't told me why either." They all flew at full throttle with the enemy hot on their heels, Andrew wondered what Lilly had in mind when as they got closer all the cargo bay and hanger doors opened.

"You better get out the way if you know what's good for you." said Lilly over the comms as every fighter and shuttle that was in the Hub launched, Andrew smiled, of course Lilly had a plan to fight. From behind the station the SS Abstrakt came into view and manoeuvred to engage the nearest pirate cargo ship.

"Ronin Flight this is Firehawk, loop back.. and arm burst torpedoes."

Miller saw it all happen from the comfort of his bridge, the Hub launched a rag tag collection of ships to defend the station and the pilots from Easton's Ronin loop back to join them in confronting his forces

"Well, this should be interesting." he said softly.

Matt flicked the switch on the burst torpedo activation console.. nothing happened, he tried again, still nothing.

"Firehawk this is White Knight, my torpedo is not responding" he reported.

"Don't worry, we will make do with what we have." by the sounds of it Andrew was having his own issues.

It took several attempts before Andrew's console worked, that was the issue with jury rigging different systems that weren't really supposed to work together, by now all the Ronin ships had levelled out and were heading back they way they came.

"Ronin flight this is Firehawk, fire torpedoes."

Corbin saw the enemy ships launch missiles and shook his head, it looked like they were dumb fired too... wait, those weren't missiles, they were torpedoes.. burst torpedoes...

"This is Omega" he said using the GalCorp fighters only frequency "Evasive manoeuvrers.. now!" and he pulled at his controls, veering away from the oncoming Torpedoes.

Miller saw it all unfold as he sat helplessly, luckily Corbin and his pilots had the sense to get out the way but the others were slow to react, the first of the four exploded and took out almost a full squadron of pirates, the other three thankfully weren't as effective but still took out a significant number of fighters

"Damn!" he shouted and punched the armrest of his chair and turned to his communications officer "Tell Corbin that I want all the Ronin pilots dead..now"

Andrew smiled at the devastation and chaos the burst Torpedoes caused, he switched to lasers and targeted the nearest enemy ship and fired.

"Ronin flight this is Firehawk, pick your targets carefully and remember everything we did in the simulators.. here goes nothing" he said as they flew into the heart of the enemy formation.

It soon became obvious that there was a big difference in ability and discipline between the regular pirates and the pilots from the SS Ramesses.

"Ronin flight this is White Knight, remember that those GalGorp Apophis Class interceptors are much more manoeuvrable than anything we have dealt with before and especially do not get involved in a turning battle with any of them" Matt said as he laced a pirate fighter with laser fire. He looked over at the SS Hades and saw it locked into battle with the SS Foxblade. They looked evenly matched but it looked like the Pirate ship had at least four fighters supporting it. The carrier could possibly cope with them but Matt wasn't going to take risks "Ronin flight this is White Knight, can anyone render assistance to the SS Hades?"

"White Knight this is Semjasa, Pollock and I are on it" and with that he saw two Battleaxes streak full throttle to the carrier.

John wasn't happy on the Bridge of the SS Hades, he had feared the battle would involve a slugging match like this but what made things worse was the SS Foxblade had a lot of its weapons at the front and could bring them to bear easier, the SS Hades had to position itself for a broadside attack. To make matters worse he was operating controls that Tessa had optimised for herself and she had an unusual way of doing things.

"Those fighters are causing issues," said Ben at the weapons console "looks like they are trying to target our cannon hardpoints." and with that one pirate fighter strafed the light laser batteries but halfway through swinging around for another try he ship blew up and through the wreckage flew two Battleaxes.

"SS Hades this is Semjasa, you focus on that gunship, we will handle the fighters" came the message through the comms, John shook his head smiling.

"Well you heard the man," he said to Ben " Target that ship with everything we have"

In the melee of battle it was was to lose your bearings, which is why Nicolae assumed Craig was flying in as tight a formation with him. It was probably more Craig acknowledging his inexperience more than anything else but he had to give the kid credit for realising this and sticking to his wingman for support. Nicolae flew in behind a flight of pirates and targeted the closest in the engines and launched a missile that hit the taeget dead on, the explosion ripped through the ship, cleaving it in half. The others scattered but one pilot, who was either very brave or very foolish, looped back and wildly fired at Nicolae's fighter. Before he could react, Craig flew in front of him, letting his shields take some hits before firing on the attacker himself. The younger pilot made short work of it.

"Hellbringer, this is Astro Ace, good work.. and thank you."

"No problem Astro Ace, you would have done the same for me." Nicolae smiled, Craig had Nicolae said as he pitched his fighter towards a swarm of pirate fighters.

"Kitten, this is Nate Dawg. Be careful" Nathan said as Kate flew through wreckage of a ship he had just destroyed

"I know what I'm doing" she said in an annoyed tone, she knew he was only being a good wingmate but it still irked her at times. They barrel rolled behind one of the Apophis class fighters. Nathan had him in his heads up display crosshairs and fired..

"Damn" he shouted t himself as the fighter jinked to avoid the shots "Kitten, this is Nate Dawg, this one is mine, watch my back" and he raced after the former GalCorp ship, firing steaks of laser, only scoring a few glancing shots on the shields. Suddenly two missiles streaked past his cockpit and slammed into the fighter the first taking out the shields, the second slamming into the engines. The missiles had come from Kate's fighter.

"A kindly reminder, we have Missiles now" he

could hear the condescending tone in her voice but she had a point. Nathan had a retort on his lips but a few shots glancing off his shields told him there was still a job to do so he turned his ship to intercept the new threat firing at him.. and armed his missiles.

Corbin Hayes was having a field day, the tattoo artist will be busy inking these scores on him, he had already took out six hub mercenary ships when a couple of Ronin Battleaxes flew past

"Well, Miller wants these guys gone, better start with this one" and he turned the steering yoke to follow.

Remy was doing his best to stay with Tamika as they were in pursuit of a pirate fighter. suddenly the targeting lock warning sounded out in the cockpit.

"Quinque this is Victoire, I need assistance, someone has a missile lock" he said with a hint of panic in his voice.

"Victoire this is Quinque, hold on, just remember your training and evade." he seen Tamika veer into a tight turn.

"Oh no, not again" said Tamika to herself, she honestly thought she had drilled this habit out of him. As she came upon Remy and his pursuer Tamika saw it was Omega. She didn't want to panic the Frenchman by telling him who was behind him but she wasn't in weapons range yet "Just hold on in here Remy." she muttered as she went full throttle.

The lead ship of the pair broke off and was executing a tight turn but Corbin stayed true, matching the Battleaxe he had a lock on as it tried to evade. .t was clear to Corbin that this was not the best of this band of pilots so he armed the missiles and pressed fire...

Tamika was just getting into position to be ready to fire when an out of control fighter, hard to tell from which side he was fighting on clipped her Battleaxe and sent her into a spin.

"Damn" she shouted as she struggled to control her craft.

The cockpit screamed with the alarm warning Remy of the missiles being fired.. he froze in panic..

Tamika just got her fighter back under control to see Remy's Battleaxe explode as the second missile slammed into his engines, his screams before the radio cut off ringing in Tamika's ears. She knew she could have stopped it, he was her wingman.. her partner... She shook her head, there would be time to mourn later, she targeted the nearest enemy and swooped closer.

Red and Alan were being pursued by two ex GalCorp fighters and the older bulkier Battleaxes were struggling to lose them.

"Pyrus, this is Redpunk, their lead has a missile lock on me" as she said this , Red saw the debris of a mercenary attack shuttle and headed to it at full speed

"Enemy has launched a missile, Enemy has launched a missile" but Red ignored Alan's warning, her flight took her so close to the debris, it felt like she may have scraped paint off her ship with it, the missile impacted on the debris.

"Hit afterburners and loop back tight ...now!" Red shouted on the comms. Alan did as he was ordered and followed her in a loop back round over the exploding wreckage just in time to see the two apophis class fighters just fly past. Both Ronin Pilots were in perfect position, Red took one out with a mix of laser fire and a missile, the second was trickier, Red had him in a missile lock, held it long enough for the other pilot to jink wildly to try and break the lock... only to bring it into Alan's field of fire where a never ending stream of laser fire ripped through the engine.

"Why didn't you fire a missile at the second fighter?" he asked.

"I ran out of missiles but I knew if I kept a missile lock on he would do something stupid, besides I wanted you to get at least one kill."

"Well, we make such a good pear don't we?" she rolled her eyes, she doubted she could ever get used to his pear puns.

"Yeah.. Yeah.. but you owe me a pear cider for giving you that kill.."

"..what about the one below your seat.."

"..the one below..?" she stopped and groped below her seat and felt a bottle under it, so that's what some of the other pilots were looking at when they climbed in their cockpits earlier "Dammit, wait till I get hold of you.." she shook her head with a smile and flew in search of more targets.

CHAPTER 42

Despite the early successes the Ronon Flight pilots were having it seemed the Hub defenders in general were suffering greatly. Unlike the highly trained ex GalCorp pilots and the Silver Blade veterens, this Hub pilots were just a rabble of pilots and soldiers in a loose alliance, it showed. Matt had tried to co-ordinate some with limited effect but he had a feeling the longer this battle went on, the worse things would get for them.

"Firehawk, this is White Knight, whats your status?" he asked as he pursued an enemy fighter, it was an old model D65 that looked surprisingly well maintained.

"This is Firehawk, currently teaching some GalCorp pilot the error of his ways." Just then an attack shuttle belonging to the defenders blew up in a hail of laser fire near Matt.

"It's not looking good is it?"

"No, We are doing the best we can but unless something big happens..." Andrew started to say.

"...I know, we need something, anything to boost morale" Matt interuppted. Yes they needed something, no matter how small, to tip the scales in their favour... but what?

Corbin once again swooped into the heart of the battle and targeted the nearest Ronin flight battleaxe, Suzanne's, and started lacing it with weapons fire, the pilot was good he thought but there was no getting away, the shields came down and his next hit grazed her engine manifold, causing her power to fluctuate...

Andrew had seen the Apophis class fighter with the custom paintjob that Omega flew swoop down on Suzanne's Battleaxe and knew he had to act.

"Brutus this is Firehawk, I will handle this one myself, don't get involved, repeat don't get involved."

"Why? What are you gonna do?" came the reply

"Just.. trust me." he said and dived towards Omega's ship at full speed.

Matt saw Suzannes ship get raked with fire from the ship that had to belong to Corbin Hayes judging by the large Omega logos on the wings, if he didn't act she'd be dead, and he couldn't let that happen, he hit the afterburners and flew direct to the enemy pilot.

"Omega, this is White Knight..." he started about to challenge Corbin before he destroyed Suzannes ship however...

"...Firehawk has a message, come get me." Andrew suddenly shouted over the comms swooping in between Suzannes and corbins ship letting his own ship take impact while getting a few hits on Corbin, as he narrowly missed hitting him head on. Corbin forgot all about Suzannes stricken fighter and turned to pursue Andrew who was heading towards the Hub itself.

"Suzanne this is White Knight, are you okay?" he asked, his voice shaky.

"I'm okay," she said, her voice pained "but my ship is too damaged to continue." then suddenly over the radio.

"White Knight this is Ellen, I will escort my sister away from the battlezone back to the SS Hades, I have already informed flight control to prepare for her," Ellen's ship ran in tight formation with Suzanne's as they flew from the battle "I will return soon." Ellen said, Matt breathed a sigh of relief, he didn't want to lose her so soon after admitting their feelings.

Cobin pursued Andrew relentlessly but couldn't geet a target lock,

"Omega this is Snap Shot, this one seems to be putting up something of a challenge" his wingman was good at stating the bloody obvious at times.

"This guy is good, but theres something damn familiar, Like I flew against him before, but where?" he said in reply and resorted to just firing randomly in the hope to spook his foe but to no avail, even when a few shots glanced his opponent did not faze him.

"That was close." Andrew said to himself, he knew a straight up fight against Omega would be suicide but he had to do something, he realised asking Marcus not to get involved may be seen as foolish but he knew what he was doing, he hoped he did anyway. Luckily Andrew had a few ideas up his sleeve.

Corbin was still trying to spook the other pilot with erratic firing but when they got to the station Andrew flew very close to the station, following every contour and corner as tight as he could making it difficult to use target lock as it couldn't register him as seperate from the station, Corbin had only saw that tactic once before, no it couldn't be, he instinctively rubbing his right wrist were the two X tattoos were, was this the pilot who flew aggressor against him? suddenly he turned a sharp corner there were two inert floating missiles. Corbin pulled up just in time. His wingman was not so lucky, Down's fighter flew straight into them. One impacted his wing, the other hit the cockpit canopy, the explosion would have killed the pilot instantly. a message came over the comms.

"Hey Omega, I see your learning from your mistakes. Sorry about your wingman, can't get the pilots these days" followed by laughter, damn it was him, Corbin redoubled his efforts, finally he would erase the one remaining blip on his career, not many counted simulator runs but he did and Firehawk was the only living being to ever beat him in any way shape or form, he had to die, now.

Well I've got him mad now, thought Andrew and opened a console he had the techs to fit into his fighter under the lightdrive controls it had the word Hop on some tape stuck to the top of the console, it was something Gareth and he worked on to allow him to easily do his lightspeed hop manouver, he hit the first button deactivating the lightdrive safety and suddenly, once he had flwown around the station, doing enough to further enrage the other pilot, who had to resort to pure line of sight for targeting due to Andrews manouvers, before heading back to the battle but suddenly instead of evading or executing any other manoeuvers Andrew simply leveled out and flew straight.

Corbin saw Andrew suddenly stop evading, maybe the other pilot was getting over confident, it was a small detail but it would be a short matter of finishing him off and returning to destroy the rest, he initiated weapons lock.

A Warning light came on Andrews console to alert him to the weapons lock, he hit the second button on the custom console that automaticly fed his current co-ordinates into the lightdrive computer.

Corbin selected and armed his missiles.
"This has went on long enough" he said to himself as we waited to get a missile lock and when he did Corbin didn't think twice and pressed the control stick trigger...

A light on the console indicated everything was ready, Andrew hit the lightdrive activation button...

Suddenly Andrew's Battleaxe vanished from Corbin's targeting computer and the missiles went harmlessly straight on through where the target used to be, he couldn't believe it, the lunatic done all that just to jump out the system, what possible reason.. suddenly his alerts were sounding, someone had weapons lock on him, but there was no-one else anywhere close enough and now he was registering hits on his shields, he looked up bewildered to see.. no it couldn't be thats impossible, the last thing he saw before his ship blew up was Andrews fighter bearing down with his main weapon blazing.

Everything went quiet in the SS Ramesses bridge when the news came in over the comms. Corbin Hayes, one of the best fighter pilots Miller had ever known was dead.

"Can you confirm the report?" he asked, a slim chance of hope crept into his voice.

"Yes sir," came the reply from the flight control officer "his transponder is no longer transmitting and there is no beacon indicating he ejected before his ship was destroyed, I'm sorry sir." Miller stood in the middle of the bridge deep in thought. He really did not want to take the risk of moving the SS Ramesses into the melee but this battle was taking too long in his opinion but he could not risk losing many more pilots, the loss of Corbin Hayes was damaging enough. Not just from a practical perspective but a morale one too.

"Take us in closer" he ordered eventually "We will make them pay for every one of us they have killed" he said to himself as he slumped in his command chair. Salma had already left the bridge to their quarters, she knew the bridge was no place for an observer in a time like this. The communications officer suddenly spoke.

"One of our pilots is contacting us"

"Well, put him on" Miller said with a sigh.

"SS Ramesses this is Supernova" Ah, David Abrams, one of the better pilots of the SS Ramesses fighter pilot contingent "Any new orders? Considering the current circumstances?" ballsy little prick Miller thought, Corbin is barely cold and here is this guy more of less assuming command of the pilots. Miller admitted he was actually impressed.

"No new orders, keep on with the attack" he said "Oh and you are flight leader now, congratulations."

"Thank you sir, won't let you down" came the reply. Miller stood up again a the SS Ramesses moved forward.

"Omega is gone, I repeat Omega is gone." came a message over the comms, suddenly the attacking forces had lost their talismanic figure, Matt smiled and shook his head, through his comms he heard Andrew.

"White Knight this is Firehawk, sorry I took your kill but I was closer and for you it was personal, for me, I just had some fun." Andrew was right, seeing Omega nearly blast Suzanne out the did make Matt emotional and going into a dogfight with someone as skillful as he was with that mindset was never going to end well, indeed it would have been a rather fatal mistake.

"Thank you, what do you say we press the advantage." Matt replied,

"Sounds like a good idea to me" Andrew said in agreement.

With their leader gone the attacking ships were trying to

regroup leaving themselves vulnerable to the Ronin and the hubs merceneries, the SS Ramesses was still staying back and the SS Foxblade was trading shots with the SS Hades, the old Hexstar gunship was only just starting to be outmatched by the carrier, suddenly a message came through, it was Nate.

"White Knight this is Nate Dawg, looks like the SS Ramesses is moving in." Matt looked, the cruiser had started its engines up and heading straight for the station. Damn, of course he must have known the the SS Foxblade was never going to beat the SS Hades but that was never the intent, it was to keep them using the carrier to defend the station. The fact that Miller was now bringing it into the battle seemed like a desperation move to get the battle over quickly.

"This is White Knight, who here still has any missiles left?" Nathan, Kate, Gareth, Nicolae, Craig and Tamika still had at least one missile each as did some of the mercenaries defending the Hub "Okay you are all with me, lets see if we can make a dent in this monster."

"White Knight this is Firehawk, you do what you need to, we will take care of the fighters" Matt let out a slow breath kicked his thrusters to full on course to the SS Ramesses.

CHAPTER 43

Admiral Miller looked on as he seen several fighters race towards the SS Ramesses, the lead one had to be Easton he thought.

"Set laser batteries to defensive fire," he ordered his weapons officer "And tell me when we are in range of the station."

"Semjasa, this is Pollock" Rob said with a sigh "We are getting too close to the SS Foxblade's weapons for comfort".

"I know, I know, but he have to knock them out to help.. watch out!" a volley of laser fire from the gunship struck out against the SS Hades.. one laser bolt grazed Rob's fighter and Phil saw a little flash in Rob's cockpit.

"Pollock, this is Semjasa, are you okay?" he asked, panic evident in his voice.

"Yeah, just a console exploded" his breathing suggested otherwise, I gotta eject, systems are failing all over that shot must have damaged the power conduits. If I don't eject now, I might not be able to.." there were small explosions just behind the cockpit area as it separated from the rest of the ship and a couple of small thrusters guided it away from the rest of the stricken ship. The cockpit section was effectively like an escape pod now and was moving to the SS Hades.

John saw the escape pod head towards the ship.

"Liana, get crews to the hanger and get a recovery shuttle out there to retrieve him" he said all, concern.

"They are already preparing for Susanne to land but I have told them to get a shuttle ready for pod retrieval too" she replied calmly. John smiled, Liana hadn't cracked under the pressure and was doing a good job.

"Ben, I want that gunship gone, now if possible" he commanded.

"Semjasa, this is SS Hades" Liana's voice came over Phil's comms " Pollock is safe and ..mostly healthy, nothing Sister Theresa can't fix" Phil breathed a sigh of relief and went after another fighter of the SS Foxblade's fighter screen, acutely aware he was flying solo, but he had to keep going.

It was clear early on that despite her joining them to be Elijah's wingmate, he was more than happy for Tessa to take the lead. She noted that while he was a bit overly cautious, he wasn't really that bad and was able to keep up with her

"Sting, this is Duo, If the SS Ramesses gets close enough to engage it's laser batteries this is going to be a short battle" Tessa couldn' disagree but that wasn't her main concern

"Duo, this is Sting, I'd be more concerned with it's Cannons. Think of what a ship like that could do to a station like the Hub" she said as she fired upon an unfortunate fighter that came across her path, a direct hit to the cockpit. Suddenly over the comm's came a voice.

"This is Brutus, needing some help over here" Tessa looked to see Marcus being chased by one ex GalCorp ship and two Silver Blades. Tessa pulled in tight behind and a few quick shots took down the trailing Silver Blade fighter, its partner panicked and fled. The Ex Galcorp fighter was a little tougher but Tessa managed to get a few hits on the fuselage as Elijah fired a few more shots into its engine before it exploded.

"Brutus, this is Sting" she said with a cold smile "may I suggest less flirting and more simulator time."

"Oh, ha ha, very bloody funny" came the response "but thanks." and Marcus pulled up alongside Tessa's fighter and he gave a loose salute before pulling off looking for a new target.

The ships accompanying Matt all called in with their remaining missile compliments, there were two Targets Matt was thinking of, the bridge or, from what he could see the conduit assembly The SS Hades had struck before had only a quick repair job on it. That made it still vulnerable and a tempting target

"This is white Knight, form up on me, we are going in"

Things weren't looking good for Alan, Red dropped back to check out his ship.

"Pyrus, this is Redpunk, looks like that last Pirate fighter has damaged one of your engines." In the last encounter an enemy fighter flew at them head on and flew in between them but clipped Alan's fighter, the enemy ship went into a spin and crashed into another ship, looked like another pirate but that wasn't the main concern. There was a deep gash down his right engine.

"I will have to turn it off I think but I can still fly on one engine." Alan replied, putting a brave face on it but Red wasn't convinced.

"No, Pyrus, transfer as much power to shields and engines as you can and get outta here, try the SS Hades or the Hub, don't worry," she then paused, she could tell he was taking the news hard by his silence "It's not your fault." she added.

"Okay, don't do anything I wouldn't dow hen I'm gone, sorry about this" he said, regret in his voice as he pulled away at high speed to the SS Hades, she stayed with him until he was relatively safe then turned back into the melee of Battle.

Things were getting chaotic near the Hub. Mercenaries, pirates and Ronin alike were locked in a struggle for dominance, Andrew had taken down another pirate when Marcus joined him

"Firehawk, this is Brutus, Was it you who took Omega down?"

"Yeah, pretty much" the matter of fact was he said it stunned Marcus, he shook his head fell in to wingman position behind Andrew. Of course he was the one to defeat Omega, laser fire impacting his shields snapped Marcus out of his thoughts and he saw Andrew, who was being fired upon too, execute a tight turn that Marcus did his best to follow.

"Marcus, this is Firehawk, when I say.. just keep flying..ignore what I do, okay?"

"Okay.." Marcus sounded confused

"Now!" Marcus did as ordered, suddenly Andrews ship just.. stopped and was slowly drifting, the pirate ships raced past, going to fast to react so instead decided to target Marcus, figuring that Andrew's ship must have had some system failure the way it just was aimlessly drifting and would be an easy target once they seen to Marcus. Indeed they were closing in on him as he weaved in and out of debris, other fighters and other obstacles to evade them.

Andrew waited a few seconds then gunned the throttle and raced on after Marcus's pursuers, cruising in behind and between them and with he just unleashed a salvo of laser fire while using the Battleaxes main gun's ability to move to target one ship then the other as he flew with full afterburners in between them, strafing both ships in a hail of relentless fire. Both pilots were so focused on Marcus they could barely react.

"Brutus, this is Firehawk, nice work."

"Oh.. wait? was I the bait?" Marcus said, slightly annoyed "You could have told me."

"I could have yes," Andrew admitted "but it was more fun this way."

The SS Ramesses was closing in on the Hub despite the defenders best efforts, Admiral Miller stood and contemplated his next move as the ship rocked from the weapons fire from the enemy fighters. He looked over to his weapons officer.

"When we are in range, focus attack on the station, don't stop until it is destroyed."

"Yes sir" The officer replied, then looked at his console intently "The SS Absrakt is approaching on our port side." This news did not please Miller, who slammed the arm of his command chair in frustration.

"Damn those useless pirates" The converted cargo ships of the Silver Blades were supposed to hold Lilly's personal ship back. It was the size of a small frigate and by the looks of it had suffered quite a lot of damage but even at full strengh it would have been no real match for the SS Ramesses. Still would rather not be engaging it, a least not until he had dealt with the Hub itself first.

The SS Abstrakt opened fire at maximum range, Matt could see its weapons fire impact on the port side shields, he noted that very few of the SS Abstrakt's weapons were still functioning but yet it was still going on the offensive. Matt prepared himself as he and the other pilots prepared for a run on the ex Galcorp cruiser themselves

The SS Foxblade was starting to struggle, Phil could see it. The SS Hades with it's big military grade canons were now in optimum position and wearing down the other ships shields. He started another run on the Gunships weapons batteries.
Suddenly a weapons lock alert sounded, he thought he had took out the last of the fighter screen.. evidently not. Phil snapped his ship into a tight turn but this guy was right behind. He continued to jink and weave to try and shake the pirate fighter off but nothing was working when an explosion rocked his ship and another battleaxe flew past.

"Semjasa, this is Ellen, do you need assistance?" damn talk about good timing Phil thought to himself.

"Yes, yes I do. Thanks.. we need to take out as many of the SS Foxblade's guns as we can to help the SS Hades."

"Agreed, I'm on your wing" Phil was surprised to hear her say that but now wasn't the time to stop and ask questions, Phil just turned his ship towards the SS Foxblade and hit the afterburners, Ellen flying on formation with him.

Matt and Gareth launched another missile each at the SS Ramesses but from what Matt could tell they weren't making a big enough dent in the shields

"G, this is White Knight, any recommendations?" he asked hoping Gareth would have an answer.

"Nothing practical unfortunately, ideally we need the SS Hades and its Cannons to come into play." Matt looked over briefly to see the SS Hades still engaged in combat with the SS Foxblade, Just then a shot from the SS Ramesses glanced off Gareth's fighter, blowing off one of the wings and putting the fighter into an uncontrolled spin.

"G this is White Knight, Eject!" Matt shouted and eventually he seen the escape pod break off to safety. The main body of the stricken fighter continued it's spin and impacted the SS Ramesses shields. Matt's scanners detected a significant weakening of the shields when that happened and launched his remaining missiles at the same spot, soon the others joined in launching missiles at the steadily weakening area of the shields.

"Shields weakening" the SS Ramesses weapons officer cried out "Admiral.. Look, the SS Foxblade.." Miller could see from the corner of the viewport the frigate rolling slowly to port, explosions on all decks. There was the now familiar sound of the SS Hades cannons.

"Sir the carrier is targeting our starboard side power conduits.." he didn't need to say more, that was the area they had hit before and was crudely patched up until the SS Ramesses could get to a repair dock, Miller turned to the navigation officer

"Turn this ship around" he aimed to present his port side to the SS Hades

"But Admiral, the SS Abstrakt?" the weapons officer said, "it is still a threat." then it happened...

CHAPTER 44

Explosions rocked the SS Ramesses.

"Shields are down, port side weapons arrays are disabled, repair teams en route." the weapons officer shouted over the chaos.

"Recall as many fighters as you can for a defence screen," Miller barked "and get those shields back up now"

On the SS Hades John pumped his fist in celebration as the cannon fire penetrated the SS Ramesses shields and hit the already damaged area of the cruiser.

"Yes! Keep going" but as he said that Ben's console sparked and fell silent

"Damn, we must have burned out the weapons system conduits I was afraid this would happen, I wasn't expecting us to be involved in such a protracted battle" Ben said as he hit his fist off the console in frustration.

"It's okay Ben, I think Andrew and the boys can take things from here" he turned to Liana who looked worried "He will be fine."

"I know he will be," she replied "Its just.. I feel so helpless sitting here"

"We all do," John said "we all do."

"This is White Knight, Anyone have any missiles left?" This was their chance to take down the SS Ramesses once and for all, everyone replied with a negative "Damn he said to himself and slammed his hand down hard on the flight console, just then the burst torpedo console came to life, Matt had an idea...

..."White Knight, this is Firehawk, that has to be the craziest idea you have came out with, but go for it," Andrew seemed amused by the idea "All fighters, clear the road for White Knight."

As he angled his fighter ready for a head on run at the SS Ramesses, Matt, despite not being religious offered up a small prayer. Either side of him was Elijah, Nicolae, Nathan and Tamika. Matt noted that in the melee of battle wingmates had largely been broken off or separated from each other, or in Tamika's case, hers was gunned down. Yet another life lost in this conflict and another good reason to end it here

"This is White Knight, here goes nothing."

"We have some starboard laser batteries and cannons back online but the engineers say the bypasses are fragile, shields are a bit trickier" the weapons officer said as Admiral Miller looked out the viewport and seen the formation of fighters fly straight at the bridge, surely not?

"Concentrate all laser fire on that group of fighters!" he shouted with an edge of panic.

"Sir, targeting systems are not functioning" the weapons officer said in a panic"

"Just fire them anyway, do something" Miller shouted back.

It looked like Miller had figured out at least part of the plan, Matt thought as a barrage of laser fire greeted them.

"White Knight, this is Duo, enemy fighter has dropped in behind us." just then Matt heard the alert warning him of a missile lock on his ship. Elijah acted quickly, turned his ship in a one eighty turn and put himself between Matt and the enemy, which turned out to be an ex GalCorp fighter and started to fire just as the missile was launched at Matt's fighter. It all happened so fast, both ships shields gave out at the same time and the enemy ship fell to Elijah's weapons fire as he put his ship in the missiles path, sacrificing himself. The explosion rocked the remaining fighters, Matt sighed. He didn't really know Elijah that well but in that moment he knew all he needed to know. His act of bravery won't go unnoticed. Shots across his field of vision snapped him out of his thoughts, an Apophis class fighter was bearing down on them from a flanking position.

"White Knight this is Quinque, I got this." Tamika said as she pulled away and flew direct at the new threat, quickly dispatching it with a few well placed shots. "Theres a few more enemy fighters closing in, I'll take care of them" she said and streaked after the incoming fighters, if anyone could hold them off it was Tamika.

"Good luck" he said to himself as he took a breath to focus himself on the task at hand. They were getting close, it was time, Matt armed the burst torpedo and scrolled through the detonator settings and selected impact so it would explode when it hits the SS Ramesses. The laser blasts were erratic and nothing shields and careful manoeuvrers couldn't handle. Matt took a deep breath, lined up the bridge viewport on his sights and fired the torpedo.

"This is White Knight, pull up, pull up pull up." he shouted as he pulled the control yoke up sharply.

Admiral Miller knew exactly what the middle ship had fired.. and where he had aimed it, there was no way the shields would get up in time So he did the only thing he could, he ran to the exit. He had thought of issuing and order to clear the bridge but that would waste precious seconds, besides, they knew what they were letting themselves in for.

The burst torpedo detonated the moment it made contact with the bridge viewport, the initial explosion blew a huge hole in it and the surrounding bulkheads and the smaller explosions devastated the forward section of the bridge and widened the hole at the front, Admiral Miller was already through to the corridor before the torpedo detonated and the emergency bulkheads came down and sealed the bridge... or what was left of it... from the rest of the ship, He picked himself up and headed to the nearest comms panel.

"relief officers to the auxiliary bridge." he said as he then made is own way to the backup command centre, he had to save the ship if nothing else.

"White Knight, this is Nate Dawg, good shot" Matt heard Nathan over the comms as he saw the SS Ramesses drift aimlessly, a gaping hole where the bridge used to be.

"All ships this is White Knight, lets press home our advantage" and he steered in to strafe the stricken cruiser.

In the auxiliary control room the crew were frantically trying to regain control, Miller marched in and turned to the officer trying to man the communications console.

"Send the command to retreat and to rendezvous at zone beta, they all know what that means" he said wearily.

"But how.." the man tried to say before Miller rushed over and done it himself.

"All ships retreat zone to beta, retreat to zone beta." and he hung his head, the battle was lost and all he could do is retreat and regroup.

"SS Ramesses this is Supernova," a voice came through the comm's, it was David Abrams, somehow knowing that at least some of his pilots are still alive brought some comfort "confirm order to retreat."

"Order confirmed, Retreat to zone beta." Miller repeated.

"Message received SS Ramesses, see you there" came the reply. Miller turned to the officer at navigation.

"Are the co-ordinates set?" he asked wearily.

"yes sir" the officer said with a nervous gulp as she brushed some hair from her eyes.

"Well, what are you waiting for?" he shouted as the ship lurched from more explosions. They needed to get out of here, regroup, the SS Ramesses and what remained of the Silver blades after this will return, this wasn't over "Lightspeed.. Now!!!"

David Abrams checked the scanners, out of the twenty four fighters that took part in the battle from the SS Ramesses, about thirteen remained. They had the fighter craft to replenish that.. but not the pilots. Miller was right, it was time to go.

"This is Supernova, All fighters retreat to zone beta," David said powering up his lightdrive. Just as he did that another Apophis class fighter came into view infront of him, the scanners identified it as Jack Reid's ship, David knew Jack would protest David's promotion to flight leader and if he was completely honest, David had already decided there would be no place for Jack in David's pilot roster "Well all but you Jack." he said to himself, and fired on Reid.

"Supernova this is Agent Orange, what are you..." Jack never got to finish that sentence as his ship exploded under fire.

"Goodbye Jack." David said as he jumped to lightspeed.

The SS Ramesses escaped into lightspeed just as Matt was leading another strafing run.

"No!!!" he screamed as he seen the larger ship vanish, "SS Hades this is White Knight, triangulate possible jump vectors..."

"SS Hades this is Firehawk, belay that order, White Knight, stand down.. " and Matt saw Andrew's fighter fly in front and facing Matt "... The battle is over.. we have won"

"But the SS Ramesses..."

"...Is badly damaged and without GalCorp support or protection." Andrew's voice was pleading. Matt sighed, he knew his friend was talking sense. In it's current state, the SS Ramesses would not be the formidable fighting machine it was and without support from GalCorp it was unlikely to such a force in the region again as a result. He looked out to the Hub and seen all the former GalCorp and the Silverblade fighters all break off and jump to lightspeed the minute they could.. some were gunned down before they had the chance to. Matt took a deep breath and reviewed the situation in his head, he was alive, as were most of the other Ronin pilots, they had saved the Hub and the SS Ramesses was on the run, severely damaged, its commanding officer and crew outlaws.

"Firehawk, this is White Knight, we won.. didn't we?"

"Yes we did." Suddenly a large carrier flanked by two cruisers jumped into the system, a message was sent out in all comm's frequencies.

"This is Captain Perez of the UES Relentless, All ships power down your weapons and engines and remain where you are or you will be considered hostile..am I making myself clear?"

"Better do as she says" Andrew said, matt reluctantly agreed and started to shut down the engines and weapons.

Captain Perez paced around the bridge of the UES Relentless, waiting to see what would happen.

"Captain" said her first officer, Commander Tsunoda "All ships are powering down and holding station where they are, what next?"

"Find out if pilots with the callsigns..." she paused to consult a datapad "White Knight and Firehawk are alive, if at least one of them is.. instruct them to come onboard, but advise them weapons will be trained on them so it would be best for them if they do not run"

CHAPTER 45

Andrew landed on the hanger of the UES Relentless, it was huge and made the SS Hades hanger look pitiful in comparison. Two armed and armoured soldiers were waiting for him as he climbed down from the cockpit and one of them grunted.

"Follow me", one walked in front, the other behind, down several corridors until they got to a door he was instructed to enter while they stood outside along with two other guards. Andrew walked in to see what looked like a conference room and Matt already there sitting on a seat.

"Well it's not a prison cell." Matt said as Andrew sat down too.

"I noticed" he replied "this is odd, I wonder what the hell is going on, we aren't under arrest but we are here for some reason"

"Don't ask me, I'm as much in the dark as you." Matt retorted "My escorts here weren't exactly chatty"

"Same here," Andrew replied as a tall woman wearing the uniform of a United Earth military captain came in, her short hair showing touches of grey. She made eye contact with Matt then Andrew.

"I assume you are Matt Easton and Andrew Douglas?" she asked curtly, they both nodded "You two have caused a lot of trouble back home," she started to pace about the room "With the amount of laws you and your people have broken, I could have you all sent some penal colony and leave you to rot," she then sighed "However in the short time that the news about all this was made public there are those already hailing you as heroes and praising your efforts."

"We never set out to be heroes, we only wanted to do what was right" Matt tried to point out but she just stared at him.

"Oh I am aware this was not your intention but it has happened none the less. There have been arrests of some high up GalCorp officials..." she started.

"..Hope Gladstone was one of them." Interrupted Matt.

"No, Director Gladstone locked himself in his office and shot himself just as the Colonial Marshals boarded Carnarvon station, but his attempts to wipe his files failed so collaborating evidence was retrieved." Perez replied.

"Well that's something" Matt said slightly deflated.

"There have been arrests at Waypoint station too, Administrator Nevland is in custody.. " Perez continued

"Oh, what has happened to.." Andrew started to interrupt

"..Obasi Adeyemi has been voted by the people of Waypoint to be the new administrator of the station. He said you would ask." she finished, looking at Andrew, who looked relieved, they sat in silence for a few moments.

"This is all fine and well but where does that leave us?" Andrew said eventually "Are we prisoners or heroes?" he saw Captain Perez pause a moment.

"Well as I said if it were up to me you would be on a penal colony but it isn't and it seems you have friends in high places" she said and then pressed a button on a control panel on the table and in the door walked a familiar face....

"Baron Chopra?" said Matt "What are you doing here?"

"Well, remember I am a retired admiral?" Chopra said with a smile "I come here with a proposition, if you are interested." he then gave a curt nod to Perez who then left the room.

"What kind of proposition?" Andrew asked.

"Mister Easton, if you remember our first conversation, I told you how much I despaired at the lawless nature of this region?" Chopra started slowly.

"I remember you saying something along those

lines yes, why?" replied Matt.

"After we spoke I decided to contact some the other influential people in the area and bring them round to my way of thinking..."

"..Which was?" said Andrew.

"That it is time the outer colonies had some protection from pirate gangs and other.. threats, in fact the success of your... Ronin is it? Was a major factor in their decision." Chopra continued

"What decision?" asked Matt.

"To sign up to become a protectorate of a security company funded by myself, but the signatures are conditional," Chopra paused a moment then continued "They would only sign up if you and your pilots were part of this company."

"What do you mean?" Matt said looking a little confused.

"What it means is, essentially I am willing to fully fund you, your men, ships.. everything to continue the job you have been doing..." he slid a datapad over to Matt, "These are the colonies that are willing to sign up and be protected by you and your people." he replied, Matt took it and read, his eyes went wide.

"Andrew, look" he said sliding it over to Andrew "It's every colony we visited and a few more besides." Andrew looked up from the datapad at Baron Chopra with a slightly sceptical look.

"Let me get this straight, you are going to pay us to continue to protect these colonies? What about the SS Hades?" he asked.

"Ideally I would hope the SS Hades would be part of the package, a mobile base of operations would be useful for you. And before you ask, replacement parts, fighters and anything else would be part of the deal." Chopra answered. "oh and the Hub will be part of the deal too, its new controller..a Miss Tamzarian.. I believe her name was, seemed most agreeable" Andrew rolled his eyes.

"Oh great.. Lilly is in charge" he muttered.

"Also I should add that, thanks to your friend Cardinal Otani, any charges against you all have been dropped, it seems the voice of the Vatican still carries some weight back on Earth," Chopra then took a deep breath "This is obviously a big decision to make and I am sure you wish to talk it over with the other. I will understand if not everyone wishes to accept the offer." Matt looked deep in thought.

"Well.." he started to say when Chopra raised a hand to stop him.

"I'm not looking for an answer right this minute, besides there is a condition to all this."

"Oh?" said Andrew looking at Matt to see if he may know what it could be but Matt shrugged in reply.

"I am taking a risk in doing this, not just in a financial way but also I am putting my reputation on the line so I feel that it would be only fair that I have a representative as part of this venture."

"As a pilot?" Matt asked, he remembered that the Baron's son.. or at least one of them anyway.. was in command of Katar Squadron, the defence force for the

Barony. Chopra shook his head.

"Yohul? No not him, no, I am talking about my daughter Richa. She would be stationed onboard the SS Hades.. if captain Adams chooses to join or onboard whatever headquarters you will have if he doesn't.. as an executive officer in theory, in practice you would see her as my representative. Does that sound reasonable? I also know that captain Adams has rather, loose ethics with the contents of his cargo bays which can't happen if he is representing my interests, someone needs to keep an eye on that" Chorpa said, Andrew nodded.

"That actually makes sense, sounds a fair condition." he said.

"well we would need to think on it and to ask the others too" Matt added, Chopra nodded and gestured to the comms panel on the table.

"Feel free to contact them, take all the time you need, I will be outside" and with that he left them alone in the room.

They sat in silence for a few minutes.

"Your going to say yes aren't you?" Andrew said knowingly to Matt.

"Of course," he replied matter of factly "You?"

"Yeah, I mean what else could I do after all this?" Andrew answered "I don't think any of us ever thought much about what we would do once this was all over." Andrew was right, what were they planning to do once it was all exposed? He continued "If we have learned anything from all this, it is that there are a lot of dangers out there and some we may not have came across yet, we gave these people hope, would be a shame to just desert them just because we got what we want out of it."

"Oddly I was thinking the same thing," Matt nodded "Let's put the proposal to the others."

Using the comms, Andrew and Matt had managed to get hold of John onboard the SS Hades and of the pilots who had been shot down, Gareth, Rob, Susan and Alan, all of which agreed to continue on with this new endeavour, although Andrew did need to convince John about the Baron having one of his people in a position of power in the group and on the SS Hades but he did relent once he realised the Baron would be paying for any repairs and upgrades.. and on an ongoing basis too. Now as time to ask the other pilots who were still out there floating in their powered down fighters, Matt keyed in the Ronin flight frequency and explained the situation...

"....So essentially, we will continue to do what we have been doing already, just getting paid for it and it will all be official and legal. Anyone not wishing to join this setup is totally free to go. We have spoken to the others and they are all staying on." Matt had just finished explaining the situation and leaned back on the chair and sighed, awaiting replies.

"This is Redpunk, You have been so good to me

since I joined and in all honesty I have nowhere else to go, I'm in. Plus who else could cope with Pyrus and his pear puns?" Andrew nodded to Matt, it was a good start.

"This is Nate Dawg, I'm in too"

"This is Brutus, Firehawk still needs the best wingman in the outer colonies, so count me in."

"This is Ellen, what did my sister say?" Matt smiled and sad

"She said she would stay on"

"Well I will too" Ellen answered

"This is Astro Ace, Sounds good to me, I'm in."

"This is Kitten, sign me up."

"This is Quinque, this is the craziest time I have ever had in all my years as a mercenary, you better believe you can count me in"

"This is Hellbringer, I'd be stupid to pass this up, count me in."

"This is Semjasa, I assume Pollock is staying?"

"Of course" Andrew replied

"Ah what the hell, why not. If he is staying, can't be the only one to leave. Okay I'm in." Tessa also said she would stay, but to continue as the helm officer of the SS Hades, not as a fighter pilot.

They called the Baron back in and told him the good news

""Wonderful to hear" he said all smiles "So what would this company called?"

."Well we should probably keep it simple like..

Ronin Security," Matt said "People already know us as Ronin Flight anyway." Andrew nodded in agreement.

"Let me contact my daughter and give her the good news" Chopra said and keyed in a requency on the comms panel, the large screen on one side of the room changed from the rotating United Earth Military logo to an image of the Baron's daughter Richa, who looked like she was back at the Barony

"Namaste father" she said with aslight smile and bowed ever so slightly

"Namaste my Richa" and he also slightly bowed "Start the preparations, they have all agreed."

"Does that include the SS Hades Father?" she asked.

"It does, so have the repair dock prepare for it's arrival. There is a lot of work to do." he replied "I will be home once I have sorted a few things out with the new Hub administration."

"Rather him than me, dealing with Lilly that is." Andrew whispered to Matt as they watched father and daughter say goodbyes and end the transmission. Baron Chopra turned to face them. "Well, I have further buisness to conduct but the Barony facilities will be ready by the time you get there, I will see you in a few days when we can formalise things further" he went to walk out "Oh, and I will tell Captain Perez, to allow you to return to your fighters and to let you and your people board the SS Hades."

"Thank you Baron, we won't let you down" Matt said with a smile.

CHAPTER 46

Andrew, Matt and the remaining operational Ronin ships landed on the SS Hades to a heroes welcome. Alan, Gareth, Rob and Susan were there with the ships crew and techs to cheer them as they landed, Susan was in a wheelchair and had Sister Theresa with her, the nun begrudgingly let the Bavarian pilot out of the medbay under the condition she goes straight back to continue treatment.

They landed in twos, the first being Phil and Ellen, who exchanged a surprisingly friendly hug

"Seems that you aren't such a bad pilot after all" Ellen quipped with a smile.

"Thanks, I think, does that mean I get the good beer from now on?" he asked, Ellen just laughed and went over to see her sister

Red and Tamika were next, as Tamika got out her fighter Rob walked up, he was holding his side and seemed in some pain

"Well, it seems us oldies survived." he said.

"Yeah, but others didn't." she said with regret.

"I know, I suppose working as a loner most of your career meant you didn't need to deal with this sort of thing." he said and she nodded then took a deep breath and composed herself.

"You are right, so, what next?" she asked

"Well, I believe celebrations are in order so, gotta plan for that.. could use some help.." he said as he indicated to his bandages in a non too subtle way, she smiled.

"Okay, okay old timer, I'll help" and they headed to the mess hall

Nicolae and Craig were next to land, Nicolae's ship was quite damaged and it was a wonder he ever managed to land, Gareth shouted up to him as he exited

"Damn, I'd hate to be the tech who has to repair that one"

"Oh I think I will ask for you personally to lea the repairs on it" Nicolae said in a manner that Gareth couldn't tell if he was joking or not. Craig came around to to look at the damage and was greeted with Phil, his hand outstretched.

"You did great today kid." he said.

"thank you" Craig replied as he shook Phil's hand, he had come a long way from that overzealous kid who sneaked onboard in order to to become a pilot "Nicolae is a good teacher." he admitted, Phil just smiled and walked over to the crowd.

Nathan and Kate landed next with Tessa and Marcus just behind them, both just looked glad to be alive. Kate ran over to Tessa as she climbed out her fighter and gave Tessa a hug. Nathan went to walk away to the main crowd, when were cheering and congratulating the other pilots that had already landed when he was grabbed by the shoulder and spun round, Tessa was there staring at him, then a smile came across her lips and she pulled him in for a hug.

"Kate speaks highly of you, I can see why now. Any friend of hers is a friend of mine." all Nathan could do was smile.

"Thanks," he said, tucking his helmet under his arm "And she is a great wingmate and a great person"

"Yes she is" said Tessa and kissed Kate, whispering to her "you're the best"

Marcus joined the others in celebration but seemed distracted.

"Probably looking for a little furry companion."

Phil quipped.

"Dammit Phil can't you give that a rest for.." Marcus was about to say when Red ran up and grabbed him by the front of the jumpsuit and in full view of the other pilots kissed him deep.

"Okay, did not see that one coming," Phil said, shock evident on his face.

"Believe it Phil," said Nicolae "lets give them some privacy shall we?"

"Yeah, lets go see if Rob needs help." Phil said in agreement.

Andrew and Matt were the last to land and received the biggest cheer from the gathered crowd, as Andrew dismounted he was nearly knocked over by a delighted and relieved Lianna who peppered him with kisses.

"I was worried this was the mission..you know.." she started to say, but Andrew just held her close. Matt looked over and smiled and then seen Suzanne, being wheeled over by Sister Theresa, he went to hug Suzanne when Sister Theresa advised him.

"Be careful Mister Easton, Miss Sommer is still under my care." So Matt crouched down.

"We did it Suzanne," he said smiling softly "we won." Suzanne just smiled back leaned over as much as she dared, kissed his cheek and replied.

"I never doubted you for a moment Matthew"

The crowd of crew, techs and pilots stayed on the hanger deck for a while as everyone shared their experiences of the battle until Rob returned and announced that were will be a celebration party in the mess hall and that it will also double as an engagement party for Andrew and Liana.

"Hey, did you know anything about all this?" Andrew asked Liana

"No," she said unconvincingly, Andrew just shook his head and kissed her anyway.

The SS Hades had set course for Baron Chopra's repair yard for repairs and for the refit that was required for it to continue to function as a mobile base for the Ronin to operate from. Most of the crew were in the mess hall enjoying the party as the ships computer handled the journey. John took a look out the bridge viewport as Ben was making some last minute checks on the autopilot settings.

"Ben, it's strange. A few short months ago we were... let's just say traders.. and look at us now. A vital part of security in this region" John said absently.

"Yeah, but look at it this way, someone else pays for ship maintenance and we get paid for our troubles. No more flying around searching for slim profits." Ben countered. John shook his head and made his way to the exit.

"Sign of the times I suppose" he mused "come on, lets get drink. We earned it I think".

"Sounds good to me" Ben said and followed John to the mess hall.

As Andrew and Liana headed to the the mess hall they came across Sister Theresa, who was heading the other way to the medbay.

"Ah, Mister Douglas, I was hoping to bump into you, do you have a moment?" she said with a slight smile, Andrew shrugged

"sure, what is it?" he said as Liana put her arm around his waist

"Well, I have been in communication with Cardinal Otani and it has been decided that This ship and it's crew would continue to benefit from my.. skills and spiritual guidance," her voice suggested that there may be something more to it but Andrew let her continue "So I have elected to stay on as a member of the crew"

"Good to hear, we are honoured to have you continue the good work you have started here. Thank you" Andrew said

"The pleasure is all mine Mister Douglas, now if you don't mind, I need to get back to my patient, she is being a little too stubborn for my tastes," she took a few steps and stopped "Oh, and if you are looking for Mister Easton, he was last seen at the hanger bay." then made her way to the medbay.

Matt stood on the SS Hades hanger deck in between the

rows of fighters, he had just spent time with Suzanne in the medbay and had just left to let her sleep as the pain medication kicked in. he looked at the varied levels of battle damage all the fighters had suffered. Tomorrow the repairs will begin but right now there was a huge party in the mess hall but for some reason he wasn't in the mood.

"Hey, I thought I'd find you here," said a voice, Matt turned to see Andrew, his arm looped around Liana "Everyone is asking where you are? Usually its me who sneaks off early."

"Sorry," Matt replied running his hand through his hair, it was needing cut "But the SS Ramesses is still out there..." he was cut off by Andrew holding up his hand.

"Yes but we will find them and we won't be alone this time thanks to our good friend Baron Chopra. We are a legitimate fighting force now." Andrew said in a calming tone, he was right. This setup the Baron had proposed would allow them to continue doing what they had been doing, just legally this time. Matt rested his back against the nearest fighter and sighed.

"I know, we were so close though to actually ending things outright" he closed his eyes as he rested his head on the fighter fuselage. Matt's eyes snapped back open when he heard more footsteps. Phil and Rob had joined them, Rob had bandages covering his right torso and upper arm, Phil looked tired but both had beer bottles in their hands.

"Guys," Phil said as he took a large drink out his

bottle "In case you didn't know there is a celebration going on back in the mess hall and there's no way you are getting out of this one," he pointed to Andrew as Liana cuddled into her fiance "At least not yet anyway"

"Ah Matt, there you are, I'm guessing you were in the medbay talking to a Bavarian girl with poor taste in guys" quipped Rob. Matt nodded and stated she should be up and about in a day or so

"You guys go on ahead, I'll catch up" Matt said eventually.

"Oh no you don't, we have had years of Andrew ducking out of parties, not you as well," said Phil as he took one arm and Rob took the other and they marched Matt to the mess hall. Phil turned back to Andrew and said "Come on, you are not getting off that easy" Andrew shrugged his shoulders and smiled, kissed Liana and followed them.

The party was in full swing, music, groups of pilots talking about their part in the battle. there was a sombre moment at the start to toast the fallen. Matt noticed Andrew flex his knee experimentally.

"Knees playing up?" he asked though he knew the answer and Andrew's nod confirmed it.

"Yeah, not surprising really," Andrew said said "but could have been a lot worse."

"Where's Liana?" Matt asked.

"She is here somewhere" Andrew replied as he handed Matt a bottle and looked around "She's talking to the bridge crew" he gestured to a table were Liana, John, Ben and Tony were listening to Tessa, it looked like Tessa was describing some manoeuvrer. Phil suddenly banged the butt of his sidearm like a hammer on the nearest table.

"A toast, to Matt and Andrew, leaders of Ronin Flight and the heroes of the Outer Colonies.." he then lead everyone in three cheers. Andrew smiled then smiled and touched his bottle to Matt's.

"Cheers" he said then gestured to the assembled crew "Enjoy yourself, you have more than earned it. Yes the bad guys are still out there, but that is a worry for another day, go.. enjoy" Matt nodded in agreement as Andrew walked towards the doorway, draining half his bottle and leaving it at a nearby table with the intention of slipping away as usual. However Phil came over and guided Andrew to the pilots table and sat him on a chair. Liana came over and sat next to him with Matt joining the table too along with Rob, Nathan, Gareth, Ellen, Craig, Nicolae, Tamika, Alan and Kate joined with Tessa. The mess hall doors opened and Suzanne was wheeled in by Sister Theresa.

"Couldn't sleep." Suzanne said as matt held her hand gently.

"She can stay for an hour" said Sister Theresa said with a tone of authority that the smile on her lips suggested wasn't genuine. Red, who had just joined the table and cuddled into Marcus had a question on her lips.

"Andrew, just how did you take down Omega?" she said curiously. Matt looked at Phil and Rob, both nodded as they knew what he was thinking. A lot of the newer pilots like Red were still getting used to Andrew's unorthodox style. Matt smiled as he looked around at the crowd gathered at the table, he felt Suzanne squeeze his hand. Yes Miller was still out there but that was a worry for tomorrow, they had more than earned the right to celebrate. Matt took a drink from his bottle as Andrew answered Red's question.

"Well," Andrew said to the other pilots gathered round the table "it was like this.."

The celebrations went on long into the night. The news story about courageous band of pilots who fought to defend helpless colonies from oppression was spreading throughout all around the colonies of Earth. They were heroes...

...They were Ronin Flight.

EPILOGUE

The refit of the SS Hades at Baron Chopra's repair docks took nearly a week, in that time the newly named Ronin Security sorted out the finer details of their new arrangement, Matt and Andrew were in the conference room going over the changes to the pilot roster. It had been decided to spilt the pilots up into two squads, Inferno Squad commanded by Andrew that would remain purely a space combat unit that had Marcus, Phil, Susan, Ellen, Red, Alan, Craig and Nicolae. Then there was Blizzard Squad commanded by Matt and had Gareth, Rob, Tamika, Nathan and Kate. While still primarily pilots would also be trained up with a secondary role as a ground unit, they were looking over their squads respective simulation tests.

"I still can't believe the dream team of Phil and Rob split," said Matt "The way they act I would have thought they would be wingmates for life." Andrew shrugged.

"Phil never really cared for ground combat much," he said absently "Oh, hows your new recruits? looked at their files yet?" After the battle of the Hub they were swamped with offers to join but in order to be fair and to also honour the contract with the Hub itself they took on just enough applicants to give them two full squadrons, the rest formed a sort of reserve unit with the job of keeping the large station safe under the watchful eye of the new administration.

"Fine actually," answered Matt looking at the personnel files of the new recruits for Blizzard, he had the most new recruits due to him looking for pilots with extra skills "there's Clint McBride, callsign Striker, as well as being a decent pilot Clint is a trained sniper. Jack Kenny, callsign Diceman, was a freelance mercenary much like Tamika, though not as experienced. Morris Richards, callsign Moric, he is former Hexstar military and like Nathan flew troop transports. We also have Scott Goldman, callsign Silver... ironic i guess but was a land vehicle technician who has some previous flight experience." Andrew nodded, having a land vehicle expert could be handy. Matt continued "We also have Leon Lewis, callsign Ludicrous and Owen White, callsign Slap Happy, both pilots came out here to become mercenaries and were caught up in the battle of the Hub, they flew on our side by the way." Matt concluded.

"Sounds like you will have a lot to keep you busy,

integrating them into the team." said Andrew.

"What about you, who are your recruits?" Matt asked. Andrew looked through his other files "Vincent Edward Devine, callsign Ved, he was one of the ones who made attack runs on the SS Ramesses in the battle, I paired him with Phil. I also have Steven Graham, callsign, Himself..?" he looked twice at the datapad "odd, but he was another who distinguished himself in the battle and rounding out my recruits is Scott Young, callsign Ice, he actually flew with Baron Chopra's Katar Squadron but asked to fly with us. I guess he is on loan to us as it were." Matt nodded and stood up, smoothed his new uniform, they went for a uniform of Grey flightsuits with black trim and the newly designed badge of a black shield trimmed in silver with one half of it black, on the silver eight pointed silver star symbolising the eight original pilots who engaged in the first battle together with a stylised 'R' in the centre, that was on the right breast of the flightsuit but on the shoulders there were similar shields but Andrew's had a red star and an I in the middle and Matt had a blue star and B in the middle to symbolise their two squads.

"Well the refit is just about finished." said John bursting in, wearing a similar uniform but like the rest of the SS Hades crew (theirs was a grey jumpsuit with the shield with the silver star and R on it on the breast and shoulders), John kept his own spin on it, still wearing his captains vest "apart from the weapons being replaced with civilian grade variants," the tone in voice suggested he wasn't pleased with that change "this ship is fully operational, systems, shields the works, she's finally running at the level she was meant to be." Just then Richa Chopra, the Barons representative, ships executive officer and essentially the day to day head of Ronin security.. at least from the business side of things. Walked in. She wore the jumpsuit and had a grey and black knee length light sleeveless zip fasten top and slits on the sides from the waist to the bottom and had the Ronin logo on the left breast and on the right, the Chopra Barony logo. Her black hair long and loose.

"I know you are unhappy with some of the modifications Captain Adams but a civilian vessel can not carry military grade weapons and you know that. The replacements are the best and most powerful a ship like ours is allowed to have. We have had this conversation many times." she said shaking her head. John held his hands up in surrender. John and Richa had been at odds from day one, just the small things mainly but Andrew could see her and Phil were going to get on well.

"Okay I promise not to mention it again.. for today anyway" as he laid the pad with the upgrades listed on the table for Matt and Andrew to see. John then held up another Datapad "Liana has kept track of GalCorp transmissions just in case of anything useful has came up, apparently the SS Amenhotep has been pulled from its usual duties to defend company interests until the SS Ramesses sister ship, the SS Horemheb is refitted to meet the new guidelines imposed on Galcorp, and also there has been suspected pirate activity near the colony of Voorbeeld."

"Voorbeeld Colony," Andrew said with interest "the SS Ramesses?" but John just handed him the pad with the data, Andrew looked at Matt and shook his head, the former GalCorp ship was not sighted.

"Better investigate anyway, they are one of the colonies who have asked for our services after all," Matt uttered "There's been no conformed sightings of Miller since the battle of the Hub." he looked troubled, Andrew sensed it and rose to put a comforting arm over his shoulders.

"The SS Ramesses was badly damaged, he can't get parts as easily as before." just then Liana came in, Matt noted she still wore her usual tall boots with the uniform but also sported a scarf that was black and grey with silver patterns on it as if to colour co-ordinate. she seemed out of breath.

"Sorry," she said panting "but the internal comms are being upgraded and had to be taken offline but we just had a report of a Galcorp supply ship attacked on the way to Luxor colony, by a group referring to themselves as the Ten Plagues I thought you'd want to know." Andrew and Matt looked at each other but it was John that spoke.

"If I were a betting man, I'd say our old friend the Admiral is trying to get replacement parts for repairs the only way he can now." he shrugged.

"John," said Matt tentatively "a couple of

questions, how much longer are the upgrades going to take and is Luxor Colony anywhere near Voorbeld?" John thought for a minute. "Just the comms and a few minor systems.." he smiled realising what Matt was suggesting "but nothing that can't be done on the go, give us an hour and we will be ready to go" he then took a moment to think "the two colonies are pretty close."

"Well," said Andrew knowingly "It would only be fair to offer assistance to our GalCorp neighbours, show no hard feelings and friendship." John get ready to set off, "Liana can you go tell the pilots to assemble in the pilot briefing room, we have a job to do." everyone in the room smiled and went to do their respective jobs, before leaving Liana walked up and kissed Andrew lovingly, he watched her leave with a dreamy smile.

later after a quick freshen up the two pilots headed to the briefing room Andrew looked at Matt deep in thought.

"A moment, I just realised something," he said looking at Matt intently "you told me once signed up to Galcorp security forces in order to come out here and help protect the innocents in the colonies, right?" Matt nodded.

"Yeah I did." he said somewhat bemused.

"What are you doing now?" Andrew asked.

"I'm part of a security force..." he trailed off and smiled "...protecting innocent colonies."

"I know you feel bad that the SS Ramesses is still out there but we will come across it again, and this time, he's the outlaw," Andrew continued "try and look at it this way, while its not the way you envisaged doing it, your finally doing what you wanted to do all along," he stopped Matt before they went in where the other pilots were waiting, even without internal comms Liana was quick, he then put his hand on Matts shoulder "surely that has got to count for something," he was right Matt thought, he is finally doing the very thing he thought he was signing up to do for Galcorp, it just took a few strange tangents, he smiled, then laughed, it was crazy how it all worked out.

"Yeah, your right. Never thought of it that way," he took a deep breath "and I have you to thank." Andrew smiled and simply said.

"I told you, my instincts told me you were a good man, I was proven right that's all. Now I do believe we have a job to do." they both smiled and walked through the briefing room door, they made their way to the podium at the the front, Matt stood in front of the other pilots, once a motley bunch of Pirates, security forces, local vigilantes, outcasts and mercenaries now a fully cohesive unit, no, more than that they were family, Matt realised he was finally were he wanted to be..he was home, he took a breath.

"Ronin Security, we have our first assignment..."

The End.. for now

ABOUT THE AUTHOR

D. D. Braithwaite was born on the 2nd of October 1980 and grew up in the Scottish town of Wishaw where he still resides with his wife Gillian and his son Corran (who is named after one of his all time favourite fictional characters). He is dyslexic and also dyspraxic (so he apologises if any little grammar or spelling errors have crept into this work) but has not let it get in the way of his writing. He is a fan of, amongst other things, science fiction, Formula One, professional wrestling and listening to the podcasts of Jim Cornette.

The authors who inspired him the most are Douglas Adams, Timothy Zahn, Aaron Allston, Michael A. Stackpole, Karen Traviss and Harry Turtledove. He also takes a lot of inspiration for his storytelling style from director/producer Dave Filoni.

Printed in Great Britain
by Amazon

18356121R10255